IAN'S ROSE

-Book One of The Mackintoshes & McLarens

by SUZAN TISDALE

Ian's Rose

Book One of The Mackintoshes and McLarens Series

Copyright © 2016 by Suzan Tisdale

ISBN-13: 1-943244-14-6
ISBN-10: 1-978-1-943244-14-0

Cover art by Dar Albert, Wicked Smart Designs

www.suzantisdale.com

Give feedback on the book at:
suzan@suzantisdale.com
Twitter: @suzantisdale
Facebook.com/suzantisdaleromance

First Edition

Printed in the U.S.A

Dedication

For my warrior princess.
Thank you for helping grandmamma write this book.

"Gradh mo Chroi"

"Love of me heart, do no' leave me."

— Ian Mackintosh

PROLOGUE

March 1356, The McLaren Keep in the Highlands

There is a special place in hell for men like Mermadak McLaren.

Those who had suffered at his hand for too many years to count, celebrated openly and joyfully at the news of his death. Many believed whoever 'twas that took the auld son-of-a-whore's life should be sainted, made king, or at the very least given his weight in gold as a blessedly deserved reward.

'Twould be no lie to say none would miss him.

As for the whereabouts of Donnel McLaren, the man who had helped the former laird steal, lie, and cheat Clan McLaren to near utter ruin, 'twas anyone's guess. Hopefully, he was burning in hell right next to the McLaren. There weren't many who were as vile, cruel, or evil as the two of them. Those few clansmen who remained were content for now to believe evil would never touch them again, or at least not for a very long while.

The McLarens had suffered through a cold, bleak, and harsh winter, living in the old granary, making plans for the future and dreaming of spring. The one thing that kept them going, even at those times when it felt God had forsaken them, was knowing Mermadak McLaren could never hurt them again.

But on this dark, windy night in early spring, Ian Mackintosh's thoughts were as far away from evil men as they could get. Nay, he was thinking only of Rose, the woman he loved beyond doubt or denial. Never in his life had he met anyone such as she. Quick-witted, wise, and always blunt and to the point when she had something to say. And God's teeth, she was beautiful. Long, wavy blonde locks that turned gold in the sunlight, blue eyes as bright and vivid as the Highland sky in springtime, and a smile that melted his heart like honey in the sun. Though she was wee, the top of her head barely reaching his heart, she was as mighty as a shield maiden from the north-lands. She possessed a body to shame Aphrodite herself and Ian wanted desperately to discover that secret paradise.

They were alone now, just the two of them, in one of the few rooms of the keep not destroyed by the fire Mermadak had set months before. The rest of the clan — those dedicated souls who had remained behind to brave the harsh winter — were hunkered down in the granary.

"I love ye, Rose, with all that I am." Ian's voice was as soft as the smoke rising from the brazier, and just as warm against her skin. "I want ye to be me wife. I want to build a life with ye, if ye'll have me."

Looking into those mesmerizing deep blue eyes of his, she had no doubt he spoke from his heart. He held her hands in his, but whose were trembling more was an unanswerable question. Though his grip was gentle, she could not help but think he was holding on for dear life. Her answer, she knew, would either make his heart soar amongst the heavens, or shatter into inestimable pieces. Before she could say aye or nay, they needed to have a very important discussion. A discussion that, in the end, could change both of their lives forever. Either for the better or for the worse; 'twould be up to Ian.

With all her heart she wanted to shout *Aye! I will marry ye!* Never had she met anyone quite like him, even if she did believe to a certain extent he was like most men, with only three things usually on his mind: food, coin, and loving. Aye, he was interested in those things, but there was more to Ian than that. He adored her, was kind and generous, and she often found him humorous even when he wasn't intending to be. He was also quite handsome. So handsome in fact that her mind often wandered to lustful and delicious thoughts of what it would be like to share the man's bed.

Aye, without a doubt, he adored her. He would protect her and love her until he took his last breath on God's beautiful earth. What more could a woman ask for in a man? Strength, honor, good looks were a welcome change to the men she'd known before the Mackintoshes arrived and changed all their lives forever.

She took several deep breaths to calm her nerves before she could speak. "Ian, I love ye with all that I am as well. I never felt this way before, not even with Almer, me first husband."

The smile that broke on his face was a blend of relief and pride. Certain that what she was about to say next would make that smile disappear, she burned the image into her memory. Every bit of his handsome face, from the way his full lips were curved upward to the sparkle in his intense blue eyes that crinkled slightly at the corners. The tiny freckle in the corner of his mouth just under his bottom lip that was often hidden, for he typically went days without shaving.

If she were to be struck dead at this very moment, she would die a most happy woman. She could take this beautiful image of him with her to keep her warm and content throughout eternity. But that would have been the coward's way out of a potentially ugly situation. And Rose was never one to behave as such.

"I fear there is somethin' we must discuss first, Ian. Somethin' of great importance."

Although he continued to smile, his eyes were filled with questions. "Great importance?" He was confident that it was not so important as to change his feelings toward her.

"I can no' give ye children," she told him sadly.

As the morning mist evaporates against sunlight, so did his smile, when the reality of her words slowly sank in. 'Twas not what he expected to hear. "Ye be barren?'"

Rose gave a slight shake of her head as she swallowed back tears. "Nay, I can get with child, but I can no' carry past me third month."

Ian had never dreamed of having children until he fell in love with Rose McLaren. He hadn't exactly led the kind of life that would allow for a wife or bairns. Those past encounters with women, now that he reflected upon it, were nothing more than moments taken to meet his physical needs.

But Rose? Somehow, without even trying, she had changed him from a whoring, warring, drinking fool to a man who looked to the future with new eyes. A future with Rose as his wife and the mother of his many children.

Pain and sorrow filled her eyes and he could feel both to his very core, just as deep as if it had been his own personal loss. Possessed with the overwhelming urge to take her into his arms, he pulled her close. They clung to one another for comfort, solace, and strength. "It matters no' to me," he whispered against her blond locks with a voice that cracked.

Although nothing was between them but the pounding of their hearts, Ian sensed something hanging in the air, something more she wanted to say but he knew his heart could not bear to hear the words. He'd not give her the chance to tell him she could not marry him.

Swallowing back his disappointment, he set any thoughts of a cottage bursting to the rafters with children aside. "I am one of many sons," he began, still clinging to her as if she were a mast on a sinking ship. "I'll never be chief, so I've no legacy to build. I'll no' need many sons or even daughters. I will be content all the rest of me days if it is just ye and me, alone in a croft, farmin' the land. As long as I can grow old with ye, spend each morn watchin' the sun rise with ye at me side and watch it set at the end of the day, me life will be complete, Rose. All I shall ever need or want, is ye."

Oh, how she wanted to believe him. "But what if ye someday change yer mind? What if ye realize later that ye do want children and I can no' give them to ye? I could no more bear that than losin' yer babe."

Squeezing her more tightly, he pressed a kiss against her head. "Then ye have me permission to remind me of this moment before ye beat me senseless."

She knew he was using humor in an attempt to assuage her worries, but this time, it did not work. Hiding her damp eyes against his chest, she murmured perhaps the one thing that bothered her most. "I could no' bear to lose yer child, Ian. 'Twould be me undoin'. 'Twould be a loss I could never overcome."

A babe of their own was the one thing she wanted most to give him, but the fear of losing his child was far stronger than that singular desire.

"Wheest, now, me love. Ye and I are neither foolish nor lackin' in knowledge. We both ken there be ways of enjoyin' one another as man and woman without the worry of creatin' a babe."

Slowly, she pulled away to look into his eyes. He was filled with hope for the future and adoration for her and 'twas as contagious as the ague. After the loss of her last babe, Almer had stopped sharing a bed with her. Not out of anger but out of his love for her. He had known how much the losses had hurt and he refused to put her through such pain again. Even after she had told him there were ways they could love one another without the fear of another loss looming over their heads, he still refused.

Now she was staring into the eyes of a man who wanted to marry her regardless of what she could not give him. Knowing what he did, he still desired her, still wanted to enjoy her as his wife. He would not turn her away.

"Ye be certain?" she asked, out of the need to hear him say it once again, to be certain she had heard him correctly.

A most wondrous, wicked smile lit his face, answering more questions than she had put to voice. "Aye, I be certain."

ONE

Scotland, May 1356, The Mackintosh Keep, Northern Highlands of Scotland

Ian Mackintosh had inherited his father's long and infamous stubborn streak. While that stubborn streak proved a useful skill on the field of battle, it was oft his undoing in other matters. Especially where matters of the heart or his pride were concerned.

Standing in the courtyard next to his older and equally pig-headed brother, Frederick, the two proud — and at times obstinate — men awaited the arrival of long over-due guests. It had been raining almost non-stop for three days and nights, only adding to the somberness of Ian's mood. Drenched to the bone, sick at heart, he wanted nothing more than to be inside the keep with vast amounts of ale to keep him company.

Torches lined the pathway to the heavy gate and along the upper walls.

They sizzled and hissed, fighting valiantly against the steady rain. The flames flickered with the gusting breeze, casting shadows hither and yon. Dancing shadows that at times Ian believed were mocking him.

Whilst Frederick was excited to be awaiting the arrival of his wife's newly discovered family, Ian was not so exceedingly cheerful. There was much on the young man's mind. More specifically, there was a woman on his mind. A beautiful woman with hair the color of honey and blue eyes that darkened if she was angry and brightened when filled with delight. Lately, those exquisite eyes were nearly obsidian, filled with sorrow. Sorrow brought on by his behavior.

A woman who consumed nearly every waking thought. A stubborn, confusing, bewildering and beautiful young woman named Rose. And as much as he wanted to spend the rest of his life with her, building a future together, it was not meant to be.

Since their return to his family's lands, he had tried to keep his distance, to stay away from the lovely lass. They had met more than a year ago, when his foolish brother had agreed to marry a young woman he'd met only once. Frederick had offered for her hand within an hour of their first meeting. Ian had done his level best to talk his brother out of it, especially after they had seen Aggie McLaren's keep for the first time, then again after meeting her father, Mermadak McLaren — may his soul now be burning in the bowels of hell for eternity.

Somehow, the young woman had won Frederick's heart, as well as every member of their family's, including Ian's. In retrospect, Ian's first impression of Aggie McLaren had been wrong and he could say without hesitation that she was the best thing that had ever happened to his brother.

Rose was Aggie's dearest friend. The two women had gone through much heartache and hell together.

He and Rose had formed a deep friendship during their time at the McLaren keep, a friendship that grew into something he had not expected. He loved her, and that alone scared the bloody hell out of him. Though he knew she felt the same toward him, had even accepted his proposal of marriage months ago, he felt wholly unworthy of her love. He believed she deserved far better than what he could offer, which was, at the moment, nothing at all. 'Twas why he had broken their secret troth. He had nothing to give her but a lifetime of poverty and: She deserved better.

"Could ye at least *pretend* excitement, brother?" Frederick asked as he frowned at Ian.

Ian's forced smile made Frederick chuckle. "Why do ye no' just go ask fer Rose's hand and be done with it?"

Ian's smile evaporated in an instant. His brother could not possibly understand his fear or hesitance. Aye, he'd asked for her hand before they had come here and she had happily agreed.

But when they'd arrived on the safe and hallowed lands of his family, he began to realize several things. One, he had no way to support a wife, not on a warrior's wages. And that was all he was good for: swinging a sword, battles, defending his homeland and his people. Two, there was no way he could give her anything but heartache. He'd not be able to give her lovely dresses such as those Frederick gave his own wife. There'd be no fancy slippers or baubles or fine linens and silks for the woman he loved more than life itself. Nay, he could give her nothing and that was the cold, hard truth.

He could not give her anything other than love.

And sometimes, love simply wasn't enough.

He would, however, love her until the day he died. There would be no other woman. No one would ever be able to take her place. 'Twas both the easiest and most difficult decision Ian Mackintosh had ever made. But Rose hadn't seen it that way. She felt betrayed, more than let down, and he could not rightly blame her. But in the end, he knew he had made the right decision. Even if it had left him feeling empty and miserable and as broken as a bit of fine glass thrown against a piece of granite.

As he brooded silently, hating the rain, the night, and for the lot life had given him, a rider approached the gates. The lad bore news that Aggie's family was several hours away, delayed by the God-awful rain. Frederick was disappointed. Ian was relieved. Now he could go and skulk and drink his misery away.

"I shall go tell Aggie the news," Frederick said. "And da and mum and everyone else who awaits them indoors."

Ian shrugged his shoulders, truly not caring about anyone or anything at the moment.

"What the bloody hell is wrong with ye, Ian?" Frederick demanded as they headed into the keep.

Standing in the narrow entryway, they left puddles of water on the stone floor as they shrugged out of their sodden cloaks.

"Ye've been in a piss poor mood fer weeks now," Frederick pointed out. "If ye can no' find yerself in better spirits before Aggie's family arrives, I'd appreciate it if ye'd stay away from everyone."

"'Twill be me pleasure," Ian said as he bounded down the steps and disappeared from sight.

Frederick stared after him for a long while. *Mayhap if Ian will no' tell me what is the matter, Rose will.*

'TWAS EASY ENOUGH TO LOCATE Rose. As soon as Frederick walked through the door to the bedchamber he shared with his wife Aggie, he regretted his decision to seek her out. The two women sat side by side on the bed and both had been crying. It took no great mental acumen to realize his brother Ian was the source of their tears. His assumption was immediately verified by the angry glare his wife shot at him.

"Yer brother is a c-cad!" Aggie informed him as if he hadn't been aware of that fact for most of his life. "He's b-broken p-poor Rose's heart!"

Frederick's anger began to flame brightly. Not at his wife, but at his brother. Aggie had suffered for years with a speech impediment, a very profound stutter that he had thought she had all but overcome. The only time it was noticeable was when she was terrified or upset. *I'm going to kill him,* he thought to himself, *fer upsettin' me wife.*

"Aggie," Rose sniffled, "I asked ye no' to tell anyone!"

Aggie gave her a reassuring hug. "Aye, but I d-did no' promise I wouldn't."

Frederick took in a deep breath and steeled himself for whatever his wife was about to say. Instinct told him this was no typical lover's quarrel, but a real and profound heartache. One that his wife felt almost as deeply as Rose.

"What did he do?"

Rose blew her nose into a bit of linen, unable to speak. Aggie took it upon herself to inform her husband of his brother's cowardice. "Did ye k-ken he had asked f-fer Rose's hand?"

"Nay, I did no'," he said.

"He did," Aggie said as she wiped her own tears away with her fingertips. "When ye were all still b-back on M-McLaren lands. They were t-to marry when ye returned."

Nay, he was not going to like this at all.

"Two weeks ago, he came to her and broke the troth! And he would no' give a good reason why!" She'd gone from being hurt to being angry. He could handle an angry wife, but not one who'd been hurt.

"Did he give any reason at all?" he asked.

"Nay, the coward did no'! He simply told her 'twas better fer Rose if they parted ways. Can ye believe he'd do such a thing?"

Letting loose a heavy sigh, he shook his head. "Nay, I can no' believe such a thing. Ian has never broken his word, at least no' that I be aware of."

Rose looked up at him, the anguish in her heart evidenced in her eyes. "One day, we were verra happy and the next, he tells me he can no' marry me." She sniffled again and dabbed at her eyes. "I do no' ken what I did."

"Ye did no' do a thing," Aggie assured her. "The fault lies entirely with that c-coward, that c-cad *he* calls brother."

He wasn't necessarily sure why his wife was behaving as though his brother's behavior was *his* fault, but he wasn't up to arguing that point. He was cold, soaked to the bone, and tired. "I be terribly sorry fer what Ian has done, Rose. I shall do me best to make it right. I will no' make ye any false promises, but I will do me best to find out what he's thinkin' inside that thick skull of his."

Rose let loose a very unladylike moan. "Do no' bother. 'Twill do neither of us any good. He simply does no' love me anymore."

"He's an arse," Aggie offered by way of consolation.

Frederick couldn't necessarily disagree with her appraisal of his younger brother.

"Why would he do such a thing?" Aggie asked, looking into her husband's eyes as if she might find some answer within them.

"I do no' ken, love. I simply do no' ken." If he did, he'd certainly rectify the situation at once. For now, he had to move on to more pressing matters. "Aggie, we've received word on Douglas. His arrival has been delayed by the rain."

Her shoulders sagged in disappointment. The wait for the arrival of the man who had fathered her, a man she'd never met, was maddening. Tears of worry filled her gold-brown eyes. He went to her, bent down on one knee and took her hand in his. They had spent most of last night discussing Douglas Carruthers' impending arrival. She worried and fretted he would not like her any more than Mermadak, the man who had raised her, had. Frederick knew nothing could be further from the truth. "Do no' fash yerself over it, sweeting. He'll love ye, of that I am certain."

"Thank ye, husband." She smiled at him. "But what are we to do about Rose and yer arse of a brother?"

He chuckled at her tenacity. "I do no' ken, but I'll think of somethin'."

TWO

Dawn came and went, and still no sign of Douglas Carruthers. Thankfully, the rain had finally lifted as the gray skies moved south. By mid morning, the sun had chased away the fog, leaving the earth to look as though fairies had bejeweled the grass and trees with tiny diamonds. Frederick assured his wife that all was well before kissing her goodbye with the promise to keep her apprised of any word from the Carruthers.

Aggie paced nervously about her chamber, her mind racing from one worry to the next as she absentmindedly chewed on her thumbnail. Her real father, a man she had not known existed until very recently, was due to ride through the gates of the Mackintosh keep at any moment. While she was curious to meet him and see for herself why her mother had fallen in love with him, she still fretted over what he was going to think of her.

No matter what her husband believed or how hard he tried to convince her there was no need to worry, she could not help *but* worry. Would he be disappointed in what he had sired? Was he visiting only to inform her he had moved on with his life and had no desire to have her in it?

As far as she was concerned, it did not matter at all that he had at one time loved her mother. That was twenty years ago. People can change over time; that she knew with certainty.

For days now, she had tried to convince herself that his opinion of her — good, bad, or indifferent — would not matter. She was married to the best of men, with two beautiful children she adored, and a good life that a year ago she'd not have thought possible. Compared to that, Douglas Carruthers' view was not important. All that mattered was Frederick, their children, and the life they were building together.

'Twas a feeble lie at best. In truth, she wanted the man to like her, to look upon her with a kind father's fondness and adoration. She wanted everything Mermadak McLaren had never given her. He'd never had a kind word to say to Aggie and his displeasure with her only increased a thousandfold after her mother's death.

According to her mother's journals — another recent discovery — the Carruthers was everything Mermadak wasn't. Kind, generous, with a strong sense of honor. They'd loved one another beyond measure even though her mother had been married to Mermadak at the time. 'Twas enough to make Aggie's head hurt when she thought about it.

And there was the matter of Rose and Ian. The cur had the audacity to break her best friend's heart by breaking a promise, a vow. Of all the men she had known in her life, next to Frederick, Ian would have been the last person she thought would break his word. Least of all to Rose, who he professed to love above all else. 'Twas an unjust deed and Rose deserved far better.

So much was happening and it seemed 'twas all taking place at once.

Still, there was much to be thankful for. Such as her children, the youngest of whom was now happily feeding at the breast of her wet-nurse, Rebeca Mackintosh. Aggie felt she owed a lifetime of gratitude to the woman who had selflessly volunteered to feed Ada when Aggie had been so dreadfully ill and nearly died. It hadn't taken long for the two women to become friends.

"Yer goin' to wear a hole in the floor," Rebeca told her as she smiled adoringly at the babe. "Besides, yer makin' me tired watchin' ye go back and forth and back and forth."

Aggie ignored her and continued pacing. 'Twas impossible to sit still, to focus on any one task, not with her mind working on what she would say to Douglas Carruthers.

Rebeca let loose a heavy breath. "Come take yer daughter," she said with a smile. "'Twill keep yer hands and mind busy."

Whenever Aggie held Ada, every worry and dread evaporated in an instant. Such a beautiful, sweet babe, with ginger hair and bright blue eyes. "She is growing well?" Aggie asked for reassurance as she took the babe into her arms.

"Aye, I believe so," Rebeca replied with an affectionate smile. "She be strong and hearty, considerin' how she came into this world."

Aggie did not like to be reminded of that dark, ugly time. Poisoned by her own half-sister, Claire, with a potion meant to kill both she and her babe. The midwife had been forced to pull Ada from her body when Aggie had been too ill to even realize she was giving birth. Days later, she finally woke, with Frederick at her side, proud to announce she was the mother of a beautiful, but very tiny, baby girl.

'Twas also up to Frederick to tell her that Claire had hung herself.

Quietly, she had mourned Claire's loss. Long ago, they'd been the best of friends.

With Ada in her arms, her thoughts turned happier, and her worries far less significant. Pressing a tender kiss against her daughter's brow, Aggie whispered, "It matters naught if the Carruthers cares fer us or no'. I have ye, yer brother and father and that is all that matters in this world."

She'd no sooner spoken the words than Rose came bounding into the room.

Out of breath with excitement and running up the stairs, Rose paused just inside the doorway.

"He be here, Aggie!"

THE CALM AND PEACE THAT came with holding her daughter evaporated all too quickly. *Nay,* she told herself. *Ye'll no' cower, ye'll no' beg fer his affections.*

Rose came to wrap an arm around her shoulders. "He looks verra nice, Aggie. And quite handsome fer a man of his age."

Whether or not he was handsome was entirely unimportant. The only things that mattered were her husband, her children, and the Mackintosh family who had accepted her as one of their own from the day she married Frederick.

Would ye like me to take Ada fer ye?" Rebeca asked.

Aggie debated on whether or not to present her children to their blood grandsire at this, her first meeting with him. The instinct to protect her children was strong. "Aye, I'd like Rose to take her."

If it turned out that Douglas Carruthers was not the kind, generous man her mother wrote about in her journals, she did not want either of her children to witness this meeting. "Would ye also make certain Ailrig stays away?"

As she handed Ada to Rose, Elsbeth, Aggie's mother-by-law, floated into the room. She was as fierce as she was beautiful and Aggie admired her greatly. "Ye need no' worry about Ailrig," she said with a fond smile. "He is with his grandfather and uncles." A moment later, she was kissing the top of Ada's wee head.

"Please, tell me they be no' playin' with dirks again," Aggie said. "The last time they tried teachin' him, John nearly lost an eye."

Elsbeth laughed and shook her head. "Nay, no' dirks. I believe they've moved on to swords. But do no' worry it, they all be usin' wooden swords."

Aggie could only hope her nine-year-old son would not cause anyone any harm, wooden swords or nay.

Elsbeth took Aggie's hand in hers. "Come, let us go below stairs and meet Douglas Carruthers."

AT AGGIE'S REQUEST, ROSE TOOK Ada to her own room across the hall while she met with Douglas Carruthers. Rose was all too happy to oblige her friend. She'd never turn down the chance to hold a babe, especially wee Ada.

'Twas a small room with a small window that faced south and one arrow window that faced east. There were multiple tables heaped with all manner of fabrics. Once Elsbeth had learned what a talented seamstress Rose was, she immediately selected this room for her and began filling it with fabrics. Rose was all too happy to create beautiful gowns and dresses for Elsbeth, her daughters, and Aggie.

Now she sat next to the arrow window with Ada cooing and gurgling happily in her arms. Rose loved the way the tiny babe smelled of lavender soap and clean linens. While it was a wonderful feeling to hold the tiny babe in her arms, her heart ached with wanting one of her own. "Ada, I be about to share a secret with ye and I'll thank ye kindly no' to tell another soul," she whispered playfully.

Ada looked up at her and cooed, as if she understood completely what her Aunt Rose was telling her.

"I was almost a mum meself," she told her. "Three times." A sense of longing slowly crept in at the memories. "Three times I got with child with me husband, Almer Gray. I lost each one before I could reach me fourth month."

Though the miscarriages had happened many years ago, the pain was as fresh and intense as if it had happened only that morn. Those had been the most difficult and tragic of times, as a young bride wanting nothing more than to give her husband a child. The disappointment at losing the first was something she believed she would never get over. The agony after the third was unbearable. Almer had done his best to assure her he loved her all the same. 'Twasn't until he lay on his deathbed that she realized he had meant it.

'Twas then she experienced an epiphany of sorts. Was this the reason Ian had broken the troth? On more than one occasion, they had discussed her inability to carry a child to term. He had been adamant that he cared not if she could never give him a child of his own. *Tis ye I love, lass. I care no' about bairns, only that I am able to spend the rest of me life with ye.*

There had not been any doubt in her mind at the time that he meant what he said. Never had she met men so honorable as the Mackintosh men. Their word was everything to them.

Just when she thought she had shed her last tear for Ian Mackintosh, new droplets began to fall. The more she thought on it, the more she believed it was her inability to carry a child that had changed Ian's opinion of her. Mayhap, after seeing Frederick holding his first babe, it triggered something in Ian's heart, leading him to realize that he did in fact want children of his own.

Suddenly she found she no longer hated him with the ferocity she'd held only moments ago. How could she hold his desire for children against him? If anyone understood the ache of wanting something you could never have, 'twas she.

Looking down at Ada, whose eyelids were growing heavy, her sorrow increased tenfold. For years now, she had convinced herself she would be happy helping other women look after their babes. Now, as Ada sighed sleepily, she realized that was not true. Nay, she wanted a babe of her own. In truth, it mattered not if she birthed the babe or adopted, she wanted a child, not only for precious moments such as these. She wanted a child she could help grow into a fine person and see his or her dreams someday come true.

Ian had told her he was not opposed to adoption, if the chance ever arose. Something had to have happened to make him change his mind. But what? She wasn't sure if she wanted to know the answer to that question.

AGGIE STOOD TALL AND PROUD, waiting for the moment Douglas Carruthers would enter John Mackintosh's private study. Two chairs sat facing one another in front of the fireplace. Over the mantle hung the Mackintosh crest with the words *Touch not a cat without a glove* carved around the image of a cat-o-mountain. On the opposite side of the room, in front of two tall, narrow walls, was the long table John used as his desk. 'Twas all neat and well organized, much like the man himself.

Behaving as if they were her personal guards, Elsbeth stood to her left, Rebeca to her right. Elsbeth kept a steady and warm hand on Aggie's back.

The air in the room suddenly felt cold, even though a fire roared in the hearth. The rain had returned, along with a strong wind that howled in through the fur-covered windows. It felt dark, ominous, as if the weather were foretelling what was about to happen.

Smoothing out the skirts of her lavender dress with sweaty palms, Aggie took deep, steadying breaths. For years, she had worn her dark hair so it covered the nasty scar on the left side of her face. 'Twas a constant reminder of Eduard Bowie, the man who had raped her more than a decade ago. But earlier that morn, she had enlisted Elsbeth's help in plaiting her dark lochs, unafraid now of letting anyone see her marred face. If the Carruthers was offended by her appearance, then 'twas something he would have to deal with. If those who loved her were unbothered by it, then it should not matter to him.

"Ye look beautiful," Elsbeth told her.

"Thank ye," she replied softly. Doing her best to untie the knots that had been forming in her stomach, she adopted the best air of nonchalance she could manage.

Quietly, Rebeca slipped a hand into hers and gave a gentle squeeze of reassurance. "He will love ye, just as the rest of us do," Rebecca whispered.

Elsbeth agreed. "Of course he will. And if he does no'? It matters no', aye?"

Aggie lifted her chin ever so slightly. "Aye, it matters no'." Her heart, however, wished for all the world that this meeting would go well. *'Tis a meeting and nothing more. Yer life will no' be changed significantly, regardless of his opinion of ye.*

A moment later, Frederick walked into the room. He bore a kind and happy smile, which brightened the moment he looked at his wife. Aggie knew she'd never tire of seeing his face or his smile.

A heartbeat or two afterward, Douglas Carruthers stepped through the door.

For the longest moment, they could do nothing but stare at one another.

He looked older than she had anticipated. Hair that had once been as black as kohl, according to her mother's journal, was now a soft shade of silver. Although he was a few inches shorter than her husband, he still seemed a formidable man. Aggie took note of the surprised expression in his gold and brown eyes. Was he happy to see her? Disappointed in the offspring he'd fathered?

The longer he stared, the more uncomfortable she became.

"God's bones," he finally spoke, his voice sounded scratchy, almost raw. The color was beginning to drain from his face. "Ye are every bit as beautiful as yer mum."

She hadn't been prepared for such a compliment, for any compliment for that matter. One of her biggest worries — that he'd take one look at her and be so appalled, he would turn around and leave — was immediately laid to rest when he stepped forward and wrapped his arms around her.

"I've waited fer this day fer more than twenty years," he whispered softly against the top of her head. "'Tis both a prayer and dream come true."

For days she had planned out every word she would say to him, thought through every question carefully. But now, with his massive arms wrapped around her as if she were the most precious treasure he'd ever held, she could not think of a single thing to say. He held on tightly, as if he were afraid to let go.

A large knot formed in her throat. Words she wanted to say, tears she wanted desperately to shed, all bound together into a lump the size of a walnut. How many times had she wished for such affection from Mermadak, the man she had always thought her true father? She took in a deep, fortifying breath, her heart awash in a combination of regret and what she could only describe as relief.

He does no' hate me, nor is he ashamed.

MUCH TIME PASSED BEFORE DOUGLAS CARRUTHERS let go of his firstborn child. A child he'd dreamed of seeing from the moment her mother, Lila, had told him she was carrying. With his heart heavy with guilt and regret, he held her away so he could study every inch of her face: a face that reminded him of the woman he had loved but could never marry.

Aggie had his coloring — hair as black as pitch with gold-brown eyes, but that was where the resemblance ended. Everything else about her was Lila McLaren through and through. He did not know if he should laugh with joyful glee or cry and beg for his daughter's forgiveness. For the life of him, he could not take his eyes away from her.

Soon he felt her grow uncomfortable under his close scrutinization. "Fergive me lass," he whispered. "I fear the moment I laid eyes on ye all me good manners and sense left me."

Aggie returned his smile, her heart awash in relief.

"I be makin' a fool of meself, aye?"

Aggie shook her head. "N-nay," she murmured.

But he didn't believe her. Looking about the room, he realized all eyes were upon them. "Would ye like to sit, lass?" he asked with a wave of his hand toward the two chairs in front of the hearth.

Aggie nodded in affirmation and gracefully took one of the chairs in front of the fire. Once he saw she was settled, he took the seat opposite her. Resting his palms on his knees, he continued to stare.

"There were many things I wanted to say to ye, lass, and now I cannot find a word to utter other than to declare once again how beautiful ye are. Yer resemblance to yer mum is remarkable."

"I fear I suffer from the same affliction," she told him. In truth, she'd been fully prepared for a less than warm response.

He took in a deep breath. "I worried, lass, that ye would hate me and want nothin' at all to do with me. 'Tis grateful I am that ye be no' stickin' a dirk into me heart."

Aye, that thought had entered her mind on more than one occasion. 'Twas true that she felt a great deal of anger toward this man, but she wanted to hear from his own lips why he had never come for her.

Frederick stepped forward and placed a comforting hand on her shoulder. "Aggie, would ye like us to leave so that ye might speak to yer father alone?"

"Aye," she replied. "But I'd like ye to stay."

Elsbeth and Rebecca said nothing as they left the room. Aggie soon realized the wind had died down, the rain was nothing more than a soft patter against the stone walls. Even the roaring fire had settled down to a subdued crackle. A sense of calm filled the room.

Frederick remained behind his wife with one hand on her shoulder. Though she was no longer the meek and timid woman she had once been, she felt stronger whenever her husband was near.

Douglas began to grow uncomfortable; he found the silence maddening. "We have much to talk about, ye and I."

"Aye, we do," Aggie replied.

"Where should we begin?" he asked. Aggie took note of the trepidation in his tone.

She decided to ask the one burning question. The question that had kept her awake at night. "Why did ye never come fer me?"

Douglas paled ever so slightly. "I did. Once."

Aggie raised a doubtful brow.

He let loose a heavy breath and rubbed a hand across his jaw. "When yer mum told me she was with child, with me child, I begged her to leave Mermadak. She refused. She said 'twas yer legacy, yer destiny to someday take over the McLaren lands. No matter how I begged and pleaded, she refused to take that legacy away from ye."

Aggie's brow drew into a fine line of puzzlement. She remained quiet and still.

"I came once, after ye were born. She was visiting her family when her time came. She refused to allow me to see ye, not even a glimpse. She also refused to go away with me. 'Nay,' she told me. '*I'll no' take away me child's birthright. I'll no' give up McLaren lands. 'Twould be a disrespect to me mother and father and those who came before me. I'll no' have me child raised as illegitimate, scorned and looked down upon because her parents are no' married.*'" His voice trailed off at the memory of that fateful night, when he had begged and pleaded to no avail.

Aggie looked to Frederick. "Was that in her journals?" she asked.

He gave a slow shake of his head. "Nay," he answered. "But that does no' mean it did no' happen as he says. She did write frequently about yer birthright, and how she looked forward to seeing ye take over someday."

Turning her attention back to Douglas, she asked, "Ye tried once, then forgot about us," she accused him. "All those years of livin' in a hell on earth, and never once did ye inquire about me." Suddenly, she felt angry. *Only once did ye try to take me away. Once. Why no' more?*

Douglas fell to his knees before her, wounded by her accusations. "Nay, lass, nay! 'Twas no' like that, I swear it." Taking her hands in his, he pleaded with her. "I wrote to yer grandminny, at least once a month. She was the only connection to ye that I had. Andoreen, she told me ye were doin' well, that Mermadak had no idea ye were no' his. She said he treated ye like a princess and that I should no' worry over ye."

Aggie withdrew her hands from his and shot to her feet. "A princess?" she asked, eyes wide and mouth agape. Years of anger sprang loose, uncontainable, as were her tears. She began tugging at the laces of her dress. "Would ye like to see how he treated me?" she spat. "Would ye like to see the scars on me back, left by his hands?"

Frederick stopped her, taking her hands away from her laces. He pulled her to his chest. To Douglas, he said, "I fear ye were lied to, Douglas. As I told ye before, Mermadak was far from kind to me wife. God has yet to allow man to create a word that aptly describes his horrid mistreatment of Aggie."

Slowly, Douglas stood, his shoulders slumped, his heart breaking with each tear his daughter shed. "I still have Andoreen's letters."

In less than half an hour, Frederick was reading Andoreen McLaren's letters aloud to his wife. They were filled with nothing but kind words for Mermadak. She bespoke often of how well Aggie was growing, how much she adored Mermadak, and what a fine woman she would grow into.

By the fourth letter, Aggie declared she had heard enough. She sat in stunned silence for a long while, playing over and over in her mind the words of her long dead grandminny.

"Mermadak was never very fond of me," she said in a low, breathless tone. "I do no' remember me grandminny very well, she died when I was nine. I do no' ken why she would lie to ye, why she would say things that were so far from the truth as to be insane."

'Twas Frederick who answered her question. "To protect the two of ye."

Aggie looked up at him with the most befuddled expression. "Protect us?" She gave a shake of her head as if she had not heard him correctly.

"Yer mother loved Douglas verra much, Aggie. I believe she sensed that if he knew the truth, knew how things really were fer ye, he would have stopped at nothing to take ye away."

Douglas nodded in agreement. "'Tis the truth. I would have. Had I known, I would have killed the man with me bare hands, Aggie. But I did no' know. By the time Andoreen died, I had moved on. I had married Eleanor, was building a life with her. But never were ye far from me thoughts or me heart. And had I known, I would have come fer ye long ago, I swear it."

Aggie studied him closely for a long while. She could detect no deception, no dishonesty. Only sincere regret and shame. She took in a deep, cleansing breath, wiped away her tears and returned to her chair.

Lies. Nothing but lies for all these many years. In her heart, she had to believe her mother did what she thought was the right thing. She could not for a moment believe that anything her mother had done had been done out of spite or malice. Desperation perhaps, but not malice.

For a moment she wondered what her life would have been like had she known the truth. Had she the opportunity, she would have run away to Douglas long ago. But then, she would not have had Ailrig — even if he were conceived by rape. She loved her son regardless of how he was conceived. Mayhap it was time to tell her sweet boy the truth. If she waited, he might feel just as betrayed as she did now.

And had she run away successfully to live with Douglas Carruthers, she would never have met Frederick nor had Ada. God had put her on this path for a reason, even if she didn't quite understand why.

"I can no longer blame ye, Douglas. Each of us were lied to, even if those lies were made with good intentions." She took another deep breath. "I do no' wish to carry these feelin's of shame or betrayal with me any more."

THREE

More than a year ago Frederick Mackintosh had made a promise to Rose McLaren. *"If me brother ever hurts ye or plays ye false, I'll kill him with me bare hands."* Hence, an easy solution to mend Rose's heart was at hand.

'Twas unfortunate that his daft and addlepated brother Ian was forcing him to keep that promise. He had reached the ends of his patience in the matter. The way his brother had treated the sweet young woman since their return to Mackintosh lands was nothing less than an abomination. 'Twas beyond time someone took the matter into hand.

The hour was quite late, long past the evening meal. Most were back in their rooms or cottages, and only a few remained in the gathering room. He soon found the object of his consternation. There, sitting alone in a dark corner, sat Ian Mackintosh. From the number of empty cups — as well as the way the fool swayed as he sat — Frederick quickly surmised his brother was so into his cups he couldn't find his arse with both hands.

Ian Mackintosh.

Known throughout the land by women as a man as *beautiful* as he was a consummate lover. He'd left a trail of broken hearts across Scotland, England, France, and God only knew where else. While women adored him, their fathers, husbands, and brothers hated him with equal passion.

Frederick stood before the drunken sot, his feet braced apart, arms crossed over his massive chest, and waited for his brother to recognize his presence. Long moments passed before that happened.

Ian clutched a cup of ale with his large hands, as if he were a man lost at sea and the cup was his last vestige of hope for survival. Listing side to side, he mumbled incoherent words that only *he* could understand in his current state of extreme inebriation.

When Ian finally noticed his brother, he smiled up at him drunkenly. "Frederick," he said with a slow inclination of his noggin. He took another pull at his ale then swept his arms out wide. The golden liquid sloshed over the rim of the cup but Ian took no notice. "Welcome to me island."

Frederick had no idea what his brother meant and in truth, he did not care. Before he could tell Ian why he was there and what his intentions were, Ian spoke again.

"I fear ye do no' belong here, brother o' mine. This island is fer the wretched and unworthy." His lips curved into a wry smile; he was apparently quite amused with himself. "Nay, brother! Men such as ye do no' belong on the island of the lost!"

Frederick let out a sigh of irritation before kicking a stool out of his way. "Ian, 'tis time we had a talk." Grabbing his brother by his tunic, he hoisted him to his feet.

Ian glowered angrily with bloodshot eyes. "What are ye doin'?" he asked, his speech slightly slurred as he struggled to free himself.

"I be keepin' a promise." Frederick smiled deviously before drawing back one mighty fist then slamming it into his brother's face.

Ian fell backward against the stone wall, as dazed and confused as he was thunderstruck. White flashes of light floated in his eyes as blood trickled from his broken lip. Shaking his daze away, he looked up at his brother with nothing short of fury and hatred in his eyes. "What the bloody hell was that fer?"

As Frederick pulled him to his feet, he answered in a calm voice that belied his frustration and anger. "That was fer breakin' Rose's heart."

Once he was certain Ian wasn't going to fall over, he hit him once again. This time his fist landed on Ian's left eye. And again, his brother fell against the wall. This time he could not keep his feet and slid onto his arse. Before Ian could question the why of it, Frederick said, "That was fer breakin' yer word. A Mackintosh *never* breaks his word."

He hauled him to his feet yet again. Ian was barely able to stand on his own, but 'twas enough for Frederick to land a third punch. "And *that* was fer upsettin' me wife!"

Ian fell to the floor, his head lolled side to side while blood trickled from his nose and mouth.

Frederick sighed disgustedly. He'd seen Ian in many a tavern brawl, far drunker than he was now, and he'd still been able to maintain his feet and fight.

Nay, the young man lying askew, bloody and defeated, was not the same proud warrior. "What the hell has happened to ye?"

FREDERICK PULLED HIS BROTHER TO his feet, hoisted him over one broad shoulder, and left the gathering room. Mumbling a curse under his breath he was appalled and disgusted at how easily his brother had given up. Hell, he hadn't fought at all. 'Twas disgraceful for a man such as Ian to behave so dishonorably, no matter his reasons.

Determined to get to the bottom of things, he carried his brother above stairs. Taking the hallway to the left, he went straightaway to Rose's room and kicked at the door. Grudgingly, he cursed his brother as he shifted his weight. "Ye're a bastard, ye ken that don' ye?"

Ian replied with an incoherent grumble.

Cautiously, Rose cracked open the door. Though he could only see one vigilant eye peering through, that eye was red and puffy from crying. 'Twas fuel added to his already burning anger.

A moment passed before she realized Frederick had someone tossed over his shoulder like a sack of leeks. Her eyes widened in time with the door she pulled open. Frederick entered the room swiftly and tossed his brother into a chair near one of the tables that held her fabrics.

"What happened to him?" Rose blurted out as she rushed to kneel before the man she loved for reasons no one could fathom.

'Twas then Frederick noticed his beautiful wife sitting in a chair in the corner of the room. She shot to her feet and repeated Rose's question. In a flash, the two women were fluttering about the room, grabbing an ewer and linen cloths, hammering Frederick with too many questions to count.

"Are we under siege?" Aggie asked as she held the ewer over Ian's lap.

"I did no' hear the warnin' bells," Rose said as she dipped a linen cloth into the water and began wiping the blood from Ian's face.

Aggie stared blankly at her husband. "Why are ye j-just standin' there? Ye should be defendin' the k-keep!"

Frederick held up his hands. "There be no attack against the keep."

Rose paused her ministrations. "Then what happened? Did he take a fall?" She looked as vexed as she was concerned.

"Rose," Ian whispered her name almost reverently. "The most beautiful woman I ever laid eyes on."

With a furrowed brow she turned her attention back to Ian. His face bore an expression of devout love and adoration. "Never has a sweeter, more bonny woman ever graced God's earth." His voice was scratchy, his tone quite sad. As if he'd lost her to the black death and was remembering her fondly.

"He's been drinkin'," Aggie pointed out as if that answered a multitude of questions.

Annoyed, Rose asked once again, "What happened?"

Looking up at his older brother, Ian answered. "He was keepin' his word to ye."

Perplexed, the two women looked to Frederick for an explanation. Hopefully one that made more sense than Ian's.

"'Tis no less than I deserve," Ian slurred before Frederick could respond. "A Mackintosh ne'er breaks his word, ye see."

Neither Rose nor Aggie had any earthly idea what the drunken man meant.

"What is he goin' on about?" Rose demanded.

Frederick ran a hand through his ginger hair before answering. "I made a promise to ye more than a year ago, that if Ian ever hurt ye or played ye false, I'd kill him with me bare hands."

Aggie closed her eyes and took a deep breath while Rose was clearly appalled. "*Ye* did this to him?"

"He hurt ye *and* he took back his proposal. Ye've been cryin' fer days now, lass," he reminded her gently. "I was merely keepin' me word when me brother broke his."

"I be ready to accept me fate," Ian told Rose. He took her hand in his. "I ne'er loved a woman as I have loved ye. I want ye to go on with yer life. Do no' pine fer me or mourn me loss."

Rose withdrew her hand from his with the level of disgust she would feel had she just fallen in a pile of warm horse dung. "Ye can no' be serious!" she exclaimed. She didn't know which of these two men confounded or angered her more. At the moment, they were tied for first.

"He must kill me," Ian told her. "He must keep his word because I did no' keep mine."

She eyed them both speculatively for a long moment. The more she stood waiting for one of them to tell her this was nothing more than a jest, the angrier she became. Once Aggie took notice of Rose's furious glower, the way her skin had turned red, Aggie suddenly swore she heard her babe, Ada, crying. Setting the bowl on the table, she scurried to her feet. "Ada needs me, as does Ailrig."

Pausing at the door, Aggie looked back to her friend. "Ye may strangle Ian, but please, do no' harm me husband. I still need him, as do me children." She did not wait for a response before hurrying out of the room and closing the door behind her.

Once she was gone, Rose looked first to Frederick, then to Ian, and back again. "Ye have both lost yer minds."

"Nay, no' me mind. Just me heart. To the most beautiful women e'er to grace God's earth."

"Be quiet!" Rose shouted at the man she knew she loved without question. But at the moment, she was hard pressed to come up with a reason why. To Frederick she said, "Ye will no' kill him."

Frederick chuckled at her ferocity. "Nay, I shall no' kill him," he assured her before quickly adding, "Yet."

Exasperated, she rolled her eyes at him. "Why did ye feel the need to," she stumbled for the right words. "To beat him senseless?"

"Someone had to."

"Frederick be the most honorable man," Ian chimed in. He leaned forward in the chair and rested his head in his hands. "Far more honorable than I. He'd ne'er hurt the woman he loves."

She spun to face the object of her consternation. "So ye *do* love me?"

His shame was too great — as was the manner in which his head was spinning — to chance lifting his head to look at her. "Of course I love ye."

"Then why on earth did ye break yer word?"

"Because ye deserve better," he mumbled. "Why is the room spinnin'?" he asked of no one in particular.

Rose thrust her hands onto her hips. "I deserve better than what?" she asked him. Her tone was sharp.

"Than me," Ian answered. He sounded entirely ashamed.

Throwing her hands up in defeat, she looked at Frederick. "Go ahead. Kill him. I no longer care."

SOMEONE WAS USING HIS HEAD AS an anvil. 'Twas the only explanation for the pounding in his skull.

Every muscle and bone in his body ached so much he was afraid to make even the slightest attempt to open his eyes. His tongue felt thick, his mouth dry, as if he'd been sucking on wool. Fighting against the incessant thudding in his head, he tried to search for some memory that would explain why he felt like he'd been trampled by horses. It hurt to think, so he stopped.

He took in slow, long breaths through his nostrils as he rolled his pasty tongue against the roof of his mouth. Images — as fleeting as a rabbit and as clear as fog — flashed in his mind, but not one of them made any sense. Perhaps if he willed his heart to stop beating and prayed to God for merciful death, he might gain some clarity in heaven. *Nay,* he silently mused. *Ye're an eejit bound fer hell.*

As he lay still, trying to make sense of his current predicament, the hammering in his skull began to slowly subside to a more bearable pace. When he attempted to lift his hands to rub his temple, only one moved. The other was weighted down by something.

Not some*thing*. Some*one*.

A warm body was nestled next to him. A small, curvaceous body that smelled like lilacs.

Too terrified to move, he wracked his brain for some memory that would explain not only *who* he was in bed with, but how it happened. After a moment, that warm body let loose with a contented sigh before slipping from the bed. He could hear her rattling about. From the sound of it, she was pouring something liquid into a cup, but why she insisted on doing it so loudly, he couldn't fathom. Whomever it was, she possessed not an ounce of mercy or compassion for his current state.

"Good morn to ye, husband."

Nay, he could not have heard her correctly. *That is no' Rose and she did no' just call me husband!*

He felt a knee sink into the bed, then a warm hand lifting his head. "Aggie brought this to ye earlier," she explained. "'Twill help ye feel better."

He was suddenly struck with such fear and trepidation, he could not respond. She poured the liquid into his mouth. It tasted awful, but at least it helped to soothe his parched mouth and tongue.

Rose giggled sweetly. "Will ye look at us? Married less than a day and already I be nursin' ye back to health."

Husband? Married? Nay!

He must have spoken his thoughts aloud, for she giggled again. "Aye, ye are me husband and I be yer wife," she told him. "Do ye no' remember?"

Oh, would that he could! He prayed fervently for some tiny sliver of a memory that would prove she was jesting, but his mind was as blank and dark as a cave at midnight. It took every ounce of strength he possessed to find the courage to open his eyes. Convinced that when he did, Rose would be laughing at him and would admit the truth: that she was simply jesting as some demented way of getting even with him for going back on his word.

But when he opened his eyes, he did not find any such expression to either ally his fears or prove he was correct.

Nay, there was no jest, no humor in her eyes. Instead, those big blue eyes of hers were filled with adoration and happiness.

Fear overtook him. He sat up so quickly that his head spun and he nearly retched. He did not let that stop him from scurrying from his bed. "This be a mistake," he declared. He was having a rather difficult time forming any kind of coherent thought, let alone the ability to put voice to what he was feeling.

The adoration he'd seen only a moment ago, turned instantly to hurt. "A mistake?" she asked.

Giving his head a rapid nod — a movement he instantly regretted — he said, "Aye! A mistake!"

She stared at him in dismay. "'Twas yer own idea, Ian. Do ye no' remember?"

He thrust his hands onto his hips only to realize he was standing before her completely naked. Immediately he began searching for his clothes. "Nay, I most certainly do no' remember!"

"I do no' ken why ye're shoutin' at me," Rose said. "'Twas *ye* that insisted — nay, *demanded* — we be married. Ye said ye regretted yer decision to break our troth and could no' live the rest of yer life without me."

He gave up searching for his trews. He needed to get out of his chamber as quickly as possible. He found his plaid lying on the floor on the other side of his bed. "I was drunk," he told her. "I was in no condition to marry anyone!"

She quirked one delicate eyebrow. "Ye regret marryin' me then?"

Were he not so flummoxed, so stupefied, and so hung over, he might have been able to have a more intelligent conversation on the matter. "Aye, I regret it!"

Without his boots or so much as a by-your-leave or a backward glance, he quit the room in such a hurry, one would have thought his arse had just caught fire.

SILENTLY FUMING, SHE WATCHED HIM leave. For a long moment, she sat on the edge of the bed, holding on to tears she was determined not to shed.

One moment she felt as though her heart had been cleaved in twain; the next, she was mad enough to tear the door from its hinges. Ian had been confusing and confounding her for weeks now. And for the life of her she could not figure out why. Last night, he had sworn on his mother's grave that he cared not if she ever bore him a child, he loved her either way. If that was not what was holding him back, then what was?

At the very least she felt he owed her an explanation. Something more than *ye deserve better than me.*

They had shared so many things, when they'd been at the McLaren keep. After Mermadak had set the keep ablaze, she had willingly stayed behind with Ian, to help tend to those who had been too injured from the fire, or too sick to travel to Mackintosh lands. Together, they had worked hard to feed those people, kept them warm through that brutal winter by living in the old granary.

But the moment they had set foot on Mackintosh land weeks ago, everything between them began to change. Gone was the camaraderie, the stolen kisses, the playful jesting and friendship they had forged. Ian no longer sought her out to share their meals together or inquired how she fared.

Then he'd come to her a week ago and said he was breaking the promise he had made to her that winter. He no longer wished to marry her.

Just like that, her hopes and dreams of building a life with him were shattered. Gone in the blink of an eye and without an explanation. At least not one that made any sense.

She'd had her fill of his brooding, his silence, and his poor attitude. "I refuse to shed another tear over this man," she blurted out.

Quickly, she jumped to her feet, grabbed her gown from the floor and slipped into it. "Ye only *thought* ye regretted yer words last night, Ian Mackintosh. But ye've yet to feel *true* regret. Ye do no' yet ken the meanin' of the word."

His only focus was to get to the loch. Hopefully, if there was a good, kind God, He'd see His way to helping him drown.

The moment his bare feet sank in the mud He regretted not grabbing his boots on his mad dash out of his room. Figuring it didn't matter, he ignored the cold muck between his toes and continued his fast forward progress toward the loch. He also ignored the curious stares of his clansmen as well as the questions they tossed his way.

Thundering across the courtyard, through the open gate, and down the hill, he finally reached his destination. Thankfully, no one was about. He pulled his plaid away, letting it fall to the grass, and walked straight into the frigid water. *What in the bloody hell have I done?* He cursed inwardly as he dove under the water. He held his breath until his lungs felt close to bursting. With a swift kick, he tore through the water, up and out, gasping for air. *Ye can no' even drown yerself, ye coward.*

The cold water did little to douse the multitude of feelings coursing through his veins or the thoughts crashing around in his mind. Pulling in a big breath, he dove under the water and swam away from the grassy bank. His muscles ached with a vengeance, as did his heart.

He loved Rose. Loved her deeply. Aye, the realization had caught him completely off guard all those months ago. He had tried to fight the new and perplexing feelings, the feelings he didn't understand at the time. But his resolve to never end up like his father and brothers — completely devoted to and besotted with their wives — gave way to his weak heart.

He broke through the surface once again and floated on his back. Closing his eyes against the bright afternoon sun, he thought back on the last year of his life.

Rose was different from other women he knew. As fierce as a cat-o-mountain and possessing an inner strength that bewildered him, his mind was unable to battle against his heart, and before he comprehended what was happening, he was in love.

He could remember the exact moment he realized he was doomed. 'Twas during the fire at the McLaren keep, when large flames tore through the roof, piercing the night sky like fingers reaching out from the bowels of hell. He'd lost sight of her, of this beautiful woman who somehow managed to perturb him and impress him at the same time.

During that long moment when he thought he'd lost her to the fire, he was quite certain his heart had been torn from his chest. Never in his life had he experienced such fear, such gut-wrenching anguish. Certain he'd lost the one person he loved more than anyone else in this world, the pain nearly brought him to his knees.

One moment he was convinced he'd lost her, so consumed with grief he could not move, but in the next, when he saw her dashing out of the keep, alive and well, the relief and utter joy was just as intense as the grief he'd felt a heartbeat earlier.

'Twas his undoing.

After that tiny moment in time, he'd never been able to deny his love for her.

Weeks later, after he confessed his feelings to her, he had proposed and, much to his relief, she had accepted.

They made plans to marry as soon as they returned to his home, to Mackintosh lands.

But when they returned and he watched Frederick's agony, his suffering, his worry that he'd lose Aggie as she lay in bed, poisoned, giving birth to a babe far too early, fear began to consume Ian. He could not fathom ever having to watch his Rose suffer as Aggie had. Nay, he did not worry she'd be poisoned. But other things, far less sinister, could take her from him. He could not bear the thought. Could not imagine having to live his life without her.

Aggie and the babe had survived and both were now quite hale and hearty. Little Ada, just as beautiful as her mum, was flourishing and it seemed things were looking up for his brother and new family. 'Twas a miracle that either had lived and Frederick celebrated that fact on a daily basis.

Ian hadn't wanted to hurt Rose, truly he hadn't. But 'twas better he break her heart now, than end up disappointing her later.

His heart began to feel heavy again. Taking another deep breath, he rolled over and dove down to the bottom of the loch. *There has to be a way out of this marriage*, he thought before planting his feet on the rocky bottom and shooting back up to the surface.

As he broke through, he caught sight of someone standing on the bank. Wiping the water from his eyes, he was able to see who it was.

Rose.

And she looked mad enough to kill.

GOD'S TEETH HE WAS HANDSOME!

It had not taken long to discover Ian had gone to the loch. As soon as she stepped into the gathering room, people were all too happy to point her in the right direction. Now she stood staring at him, all braw muscle and power. The sight of his bare bottom was enough to make her want to swoon. Or take a nibble out of each crescent moon shaped buttock that bounced in the water.

His wet blonde locks clung to his neck and shoulders: unparalleled muscular shoulders that looked as though they'd been carved from granite. Hard, sinewy, powerful shoulders, and a chest she wanted very much to feel pressed hard against her own.

Aye, he was a braw warrior, as beautiful as he was stupid.

Pushing away her physical desire, she glared at him. Determined to have both a sensible answer as to why he'd broken the troth, as well as the last word, she called out. "I want to have a word with ye, Ian Mackintosh."

He looked terrified. *Good,* she thought to herself. *Ye should be.*

If she thought he'd swim right up to her and beg forgiveness, she'd have a long wait.

She could well imagine him being stubborn enough to refuse to get out of the water. Stubborn enough to wait until the loch froze over, and then he'd probably still remain.

"Are ye afraid to talk to me?" she asked.

"I be naked," he shouted back.

Resting her fingertips on her hips, she shook her head. "We be married now, Ian. I believe it be perfectly acceptable fer me to see you naked." Though she might not be able to hang on to her anger or frustration, especially if he got close enough for her to reach out and touch him. Mayhap 'twas safer for him to remain where he was.

"Why did ye break our troth?" she asked. Her tone was demanding, insistent.

"I told ye why."

She took in a deep breath, hoping it would quash some of her ire. It didn't. "Nay, ye have no' told me why. All ye said was ye could no' marry me. Ye never bothered with the *why* of it. I demand to ken *why*."

She watched his Adam's apple bob up and down, could see clearly that he was looking for either the courage to speak or the words.

"Why?" she asked once again, but not with as much anger in her tone.

"Ye deserve better than me, Rose," he told her.

"Of course I do, ye eejit! But for reasons I can no' explain, I do no' want better."

He began to slowly swim back to the bank. He stood upright, the water barely covering his nether regions. "I am goin' to ask our marriage be set aside, Rose. 'Tis fer yer own good."

If he'd been close enough to strangle, she would have. Aye, she knew he was bigger and stronger than she, but she still would have liked the opportunity to try. All the hurt she thought she'd set aside came back in one painful beat of her heart.

"Do ye remember nothin' from last night?" she asked, her voice cracking.

He needn't answer. From his expression, he could not remember a thing that had transpired. 'Twas probably a good thing for her that he didn't. For if he did, he'd probably be so angry with her he would be tempted to strangle the life right out of her.

"Ye said ye loved me, Ian. Ye said ye regretted breaking our troth. Ye begged fer a second chance. Begged fer me fergiveness." She choked back tears, refusing to shed them lest he see how hurt she truly was. "Ye begged me to marry ye that verra moment. Insisted upon it, fer ye could no' bear to live another minute without me by yer side. Ye would no' quit yer shoutin' until Frederick woke yer father to marry us."

That much was true. It had happened just as she described. However, she left out the part where he passed out before his father arrived. She had helped Frederick pour his drunken carcass into his bed. But when she had tried to leave, he grabbed her around the waist and pulled her down next to him. *"Gradh mo Chroi,"* he had whispered into her ear. *Love of me heart, do no' leave me.*

How many times had her mother told her that a man sometimes needed the aid of strong drink before he could say what was truly in his heart? Rose hadn't believed it until last night. Now she was left feeling very much the fool.

"I liked ye better when ye were in yer cups. At least then ye spoke what ye really felt."

She had allowed him to make a fool out of her, something she had sworn she would not allow the first time she'd ever met him. That seemed a lifetime ago, that moment when she first saw the blonde-haired, blue-eyed Adonis. Regret, frustration and humiliation took over now. Scooping up his plaid, she left him in the loch and stomped away.

"Rose!" Ian called out. "Bring back me plaid!"

"Ye can go to hell, Ian Mackintosh! And ye can go there as naked as the day ye were born!"

HE COULDN'T RIGHTLY BLAME HER FOR being angry with him. However he *could* and did blame her for leaving him naked in the frigid loch. "Rose!" he called out again. "Bring back me plaid. Now!"

Too hurt and angry, she ignored him and continued back to the keep.

"How dare she?" he ground out as he pounded his fists into the water.

Anger bubbled upward from his stomach. Could she not see he was doing her a favor by putting her aside? 'Twas the merciful thing to do, considering he had nothing to offer her as a husband. She was far too stubborn for her own good. He knew he'd hurt her, but at the moment, his male pride got in the way of any sort of common sense.

If she hoped to humiliate him by leaving him in the loch without so much as a leaf to cover himself with, she was sorely mistaken. Not once in his entire life had he even been tempted to hit a woman. But now? He was sorely tempted to find her and take her over his knee.

"Bloody hell," he growled out. A moment later, he was out of the water and heading back to the keep.

EVERY PEBBLE, EVERY MUD PUDDLE, AND every crude remark made by his clansmen as he exploded through the courtyard and into the keep only fueled his already burning anger. An older woman was spreading fresh rushes on the gathering room floor when he stormed in. "Och, Ian!" she giggled. "Ye seem to have fergotten to cover yerself, lad!"

His face was already purple with rage, so she did not notice how it burned with humiliation.

"I do no' mind though!" she said with a smile. "But ye might want to cover yerself fer the sake of the children." Tugging a small drying cloth from her belt, she tossed it to him. He caught it with one hand and used it to cover himself.

"Where. Is. Rose?" His words were clipped, heated.

"I believe she went above stairs, lad."

Ignoring the whistles and comments as they pertained to his bare arse, he took the stairs two at a time. He went first to her room, threw open the door, but 'twas empty.

He spun around to head back to his room, when he saw her at the end of the hall. Her eyes widened in surprise first, before he caught a fleeting glimpse at her fear.

"Woman!" he shouted.

With nowhere to run, she turned around and went back into his chamber. He was at the door before she could bar it. Pushing through, out of breath and furious, he stood in the doorway and glowered at her. "Did ye find it amusin' to leave me in the loch without so much as a leaf to cover me nakedness?"

Slowly, she backed away, looking more fearful as the moments passed.

"I asked ye a question," he said as he took a step forward.

She cleared her throat before answering. "'Tis no more than ye deserved, ye pigheaded lout!"

He quirked a brow at her insult. "Just because ye be me wife does no' mean ye can do as ye please. It does no' give ye the right to leave me naked, to force me to walk all through the keep without a stitch of clothing. It also does no' allow ye to insult me."

Even if he had not spoken a word, she would have been able to tell just how angry he was. His eyes pinned her in place, the vein on the side of his neck pulsed and throbbed. He was standing over her now, his hands clenched into fists at his side. At the moment, she was unable to determine if he planned on hitting her. Believing they were married, he might just believe 'twas his right to do so.

Mustering courage, she pushed her fear aside, fully prepared to admit they were not.

"As me wife, Rose McLaren, ye shall show me the respect I deserve as yer husband. Do no' ever tempt me patience like this again, or else I'll give way to me anger and give ye the spankin' I be certain ye deserve."

Her eyes widened in surprise. "Ye would no' dare!"

"Because we be newly married, I will nay give in to the temptation to do just that. But mark me word, ye'll no' be so lucky next time."

"Next time?" she scoffed at the idea. "I thought ye were setting me aside? I thought ye wanted out of this marriage?"

Her questions stopped him dead in his tracks. 'Twas as if he had forgotten what he'd said earlier. "I fear the beatin' Frederick gave ye last night did more damage than I previously thought," she told him. "One minute ye can no' stand the sight of me and want to cast me aside, the next ye speak as if ye think we'll be married a good long while."

He turned away from her, clenching and unclenching his hands. He had no desire to admit she had a valid point. He'd been so furious that he had forgotten he wanted to end the marriage.

"I AM NO GOOD FER YE, ROSE," he told her pointedly. "I can no' give ye the things a woman wants, like beautiful dresses, fancy slippers and baubles. Hell, I can no' even give ye a decent home."

She stared at him in stunned silence. *So that was what all this was about?* She had never been more thoroughly convinced he was an idiot.

"Ye deserve far better than me."

He was an exasperating man. "Of course I do!" she replied. "Every one kens that."

He had no good response. Instead, he stood next to the cold hearth with his head hanging low.

"So *ye* decided to break our troth, to set me aside, because ye can no' give me things I never asked fer?" she demanded with a shake of her head. "Ye be just as addled as Frederick said ye were. Ye're also quite selfish. And a coward."

His head shot up so rapidly she was surprised he didn't snap his neck.

"Aye, I said it." She crossed her arms over her chest. "Instead of takin' it as a challenge, ye surrendered. Instead of doin' what most men do — work verra hard to make a happy and safe home fer their wives, work hard to give them what they can — ye took the coward's way out by surrenderin'." She shook her head in disgust. "Nay, ye be no' the man I thought ye were, and all the things I heard about ye must be lies."

"What things?" he dared to ask.

She gave him a casual shrug of her shoulders. "That ye have stared into the face of death and no' even flinched. That ye be a brave and powerful warrior who never backs down from a fight or a challenge."

She was poking at his male pride and his ire began to show. "Those things are all true."

She shrugged her shoulders again. "I've also heard ye be a fine lover, that ye can please a woman until her toes curl and her eyes cross. But I fear that is probably no' true either. And I fear we'll never find out, since ye're settin' me aside."

The space between them disappeared in two long strides. He leaned down to look her directly in the eye. "Believe me when I say that if I were to take ye to me bed, ye'd be more than just *pleased*. Ye'd be thoroughly and most assuredly loved until ye could no' walk."

With a raised brow, she challenged him. "Prove it."

LIKE ANY GOOD WARRIOR, HE met her challenge the only way he knew how: head on. In the span of three fluttering heartbeats, Ian had his arms wrapped around her waist. Without permission or warning, he pressed his lips to hers.

He took soft and tender possession of lips he'd kissed before, but not with the fervor and intensity of this moment. Languid. Slow. Treasuring every ragged breath she was trying so desperately to conceal. He reveled in her soft moans of pleasure.

Surrender was inevitable.

Whether he surrendered to her or she to him, 'twas not important. What was important was that he had decided he would never set her aside, would never let her go. He was going to make her his, for now and forever. She was his wife, and soon they would consummate their marriage, sealing their fate, their destiny to one another for all eternity.

The kiss left her breathless, with legs as sturdy as hot honey. Every square inch of her felt warm with thrilling anticipation. And he'd only begun to kiss her.

His hands spanned her dainty waist before he began to gently caress her back. She swore she could feel how hot his fingertips were, even through her chemise and gown. Shivers of delight trailed up and down her spine, spread to her stomach, her chest.

Unable to deny the need to touch him, she wrapped her hands around his neck and pulled him closer, wanting with desperation to feel every square inch of his body with her palms, her fingertips, and her tongue.

Ian's hands found their way to her braid and made quick work of unbinding it. 'Twasn't until she felt his long fingers combing through her locks that it even registered in her mind he'd done it. Those wonderfully hot lips of his soon left hers and began an exploration of her cheek, her chin, and next, her earlobe.

Grabbing her hair tightly betwixt his fingers, he pulled her head back so he could leave hot kisses along the length of her neck. There was no denying the immense pleasure he was deriving from making her mad with desire, just as she would not deny she took great pleasure from those fiery kisses.

Everything she knew about loving a man she had learned from her first husband. Though she might not have had as much experience as Ian, she was not without her own knowledge from which to pull. Though her first husband had been much older than she and not built anywhere near as nicely as Ian, she felt confident in herself.

But this kiss, these kisses? Nay, Almer had never kissed her like this. These were far different, far more passionate, more intense.

"Wife," Ian whispered against her neck, "I dare say I shall never grow tired of kissin' ye."

Wife.

He had called her *wife*.

He believed they were well and duly married.

For a brief moment, she was tempted to remain quiet and not correct him, for she was fearful that if she did tell him the truth, he might be so thankful he'd leave her.

But she knew she could not lie to him, not now. The moment was too important. She could very well have him thinking they were about to consummate their marriage, only to have him learn the truth later. How would he look at her then? Nay, she could not stand the thought of his disgust or doubt or skepticism.

"Ian," she whispered in a voice she barely recognized as her own, "though I wish nothin' more than for you to continue, I fear we can no'."

His lips were on her neck, his tongue making slow, circular motions that were driving her to the point of madness.

"Pray tell, wife, are ye no' enjoyin' me kisses?"

She sucked in a sharp breath when he blew a hot breath against her tender skin. "Oh, Ian, I am."

"Then why must we stop?" he asked as he took her earlobe betwixt his teeth and nibbled.

"Because we are no' exactly married."

An interminable, painfully long moment passed as she felt him grow rigid with confusion. "What do ye mean, *we're no' exactly married?*" She could feel his breath against her neck.

Unable to speak at first, she had to clear her throat before she could answer. "I mean," she paused, searching for the best way to describe exactly what had happened the night before. "Well, ye see, ye were verra into yer cups. And ye kept demandin' that someone find a priest to marry us. And, well, ye see, ye *were* verra drunk…" she trailed off, for she could feel his spine stiffen, and was certain he would be as angry as a poked bear.

Another long moment of silence passed between them before he let her go, stood taller, and looked her in the eye. "Were we married or no'?"

"No' exactly," she said, diverting her eyes to his chest, for she could not bear to look at him. Shame and humiliation built.

"Ye said that. Now explain yerself."

There was no easy way to explain it, so like any good woman, she decided to confront the issue head on. "Ye were verra drunk," she began.

"Ye said that and I ken I was drunk," he reminded her. He sounded perturbed and she knew he was going to be downright furious by the time she explained it all.

"Ye were *verra* drunk and yellin' fer someone to fetch Father MacBrodie. Well, he was no' here, ye see, so ye demanded we wake yer da. As chief he can marry a couple, ye ken."

"I ken," he said.

Chancing a glance at his face, she could see a tic begin to form in his jaw. "Well, we did no' want to wake yer da, so Frederick said that as chief of Clan McLaren, he could marry us." That much was true. "Well, ye started sayin' vows, that ye'd love me until ye took yer last breath on this earth and then beyond. Ye promised to cherish me all the rest of yer days."

"And?" he asked with a skeptical tone and raised brow.

"Well, before I could make ye any promises, ye sort of passed out."

His eyes widened in disbelief. Unable to form the words, his mouth opened and closed repeatedly.

"We carried ye up here and put ye to bed. But ye would no' let me leave. Ye kept professin' yer love fer me and begged me to no' leave ye." She was speaking so rapidly it was difficult for him to keep up. "And then when ye woke this morn, I thought only to jest with ye fer a moment. But then ye got so angry and said ye regretted marryin' me, and I was so hurt, I was no' goin' to tell ye."

Finally, he moved. He took a few tentative steps away, a look of utter disbelief etched on his face. Agitated, he ran a hand through his blond locks. "So we be no' married?" he asked, still unable to believe what he'd just heard.

"Nay," she whispered. "We be no' married."

THERE WAS NO MISTAKING HER PAIN, for her blue eyes grew damp, her bottom lip trembled. Ian knew her sorrow was real. It had not been easy for her to admit the truth. Valiantly, she held the tears back as she stared at her feet and worriedly worked her fingers together.

He had two choices.

One, he could use this moment as an excuse to walk away now and forever. Let her go so she might make a life of her own, with someone else who could give her all the things he felt certain she deserved.

Or two, he could swallow his bloody pride and do as she suggested; use his current lack of financial stability to propel himself forward. Work from sunup to sundown every day for the rest of his life to give her all those things he wanted her to have.

Letting loose a frustrated breath, he found a plaid on the back of a chair, wrapped it around his waist and shoulder. Next, he grabbed her hand and pulled her out of the room.

Astonished, she hurried behind him. "What are ye doin'? Where are ye takin' me?" She sounded afraid.

"To find the bloody priest!"

Dragging his soon-to-be-wife down the stairs and into the grand gathering room, he began shouting, "Where be Father MacBrodie?"

Several sets of fearful eyes looked back at him. Uncertain as to why Ian seemed so angry, people began flurrying about like leaves in the wind, unwilling to find out.

"Ian, slow down!" Rose demanded. "Ye're scarin' people!"

"Where be Father MacBrodie?" His voice boomed through the room, echoed off the beams and walls with ferocity.

No one answered. Instead, they fled for safety.

"Bloody hell," he muttered under his breath as he headed toward the door.

He was about to pull it open when his father called to them from behind. "What in the name of God is goin' on?"

If Rose had thought Ian sounded furious, 'twas nothing compared to John Mackintosh's thundering voice. The man was taller than Ian, broad as a barn and as strong as an ox. When Rose first met him, he had scared the daylights out of her. But she soon learned that he was a kind and gentle man. Unless he was angry. Then 'twas best the rest of the world get out of his way. That must have been where Ian got his temper from.

Ian spun around, still holding on to Rose's hand. "I need Father MacBrodie. Now."

John's scrutinizing gaze made Rose's legs quake with fear while Ian seemed unbothered by it.

As if he understood everything that was happening, John gave an approving nod before answering. "He be at Seamus's givin' him last rites."

Rose's heart felt heavy at that news. Seamus was a sweet old man who had lost his wife years before. "We can no' bother Father MacBrodie *now*," Rose politely informed them. 'Twould be shameful to interrupt a priest while he was giving last rites.

Both turned to look at her as if she'd lost her mind. She began to shrink under their gazes.

"What kind of man do ye think I am?" Ian asked.

"I imagine he'll be done by the time ye make yer way to Seamus's cottage," John said. "Ye'll no' be interruptin' anythin'. I'll get Elsbeth and we'll meet ye there."

Before she could utter a response or argument against seeking out the priest at this most sorrowful time, Ian was hauling her out the door.

With legs as long as his, it was quite easy for him to thunder across the courtyard quickly. Rose, however, was not thus blessed and had to run to keep up with him.

Out of the courtyard, they turned left to head for Seamus's cottage. Clutching her skirts in one hand, Rose did her best to keep up with this man she loved but could not say *why* she did. As far as she was concerned, he was as foolish as he was handsome, as hot-headed as he was generous. 'Twas enough to make her question her own soundness of mind.

"Ian, please slow down!"

"Why?" he asked without bothering to look back at her.

"Because I can no' keep up with ye, ye big lummox!"

Beyond frustrated with him at the moment, she tried yanking her hand from his tight grip. While she could guess why he was in such a hurry, she was not certain she was equally enthusiastic about the idea. This was not how she had imagined her wedding day: hauled through mud puddles by an angry groom, who still wore no boots.

"Ian, please!" she pleaded with him.

Reluctantly, he stopped and turned to face her.

Och! Those big blue eyes of his were enough to melt her heart like butter left in the sun. But when they were filled with intense anger, as they were now, 'twas enough to make her want to run screaming and hie herself off for safety.

"Would ye please tell me *why* ye're in such a hurry to find the priest?"

Judging from his perplexed expression and raised brow, he thought it a most daft question. "To marry us."

She had expected as much, but considering how angry he seemed, she thought it best to ask for clarification. "And ye mean to do that now? With ye half naked and no boots? And besides, ye have no' even asked fer me hand yet!"

"Of course I have!" he exclaimed.

"Nay," she said, giving a slow and thoughtful shake of her head. "Ye broke our troth, remember? And now ye're draggin' me to find a priest. Do no' look at me as if I've lost me mind, Ian. Ye be the one who keeps changin' *his*!"

Cocking his head to one side, he asked, "Do ye wish to marry me or no'?"

She took a deep, cleansing breath before answering. "That depends."

His scowl increased, forming tight lines around his eyes. "Depends on what?"

"Do ye plan on always bein' so temperamental? Do ye always plan on changin' yer mind as quickly as the weather?" Considering the events of the last few weeks, she thought it a most reasonable inquiry. "Besides, ye've yet to ask me proper."

It was not her intent to vex him or instigate another argument betwixt them. However, she thought it important to set matters straight before they reached the priest.

"Again, I ask ye, do ye wish to marry me?" The slight tic in his jaw increased in time with the beating of her heart.

"Will ye always be this temperamental? Will ye always be this pig-headed and obstinate?"

"Aye, I will," he replied. "Because I fear *ye* will vex me to the point of madness each and every day of our lives. But I find I love ye enough to live with that flaw."

'Twas her turn to be angry. "Flaw?" she asked with much exasperation. "If ye find me so flawed, why are ye in such a hurry to marry?"

"Because for reasons I cannot begin to fathom, I love ye. When ye're no' vexin' me to the point of madness, I find ye sweet, bonny, and generous. Ye have the ability to amuse me *while* ye're vexin' me. And I do no' wish to spend the rest of me days without ye, wonderin' what might have been betwixt us."

Tears flooded her eyes and trailed down her cheeks. 'Twas most refreshing to hear him say those sweet words while sober. With the sleeve of her dress, she swiped away her tears and smiled up at him. "Ye vex me as well, ye handsome lummox."

A broad, much relieved smile formed on his lips, making his eyes twinkle in the sunlight. "So ye'll marry me then?"

"Aye," she replied with a sniffle. "I'll marry ye on one condition."

His smile faded. "What condition?"

"Ye will at least put on yer boots?"

FOUR

"What about the banns?" Father MacBrodie asked, aghast at the notion of marrying anyone without following proper procedure. They were standing in the courtyard, he and Ian and Rose. Ian was determined to marry Rose immediately. Father MacBrodie was just as determined to see that rules were followed according to the law.

Appearing as round as he was short, he had to lean his head back in order to look into Ian's eyes. Though he was as pious as the day was long, he was not afraid of putting a Mackintosh in their place when the occasion called for it.

"We do no' need banns posted," Ian assured him. "I have me family's blessin'."

Father MacBrodie cast a glance at Rose. "What about *her* family?"

Rose smiled thoughtfully. "The Macktinoshes *are* me family."

The older man eyed her suspiciously, staring into her eyes as if he could sense a lie from a thousand paces.

Her smile faded. "Both me parents be dead, ye ken. I've no brothers nor sisters, save fer Aggie. Though we share no blood, we share a bond just the same."

Unimpressed, the priest asked, "How long have ye known this man?"

"More than a year now," Rose answered. She was growing more and more uncomfortable under his scrutiny.

"Are ye aware of his reputation, lass?" he asked before turning to stare Ian down. "As a scoundrel? A man who has no compunction in ruinin' an innocent lass's reputation? As a womanizer of near biblical proportions?"

He may have meant it as an insult, or a simple statement of fact. Ian took it as a compliment and smiled proudly. A deep blush came to Rose's cheeks. Aye, she was well aware of Ian's past, but she was confident he would no longer chase women after they were married. "I ken what he was, Father."

"Are ye no' worried he'll break yer heart, lass?"

Smiling cheekily, she said, "Nay, fer he kens I'll kill him while he sleeps if he even thinks to."

Somewhat satisfied with her answer, he offered the closest thing to a smile he ever volunteered. Then he glared at Ian, "Be there a reason why ye're in such a hurry? Have ye by chance already endangered this young woman's soul by taking her to yer bed outside the bonds of marriage?"

Ian's lips curved into a devilish grin as he leaned in to whisper into Father MacBrodie's ear. "Nay yet. But married or no, I intend to take her to me bed before this day is out." He righted himself before adding, "Ye can either marry us this day, or ye will be the one to blame if her soul is endangered."

AFTER THEY EXCHANGED THEIR VOWS, a loud cheer exploded from the crowd.

There had been no time to prepare a celebratory feast, for which Ian was ecstatically grateful. He'd been waiting for more than a year to take Rose to his bed. They could observe their union with the clan on the morrow. But for now, for tonight, he wanted her all to himself.

Scooping her into his arms, he carried her into the keep and above stairs to his — nay, 'twas their's now — chamber. Pausing at the door, he offered her a tender kiss and his most devilish smile.

"Ye seem to be in a hurry," Rose teased.

Laughing, he pushed open the door with his booted foot and carried her inside. "I've been waitin' a very long time fer this night."

"And ye be certain ye ken what ye're doin'?" she asked playfully.

Shutting the door with his foot, he carried her to the bed, and in a frolicsome fashion, he tossed her onto it. "I think I have the way of it," he said as he began shedding his clothes.

Rose, no naive lass, happily watched as he removed first his plaid, then his boots, which were quickly followed by his tunic and trews. What sprouted forth surprised her. Not only was he more than amply endowed, the endowment appeared quite ready, willing and able to bestow itself upon her.

Past experience — though she knew 'twas not nearly as much as Ian possessed — told her that she should probably hurry and remove her clothing before 'twas too late. Many times, her late husband had found his own release before she had a chance to warm to the idea. Mercifully he had explained 'twas an affliction all men suffered from, especially when loving a woman as beautiful as she. Rose could not begin to fault Almer, for he was such a dear, sweet man.

Quickly, she began to unlace her dress whilst she pulled her woolens off with her toes.

"Wait," Ian said as he climbed onto the foot of the bed like a wolf about to devour its prey. His blue eyes were dark with a smoldering desire that nearly stole her breath away.

He lay beside her and hooked one finger under the laces. "I've been dreamin' of slowly relievin' ye of yer clothes fer an age, wife." Ever so slowly, he tugged at the lace, slowly, methodically pulling it free from the first grommet. "Though I must admit there were many a time where I could have simply lifted yer skirts and taken ye in an instant." He looped his finger around the lace again and tugged ever so slowly. "But tonight? Tonight I wish us to take our time."

She too had been thinking of this moment for an age. Almer's words echoed in her mind... *Ye're too beautiful, Rose, and that be why at times I can no' hold onto me seed fer more than a few heartbeats and leave ye behind.* Determined not to be left behind *this* day, she felt it necessary to voice her worry. "Are ye certain?"

"Certain of what?" he asked, as he pulled the lacing through another grommet, paying no real attention to what she was asking.

How does one broach this subject without insultin' a man's pride? She hadn't a clue. Being blunt and honest had served her well over the years and she prayed it would serve her now.

"Ye ken I be no' an innocent lass who does no' ken the way of lovin'," she began.

Ian's finger paused for a brief moment. "I ken ye have been married," he replied rather abruptly. This was his wedding day and he would prefer that Rose not bring up any old memories of past lovers. She was his now and that was all that mattered.

Clearing her throat once, she pushed forward, broaching what she knew would be a difficult topic. "I ken there be times when a man can no' hold himself back. He can get far too excited far too quickly."

With his brow furrowed, he finally turned his attention to her face.

"I want ye to ken that I understand that. However, I also need ye to understand I'd prefer no' to be left behind. This be *me* weddin' day and I, too, have been lookin' forward to it for a verra long while now."

From the expression on his face, she could see he was confused.

"I was married once before, Ian," she told him. She felt her face grow warm with embarrassment, but refused to back away from the topic. "I would like to ken aforehand, well, I be wonderin', when ye, well, I—" Pausing for a moment, searching for the right words, she began to feel less confident. Especially when he was looking at her with such a confused expression. "If ye finish before me, how long do ye think 'twill be before ye can do it again?"

Understanding settled in quickly and his eyes grew wide with a blend of horror and insult. "Are ye inferrin' that I'll find me own pleasure before ye find yers?" He found the thought repulsive.

"Ye need no' shout at me, Ian," she told him. "I *was* married afore ye. And Almer explained the way of it to me and I'll no' fault ye fer somethin' all men are afflicted with."

He shook his head once, as if it would help him gain some clarity. *Affliction? Fault?* Not wanting to argue with his beautiful wife on their wedding day, he decided to practice some patience and not jump to any conclusions. "Please, pray tell, me love, what exactly did Almer explain to ye? To what *affliction* are ye referrin'?"

She did not for a moment believe he was as calm as he was trying to appear. Male pride, especially when it came to matters of loving, was not something any woman wanted to injure or insult. But he was at least making the attempt to have a civil conversation, so that had to count for something. "There were many times when Almer found his own pleasure before I was even under the covers. He explained 'twas an affliction that most men suffer from. He was very kind about it, ye ken, in helpin' me to understand 'twas because he found me so beautiful that sometimes all he had to do was look at me and ..." she let her words trail off to give Ian a moment to mull it over. "Now while I understood it and could no' rightly blame him, ye see, I was still often left wantin' a wee bit more if ye get me meanin'. Verra often afterwards, he would say *'let me catch me breath lass and we'll try again'*. But then he'd fall asleep and 'twould be days before we *tried again*."

It took every ounce of strength and kindness he owned not to break down and laugh his fool head off. He knew that Rose had been all of fifteen when she married the much older Almer Gray. In truth, there had been a few times over the past year where Ian himself could very well have spilled his own seed just by looking at her. However, he was neither a young lad nor an auld man. Never in all his years had he ever left a woman *wantin' a wee bit more.*

Not wanting to impugn her dead husband or tarnish the fond memories he knew she held for the man, Ian took a far more tactful approach. "As ye said, no' all men suffer from that affliction," he pointed out as he turned his attention back to the leather laces that stood between him and paradise. "I be no' one of them. I can promise ye, that ye'll *never* be left wantin' a wee bit more."

Rose quirked a brow and studied him for a moment. "Ye sound quite sure of yerself."

"I am," he said as he pulled the lace through the last grommet. "And I'll be more than happy to prove it to ye."

INTENTLY, IAN SLIPPED HIS HAND THROUGH the opening of her dress, brushing his palm over her chemise and the taught peak of her breast. At which Rose sucked in a deep breath that in turn made him smile. Slowly, ever so slowly, he continued the sweet ministration as he stared at her face. She had closed her eyes, her lips formed a sensual, pouty 'o' as she lay on her back with her arms at her sides. When he ran the pad of his thumb over the bud, she arched her back and sucked in another deep breath.

Pressing his lips to her neck, nibbling the tender spot, he turned his attention to her other breast, showing it just as much attention as the first. When Rose tried to sit up, he tossed one leg over hers. "Wheest, wife. I am enjoyin' meself."

Short of breath, as if she'd just run across the entirety of Scotland, she said, "Let me get out of me dress."

"No' yet," he whispered against her neck.

Slowly, he moved his hand down her stomach before returning to her plump breasts. All the while, he trailed kisses from her ear to that very soft and tender spot at the base of her throat.

While she could certainly appreciate his attempts at *warming her* to the idea of joining, she would have much preferred to be done with the warming part and get straight to the joining part. All thoughts of hurrying, however, fell to the wayside when he took her breast into his mouth.

Had Almer ever paid such attention to her breasts? Nay, she was quite certain he hadn't, at least not in the manner in which Ian was. Wickedly, he licked and twirled and flicked his tongue across the peak wondrously. Her stomach felt warm, her legs as sturdy as water, all the while her heart pounded against her chest.

With her attention focused on what he was doing to her breast, she hadn't realized he had taken his leg away from hers, allowing his free hand to make it's way under her dress and chemise until she felt his fingertips caress her inner thigh as softly as a butterfly against her cheek. Tenderly, he drew his fingers up and down her thigh, all the while he suckled at her breast.

'Twas torture, to be certain. But wickedly delightful torture.

He found the nub at the apex of her legs and 'twas all she could do not to fly from the bed. Nay, Almer had never done *that*.

Ian chuckled against her skin and whispered something. She couldn't hear him over the pounding of her heart or her own heavy breathing. Filled with that all too familiar aching need, she was soon begging him not to stop.

Blessedly, he didn't. He continued with his ministrations as he whispered sweet words against her skin. The ache built as he kissed the tender skin from her neck to her breast until her release hit with such intensity she thought her heart would explode.

Out of breath with her heart pounding and her body pulsing and throbbing, she could not help but smile. He gave her no time to bask in the warm sensations for he was soon lying atop her. "I promised I would no' leave ye behind," he whispered with a good measure of pride and devilishness.

Nay, not once for the remainder of the afternoon, did he leave her behind.

DAWN HAD COME AND GONE WHILE they slept wrapped up in one another's arms. Rose's blond hair was tousled, splayed across her pillow as well as Ian's shoulder, where she rested her head. Ian woke first, immediately taking delight in the knowledge that he would wake next to this lovely woman each and every day for the rest of their lives. Hopefully, they'd live to be one hundred.

Closing his eyes, he listened to her soft breaths that tickled against his chest. 'Twas remarkable he could draw such comfort from something so simple as listening to someone breathe. 'Twas also remarkable how anyone as wee as his wife could bring him to his knees with just a smile or seductive word.

The more he thought on what had transpired betwixt the two of them last night, the more intent he became on having her again. He knew it probably wasn't proper to join with his wife five times in less than a day, but he cared not. He'd never grow tired of hearing her soft sighs, the moans of pleasure, or hearing her call out his name when she found her release.

With a featherlight touch, he began to caress her bare arm with his fingertips. She mumbled something incoherent and snuggled in closer to his side. Feeling mischievous, he took a long strand of her hair, using it to tickle the tip of her nose. She swatted it away with a sleepy hand. Resisting the urge to chuckle, he tickled her again.

This time when she swatted the imaginary fly, she ended up slapping his chin and cursing. "Go away, bloody fly."

'Twas impossible for him not to chuckle outright.

Ian was more than ready to love his wife again when Frederick called out to him behind the door. When Ian did not answer, his brother began pounding on it relentlessly.

"Need I remind ye it be me weddin' night!" Ian shouted from the bed, hopeful that his brother would take the hint and leave. Turning his attention back to more pleasurable pursuits, he pressed his lips to Rose's.

"That was last night," Frederick called back to him. "It be a new day, brother!"

While Rose found a measure of humor in her new brother-by-law's jest, Ian grew more frustrated. "Go away, Frederick!" he called to the door. To his wife, he said, "I have more thrillin' adventures to tend to."

The pounding continued.

"He will no' go away," Rose told him. "Ye ken that."

With a heavy sigh of resignation and a muffled curse, he jumped from the bed and, as naked as the day he was born, stomped to the door and yanked it open.

He wasn't prepared to see his sister-by-law standing next to his brother. Aggie shrieked with embarrassment, her eyes as wide as trenchers, before quickly turning away from him. Ian burned red with shame.

"Fer the sake of Christ, Ian, cover yerself!" Frederick boomed. "Ye haven't shown yer wanker to this many people since ye were a wean!" He was, of course, referring to the events of yester afternoon.

Hurrying to the bed, Ian attempted to grab a blanket to cover himself. Rose, consumed now with laughter, pulled the covers from his grasp. "Need I remind ye, ye took an oath yester afternoon?" Ian asked through gritted teeth.

"Would ye prefer yer brother see *me* naked?" she coyly asked before bursting into another fit of giggles.

"I'd prefer to see neither of ye naked!" Frederick called from the doorway. He took note that his wife was not so much embarrassed as she was amused. Her shoulders shook and he knew it was taking a good effort not to allow her concealed laughter to escape.

Having found his plaid and covered himself respectfully, Ian told his brother 'twas safe to enter.

Rose quit laughing and shot him an angry glare. He knew very well she didn't have a stitch of clothing on under those blankets. He returned her glare with a look that said *all be fair in love and war.*

"Is yer wife dressed?" Frederick asked. He was always the smarter one.

Ian rolled his eyes toward the doorway. "Give us a moment."

While Frederick and Aggie waited patiently in the hallway, Rose and Ian hurried to dress. "What does he want?" Rose asked as she pulled her chemise over her head.

"I do no' ken, but it sounds verra important." Admittedly, his curiosity was piqued. But when he caught sight of his wife's bare thigh as she pulled on woolens, his thoughts turned away from his brother's important news to Rose's soft, creamy flesh.

It had better be important, he mused with a curse. Knowing the pleasures he could find with Rose, he was reluctant to let anyone interfere. Still, were it not for Frederick's interference, they would never have been married. He owed his older brother a great deal at the moment. Giving Frederick a wee bit of his time seemed wise.

Once they were dressed, Ian opened the door to let his brother and sister-in-law inside. With a wide flourish, he said, "Welcome to our castle, brother. What is mine is yers. Though I dare say that be no' much at the moment." Smiling broadly, he went on to add, "We've made piece with the mice. What they lack in might, they make up for in food. 'Twas a peace accord made out of necessity."

Rose laughed at his jest. "They've far better food stores than we, the little buggers."

Aggie found their light humor infectious and could not help but laugh as Ian offered her a seat. A wobbly, three-legged stool. "Ye may take me throne, me Queen."

Aggie giggled and rolled her eyes. "I see marriage has yet to rid ye of that boyish sense of humor," she said as she sat down.

Ian leaned down to whisper in her ear. "Did ye expect it to?"

Frederick let loose with a short, frustrated sigh. Crossing his arms over his chest, he said, "Ian, we need to talk and it be a verra serious matter."

Ian's smile faded as his brow furrowed. His first thought was that the Camerons were on the offensive and preparing to lay siege once again to the Mackintosh keep. Dread began to displace his good humor.

Sensing his unease, Rose came to stand next to him. "What be the matter?"

Frederick went to stand next to his wife. He placed a hand on her shoulder. Aggie smiled wanly as she patted it. Something unspoken passed between them. 'Twas a language Ian had witnessed countless times before but could never understand.

"We've a proposition fer ye both," Frederick said.

"While it was an easy decision to come to, it be no' made lightly," Aggie added.

Ian and Rose were equally intrigued but remained silent.

"As ye ken, Aggie's father-by-blood is here. He be quite fond of her." He gave his wife's shoulder another gentle squeeze before adding, "As I knew he would be."

Aggie smiled ever so slightly. Rose sensed something was wrong. "Aggie? Why do ye no' seem happy?"

"I am happy that he is fond of me," Aggie replied. "He is a good man. I fear I was no' quite prepared to like him as much as I do. But there is more to it than just the two of us bein' fond of each other."

"Such as?" Rose asked.

"'Tis a verra long story," Aggie said in a low tone. "But apparently, I have just inherited a grand keep with much land. It be a three-day ride from McLaren lands."

"That is wonderful news!" Rose exclaimed. "I be so verra happy fer ye."

Frederick and Aggie stared at one another for a long moment as silence filled the room. If either Ian or Rose had just been gifted a grand keep and lands, Ian imagined they'd be dancing around like fools. He found their reaction quite odd.

Frederick was the first to speak. "Aggie has grown quite fond of Mackintosh lands."

"And her people," Aggie added.

Frederick smiled at her fondly. "And her people," he said. "But this is an opportunity neither of us feel we should ignore or walk away from."

"And ye'd like us to go with ye?" Ian asked with a broad smile. He was never one to back down from an adventure.

"Nay," Frederick said. "Ye'll no' be goin' with us."

It took less than a heartbeat for everything to sink in for Ian. "Ye'll be leavin' us." His voice was nothing more than a stunned whisper. It hurt that Frederick no longer wanted him at his side as his second in command, his friend. He clenched his jaw tightly. How could his brother not want him to go along? It made no sense.

"Not until next spring," Frederick said. "Ada is far too young and weak yet to make such an arduous journey."

Of all his brothers, Frederick was by far his most favored. He was Ian's closest friend and ally, and next to their father, the one man Ian admired above all others. To learn he would be leaving *and* he was not welcome hurt his heart as much as the punches Frederick had inflicted just two days ago.

"Of all our brothers, ye be the one I love the most," Frederick said unexpectedly. "Though I trust all of me brothers with me life and the lives of me wife and children, ye be the one I trust most to do what we are about to ask."

Ian's head and heart began to feel like an inflated pig bladder being kicked around the hills by heavy-footed children. "I fear I do no' understand ye," Ian said betwixt clenched teeth. "Trust me to do what?"

Frederick stood a bit taller. "We want ye to be chief of Clan McLaren."

ROSE GASPED ALOUD WHILE IAN stood dumbfounded. Quite certain he had not heard Frederick correctly, he said, "Ye want me to do what?"

"We want ye to return to McLaren lands, ye and Rose. We want ye to rebuild the keep, build a band of warriors, and as their chief, to reestablish the clan as a whole."

Aye, Ian had heard him correctly. Still, that did nothing to dull his utter astonishment. He ran a hand through his blonde locks and began to pace about the small room. "Me?" he said to no one in particular. "Ye want *me* to be the McLaren?"

Frederick gave a short nod. "We do. We would like ye to help build a legacy we can leave to Ailrig."

"Ailrig?" Ian asked.

"By rights, McLaren lands would be his to inherit when he be old enough. Aggie and I had planned on returnin' next year to begin rebuildin'. But her blood father's gift? 'Tis Aggie's by right of birth as well. We would like to go there and claim that legacy fer Aggie and fer Ada. I can no' be in both places at once. McLaren lands need ye more than I at the moment."

Ian studied Aggie for a long moment. When he'd met her more than a year ago, she'd been a very poor, mute young woman raised by a most brutal man. My, how things had changed. She'd gone from having less than nothing to not one, but two keeps and the lands that went with them.

"So I would be temporary chief?" Ian asked for clarity's sake.

Frederick chuckled softly. "'Twill be many a year before Ailrig be ready to claim it as his own. I ken this be a tremendous undertakin', Ian. To ask ye to build somethin' ye'd never be able to pass to yer own children."

"Ye did no' tell him?" Rose whispered softly.

Ian stopped pacing long enough to look at her. He realized two things in that short moment of time. First, he now understood how an unspoken thing could pass betwixt husband and wife so easily. And secondly, he loved Rose more than he had previously believed possible. He could give her the world now.

Frederick waited patiently for one of them to explain.

"There will be no children for Rose and I to pass anythin' on to."

Thankfully, Frederick did not press for more information.

"Still, 'tis an awful lot I ask of the both of ye. Ye'll be buildin' somethin' ye'll nay get to keep forever. Unless Ailrig decides later in life 'tis no' somethin' he wants."

Ailrig was all of nine summers now. Not a one of them knew what the future would hold for any of them, let alone a boy of nine.

"Ye be right, Frederick," Ian agreed. "'Tis a tremendous undertakin', to be certain. But 'tis also a tremendous opportunity fer Rose and me."

Aggie left the stool to stand before Rose. "Frederick and I could no' trust this to just anyone. Ye have been the closest thing to a sister I've ever had, Rose. Truly, I do no' wish to leave here, to leave ye or Ian or anyone. But Frederick believes we should at least make an attempt at what Douglas has given me." Tears pooled in her eyes as she wrapped her arms around her friend. "If I had me own way, we'd never leave here. But I keep thinkin' of me mum. McLaren lands were *hers*, ye ken. To ignore that, to let them fall to ruin, to allow neighborin' clans to take that land? 'Twould be a travesty to her memory."

Rose was just as stunned as her husband. Certainly he would not consider leaving here. They'd already made plans to ask his father for a wee cottage, where she would plant a garden and flowers, and they would spend the rest of their lives simply loving one another. Nay, he could not even consider the proposal.

She should have known better.

His brother had just given him the chance at a much brighter future. If he took what Frederick and Aggie were offering him, he'd be able to give Rose everything he felt she deserved. And in his mind and heart, he wanted to give his wife the world.

"I shall give ye some time to think on it," Frederick said as he started for the door.

"I need no time," Ian said with a wide smile. "We shall do this fer ye."

Rose pulled away from Aggie's embrace. Seeing the look of surprise and desperation in her dear friend's eyes, Aggie said, "Ian, do ye no' think ye should discuss this with yer wife?"

As soon as he looked at her with that wide, proud smile, Rose knew she'd not ever be able to change his mind. In that tiny moment, she knew she was destined to return to those lands she had grown to hate and fear. The rundown keep. The land where 'twas impossible to grow anything more than weeds. The lands that held more bad memories than good. 'Twas that smile of his that was her undoing: the one she knew in her heart she'd never be able to deny a thing on God's earth. So proud, so utterly happy, as if he'd just been handed the world on a golden salver by all the old gods.

"If this be what me husband wants," she said, choking back tears, "then we shall do what ye ask."

FIVE

The following days seemed to fly by as Ian and Rose prepared for their future. A future that Ian was far more excited about than Rose.

Ian spent his days in meetings with his father and brothers, planning the route back to McLaren lands, discussing what supplies would be necessary, as well as the design of the future keep.

Weeks ago — almost immediately after Aggie had agreed they could use the money found in her father's old office to rebuild her clan — Frederick had began to put in place plans for a new keep. He had gone to Inverness and met with a well-known and respected carpenter, Ingerame Macdowall, whom he hired immediately. Ingerame would be the lead carpenter on the project, responsible for hiring a team of laborers and carpenters of his own choosing. Frederick had the perfect spot in mind. 'Twas a mile away from the original keep, with more fertile ground, and more importantly, as far away from the glen as it could be. He'd also spent many a night drawing up plans for a much grander and heavily fortified structure. And the bloody roof would never leak.

Almost immediately after being hired, the carpenter and his team of laborers set out for McLaren lands. The idea was that Frederick would meet him there later in the autumn.

But with the recent turn of events and changes in leadership, 'twould now be Ian and Rose meeting the man, and much sooner than originally anticipated.

A swearing-in ceremony was held on the same evening Ian accepted the position. In front of his family and new clan, he swore an oath to protect each and every one of them, to lead with a firm yet fair hand, and to do a damn sight better than their last chief.

While Ian was busy planning, Rose was busy organizing the packing of all the supplies and meeting with the women who would be making the journey with them. Most were McLarens, but a handful of the women were the wives of the Mackintosh warriors who had volunteered to go.

Ian chose his older half-brother, Brogan, as his second in command. Brogan looked very much like Frederick, resembling him in coloring and build. However, that was where the resemblance ended. Brogan was a quiet man, speaking only when he believed he had something intelligent to say. He did not sing as Frederick did, nor did he play any musical instrument. He was also not as jovial or as quick to smile. But he was just as honorable and as good a warrior. He exuded power and strength and led by example more than by boisterous words.

The next man Ian chose to help turn the McLaren men into a strong fighting force was his long time friend, Andrew the Red. Rose did not find the man quite as humorous or as brave and wonderful as Ian found him, or for that matter, as the man himself did. She tolerated him only because Ian both admired and trusted him.

Both men swore their fealty to both Ian and to Rose. Never would they take their duties lightly.

THERE WAS NOT A MOMENT'S PEACE to be had on the long journey west. At least not in Rose's mind. At Ian's insistence Brogan and Andrew the

Red were made her personal guards for the entire excursion. "Ye're far too valuable to me to take a risk," her husband explained. "I can no' be with ye at all times. 'Tis dangerous land we trek across."

Rose thought it quite senseless, the need for personal guards. And she told him just that as they stood in the courtyard one cool afternoon. Brogan stood to Ian's left, Andrew the Red on his right. They were a formidable sight, these three men. Well muscled, with broadswords dangling from their hips, anyone else would probably have simply agreed with her husband and run away. But Rose was not *anyone else*. 'Twas one of the things Ian loved most about her: her fierce determination and inner strength.

"I wonder how I was able to live me life all these years without guards?" she asked, her tone dripping with sarcasm.

"Ye have never been the wife of a clan chief before," Ian explained. "Ye're no' only valuable to me, but to the entire clan." Admittedly, he admired her independent streak. But on this, he would give no quarter.

"Come now, lass," Andrew the Red said, flashing a bright smile at her. "Our company can no' be so bad, can it?"

If he thought he would alter her opinion by charming her, he was sadly mistaken. "Ye think ye can change me mind with a smile? I am no' some half-witted young lass who can be swayed by a man's charm" she told him, her tone blunt and firm. "Better men than ye have tried. Ask Ian."

Andrew's smile evaporated instantly. Ian chuckled outright at his wife and his friend's response. "She be tellin' the truth, Andrew."

"I can take care of myself, Ian. Ye ken that as well as anyone," she told him.

"Aye, I ken verra well ye can. But our current situation calls fer more protective measures. Remember, ye be the wife of a clan chief now."

"So ye've reminded me. Repeatedly." Crossing her arms over her chest to mimic her husband, she was not quite ready to give up the battle. For days now, that was all he'd spoken of, being the chief of her clan. She wished she could be as excited about the future as he.

"M'lady," Andrew addressed her formally as he took one step forward, "I think what yer husband is tryin' to say is that he cares a great deal fer your safety. We all do. I've sworn to protect ye, with me own life if necessary. 'Tis me great honor to do so."

"I ken verra well what me husband is sayin', Andrew," she informed him as politely as she could manage.

"Then allow us to do our jobs," Andrew said unflinchingly.

Ian decided 'twas best to step in before things escalated between the two of them. "Rose, if anythin' were to happen to ye on our journey west, I could no' live with knowin' I did no' do all that I could to protect ye."

When he spoke from his heart like that, Rose could not deny him anything. Reluctantly, she acquiesced. "Verra well then," she said. "But hear me now. I will no' spend the rest of me life bein' surrounded by yer men. 'Twill drive me to madness."

Andrew was about to speak again when Ian stopped him with a hand on his shoulder, pulling him back and away from Rose. "I thank ye fer understandin'," he said with a smile.

Realizing he would not give in, Rose let the matter rest, with the belief that once they reached McLaren lands, the need for guards would pass. She could not have been more wrong.

"I shall return to me duties," Rose said. Giving a nod to all three men, she left them in the courtyard.

Once she was out of earshot, Andrew said, "Why did ye no' tell her she'd be guarded the rest of her days?"

Ian turned around to face his brother and friend. "Because had I told her, I would never get her to leave this keep."

Andrew raised one brow in confusion.

Brogan slapped him on the back. "Ye have never been married, lad. A man must choose his battles wisely when it comes to his wife."

Andrew scoffed at the notion. "Bah! A wife must always do what her husband says."

Ian and Brogan exchanged knowing glances before bursting into a fit of laughter.

"If ever ye marry, make sure to explain that to yer wife," Ian said.

"And let us ken if ye're successful with such an opinion," Brogan offered.

They left Andrew in a state of confusion. "But that is the way of things," he called out to them. "Every man kens that!"

Ian and Brogan paused and turned to face him. "Aye, every man kens it. But every woman kens it is just a pack of lies."

"Bah!" Andrew said, waving the two men off. "Ye're both daft."

Smiling, the two men left him alone once again.

Mumbling to himself he said, "If ever I am blessed with a wife, I'll no' let her rule over me like Ian does."

It TOOK TWO WEEKS TO PREPARE the tangible necessities for the journey west. But 'twas impossible to prepare for the pain of saying goodbye to her family. Rose was quite certain 'twould take a lifetime to get over the heartache of leaving her closest, most treasured friend behind, as well as all the new friends she had made since her arrival.

They said their goodbyes the night before they were to leave. Alone in Rose's old room, the two women sat and talked for hours, remembering all the good times they had shared, along with some of the bad.

Rose's room was empty now, save for the furniture. Elsbeth had insisted she take the fabrics and supplies with her to the new McLaren keep. 'Twas a gesture that meant the world to Rose. If they grew low on funds, she could always sell her talents as a seamstress.

"Ye have been the closest thing to a sister I ever had," Rose said as she wept and held on fiercely to Aggie. "I do no' ken what I shall do without ye, or Ailrig and Ada."

Aggie was just as bereft. "If I could, I would leave McLaren lands to fall to ruin. Let the Bowies and other clans fight over it." She pulled away, wiping her tears with a bit of linen. "But I can no' do that to me mother's memory."

Rose's mother had left her nothing more than memories, a few bone needles, some blankets, and unfinished dresses. But those few things had meant the world to her. 'Twasn't a keep and lands, but 'twas just as important. "Ye can no' turn away from what yer mother wanted, Aggie." Rose agreed. "I just wish we were goin' with ye, to *Am boireannach dubh-ghlas.*"

The keep was named *Am boireannach dubh-ghlas* The Dark Grey woman. Neither Rose nor Aggie necessarily liked the name. Hopefully the keep was not as dark and foreboding as its name.

Aggie began to cry again. "I wish the same!" she cried as she pulled Rose into another warm embrace.

"Please, promise me we'll see each other again," Rose said as she held her friend close.

Aggie nodded rapidly. "I do so promise. Next spring, we shall come to visit ye before we go to *Am boireannach dubh-ghlas.*"

A year seemed an eternity at the moment.

"And Frederick has promised to write to ye fer me," Aggie told her. "We shall write to ye every day."

Rose could barely read and write, but knew that, with Ian's help, she would be able to write to her friend and sister. "And I shall write to ye as well."

"We shall always be sisters," Aggie declared. "Our bond is stronger than blood."

Sniffling, Rose pulled away to look into her dearest friend's eyes. "Our bond is stronger than blood."

SIX

The auld McLaren keep had been deserted for some time now. He knew because he'd been watching from a careful distance and with a wary eye. Today was the day he decided to give it a closer inspection, and he was fully prepared to kill anyone who might cross his path. There was far too much at stake to take any chances.

For weeks, he'd been living in the woods near the glen, watching from a safe distance. As far as he could tell, the last of the McLarens and bloody Mackintoshes had left days ago. They'd loaded one wagon with what appeared to be very meager belongings, the last of the horses, and taken off, heading north.

His stomach grumbled, hungrier than he could ever remember being. The last good meal he'd partaken of was in Edinburgh, two months past. He'd survived the winter — albeit barely — in Edinburgh and had left as soon as the snows had melted, on a horse he had stolen from a drunken lout. Hundreds of miles away now, he felt confident that he needn't worry about anyone coming after him.

Deciding now was as good a time as any, he left the safety of the wood.

The gates stood wide open, another sure sign no one was about. Cautiously he crept through the gates and into the courtyard. An eerie quiet had befallen the place. He very nearly came to shitting himself when he neared the burned out keep and a tiny bird who had decided to take up residence in the eaves, flapped it's wings. With a start and a pounding heart, he cursed up at the ugly bird who began to chirp it's warning. "Ye will no' be laughin' when I eat ye fer me supper," he cursed. The bird stared at him, chirped a few times before settling back to building his nest.

Nary a soul remained, save for the rats that had taken up residence in nearly every spot imaginable. From the abandoned granary to the stables and burned out shell of the keep, the blasted things were everywhere. Just what they were dining on, he couldn't rightly say. He himself had been hard pressed to find little more than grouse and the occasional rabbit to eat.

With due diligence, he made his way inside the keep. The roof had collapsed some time ago; the beams lay scattered across the stone floor of the gathering room. One heavy, blackened beam lay across the staircase, barring any entry to the floors above. The air was dank, musty, and smelled of decaying wood.

Stepping through puddles of water, undoubtedly left by the last rain, he headed to Mermadak's private room. The door was ajar and groaned in protest when he pushed it open. It scraped against the hard stone floor and stopped, allowing just enough room for him to squeeze through.

The moment he pushed through, an eerie sense of foreboding settled in, making the hair on the back of his neck stand at attention. Where the rest of the keep had fallen into decay and rot, this room seemed almost untouched. A thick layer of dust covered every surface, and a creeping vine had sprouted up through the floor near Mermadak's desk. Other than that, one wouldn't be able to surmise the condition of the rest of the keep based on this one room alone.

There was a door on the opposite side of the room that was also ajar. A strong breeze came in from seemingly nowhere and began to stir up bits of dust and debris. For an instant, he could have sworn he heard someone whisper something incoherent, and it sent a chill up and down his spine. A forewarning from the world beyond, mayhap? Mermadak reaching from the pits of hell to warn him to leave this place at once?

Nay. He'd not leave, not now. There was too much at stake to run away now. 'Twas just his mind playing tricks on him. But just to be certain, he unsheathed his dirk.

Taking a steadying breath, he made his way to the large desk. Using the tip of the dirk, he began to pick through the parchments, afraid for some unknown reason, to allow his hands to touch them. Nothing in them seemed of any significance to the matter at hand. He was here to find the fortune Mermadak had hidden away.

How many hours had he spent in this room? Countless hours to be certain. He'd been one of Mermadak's messengers, one of only two men the laird trusted. It had been he who had collected much of the silver and gold from those men the McLaren had blackmailed. It had been he who had broken a leg or two when a victim developed a backbone and threatened to stop paying. Together, the three of them had collected vast amounts of money. How much, he was not sure, but he knew he alone had collected hundreds if not thousands of groats, merks, and sillars over the years.

It was hidden in this room. He *knew* it as well as he knew his own name. But where? That was one thing Mermadak made certain of: none would know where the money was kept. He might have trusted him enough to do his dirty work, but he'd never trust him with the location of their spoils.

He scoured the shelves, the walls, and even the floor, looking for any sign of a hidden compartment. For an hour, he was on his hands and knees, clawing at things that looked as though they should move but didn't. The longer he searched the angrier he became. It was here, he knew it, could feel it to his very marrow.

Soaked in sweat, despite the cool breeze that continued to linger, he finally stood. Panting with anger and frustration, he scanned the room, cursing all the world for the lot he'd been dealt.

Then he saw it.

The mantle.

SEVEN

It had been a long, difficult journey. Weeks of traveling halfway across Scotland had not been easy — facing mountains, rivers, and all manner of terrain and weather. The most terrifying part of their journey was when they had to pass through the southern tip of Cameron lands. The Mackintoshes and Camerons had been feuding for decades. They would most assuredly have been slaughtered had any of the Camerons discovered they were passing through, no matter if it had been for less than half an hour.

They pushed forward during the day, as fast as they were able, considering their large numbers and the heavy wagons, the cattle, pigs, and other animals. Many of Ian's followers were on foot, which slowed their progression even further.

Whenever Ian was off tending to one problem or another, Andrew the Red and Brogan would fall in to ride on either side of Rose. At first, she did not like being singled out, but she was now the wife of a clan chief.

Certain precautions had to be made to insure her safety at all times.

She'd grown fond of Brogan, simply because he rarely spoke. When he did, 'twas always to say something kind and thoughtful.

Andrew the Red however, was an altogether different story. He talked incessantly, to the point of giving her an ache in her head. He seemed to have either an opinion or story on nearly every topic, from how to cut stone properly to how to brew the best ale. He was a tremendous pain in her arse. Ian seemed either not to notice or to care. Andrew was his friend and that 'twas all that mattered.

At night, Ian and Rose slept in a small but comfortable tent. Many times they fell into the soft pallets far too exhausted to move, let alone make love. However, come morning, well rested after a good night's sleep, she would wake to her husband nuzzling her neck or caressing her breast. 'Twas a wonderful way to wake each morn, being loved quite thoroughly. Ian was attentive and generous in that way. Though there were times when she wished he would spill his seed inside of her. But he had made a promise to do everything they could to avoid getting her with child. So far, it seemed to be working. Their lovemaking would leave her in a most happy mood for the remainder of the day.

And Ian hadn't lied when he had told Rose she would know the plans by heart and be sick of hearing about them before they arrived. She imagined she could recite it all in her sleep.

Today was no exception. Brogan estimated they were less than an hour from their destination. "Soon, sister, we shall come upon a large hill," he began with a level of excitement she'd never witnessed in him before.

"And just over that large hill will be the spot where we shall build the new keep," she finished for him.

Brogan smiled thoughtfully and nodded. "Have ye given any thought to what ye'd like the keep to look like?"

'Twas the most he'd spoken to her in weeks and it took her aback. "What *I* would like it to look like?" she asked. "Ian has already drawn up the plans."

"True, but a man never thinks of the things that make a home a home," Brogan pointed out. "He thinks of the number of logs, pegs, and shingles. He thinks of stone and mortar and the like."

Rose was not quite certain what he was asking and since she'd never heard him string together so many words, she remained quiet and listened.

"But a woman? A woman thinks of the seemingly little things that are just as important as how soundly it is built. Tapestries on the walls, flowers in the gardens, how the furniture should be arranged ..." His voice trailed off, his eyes on something only he could see.

Remembering that Brogan had lost his wife three years ago to the wasting disease, Rose understood then, what he meant. And the far away look in his eyes? He was thinking of his wife.

After some time, he gave his head a hard shake and turned his attention back to Rose. "A woman, she is what makes a house a home. 'Tis no' the timber and stone, but her heart and what she puts into it. Without it, 'tis nothin' more than four empty walls."

Suddenly, she felt sad for him. 'Twas quite evident that he missed his wife a great deal.

"I lost me first husband," she told him. "Though 'twas no' some great marriage filled with romance and wonder, I still loved him." For a tiny moment, she tried to imagine her life without Ian, but the thought made her ill at heart.

Brogan smiled wanly. "Alaina was a beautiful woman and I loved her verra much. I have no desire to take another wife or to love again."

"I would feel the same were I to lose Ian," she said.

Ian raced toward his wife and brother, excited and relieved; he was grinning from ear to ear. "We be almost there!" he shouted as he approached, pulling rein quickly, angling his horse in between Andrew the Red and Rose. "It be just beyond that hill," he informed them.

His smile as well as his excitement was contagious.

"Be it as beautiful as they told us?" Rose asked.

Ian leaned across his saddle and kissed her soundly. It left her breathless and wanting more. "Aye, lass. Next to ye, it be the most beautiful thing I've ever seen."

When he spoke thus, with such sincerity and adoration, it brought forth a delightful tickling sensation in the pit of her stomach. Oh, how she adored this man, loved him with all that she was. She could not help but blush and smile all at once.

"Andrew, spread the word to the rest," Ian directed before turning to face his wife. "Rose and Brogan, shall we go up together?"

Returning his smile and just as excited as he to see what lay just beyond that rise, the three of them raced to the top of the hill. What lay ahead stole Rose's breath away.

It seemed to go on for as far as the eye could see. At the bottom of the hill on rich flat land, lay lush, green grass that stretched on forever. Flowers of every imaginable color dotted the land. Beyond the flat, wide-open glen, lay the largest forest she'd ever set eyes on. Running perpendicular between the grass and the base of the hill, was a wide bubbling stream; she could see neither where it began nor ended.

"Who are they?" Rose asked when she spied a rather small encampment at the edge of the woods. She could see some ten men there, as well as a few tents nearby.

"Those be the carpenters Frederick sent ahead of us," Ian explained. "It looks as though they've already begun work."

Below them, men had begun to clear out part of the forest. Massive logs were stacked as high as a man's head, already cleaned and scraped and ready for use.

Moments later, two men on horseback came bounding across the hill from the north.

"Good day to ye!" Ian called out as he slowly pulled his horse away from Brogan and Rose.

Either out of instinct or habit, Brogan rested a palm on the hilt of his sword. "Get behind me, Rose," he whispered.

Though she didn't think it necessary, she did as he said, and led her horse to stand behind him. "Are ye no' bein' a wee bit over-protective?" she asked. "Clearly they be with the men below."

Brogan ignored her. Giving a quick scan of their surroundings, he kept a close eye on the two men. Moments later, Andrew appeared with three other mounted men who all drew in to protect Rose.

In silence, and on full alert, they watched as Ian met the strangers.

AFTER CASTING A QUICK GLANCE TO see that his wife was well protected, Ian turned to watch the men approach. One appeared young, mayhap twenty years old. He was slender with long blonde hair. The other was an aulder brown-haired man with a scowl as mean-looking as a rabid dog. Both had swords drawn and at the ready. They slowed their pace as they drew nearer to him.

"Identify yerself," the blonde man said as he pulled his horse to a stop some ten paces from Ian. They stood facing one another on the crest of the hill. The warm breeze picked up, billowing tunics and hair.

"I be Ian Mackintosh, newly appointed chief of Clan McLaren," he answered in a firm voice. "And who might ye be?"

While the blonde man's shoulders relaxed in relief, the brown-haired fellow remained stern-faced. "We were expectin' ye days ago," the blonde said. "I be Charles MacFarland and this be Rodrick the Bold. We be yer sentries."

"We were delayed a bit by rain. I did no' want to risk our wagons bein' stuck or damaged," Ian explained as he kept a close eye on the man named Rodrick. There was something about the man, his scowl or his countenance, that did not sit well with him.

Charles gave a nod of understanding. "Well, I fer one be glad ye're here. As ye can see, we've been workin' hard to clear out the forest as Frederick directed," he said with a nod toward the glen below. "We also have twenty men workin' in the quarry. We've a wee bit more to clear before they bring the stones in. Fer now, they be stockpilin' them."

The moment Aggie had agreed to rebuild her clan, Frederick had set to work finding the best carpenters and laborers. From as far away as Inverness, he had found many men willing to come to this part of the country. Ian knew that over the next weeks and months, more men would be arriving. He was grateful for his brother's foresight.

"We have brought some one-hundred and twenty-five men with us," Ian told him. "I reckon things will move along quickly now."

Charles smiled, showing a slight gap between his otherwise straight teeth. "I reckon ye be right," he said. "Come, I'll take ye to meet Ingerame."

Ian recognized the name at once. Ingerame Macdowall was the man Frederick had hired as their main carpenter. Ian had not yet met the man. But from what Frederick had told him, he was a good man that could be trusted. "Let me see to me wife while ye let Ingerame ken we be here."

'Twas then that Rodrick the Bold decided to finally speak. His voice was as deep as his scowl was fierce. "I will let him ken ye're here," he said as he started to pull away.

Ian was not about to let the man dictate anything to him. "Nay, Rodrick," he said. "I should like ye to continue with yer duties as sentry." He gave him no time to respond or argue. "Charles, ye go and let Ingerame ken we've arrived."

Apparently Rodrick was not used to either receiving nor taking orders. Scowling, he took in a deep breath through flared nostrils, staring long and hard at Ian. A lengthy moment passed with Rodrick and Ian staring one another down. Rodrick blinked first. Pulling hard on the reins, he turned his horse around and raced away, along the ridgeline of the hill.

Charles and Ian watched as he rode away. "He be a hard man, that one," Charles said. "He likes to think he be smarter than everyone else and thinks of himself as the man in charge."

"And what do *ye* think of him?" Ian asked.

Charles chuckled before answering. "Well, he has some good ideas on occasion."

Ian sensed there was more the young man wanted to say. "And?"

"He can be fiercely loyal once ye get to know him." And that was as far as he was willing to go.

ONCE IAN HAD GIVEN THE ORDER for the wagons to be brought over the hill, he and his wife rode into the encampment. A gangly young lad of no more than four and ten came running up to greet them. "Ye be the McLaren?" he asked, bright blue eyes staring up in awe.

Being referred to as *The McLaren* was not appealing to Ian in the least. It simply did not feel right or proper and he doubted he would ever find any enjoyment in it. "Call me Ian," he told the boy as he slid from his horse.

"I be Robby," the lad informed him as he took the reins.

Ian stretched a bit before helping Rose down from her mount. "This be yer mistress, Rose Mackintosh," he said by way of introduction.

Robby offered her a bow before taking the reins. "'Tis me great honor to meet ye, mistress."

A dark flush came to her cheeks. She was no more used to being referred to as mistress than Ian was as The McLaren. "Ye may call me Rose."

The boy's eyes opened wide in amazement before he looked to Ian for approval. Ian gave a slow shake of his head. "Ye shall always refer to her as mistress."

Before Rose could voice her protest, Ian pulled her into his arms and kissed the tip of her nose. "Before ye argue again over this, 'tis a sign of respect. Ye be the mistress of the keep, such as it is in its current state." He smiled fondly before kissing her lips. "And even if ye insist, 'twill be me order they listen to and no' yer request."

They'd discussed it before, this insistence of his that she be referred to as mistress. It felt just as awkward now as it did in the beginning. "It still does no' feel right or proper, Ian."

Though he could well understand her reluctance, he could not acquiesce. "Ye be me wife. I be the interim chief, fer at least the next ten years or so. Ye be the mistress of this keep, Rose Mackintosh. If everyone be referrin' to ye as Rose, they'll no' be respectin' ye as ye deserve."

She quirked a brow at that last part. "But 'tis perfectly acceptable fer ye to be called *Ian* instead of *The McLaren*?"

He shuddered, aghast. "'Tis no' the same."

"How be it no' the same?"

He smiled devilishly. "Because I *detest* the title. The men will respect me because I shall demand it, no' because of me title."

Just how that was any different from her own argument, she could not begin to guess. Men were a most confusing lot.

Deciding the topic closed permanently, Ian slipped his hand into hers. "Now let us go see Ingerame Macdowall."

"Leona!" Ingerame Macdowall shouted above the loud din of tools scraping against a newly felled tree. "Leona!"

He had been shouting for his daughter for what seemed like hours. He was busy carving out large pegs to be used later, his voice booming and echoing through the clearing. "Confound it, Leona! Where the bloody hell are ye?" Raising his head up from his project, he found himself staring directly into the eyes of Ian Mackintosh.

Charles made the introductions. "Ingerame Macdowall, this be Ian Mackintosh, our new chief and laird. And this be our mistress, Rose."

"Ingerame," Ian said, looking displeased with all the shouting.

"Ian," he replied as he stood up and wiped his hands on his heavy apron. "Fergive me shoutin'," he said. "I've been lookin' fer me daughter fer hours now."

Ian didn't think bellowing and shouting was the same as looking, but he'd remain mute on the matter for now. "How old be yer daughter?" he asked, hoping she wasn't a little girl lost.

"Bah! She be an auld maid, ye ken. Nearin' two and twenty!" He shook his head as if he were ashamed of that fact. "She'll never marry, that one. I could no' give her away."

Instantly, Rose found she did not like the man, for he was speaking so unkindly about his own flesh and blood. His assertion begged the question *why*. But before she could ask it, he was rambling on about his unmarriable daughter.

"Me wife— God rest her soul — could only give me but one child. Betimes I think I'd have preferred she had no' given me any. Some think the lass be tetched, but I ken the truth. She be a witch as sure as I be standin' here. But what is a father to do?"

"A *father* could be a bit more kind and encouragin'," Rose told him sternly. "A *father* would no' speak so unkindly of his only child."

If she thought to put the man in his place, or hoped for any sign of shame or regret, Rose was sadly mistaken. Ingerame Macdowall did not so much as bat an eye. He was wholly unapologetic. "Ye'll think differently once ye meet her."

Ian was growing impatient. "Would ye like us to help ye find yer daughter so we might talk without distraction?"

Ingerame waved his hands in the air. "Nay, now is as good a time as any. Knowin' Leona, she'd be halfway to France and no' even realize it."

He dropped his chisel and hammer on a tree stump he used as a workspace and once again wiped his dirty hands on his apron. "We only arrived three weeks ago, but we've made good progress."

Rose had no desire to remain in the man's presence a moment longer than necessary. She took the opportunity to leave. "If ye'll excuse me, I'd like to see to settin' up our camp." In truth, she hoped to find this mysterious Leona and see for herself why Ingerame thought so poorly of her.

EIGHT

Rutger Bowie had never been one to hold any delusions of grandeur when it came to his clan. They were a ruthless lot of marauders, ne'er-do-wells, bandits, and thieves. He sat at the high table in the gathering room, looking out at the clan of misfits with a good measure of pride. Tonight, they feasted like kings only because four of his men had the wherewithal to raid a neighboring clan and divest said clan of a few head of their precious cattle.

Oh, they did not possess the refinement or grace of kings, as evidenced by the way they shoveled food into their greasy mouths whilst telling one bawdy tale after another. Ruthless and disgusting as they may be, they were his people.

The Bowies would never be heralded as great inventors, harbingers of peace, or in any other positive light. Nay, if they were to be remembered at all, 'twould only be in stories meant to scare small children. The proof lay in the legacies of their former chiefs.

And none were as insane or ruthless as Eduard Bowie.

That name alone was enough to make Rutger shudder. To say Eduard ruled with an iron fist would have been a tremendous understatement of fact. 'Twas more than that he ruled heartlessly and without mercy. Eduard Bowie was the stuff nightmares were made of. The man took what he wanted when he wanted, no matter who might be the rightful owner. People in general had been terrified of the man. And his clansmen? They hated him passionately. However, they knew that a revolt of any kind would be met with brutal death. He had possessed too many loyal men who would do his bidding, no matter how disgraceful or cruel that bidding might be.

Silently, Rutger raised his cup of *usaige beatha* to the woman who had taken Eduard's life. As far as he was concerned, that wee lass had more courage in her little toe than all of Eduard's men combined. Though it *had* been a horrible way for any man to die — a grappling hook to his neck— 'twas no less than the bloody son of a whore deserved.

He'd oft thought of sending Aggie Mackintosh a letter of thanks for killing Eduard. Were it not for her, he would have lived a verra long time and Rutger would be nothing more than another member of the clan simply praying for their chief's death.

NINE

efore the afternoon was out, tents had been erected, wagons unpacked, goods stored, and camp set up. It amazed Rose no end how everyone came together to do more than their fair share of hard work. The air around them sizzled with excitement and anticipation.

Fires for cooking were started, tables set up for food preparation, and much ale was poured and drunk.

From atop the hill, Ian stood in the early evening light, looking down at his new clan. An overwhelming sense of pride enveloped him as he watched his people happily working together.

His people.

'Twas odd for him to think of himself as the chief of any clan. Odder still, this one in particular. He did not worry about the Mackintosh men, for they were a fierce and loyal lot, not afraid of hard work or a challenge. Nor did he worry about those Frederick had hired to build the keep, for they were being paid well for their work. Neither did he worry about his beautiful wife. Rose was strong, and betimes just as stubborn as he. There was not a doubt in his mind that she would have no trouble being the mistress of the keep.

Nay, he worried about the McLarens and them alone.

Never had he met a sorrier, more hapless and lazy lot of individuals. 'Twas the men's attitudes that bothered him most. He'd seen their lethargy and idleness first hand and on countless occasions. Not one was ever bothered by sitting back and watching women — his Rose and Aggie in particular — doing the work of ten men. Where was their pride? Their honor? He would have to lose both arms and legs before he'd let a woman work as hard as those two women had in the past.

He could name only a few of them, for he hadn't bothered to learn their names. Even though they'd just spent the last three weeks travelling together, he was certain that once the hard work began, they'd leave without so much as a by-your-leave.

There were, by his count, only forty-three McLarens. Of that number, more than half were women. He was certain that if they all left on the morrow, none of them would be missed. He reckoned they could be replaced with only five good men and still get the same amount of work done.

Nightfall was fast approaching when he caught sight of his brother Brogan walking up the hill towards him. Though they were not as close as he and Frederick, they were still brothers and allies. He admired Brogan's ability to look at a problem from more than one angle; he was also quite intelligent. Knowing he was still grieving over the loss of his wife, Ian had been careful not to talk too much about Rose. If their roles were reversed and Ian were the grieving widower, he would not want to be constantly bombarded by someone else's happy marriage.

"Ian," Brogan said as he crested the hill. "'Tis a good, warm night, aye?"

"That it is," Ian said as he slapped him on the back affectionately. Brogan winced ever so slightly, then began pulling at his tunic to help cool his skin.

"It be no' *that* warm," Ian remarked sarcastically.

"Do ye think me weak?" Brogan asked. "I worked all afternoon with me tunic off and now I suffer the affects of the sun."

Ian grimaced, knowing full well how badly skin burned by the sun could hurt.

"I fear I be no' used to all this sunshine," Brogan said. "It rarely shone back home, aye?"

Ian chucked. "Aye, that be true. I imagine it will take us some time to get used to. Ye should seek out Rose. She will have somethin' to help ease yer pain and soothe that burnin' back."

Brogan shrugged as if it were nothing more than a nuisance, even if his back burned as hot as the cooking fires below the hill.

Sensing his brother's reluctance to admit to any kind of injury, Ian rolled his eyes. "'Twill no' injure yer reputation as a whoreson to get a balm fer yer back, ye stubborn eejit."

Brogan ignored him and changed the subject. "Would ye like me to call everyone together so ye might talk to them about yer plans and what ye expect from them?"

"Aye," Ian agreed with a nod. "We shall sup together and afterward I will address them."

Feeling somewhat devilish, Brogan said, "Ye'll make a fine McLaren."

Ian glowered at what he considered an insult. "Ye're either verra brave or a foolish bastard. Either way, I'll kick yer arse up over yer shoulders if ye ever refer to me as the McLaren again."

Rose was very proud of the fine meal she and the other women had prepared for their first night. Everyone had their choice of roasted duck, venison, or fish, along with savory vegetables, fruits, and sweet cakes. Copious amounts of ale and wine were poured and everyone — save for Rodrick the Bold — seemed in fine spirits. Rodrick sat alone on a log, away from the rest of the clan, watching everyone with either a scrutinizing gaze or a scowl; she didn't know him well enough to ascertain which it was.

There were not enough tables and benches for everyone to sit around, so many took seats upon the ground, or on felled logs. Fires roared and crackled whilst a few men took out lutes and drums to play lively tunes.

Rose knew each of the McLaren women, and had built fast friendships with those Mackintosh women who had followed their husbands to these new lands. Most of the carpenters and laborers were single. Only a few had brought their wives with them. Rose made a point of seeking each of the women out to welcome them to the clan. She was also eager to meet Leona Macdowall.

Ian was also quite proud of what his wife and the clanswomen had been able to accomplish in such a short amount of time. Seated at a table, surrounded by his men, his attention was more on his beautiful wife than whatever the men were discussing. He watched as she stood talking with a small group of women. What they were saying, he could not hear. Occasionally, that brilliant smile he'd grown more than fond of, broke over her face. Instantly, his desire flared and he wanted only to seek out their tent and love her all the night long. Though he had explored nearly every square inch of her luscious body, he imagined he'd never grow tired of daily discoveries.

'Twas Andrew the Red's voice in his ear that broke through his thoughts. "Are ye ready to speak to yer people?" he asked, his speech slightly slurred from too much ale.

Inwardly, Ian sighed, then gave a curt nod. Frederick and Brogan were always far better with words, and he hoped he wouldn't muddle things. It had been Frederick who had addressed them weeks ago, back on Mackintosh lands. It had been Frederick who told them of their plans, of what they hoped to accomplish in the months and years to come. Nightly, Ian prayed these people would continue to follow him, that he could lead as well as his brother.

"Stand on the table so they can hear ye," Andrew suggested as he stood to allow Ian more room to leave the bench.

Swinging his long legs around, Ian stood tall and stretched for a moment before climbing onto the table. As he stood in the center, Andrew let out a loud whistle to draw everyone's attention. "Yer chief wishes to speak to ye!" he shouted over the din of conversation.

Ian grimaced slightly at Andrew's bold behavior. He knew he was only trying to help, but perhaps he needn't help quite so much. The people soon grew quiet. Taking a deep breath, he addressed his people for the first time as their chief.

"I wish to first thank me wife and the fine women who prepared a feast fit fer a king," he began. The crowd clapped and cheered and tankards were pounded against the tops of tables. Looking directly at his smiling wife, he held out his hands for her to join him. Brogan and Andrew assisted her up to stand next to Ian. Taking her hand in his, he said, "My wife, yer mistress, Rose Mackintosh of Clan McLaren." Another cheer erupted through the crowd who had drawn closer in order to hear their chief speak. Ian noticed a few of the single men were smiling a little too fondly toward his wife, but he ignored them. It made sense for men to stare, for she was quite beautiful to look upon. But if any of them were to so much as step one toe out of place, he'd have no problem beating them senseless.

"We have travelled a long while, over rough terrain, through rivers and over mountains, to reach this most beautiful of places," he began. "Just as our journey here was no' easy, neither will it be an easy task rebuildin' Clan McLaren to its former glory. But with hard work and our determination and strong will, together, we will prevail, no matter what obstacles may come our way." The McLarens cheered more loudly than the others. He eyed his Mackintosh brethren for a long moment. Clearly, they were not as excited as he or the others.

"I must admit that I do no' ken much about the history of Clan McLaren. I do know that fer a very long time, 'twas run by a ruthless man known as Mermadak. The McLarens who stand with ye today, ken all too well what kind of man he was. To ye, I promise that as long as I live, ye'll never endure again that which ye endured at his hand." The McLarens broke out into another cheer, even louder than the first. "To the Mackintoshes," he began, raising his hands once again for quiet. "I ken 'twas no' easy fer ye to leave our homelands to come here, to help rebuild a clan who until recently, ye'd never known. To each of ye, ye have me undyin' gratitude and thanks, as well as Frederick's and his Aggie's."

The Mackintoshes burst into a roaring cheer, waving hands and swords in the air. "Fer Aggie!" they shouted. "Fer Aggie!"

Ian looked to Rose, who was smiling as proudly as if the cheers were meant for her. When he looked out again, with the Mackintoshes and McLarens now cheering *fer Aggie'* in unison, he knew these people were not here for him, but for his sister-by-law. 'Twas a slight wound to his pride, but he'd rather have them here for Aggie than not here at all.

As the crowd began to quiet, someone shouted, "Ian! We will follow ye anywhere! Our new chief! The new McLaren!"

Grimacing inward, he painted a smile on his face. Would he ever get used to being referred to as the McLaren? He prayed to God he did not.

TEN

Two days passed before Rose had the opportunity to meet the elusive Leona Macdowall. She was not at all what Rose had expected.

She was a strikingly beautiful woman, with long, wavy blonde hair. Why her father believed she was unmarriageable, Rose could not understand. Only slightly taller than Rose, she possessed a far more buxom figure, and a very sweet, nearly melodic voice. The only thing Rose found unusual about the young woman's appearance was the fact that one eye was a dark green and the other a pale blue. Could that be the reason?

Highlander men, by nature, were superstitious. Mayhap they thought her different colored eyes were a sign of the devil or a bewitchment. 'Twas wholly ludicrous, by Rose's way of thinking. She found Leona Macdowall soft-spoken and good natured, even if she were easily distracted.

"I shall be happy to assist ye in any way I can, m'lady," Leona said as they stood near one of the cooking fires.

"I shall be glad fer it, Leona," Rose said with a smile. "I look forward to gettin' to know ye better."

Leona simply returned the smile, gave a slight curtsey and walked away, leaving Rose perplexed. Had she not just expressed the desire to get to know her better? The young woman had left before Rose could ask even the simplest question.

In the few short days that followed, the new Clan McLaren had settled into a routine. With the influx of extra men, they began erecting the wooden wall. Though 'twas not meant to be a permanent structure 'twas built as soundly as if it were. While teams of men felled the massive trees, other teams worked to remove limbs and branches before scraping the bark away. The top of each beam was cut to a fine, sharp point.

While those men made the beams, another team worked to dig the holes in which those heavy beams would be set. And less than a mile away, men were busy quarrying stone.

'Twas dirty, back-breaking work, but none complained, at least not in excess.

The women were just as busy ensuring the men were well fed and had clean clothes, as well as tending to the occasional cut hand or broken finger.

Ian was as proud as any man could be, though he did his best to maintain a serious facade. Rose knew he worried that if he seemed more the men's joyful friend, he'd seem less their fearless leader and chief. Only at night, when they were alone in their tent, would he let his guard down.

"The McLaren men be workin' just as hard as the Mackintosh," he told her. They'd been there a week now and much had been accomplished.

"Why do ye find that so hard to believe?" Rose asked him. He was sitting on a stool whilst she struggled to remove his dirty boots.

He looked at her with a good measure of disbelief. "Ye've met the McLaren men, have ye no'?" he asked sarcastically.

She tugged the first boot free and set it next to the entrance of their tent. "Aye, I have. Apparently it be ye who has no'."

"I be referrin' to the same McLaren men who stood by and let ye and Aggie do the work of ten men," he said, referring to how things had been when they had first met more than a year prior.

Freeing the other boot, she set it next to its partner before standing to her full height. "Nay, ye be referrin' to the cowards that followed Mermadak. Most of them be dead now, thanks to Rowan Graham — may the man be someday sainted fer comin' to us in our hour of need."

It had been Frederick's long-time friend and ally, Rowan Graham, and his men, who had wrested the old McLaren keep from the Bowie. Mermadak had convinced Eduard to kidnap and kill his only son-by-law, Frederick. In return, he gave Eduard the keep and all the McLaren lands. Eduard's plans failed — and failed miserably, for Aggie McLaren-Mackintosh killed the bloody bastard with her own hands. Rowan Graham had come to their rescue by seizing the McLaren keep and taking it back from the Bowie.

Ian continued to look at his wife with an expression that questioned her soundness of mind.

Rose rolled her eyes as she rested her hands on her hips. "Do no' look at me that way," she admonished. "I've no' lost me mind."

Ian quirked a brow.

"The men that be here now? They were at one time good and hardworkin' men. But after all those years of livin' under Mermadak's rule, they lost hope. They gave up, ye see. Would *ye* have worked from sun-up to sunset fer him?" She already knew the answer. Ian had grown up inside the powerful yet loving arms of a very strong clan. "Nay, ye would no'. The men that be here workin' alongside ye now? I grew up knowin' these men. I remember how things used to be. So do they. They have ye to thank fer givin' us hope fer a much better future, Ian. As do I."

Ian hoped that his wife spoke the truth.

It DID NOT TAKE LONG TO REALIZE Rose was correct in regards to the McLaren men. The following morn, Ian woke just after sunrise. After making love to his wife slowly and with much passion, he dressed quickly, grabbed a bannock from their small table, and left her to sleep in the tent.

'Twas a brilliant morn, with the sun casting shades of bright golds and yellows across the land. Until he met Rose, married her, and moved to this place, he'd never been one to enjoy early mornings. Nay, he much preferred to drink and carouse all through the night and to sleep the mornings away.

But now, everything was different. He was the chief of this hardscrabble clan. He was now a man who possessed dreams and goals which he intended to work very hard to make them come to fruition. Save for a few women who were readying fires in order to prepare the morning meal, he saw no one else as he made his way across the clearing.

As soon as he walked into the forest he caught sight of men already fast at work. And every one of the dozen men were McLarens.

From the looks of things, they'd been at it for some time. Two men to a timber, six in all, were scraping bark from the massive logs. The other men were scooping the remnants into wooden wheelbarrows and carrying them off to add to the large, growing pile near the entrance. Covered in sweat — a few of the older men looked as though they might keel over from the exertion — out of breath and hard at work.

But every single one of them bore a proud, beaming smile.

Ian was struck at once with the realization that these men were much like him. They too had dreams and goals.

As he approached, the men all looked up from their work to offer him a quick nod or a warm greeting. "Good morn to ye, m'laird," one of the older men called out as he steered his full wheelbarrow toward the pile of branches and bark.

Feeling a bit ashamed for not remembering the man's name, Ian returned his greeting, patted the man on the back. "Fast at work already, I see."

"Aye m'laird. Ye never ken how long the weather will hold, aye?" the gray-headed man said with a smile as he went on his way.

The mood amongst these men seemed light and merry. Cheerful laughter echoed from farther inside the dense forest. Try as he might, he could not find a Mackintosh man among those already up and at work.

He stood for a long moment, looking from one man to the next. A sense of pride blended with disbelief came over him. Had he not witnessed it with his own eyes, he would never have believed a McLaren would or could work as hard as these men obviously were.

A familiar voice called out from behind him. "Ye never believed a McLaren man kent what hard work was, did ye?"

Ian spun around to see Eggar Wardwin standing but a few feet away.

"Eggar?" he asked, unable to hide his surprise at seeing the man. A tall, lean man with brown hair and hazel eyes, Eggar Wardwin had had the unfortunate experience of once being married to the infamous Claire. The woman who had nearly killed Aggie. Eggar had stayed behind last spring with a handful of other McLarens.

"M'laird," he said with a slight inclination of his head.

Ian studied him closely for a moment before extending his hand in greeting.

Eggar was relieved at the offering and gladly accepted. "I pray it be all right that I am here."

"'Tis mighty glad I am to have ye here," Ian admitted. "How fare ye?"

With a quick shrug, Eggar said, "Well enough, I reckon." He took a deep breath and let it out in a whoosh. "I heard about Claire and what she did."

Ian's jaw ticked at the memory. Claire had poisoned Aggie, nearly killed her. It had forced her into early labor. A birthing that went on for hours, with Aggie unaware of what was happening to her. Ian had witnessed only part of that long, ugly night and was glad he'd never have to witness his own wife in such agony or despair.

"What Claire did does no' reflect upon ye, Eggar. None will hold her actions against ye."

He was relieved to hear it, though his smile did not quite reach his eyes. "I thank ye, m'laird."

The McLaren men respected Eggar. Mayhap he could use the man to help bring the Mackintoshes closer to the McLarens.

"We arrived a few weeks ago," Eggar explained. "We were out huntin' and noticed strange men fellin' trees. Rodrick nearly ran us through. Tried to run us off our own land."

That information made Ian feel better about keeping Rodrick on sentry duty. The man took his duties quite seriously.

"But once we explained who we were — and that took a good long while — he took us to Ingerame. The next day, we packed up what little we had and came here. Have no' left since."

"How many came with ye?" Ian asked.

"Nine."

The image of Rodrick the Bold holding nine men at sword point amused him. There had not been too many opportunities as yet for him to interact with Rodrick. Though Charles McFarland did not much care for the man, the more Ian learned of him, the more impressed he became.

"I should like to meet with them. So much has happened these past months, I fear I do no' remember who stayed and who went with us," Ian said. He was growing more ashamed of himself for not remembering most of the names of the McLarens who had ventured east with them last spring. Seeing how hard these men were working intensified that feeling.

"Would ye like to meet with them now?" Eggar asked.

"Aye, I would."

Eggar let out a shrill whistle betwixt his teeth. Moments later the McLaren men came running.

For the next hour, Ian took the time to learn each of their names and to get to know them a bit better. When he was finished, he thanked them for their fealty to Clan McLaren.

"When we heard ye were now our laird and chief, we could no' have been more happy," Milton McLaren said with a proud gleam in his eyes. He was at least fifty, with skinny arms and legs affixed to a rather large belly. His light brown hair was streaked with gray and one of his front teeth was missing. "'Tis we who should be thankin' ye, m'laird, fer givin' us our clan back."

Ian was about to express his gratitude to them, when Milton went on to say, "We reckon ye'll be the best McLaren we've had in a good long while."

"To the McLaren!" One of the men shouted.

Ian blanched inwardly. "Please, call me Ian."

Thus far, the weather had cooperated quite nicely. 'Twas a sunny summer morning within a month of their arrival when construction began on the foundation to the tower. Large stones had been quarried and carried in on the wagons, massive holes dug for the foundation, and pulleys erected to help offload those stones.

The tower would be a square structure, three stories tall, with arrow slits and small rectangular windows. Ian and Ingerame were hopeful they could erect the tower before winter arrived.

With the good weather and good attitudes of all, everything was running as smoothly as Ian could ever have hoped for. Though he was nowhere near as pious as his older brothers, he could not help but feel that God agreed with their plans. The good weather, the ease with which everything was moving along, was proof enough of His acceptance and blessing.

He should have known better.

The first rift in their little bit of paradise came when the weather decided to take a turn from God-blessed to God-forsaken. Rain came down in torrential sheets as the wind whipped and tore at anyone or anything in its path. People took shelter in their tents, huddled together and soaked to the bone.

Ian and Rose took refuge in their own little tent that sat slightly apart from the others. With nothing better to do, and a sexual appetite that shamed even the ancient gods of old, Ian set about wooing his wife. 'Twas the only ray of proverbial sunshine in the otherwise dark, stormy afternoon.

"Have I ever told ye how fond I am of yer breasts?" he asked as he slipped a hand through the open bodice of her dress.

"Once or twice," she giggled.

Brushing the pad of his thumb over a taught peak, he whispered against the soft skin of her cheek. "Then I have been remiss in me duties as yer husband." He pressed his lips tenderly against her skin. "Be there anyway I can make it up to ye?"

She took in a deep breath and let it out slowly, thoroughly enjoying the way his warm hands felt as they caressed her breasts, the way his lips brushed against her neck. "Oh, I am sure together we can think of somethin'," she cooed.

He had just scooped her into his arms to lay her on their bed, when a voice sounded outside their tent. "R-Rose? Are ye th-there?"

Ian was about to tell whoever it was to go away. Rose silenced him with a look of concern and a finger to his lips. "That be Leona," she said.

Reluctantly, he set his wife on her feet and went to open the flap of their tent. He had yet to meet Leona Macdowall. Before he could demand to know what the bloody hell she was doing out in this weather, he was taken aback by her appearance. There stood a young woman who Ian thought the spitting image of his wife. Save for her odd colored eyes and very ample bosom. "Och! M'laird, I did no' ken ye were here."

Before she could leave, Rose was pulling her inside. "Come in out of the rain!"

Leona quickly stepped through into the warmth of the tent. Shivering from head to toe, she looked as though she'd just fallen into a loch.

Rose took the wet shawl from Leona's shoulders and draped it over the stool next to the brazier. Ian grabbed a warm fur from the bed and offered it to her. Through chattering teeth, she apologized. "I-it b-be r-rainin' t-t-too hard to g-get t-t-to me own t-t-tent."

"We need to get ye out of those wet clothes or ye'll catch yer death fer certain," Rose exclaimed as she handed the fur to her husband. "Turn around, Ian."

Seeing that his wife was in complete control of the situation, he did as she bid, stepping to the opposite side of the tent. "It has been rainin' fer some time, Leona." He spoke to the tent wall. "Where have ye been?"

"P-pickin' f-flowers," she replied.

"Flowers, ye say?" Was she not a wee bit old to be off picking flowers when there was so much work to be done? He could hear the sound of wet clothes hitting the floor and much shuffling of feet.

"Aye," she answered.

"Do ye no' have more important things to do, lass? Is there no' enough work to be had by all?"

Silence filled the small space. It seemed to stretch on forever. "Well, lass?"

'Twas his wife who answered, and she did not sound at all pleased. "She was pickin' flowers fer our healer," Rose explained. "Our healer be too auld to be walkin' around the countryside. Leona volunteered to help."

She left him feeling quite the cad and Ian was glad his back was to them so they could not see his face burn red with embarrassment. "I apologize to ye, Leona," he stammered.

"This dress should work fer ye, at least long enough until yers gets dry. I reckon the rain will lighten up soon enough," Rose said hopefully.

Ian could hear the dress being pulled over Leona's head. A moment later, Rose said, "Oh dear."

He was not about to ask what the problem might be or if he could offer any assistance. The moment he heard Rose declare the dress would work, he knew it wouldn't. Although Leona appeared to be about the same height and build as his wife, there was a distinct difference between the women. More specifically, *two*. And though he was passionately in love with his wife's breasts, and hadn't been tempted in the least by another woman since he'd met her, he was not blind. He knew the dress would be far too small to accommodate the ample bosom of Leona Macdowall. For the life of him, he could not understand why any man had yet to offer for the young woman's hand.

More scuffling and shuffling came from behind him as he began to rock back and forth on his heels. "That be much better," Rose declared before giving her husband permission to turn around.

Rose had pulled one of his tunics over the dress, no doubt to cover up what his wee wife's dress could not. Grabbing the fur once again, Rose wrapped it around Leona's shoulders and sat her next to the brazier. "Are ye hungry?" Rose asked.

Leona gave a slight shake of her head. "Nay, but th-thank y-ye."

Pouring a generous amount of wine into a wooden cup, Rose handed it to the semi-frozen young woman. "Drink this. 'Twill help warm ye up a bit."

Leona took the offered cup and sipped slowly at its contents. "'Tis v-verra good," she murmured.

Rose pulled the other stool away from the wall and sat across from Leona. For a long moment, she studied the young woman closely. "Did ye manage to get the flowers Angrabaid needed?"

She nodded in affirmation. "I left them in the c-cave. I d-did no' want them to g-get damaged by the r-rain."

Both Rose and Ian looked at her with furrowed brows. "What cave?" Ian asked.

"Near the quarry," she told him.

Ian shook his head, hoping he could shake some sense of what she'd just said into his head. "If ye were in the cave, lass, why didn't ye *stay* in the cave?"

A deep blush came to her cheeks. "'Twas otherwise occupied," she said.

Ian and Rose cast curious glances at one another. "Occupied? Were they strangers? People we need to worry over?"

She was hesitant to answer. "N-nay."

'Twas like pulling teeth to get to the bottom of things with this young woman. "If they were no' strangers, then why did ye no' stay?" Ian pushed forward.

Leona looked first to Rose, then to Ian, and back to Rose as if she were trying to ascertain something. Mayhap she did not trust them.

Finally, after a few more sips of wine, she answered. "They be the men workin' in the quarry. If me da found out I had spent any time at all in a cave, alone with men, no matter the reason, well, he would have no' liked that at all."

So she would rather risk life and limb, battle a horrendous storm, rather than wait that storm out in a cave filled with men.

While his wife nodded and looked as though it all made perfectly good sense to her, Ian was left dumbfounded. Aye, Leona Macdowall was an odd creature indeed.

It rained for three solid days, non-stop. Everything and everyone was soaked through. Mud and rain had begun to seep into the tents, and the pit for the foundation of the keep was filled to the brim with muddy rainwater. No one gathered at night to sup together, for the rain kept them in. After he had seen Leona safely to her own tent, Ian and Rose locked themselves away from the rest of the world. They made love as frequently as either wanted — or later as either was able.

While he'd once dreamed of being hidden away with Rose, enjoying her company and her loving, by dawn on the fourth day, he was ready to go mad. Not from boredom, for he'd never grow bored of his wife. Nay he worried about losing all the progress they had made over the past weeks. He also worried about their food stores and running out of fresh meat.

"I have had about enough of this rain and mud," Rose declared as she lifted another rain-soaked fur from the floor. "'Tis seepin' in and soakin' everythin', includin' me fine spirits." She gave the fur a good shake and hung it on the line Ian had strung up for her days before. The line sagged with the weight of countless furs and blankets. "Mayhap when the rain lets up, ye could ask the men to make us planks to use as flooring?"

He had more important things on his mind than wet floors. Only half listening, he looked at the parchment before him for the thousandth time in the past three days. Rose took his grunt to mean he'd heard her and agreed.

"I do no' ken why ye keep lookin' at those plans," she said as she threw another piece of wood on the brazier. "Surely ye have them memorized by now."

Soon, she realized he was not paying any attention to her. Typically, she would have gone to him, wrapped her arms around his neck and made a suggestion about what to do with the rest of the afternoon. But they had already made love twice that morning. Though she truly enjoyed loving her husband, well, there was only so much loving a woman could do in one day.

JUST WHEN THEY HAD BEGUN TO dry everything out, the rain would return. Rose had grown up here and therefore was accustomed to the fickle weather. But even this amount of rain was highly unusual. No matter what she did to keep the water out of her tent, 'twas to no avail.

She was not the only one suffering from this problem.

One afternoon in early August, she and the other women met around the main cooking fire. The rain had let up, but the air was still filled with a seemingly ever-present fine mist. Everywhere they were able, they'd hung up lines to dry clothes, blankets and furs.

"'Tis because the men are no' the ones havin' to dry everythin' out, or to fight the weather to cook a meal," Ronna, one of the McLaren women said. "If 'twas them havin' to struggle with it, they'd find a solution right quick." Ronna looked tired, older than her years, and not very hopeful that the problem would be resolved any time soon. Her brown hair was twisted into a braid, her brown eyes dull, as if she'd given up hope for more than just having dry floors.

Della Mackintosh agreed. "'Tis the way of things. Always has been, always will be." Della was in her late thirties, the mother of four boys, three of whom were old enough to help in the woods with their father.

"In their defense," Rose interjected, "they have been very busy at the quarry, in the woods, and workin' on the tower. All those things are equally as important as what we do."

They could not argue that point, but it did nothing to solve the problem at hand. "I have asked Ian once again fer planks fer our tents."

"And what does Ian say?" Ronna asked.

Rose was hesitant to tell them but she had no choice. "He says they will get to it when they get to it. Fer now, we must be patient. The tower is their first priority at the moment."

"Bah!" Ronna chortled.

As they discussed possible solutions, Rose caught sight of two young men she knew. Kerchar McLaren and Rory Mackinlay. They had just walked up to the wagons where they kept the food stores and began removing the bags and barrels, setting them on the ground.

"What on earth?" she asked as she made haste to stop them.

"What are ye doin?" she demanded rather loudly.

Kerchar looked up as he placed a bag of barley on the ground. "Ian's orders," he told her. "We need the extra wagon down at the quarry."

Angrily, Rose tried picking up the heavy bag of grain. 'Twas far too heavy. "Ye can no' just set things upon the ground! 'Tis too damp. 'Twill spoil!"

The two young men looked perplexed, and neither truly wanted to insult their mistress. But neither did they wish to make Ian wait for the extra wagon. "I be sorry, mistress," Kerchar said. "Where would ye like us to put them?"

Rolling her eyes, she was tempted to tell him to give a message to her husband, directing him as to where exactly he could put their food stores. Deciding 'twas neither ladylike nor polite, she instead told them to put the items on the long table near the cooking fire. Eager not to distress their mistress or their chief, they hurried to do as she had asked.

As the two young lads were hauling items from the wagon to the table, two other men appeared with a team of horses. Giving a polite nod to Rose, they began hooking them up to the wagon. Rose's band of women were now standing beside her with mouths agape. "What …" Della couldn't form the question.

Rose sighed and put her hands on her hips. "Apparently, they need more wagons fer the quarry."

"But…" Again, she was too stunned to voice her thoughts. All they could do was stand by and watch as the last of the dry spaces to store food was taken over.

Rose loved her husband. Truly she did. But this, this was just unacceptable . As they watched the men hitch the team to the wagons, an idea began to form in Rose's mind. Turning to face the women, she said, "My friends, 'tis time we took matters into our own hands."

ELEVEN

ose had been fast asleep when Ian came to bed and he left before she was awake. It had been like this for days now — days of having no time alone with her husband to discuss important matters.

The men had erected tents near the quarry, where they would take refuge whenever the rains came. The moment the rain let up enough, they immediately went back to work. When she did see Ian, he was often too exhausted or too preoccupied to talk. She had requested just a few moments alone with him on numerous occasions. "I promise, Rose, I will try to set aside some time fer ye later," was always his response.

She pretended not to be hurt or insulted by his lack of attention. Logically, she knew he was very busy, with important duties, a keep to build…but that did very little to ease the ache in her heart.

Her plan had been quite simple; go to the auld McLaren keep, dismantle the granary, and bring those planks back by wagon. It would save time for everyone and it would solve the problem of ruined clothing and spoiled food. If Ian had given her just a few moments of his precious time, she could have explained it logically to him. But once again, he was gone before she woke.

"Enough is enough," she declared as she stepped out of bed onto a still soggy floor. Reasoning that neither her husband nor his men could be bothered, she dressed quickly and set about enlisting the help of her clanswomen.

Ronna, though aged and oft tired-looking, was all too willing to help, as was Della.

"I agree," Ronna said, "that me grandchildren will be grandparents before our men get around to planks fer floors, or even buildin' huts fer us."

At this point, Rose could not say she disagreed. "I pray ye're no' right, Ronna," she said as they sought out more women to help. "I fear I'll strangle Ian in his sleep if he makes me wait that long fer a sound roof and walls that do no' leak." 'Twas neither an exaggeration nor bold boast.

Soon, they had rounded up ten more women of varying ages, who were all too eager to help. "Who among us kens how to ready a team of horses?" Rose asked as they made their way to the corral where the horses were kept.

"I do!" Anna Markland piped up. "I help me husband all the time."

"Verra well then, Anna, ye shall be in charge of the horses." She smiled at the young woman. "We shall need tools to help dismantle the granary. I fear all I have is a hammer."

Liza Markland, sister-by-law to Anna, slowly raised her hand. "Me husband, he has spare tools in our tent."

"Good!" Rose said cheerfully. Thus far, things were going quite well. "I'll need someone to help Anna with the horses."

"But we have no wagons," Ronna pointed out.

Rose looked around the encampment and spotted two empty wagons sitting near the tower. "Oh, but we do!" she exclaimed happily as she pointed.

"Now, we shall go get our tools, and any weapons ye can find. Anna, can ye also ride?"

"Aye," she said as she backed the first horse up to the wagon. "So can Liza, and I believe Lena can as well."

Liza and Lena said they could in fact ride and ride well. "So be it," Rose said. "Let us gather our tools, weapons and a lunch, and meet back here in a quarter of an hour."

ROSE RETURNED TO HER TENT, grabbed the hammer, the *sgian dubh* Ian had given her a long time ago, as well as two dirks and a sword he kept in the tent. Feeling quite strongly that she was doing the right thing, she headed back to the meeting place. On her way, she saw Leona near one of the cooking fires.

"Leona, I need yer help."

As was typical, the pretty young woman seemed distracted as she stared into the fire. Rose approached cautiously. "Leona?"

Slowly, she looked up and bid Rose a half-hearted good morn. Rose was pressed for time. If it had been any other day, she would have asked if something was the matter and offered any help she could. But the other women were waiting for her. "Leona, if Ian asks where I am, please tell him we went to the auld keep and should be back before nightfall."

Leona nodded and gave her a smile. "Aye, I will."

'Twas never easy to tell if the young girl was listening or not. Rose was about to ask if she understood when Ronna and Della called for her. "The auld keep, Leona. We're goin' to the auld keep."

"I heard ye," she replied without looking up.

With very little time to waste, Rose thanked her kindly and left her staring blankly into the fire.

THERE HAD BEEN NO ONE manning the gate when the band of determined women headed off that morning. Most of the men were working in the quarry and only a few were patrolling farther out. With light hearts, the group made the mile long journey to the auld McLaren keep in very little time.

For Rose, and Ronna McLaren, the lightness in their hearts faded the moment they set eyes on the auld keep. Not-too-distant memories trickled in, leaving Rose feeling sad and angry all at once. Sad for the days of her childhood when things hadn't been quite as bad, and heavy-hearted with missing Aggie.

Rose's skin turned to gooseflesh as they filed through the gate, seeing the keep lifeless, marred still by a fire set nearly a year past. The cheerful banter among the women faded and an eerie silence filled the air.

"I never thought I'd see this place again," Ronna remarked in a barely audible whisper. "Truth be told, I never wanted to."

Rose felt much the same way.

Beyond the main keep was the granary. 'Twas just as dilapidated as she remembered; however, the wide wooden planks it had been made from seemed to be in good enough condition to be useful.

Anna led the team and wagon across the empty yard, coming to a stop next to the auld building. The women sat in silence as they stared at the project before them. When Rose had first come up with the idea, it had seemed an easy enough task. But now that they were here, and she could once again see just how large the building was, a sense of dread settled in.

Not quite ready to give up, she took a deep breath and jumped down from the wagon, bringing her hammer with her. "'Tis a bit bigger than I remember, but we shall no' let that stop us." She tried to sound less disheartened and more a hopeful leader.

While the women climbed out of the wagon, she went to speak to the three on horseback. "I doubt we'll have any troubles, but if we do, I need ye to run back to camp and tell Ian and the others."

Anna appeared not only fully prepared but also fully capable of defending herself against any intruders. Liza and Lena seemed a little more worried about the prospect. "Just patrol where we discussed earlier. Blow the horn fer a warnin' then ride as fast as ye can. We shall be fine, but. 'tis best to be cautious."

With the most serious expression, Anna patted the horn that hung around her neck then the sword that hung at her waist, signifying she was absolutely ready for anything. "Come ladies, we've work to do," she said as she tapped the flanks of her horse.

Rose listened to Anna give bits of advice as the trio pulled away. "The trick, ye ken, is never to panic, as well as to remain as quiet as a church mouse..."

Feeling mayhap a bit safer than she ought, Rose returned to the group of women who would, for today at least, be carpenters and laborers.

"We should begin inside," she said as she led them in to the interior of the granary. In each corner of the building sat tall, square bins that were meant to store grain. Old, decrepit looking ladders rested against each of the structures. Scattered about the room were remnants and reminders of the winter when this large building housed some fifty men and women. Rocks placed in circles still contained the charred remains of old fires; a few pieces of broken pottery were the only things left to prove people had once lived in this place.

"Let's dismantle the bins first," Rose suggested. Her hammer in hand, she took the ladder up to the top of the first bin. Studying it for a moment, she realized she was far too short to reach the very top of the bin. Twisting her bottom lip, she felt the stirrings of doubt begin to creep in.

"Start in the middle," Della suggested from the bin opposite Rose. The woman had already climbed up the ladder and was working a heavy iron bar betwixt two pieces of wood. "We can no' get it all, but we'll settle fer what we *can* get."

Della's positivity was contagious. Rose pushed all doubt aside when Maribet Mackintosh tapped her on the leg with an iron bar. "This might work better than yer hammer."

Exchanging one tool for another, Rose set about working the bar between the planks. Back and forth, sliding the bar from side to side, she was ready to give up hope when she heard the plank moan before it gave way just enough to offer a glimmer of a chance they would be successful. It seemed to take forever before she was able to work the plank free on one side. Still, 'twas progress.

After much struggling, elbow grease, and a wee bit of cursing, the first plank finally broke free. It nearly knocked her from the ladder, but thankfully, she was able to keep herself from falling to the ground. Maribet caught one edge of the heavy piece of wood before it had the chance to land on her head.

"Bloody hell!" the young woman cursed.

"Mayhap ye should no' stand so close," Rose offered after apologizing.

Maribet cast her a stern look before bursting into laughter. "Mayhap I should work at dismantlin' and let ye catch. Della has two planks down and is workin' on her third."

Rose looked across to see that Maribet spoke the truth. Giggling, she said, "I let her have the easy one, with the rotted wood."

Della chimed in. "Mayhap ye should take the rotted wood, m'lady. We do no' want ye hurtin' yer pretty hands."

Unable to contain her laughter, Rose leaned her head against the bin. She knew Della spoke in jest, for 'twas a conversation they'd had many times over the past weeks. *'Ye do no' work like any mistress I've ever kent,'* Della had told her numerous times. *'I've never seen such worn hands on a lady before.'* The jests were her way of complimenting Rose, in her own round about way.

At the end of the first hour, Rose had dismantled four boards to Della's nine. Covered in sweat and grime, both women eagerly gave over their tools for a quick rest, allowing others to ascend the ladders and take over.

Working in teams, while four women dismantled the bins, the women on the ground loaded the planks into the wagon. 'Twas not as easy as Rose had anticipated, but together, they worked diligently and proudly. By the end of the day, they had a sizable amount of lumber loaded into the wagons.

"Our men will be verra proud of us," Rose declared as she looked over the contents of the wagon. "Verra proud indeed!"

"WHERE THE BLOODY HELL IS me wife?" Ian shouted as he stormed through the encampment. When she had not brought him his noonin' meal — as she'd been doing for weeks now — he thought mayhap she'd simply gotten too busy with something else. And when a handful of other men began to wonder where their wives were, they concluded their women must be together. But what could be so important that they'd forget to feed the men? Ian had volunteered to go back to find out.

Rose was nowhere to be found. He began asking every woman he came upon, if, by chance, they knew where his wife was. After the fifth

"I do no' ken" he began to worry. Worry turned to an unsettling anger and frustration, thus his need to shout at the top of his lungs.

A younger woman, whose name he had yet to memorize, hesitantly came to him. "M'laird, I saw her leave early this morn with Della, Ronna and a few others," she stammered.

"Where did they go?"

Shrugging her shoulders, she answered as best she could. "I do no' ken. I only saw them leave and head south."

Perturbed, Ian ran a hand through his hair. "And ye did no' think to ask them what they be doin'?" His voice was harsh, filled with frustration.

The young girl's shoulders fell as she stared at the ground. "But she's our mistress," she murmured. "I did no' think it me place."

He felt ashamed. 'Twas no' her fault his wife had left without telling anyone where she was going. "I be sorry, fer yellin' at ye. Please, if ye find anyone who kens where they went, find me and tell me at once."

The girl gave a nod and a curtsey before scurrying off.

Ian found Della's youngest boy and sent him back to the quarry to fetch Brogan and Andrew the Red.

As he paced nervously around the encampment, a sense of unease came over him. It had been his decision to not have men at the gates. His decision as well to only have a few men on patrol. Plagued with guilt, angry that his wife had left without word, he was soon consumed by anger. He had been so focused on building the tower and other buildings that he had not taken the time to think of any scenario that would require strong defenses. Daily training had been replaced with daily, non-stop work on the tower and wall. Not once had he stopped to consider the actual safety of his clan.

He had even dismissed the idea of Brogan and Andrew protecting his wife. She was among her clanspeople. What would she need protection from? Apparently, from her own foolish and stubborn self.

Brogan and Andrew came racing into the encampment on horseback, worry etched into the lines of their faces. "What happened?" Brogan demanded as he slid from his horse. "The boy said Rose be missin'."

Quickly, Ian filled the two men in with all he knew at this point. "They left without word, apparently," he explained. "Why would she do somethin' so foolish?"

Whatever thoughts Brogan or Andrew had on that particular matter, they kept to themselves. "I shall call all the men back," Andrew offered. "We shall form a search party."

For once, Ian did not think about towers or quarries or work. His only concern was his wife.

"WHEN WE GET BACK TO CAMP, I'll have me boys help unload," Della said from the back of the wagon. "I can no' wait to have a dry floor!"

Rose was just as excited about the prospect as the rest of the women. "I fear we will no' have enough wood to go around, though," she said. "Mayhap when the men see how easy 'twas to dismantle the bins, they'll go back and get the rest fer us." That was if she could get her stubborn and distracted husband to let go of a few men for a few hours. Hopeful that once he saw the kind of progress ten women had made in a few short hours, he might not be against the idea. There had to be a way to get through his thick skull. Mayhap coming back with a wagon filled with wood would be the one thing to help him see the errors of his ways.

"There be home," Rose said over the sound of the creaking and groaning wagon. She could just make out the tall wooden wall and the gate. "'Twill no' be long now and we will have dry floors and verra thankful husbands."

Little did she know there was nothing further from the truth.

PROUD AND HAPPY WERE AS far from what Ian felt than the moon was from the earth.

As they pulled the wagon through the gates, the women were met by furious husbands.

Rose took one look at Ian, and for the first time since meeting him, she was actually afraid. Oh, she knew he'd not lay a hand on her in anger. But from the glower on his face, he was mad enough to bite his sword in half.

Tamping down her fear, and pushing away any good sense she might previously have been using, she offered him her brightest smile. "Ian!" she called out to him. "Ye be back early. We have a surprise fer ye!"

Like a hoard of angry bees, the men stormed forward, each one after his own wife. Ian appeared to be the angriest of all, if his purple face and piercing gaze were any indication. "Where. In. The. Bloody hell. Have. Ye. Been?"

He gave her no time to respond. "We have been worried sick!" he shouted as he grabbed her about the waist and lifted her out of the wagon. "Ye hie yerself off and do no' tell a soul where ye're goin'? And ye take nine innocent women with ye?" He was certain that whatever they had done, Rose had been their fearless if not addlepated leader. "Ye will never put me through such anguish and worry again, wife!"

Rose knew there were times she should simply let her husband be angry; like water boiling in a pot, it would eventually run dry. Knowing that and allowing it were two totally different things. They were standing in the middle of a crowd of people. He was showing her not an ounce of respect. When he finally stopped his tirade long enough to draw breath, she took the tiny opening to let off a wee bit of steam of her own.

"Are ye quite finished?" she asked, crossing her arms over her breasts.

He looked as though she had just slapped him. Stunned that she dare utter a word at that moment. Rose ignored him.

"I *did* tell someone where we were goin'," she informed him in a stern, sharp tone. "I told Leona and I even told *ye,* days ago, what me plans were, but *ye* were too busy to listen."

Until she uttered those words, she did not think his face could grow any darker. But it did.

"Ye told me? I think not, wife of mine! If ye had, I would no' have been worried to the point of madness! Do ye have any idea how unsafe it is to venture far from these walls? Do ye have any idea the worry ye set upon me and the other husbands?"

Rose stepped forward, and with her index finger, she jabbed his chest. "Do *ye* have any idea the work these women have done since arrivin'?" she demanded. "Do *ye* have any idea how hard it be to keep food and kin *dry* in this weather? Can *ye* count the number of times we all asked fer planks to help keep us and our food stores off the ground and safe?"

He tried to respond, but she'd not allow it. She was furious with him, for a whole host of reasons. He'd ignored her pleas, had ignored her concerns. "Nay, ye can no' tell me because ye do no' listen! We took it upon ourselves to get the planks we needed, because neither ye nor the other men here give one rat's arse about what we have to endure on a daily basis."

The other women had backed away from their husbands to stand with Rose. A united front of sorts, just as angry as their mistress was with how their men were behaving. "Because ye would no' help us, we solved the problem ourselves," Della chimed in, shooting her husband a most furious look of contempt.

"Aye! No' that ye care, but we have worked hard all day dismantlin' the bins from the auld granary," Ronna added.

Ian's eyes flew wide with shock. "Ye went all the way to the auld keep?"

Rose nodded. "It be a mile away, Ian. 'Tis no' as if we rode all the way to Inverness."

How far they had gone did not matter. Before he could manage to explain to her why he was so angry, his wife spoke once again, summarily dismissing him and thus ending their conversation. "Now, if ye will excuse me, I be tired and dirty." And with that, she headed to their tent, leaving a very angry husband behind.

How dare he humiliate me in front of the clan? Rose fumed all the way back to her tent. *Ian Mackintosh be a stubborn, pigheaded man and an eejit to boot!* Storming inside, she sat on a stool to remove her boots. As she pulled off her second boot — silently cursing her husband to the devil — Ian entered the tent.

Weeks of pent up frustration came spouting forth and she could do nothing to stop it. "Have I once complained of anythin'?" she demanded before he could say a word. "Have I once complained of havin' to bathe in the freezin' cold loch? Have I once complained of ye workin' from sun-up to long after dark?" she tossed her boot to the floor. "Me only complaint in these past weeks, nay *months*, is wet floors. Wet floors, Ian! And I do no' complain because 'tis a harsh life I do no' want to live. It be no' healthy to be constantly damp or soaked to the bone. This one thing, one thing I have asked of ye and ye were too busy to help."

Shooting to her feet in exasperation, she continued with her tirade. "I be no' a fool or an impulsive woman, Ian Mackintosh. I left a home — the only home where I felt safe in a verra long while, and left me one true friend as well — to follow ye across Scotia, to build a life with ye. I have been workin' just as hard and just as long as ye, and what thanks do I get? None! And when I ask fer a small thing, planks to keep us off the muddy ground, planks to keep our food dry, what do ye do? Ye start takin' our wagons, and yer men set to tossin' our precious food on the ground."

She was hard pressed to remember a time in her life when she had been this furious with anyone, let alone the man she loved beyond all measure. "If anyone is to blame fer me bein' so desperate as to go back to that place that holds so many ugly memories, 'tis *ye*, Ian Mackintosh. 'Tis *ye*."

Loathe as he was to admit it, his wife had a point. But if she thought to make him feel guilty for not listening to her earlier pleas for assistance, she would have to wait a very long time for an admission of culpability. Or an apology.

The matter at hand was not wet floors or mud or his lack of understanding. Nay the point was she had left without escort and without leaving word. He could not count telling Leona Macdowall as *leaving word*. The woman was as addlepated as her father had said she was.

"Had ye come to me—" he began to explain before she cut him short.

"What would ye have done today that would be any different than the other times I asked?" she spat out angrily.

Though he was furious that she had taken such a dangerous risk today, his fury began to subside when he saw how hurt she was. Aye, she was angry, that much was evident in her pursed lips and the fury blazing in those lovely eyes. But for the first time, he could actually see her pain.

"I will only apologize fer raisin' me voice in front of the clan," he told her. "I will no' apologize fer bein' worried or scared half out of me mind that somethin' bad had happened to ye."

To Rose's way of thinking, his half apology was a step in the right direction, but he had far to go. "Then ye do no' see the entirety of our problem."

Raising one brow, he bade her explain herself.

"Ian, I love ye. But these past few weeks I feel as though I am the least important person in yer world."

That stung like a slap to his face. "Ye ken that is no' true. Ye ken how much I love ye."

Letting out a slow, sorrowful sigh, she returned to the stool. "I *ken* ye love me, Ian…" her words trailed off. There was more she wanted to say but was reluctant.

"But?"

The last thing she wanted to do at the moment was cry, but tears welled in spite of her resistance. "The only time ye show me any kind of attention is when we're lovin' one another. I fear I need to be more than a vessel to slake yer lust." That fact had been bothering her far more than she cared to admit. While she did enjoy loving her husband, it had gotten to the point where that was the only time she felt she had his full attention. "A marriage needs to be more than that," she told him. "We were supposed to be partners in all things. When ye ignore me, it hurts."

Damn it all if she did not succeed in making him feel the one thing he refused to feel: guilt. "Rose." He whispered her name before sinking to his knees and taking her hands in his. "Ye are never far from me thoughts. I have been workin' to build *us* a home, lass. To build a legacy fer us, fer Ailrig's future. I have been an arse, I suppose, in ignorin' yer pleas fer help. But ken me heart, wife," he said as he placed her palms against his chest where his heart was pounding mercilessly. "Ken that ye are everythin' to me, me entire world. I can no' bear the thought of anythin' happenin' to ye. When I did no' ken where ye were this day, I nearly lost me mind with worry. Never in me life have I felt so useless or so guilty. If anythin' had happened to ye, 'twould have been no one's fault but me own."

He spoke from his heart, truthfully and most sincerely. A tear streamed down her cheek and she began to feel a bit guilty herself. His worry was partially her fault, for she had chosen a less than reliable person to give her husband such an important message. "I be sorry fer makin' ye worry, Ian."

He pressed his lips to the tips of her fingers and smiled. "'Tis only because I love ye more than me own life that I worry, wife. I worry ye'll no' be truly proud of me until the tower and keep are built."

"Nay," she exclaimed. "That be no' true! I could no' be more proud of ye, Ian Mackintosh. We have accomplished much in these past weeks. Far more than even I had anticipated. Ye have much to be proud of."

Her kind words did nothing to soothe his guilt. "I fear I have no' done a good job at bein' chief. I have no one mannin' the gates, I have only a few men on patrol, and we have no' trained since our arrival. I have sacrificed our safety in order to build."

Rose placed a warm palm on his cheek. "One sign of a verra good chief is that he can see the errors of his ways and fix them."

He snorted in disbelief.

"Speakin' as a woman who has had the verra worst of chiefs, I can tell ye that ye've already done more to help our clan, than any chief has done in a good, long while."

She had him there. Compared to Mermadak, Ian was a saint and the best of all chiefs. He smiled fondly and thanked her. "I ken I be no' the easiest man to live with, Rose. But I promise, from this day forward, to listen to yer concerns and do what I can to help ye as much as ye have helped me."

Her heart felt near to bursting with relief as well as pride. Pushing herself to her feet, she began to unlace the bodice of her dress. "Are ye in a hurry to return to yer work?" She all but purred the question.

Heat and desire flamed in his groin as he watched her seductively unlacing her dress. "Nay," he answered, his voice low and filled with desire.

"Good," she said as she slipped one sleeve off her shoulder. "I want to apologize fer makin' ye mad with worry."

As far as apologies went, Rose's was, by far, the nicest one he'd ever received.

As he lay on their bed, with her nestled in the crook of his arm sound asleep, he had never felt more alive or more determined. His wife had been making great sacrifices of her own since the day after they married. 'Twas high time he showed her just how much those sacrifices, and she herself, meant to him.

Quietly, he eased himself from the bed and dressed. Before he left the tent, he paused to look down at his beautiful, loving wife. "Ye're too good to me, woman," he whispered softly. "And I do no' deserve ye."

He was tempted to climb back into bed and show her once again just what she meant to him. But he had important work to do. And it had nothing to do with towers or granaries or walls.

Nay, he needed to find Ingerame Macdowall. 'Twas beyond time he built Rose a home. One with stone walls, a roof, and dry floors.

ROSE SLEPT THROUGH THE EVENING meal and did not wake until morning. When she began to apologize for laying abed like a lazy lout, Ian silenced her with tender kisses, which led to some very tender love-making. 'Twas after the morning meal before she woke again and climbed from her warm bed.

She found Brogan and Andrew the Red waiting for her. The two men fell in step behind her as she went to find Leona. "Why are ye followin' me again?" She tossed the question over her shoulder, certain she already knew the answer.

"Ian's orders," Brogan replied.

Knowing it would do no good to argue with them, she decided to ignore them completely. 'Twasn't their fault her husband was as stubborn as an ox.

The tent Leona shared with her father was empty.

"If ye're lookin' fer Leona, she left after the mornin' meal," Brogan said. "Saw her head toward the creek."

Forgetting that she had decided to ignore them, she thanked Brogan and headed toward the gates. Today, they were closed. Rose smiled prettily at the guard. "I should like ye to open the gate," she told him.

The guard looked first to Brogan for approval. Ire slowly crept into her stomach, but she bit back the harsh words. Apparently, Brogan approved, for the guard opened the gate a moment later.

"I suppose me husband told ye no' to let me out of yer sight?" she asked as she walked around a large puddle.

"Aye, he did," Andrew chuckled. "Ye took ten years off his life yester day."

She made a mental note to discuss Brogan and Andrew's presence with her husband later. Knowing he meant well helped to soften her ire.

Scanning the creek in both directions, she could not see Leona anywhere. The creek snaked around the hill in both directions. A few trees were scattered here and there along the pebbly banks. "Where do ye suppose she goes each day?" She was thinking aloud, not asking anyone in particular.

"Knowin' Leona, she's half way to Italy by now," Andrew said, chuckling at his own jest.

Rose spun to face him. "Ye ken her well, then?" she asked.

His smile faded rapidly. "Nay," he answered.

"Then why would ye say such a thing?" she asked him.

He cast a glance toward Brogan, as if seeking assistance. Brogan wasn't giving any. "I only ken what her father says," Andrew explained. "He says she be tetched, ye ken. Wanders off fer hours, sometimes days at a time."

Rose was growing rather impatient with Ingerame Macdowall and his opinion of his daughter. Even if she were a little forgetful, it did not give anyone the right to insult her. "And have ye ever taken the time to get to ken her? Mayhap ask her where she goes?" She shook her head in disgust when another thought entered her mind. "And why, pray tell, is Leona allowed to wander off fer hours or days at a time without escort? Why does no one care about her safety?"

In truth, neither men had a good answer. Brogan looked positively ashamed of himself, while Andrew behaved as if the thought never entered his mind.

"'Tis her father who is to blame," Rose said. "No father should be so cruel to his only child, let alone a daughter. Have neither of ye learned anything from Aggie's plight?"

Andrew's eyes grew wide. "Do ye think he beats her like Mermadak did Aggie?" Though he had not witnessed the horrors Aggie had suffered, he had heard the stories.

Frustrated, Rose threw her hands in the air. "It does no' matter if he beats her, ye eejit! Words can hurt as much as a fist. I suggest ye both remember that, and perhaps show the poor girl a bit of kindness."

Now that they were duly chastised, Rose turned and headed back toward camp. *Stupid men.*

WORRY BEGAN TO SETTLE INTO Rose's heart when the nooning meal came and went and there was still no sign of Leona. Much to her relief, Brogan had agreed to go in search of the girl. He returned two hours later, empty-handed.

As she and the women began to prepare the evening meal, her worry turned to dread. She was about to send word to Ian, who had spent the day at the quarry, to request a search party be sent out for Leona, when the absent-minded girl seemed to appear out of nowhere.

Relieved to see her, Rose dropped the large wooden spoon she had been stirring stew with onto the table and ran to Leona. Without thinking to, she wrapped her arms around the young woman and hugged her tightly. "Leona!" she exclaimed. "I have been so worried about ye!"

Leona stood frozen, either unwilling or incapable of returning Rose's embrace. "Ye were?" she asked, sounding quite dumbfounded.

Rose stepped away, her warm smile fading. "Of course we were," she told her. "Ye can no' just leave without tellin' a soul where ye're goin'."

Tilting her head to one side, she studied Rose as if she were some foreign creature she'd never seen before.

"Leona, if ye find there be times when ye need to be alone fer a spell, I understand. But please, tell me first so I do no' worry."

Leona's slow nod of affirmation came a few moments later.

"Now, come help us with the evenin' meal, and if ye want, ye can tell me where ye've been and what ye've seen."

Taking Leona's hand, she led her back to the large bubbling pot. Uncomfortable silence filled the air. Realizing the young woman did not feel at ease speaking, Rose did much of the talking.

"Ye'll have a real home soon enough," she said as she began slicing loaves of bread. "We shall all have our own cottages before winter sets in."

Leona remained quiet, but picked up a knife and began to help slice a loaf of still warm bread.

"Are ye no' excited about havin' yer own home?" Rose asked.

Leona shrugged her shoulders with indifference.

Beyond a shadow of a doubt, Rose knew this young woman was not as addlepated as her father wanted everyone to believe. Mayhap she only needed a friend. "Leona, I want to be yer friend. If ye ever need anyone to talk to, I want ye to ken ye can come to me."

Snorting in a most unladylike manner, Leona said, "Do ye no' ken that I be tetched? A witch?"

Rose laughed. "Ye be as tetched as I and just as much a witch."

Leona cast her a suspicious look.

"I ken Ingerame be yer da, but in truth, I do no' care fer him much," Rose told her bluntly.

Finally, something akin to a smile began to appear on Leona's face. She leaned in ever so slightly. "Truth be told, I do no' care fer him much meself."

TWELVE

Within a week of the women's trip to the auld keep, many changes had taken place. Several cottages sprang up across the wide-open space next to the woods. While many of the men still worked in the quarry, Ian had pulled twenty-five of them away to work on the much needed homes. Construction also began on building platforms along the top of the wood wall for guards to man. Sentries at the gates were doubled and around the clock as well as mounted patrols were set up along the borders.

Everyone worked together and in unison to build the small cottages. Couples with children were given first priority, at Rose's behest. "The children have suffered more than the rest of us. It be no' healthy fer them to continue to sleep in tents."

Ian recognized the wisdom in that; the clan must come first if he wanted them to follow him. Things between he and his wife had improved immeasurably, even though he hadn't realized their marriage needed any improving. Still, he was grateful, for she smiled far more often, which pleased him a great deal.

By late September, families were moved into their new homes, as more were being built. Knowing that winter would be here far sooner than any one wanted, Ian ordered the construction of the armory. 'Twould not only be used to house weapons, but also the good number of unmarried men. 'Twas a long, narrow building with plenty of space for pallets and beds. His goal now was to ensure that everyone had a warm, dry place to live out the winter. God willing, it would not be anywhere near as harsh as the last.

On a rather foggy afternoon near the end of September, messengers from Ian's father arrived. Three young men in their early twenties Rose assumed, all looking beleaguered and road weary.

Excitedly, Rose and Leona ushered the three men to sit at a long table, while a lad was sent to fetch Ian, Brogan, and Andrew the Red from the quarry.

Rose set about preparing trays filled with dried meats, fruits, cheese and bread while Leona served them ale.

"How fares everyone at home?" Rose asked, excited for any word about or from Aggie.

"All be well when we left," the shorter of the three men replied before taking a long pull of ale.

"But the Camerons have been eerily quiet far too long fer John and Frederick's liking," offered the tallest of the three.

"Bah!" the shorter man scoffed. "We have no need to worry over the Camerons, I tell ye. They be no more dangerous than a flea on the backside of a mongrel dog!"

Rose didn't care much about the Camerons, clan wars, or anything else at the moment. All she wanted to know was if Aggie fared well. She sliced apples while the men argued back and forth over whether or not the Camerons would attack, and if so, when. 'Twas enough to make her head spin.

After filling two more pitchers of ale, Leona left them on the table and came to stand beside Rose. "Have ye ever seen men argue as much as they?" she asked, her tone filled with disbelief.

"They be Mackintoshes," Rose answered. "'Tis what they do. Argue, fight, and love their women, all with the same level of passion."

Leona quirked a curious brow at her mistress before turning her attention back to the men. "I do no' think I have ever seen Ian or Brogan argue like that before."

"'Tis because they have more important things to do," Rose explained. "Ye've seen them fret and worry over the plans fer the keep, aye?"

Leona nodded and said she had.

"Well, if they did no' have that to keep them busy, they'd be frettin' over somethin' else, like those three." She placed the sliced apples on a tray next to a round brick of cheese. "A Mackintosh will study a thing over and over again until there be nothin' else to learn from it. Unless it be a woman." Rose smiled fondly, thinking of how well Ian had *studied* her these past months. "He'll never give up his exploration of *that* particular thing. A Mackintosh will never leave ye wantin' fer more, of that, ye can be certain."

Leona blushed from head to toe. Aye, she knew how a man and woman joined, knew what went where. But to hear her mistress speak so candidly on the subject was shocking. Stammering, she said, "I think they need more ale." She left Rose and went to fill two more pitchers from the cask.

Ian soon returned with Brogan and Andrew. There was much joyful backslapping and hearty embraces exchanged betwixt the six men. Rose waited anxiously, wishing they would all simply be quiet so she could ask if there was news from her friend.

The men sat and ate, talked, drank, and talked more, all the while Rose grew more and more impatient. After nearly an hour, she could bear no more. Coming to stand behind her husband, she interrupted the conversation. "Pardon me, but have ye any news fer me?"

The chatter came to an abrupt stop as all eyes turned to her. Andrew especially looked perturbed that she had disturbed them.

Ian chuckled loudly. "Lads, me wife has left her most treasured friend back on Mackintosh lands. She has been waitin' fer some time fer word from her. Have ye any?"

The shorter of the men — Roger, whose name she gleaned from their conversation — smiled up at her. "We do!" he said as he lifted a pack from the ground and set it on the table. "I have letters fer ye, from Aggie, Elsbeth, and even Ian's youngest sister, wee Margaret." He dug through the pack for a time, before finally withdrawing a large bundle of letters. Leaning across the table, he handed the heavy stack to her. Gratefully, she took them from him and held them to her breast. Choking back tears, she smiled and thanked him.

Ian swung his long legs around and stood. Pressing a tender kiss to the top of her head, he said, "Rose, go. Read yer letters. The men and I can take care of ourselves."

She didn't even make an attempt to argue.

ALONE IN HER TENT, SHE lit a candle and sat at Ian's makeshift desk. Carefully, she untied the twine that held the letters together. Carefully, she picked through until she separated all of Aggie's letters from the others. Thankfully, Aggie had written the date on each one, just above the Mackintosh seal. Setting Elsbeth's and Margaret's aside to read later, she organized Aggie's letters by date, and chose the first one.

Carefully, she took a small dagger from the desk and broke the first seal. Pressed into the letter was a sprig of tiny yellow flowers. Her eyes grew damp before she even began to read. She could hear her friend's voice as she read, as clearly as if she were sitting next to her.

The Ninth of June, 1356

My dearest sister,

As ye ken, I be no' verra good at readin' or writin'. But with Elsbeth's and Frederick's help, I hope to improve.

Our lives are n't the same without ye here, me sweet friend. You've only left this mornin' and everythin' seems different. I have no one in whom to confide or voice me worries, save for Elsbeth. While she is a fine woman, she is not ye.

Frederick says I canno' send a letter to you every day for 'twill cost us a fortune with the messengers. But he did no' say I could no' write to ye every day. I imagine the messenger will have dozens of letters to give ye when he leaves next month.

This will be the first night in an age where ye and I did not sit by the fire after the evenin' meal. We have rarely ever been apart, ye and I, fer more than a few days at a time. I doubt I shall ever get used to ye bei'g so far away.

This is no' how either of us imagined our lives to be, but I be no' complainin'. If I had never met Frederick or yer Ian, I imagine I would have died long before now. So 'tis bittersweet feelin's I have as we both take far different paths than either of us ever intended.

I have nothin' else to say right now other than there is now a rather large empty hole in me heart. Ye are missed.

Aggie

By the time she was finished reading the first letter, tears were sliding off her cheeks. Her heart ached with missing Aggie and the children. Using a bit of linen, she wiped away her tears and opened the next letter. Inside were more dried flowers, this time, a sprig of lavender.

The Twelfth of June, 1356

Rose,

So many things have changed since ye left us only a few short days ago. Ada has gotten her first tooth! She neither fussed nor cried and we only discovered the tooth when she bit down on poor Rebecca. 'Twas very embarrassin'! But I admit I was glad 'twas Rebeca's breast she bit and no' mine!

Ailrig is doing well. He certainly has taken to the role of older brother quite well. He watches over Ada as if she were his verra own. Sometimes he speaks to her when he does not ken I am there. He swears to watch over and protect her, to be her champion all the days of his life. But then I also heard him say the verra same thing to a pretty little lass of nine just this morn. While the Mackintosh men are the finest example of honorable and good men any lad could ever have, I fear their other qualities are also rubbin' off on me son.

Frederick is doing well. He is constantly makin' plans for our leavin' next spring. I admit he is far more excited about goin' to Am boireannach dubh-ghlas than I. If I could have but one wish, it would be to stay here for the rest of me life and have ye and

Ian return to us. But I fear I love me husband more than I love the next beat of me heart. Therefore, I will go wherever he wishes. I know also, in me heart, that God has a plan fer us, bigger than any we could imagine.

Douglas, his wife and children have welcomed all of us into their family. I was no' sure what to think of his wife at first, because she was almost as mute as I used to be. But the more time we spend together, the more she opens up and the more I like her. She kens all about the love me mum and Douglas once shared. She admits to bein' quite jealous of it in the beginnin', but, as she put it, 'Douglas loved her out of the dark place of jealousy and into the light of love and life.' I can understand well what she means by that, fer that is how I feel about Frederick.

As for Douglas, he seems a good and honorable man. Nothing at all like Mermadak. Douglas is kind, generous, and often reminds me of John. They are a bit like day old meat pies: a bit hard on the outside but soft and warm on the inside.

I still canno' call him father or da, at least no' when I speak to him. It simply seems far too odd. Frederick declares that in time I will call him da with great affection, just as Ailrig did him. We shall see.

I must go now, to collect herbs from me garden. I shall write to ye again soon.
With love and devotion,
Aggie

By the time Rose finished reading the last letter, the sun had begun to set and her eyes were red, her skin blotchy from crying. Oh, how she wished she could go back to Mackintosh lands and see her friend again. 'Twould be at least nine or ten months before she and Aggie met again. At that quiet moment, nine months seemed like a lifetime.

Ian and the men took turns each week to hunt. Blessedly, they had been able to find enough fresh meat to see them through one week to the next. On this particular day, the men returned from their best hunt yet. 'Twas enough meat to see them through the next two months.

"Let us feast this night," Ian declared as he looked over the numerous deer, pheasants, and even a few geese. "Let us celebrate this good bounty."

Rose and the womenfolk agreed a feast was in order. "And tomorrow, can we take a day of rest?" she asked her husband.

"Aye!" he agreed cheerfully. "Tonight we feast, and on the morrow, we shall rest."

And feast they did, like kings. Roast pheasant, goose and venison were plentiful. Breads, cheeses, fresh fruits, and roasted vegetables. Sweetmeats and sweet cakes, and enough ale to drown a whale.

Stories were told, songs of glory were sung, and more ale, wine and whisky consumed. Rose was feeling quite happy and gay, having consumed her fair share of wine. Ian was looking at her with drunk eyes full of desire for most of the night. More than once, he pulled her onto his lap and kissed her soundly, more passionately and shamelessly than was proper.

Long after the midnight hour, she leaned in to whisper an offer he found he could not refuse. "Take me to our bed now, Ian, fer I fear I can no' go much longer without havin' yer naked skin against mine."

Wattle and daub huts had sprung up all around the keep. They were by no means spectacular in appearance or amenities, but no one cared much. With solid walls and thatched roofs above and around them, 'twas a merciful blessing to be out of all the mud and muck and rain.

Men, women, and even children worked side by side to help build the homes. 'Twas hard work, but no one complained. While the women wove branches together for the wattle, the children worked on making the daub in pits of mud and limestone. The men framed out each hut, carefully assembling the walls, fireplaces, and roofs.

'Twas during the construction of these homes that Ian came to know Charles McFarland and Rodrick the Bold. He pulled the two men away from their duties as sentries to help with the construction.

While Charles was amenable to the change, Rodrick was less so. "I be a warrior," he told Ian, "no' a laborer."

"But both are equally important here, Rodrick," Ian explained. They were in the forest gathering more slender branches for the wattle.

"Bah!" Rodrick groused. "Ye may think that now, but ye'll be singin' a far different tune when the Bowies attack."

Ian wound a length of twine around a large bundle of branches. "Ye speak as if ye ken an attack is inevitable."

"Where the Bowies be concerned, an attack is always inevitable."

Ian gave his complaint careful consideration. During his time at the auld McLaren keep, the Bowies had only attacked once, and that was at the behest of Mermadak. "Mayhap they be no' aware we are even here," Ian offered.

Rodrick's expression said enough. He thought his current laird insane or the most unintelligent man he'd ever encountered. "The Bowies ken," he argued. "Trust me. They ken well we are here."

"And how can ye be so certain?" Ian asked as he tied off the last length of twine. Aye, he was very interested in finding out what this man did or or didn't know.

"'Tis me job to ken these things," Rodrick told him. "I ken I be neither a Mackintosh nor a McLaren. I may have come here with Ingerame ..." his words trailed off as his cheeks turned bright red.

"And?" Ian asked as he hoisted the bundle up and placed it on the back of a wagon.

Reluctantly, Rodrick explained himself. "Fer reasons I canno' begin to comprehend, I like ye, Mackintosh. I like the other people here as well. I am a warrior and I feel it be me duty to help protect the lot of ye."

Ian appreciated his honesty and how hard it had been for him to speak the truth. "Verra well," he said as he began to bundle more branches together. "Go seek out Brogan and tell him I said we are to use ye on patrols." Truth be told, Ian would rather have the man on patrol than grumbling beside him all the day long.

The man sighed in relief and then did something remarkable. He smiled.

Ian found it unsettling. He was used to the man's glower.

Without so much as a thank you, Rodrick spun around and left.

THIRTEEN

utger Bowie was faced with a dilemma. The coffers were growing empty and the larder bare. The coin he had inherited after his cousin Eduard was killed had not lasted nearly as long as he would have hoped. His brother, Collum, had warned him months ago they'd not be able to continue with the nightly feasts or the endless number of women he'd taken to his bed, without a means to replenish the reserves.

Oh, how he hated his younger brother's sensibilities.

Just when he had begun to believe they might have to do something *sensible*, such as learn to become farmers or whisky makers or some other too-boring-to-think-about way of making a living, a man appeared at their gates.

A McLaren man.

A man with a story that at first seemed so utterly outrageous as to border on the insane. But there was *something* about the man, in the way he told the story with such hatred and vehemence toward Aggie and Frederick Mackintosh, that it left him to wonder. According to this fellow, Mermadak McLaren had swindled dozens upon dozens of his fellow Scotsmen, as well as Englishmen and Frenchmen. Over the years, he had somehow managed to accumulate a vast fortune. If what the McLaren man said was true, it amounted to at least fifty-thousand groats.

Fifty-thousand groats.

He and his clan could live like kings for generations on that kind of coin.

Thus, an idea began to form in his mind. A way out of his current state of poverty and distress.

FOURTEEN

October arrived peacefully enough, weather wise. The days were growing shorter, but oh those days were brilliantly beautiful. Bright, crisp mornings that put a spring in a man's step. Tips of blazingly green leaves were just beginning to turn, bringing forth the promise of a dazzling autumn.

More huts were springing up, filling the future courtyard almost to the brim. It had been Eggar Wardwin who had suggested a more organized plan of lining the little huts up in straight rows so it would be easier to make one's way from one point to another. Ian agreed. Ingerame Macdowall, however, was against it. Ian suspected 'twas only because Eggar had thought of it first.

The two men did not get along well, not well at all. Ian soon learned that Eggar was in fact, the better of the two men. Eggar did his level best to avoid Ingeramc whenever he could.

On this particular bright, sunny morn, Ian found the two men standing at the base of the tower. Neither of them looked happy.

"All I be sayin' is that 'twould make more sense to build the foundation fer the second tower *now* instead of waitin'," Eggar said, his consternation showing in his pinched face.

"And I be sayin' ye are no' the lead carpenter. Ye have no experience in matters such as these."

Eggar closed his eyes and Ian wondered if he weren't silently counting to one hundred or plotting Ingerame's demise.

"At least I be smart enough to ken ye do no' put the latrine next to the granary!" Eggar's temper flared, born of frustration with Ingerame's constant reminder of just who was in charge.

Ingerame's face burned bright red. "That was no' me mistake! The men did no' build it where I told them to!"

Before they came to blows, Ian stepped in betwixt them. "Lads, it be far too beautiful a mornin' to be fightin'. Now tell me, what be the matter."

They both began to explain at once. Ian held up his hands to stop them. "Ingerame, ye first."

Looking as pleased as a peacock strutting for a peahen, Ingerame pulled his shoulders back. "Eggar gave an order to the men without first speakin' to me."

"And what order was that?" Ian asked. He noticed a slight throb began to form in his temple. Being laird was not always easy.

"To start buildin' the foundation fer a second tower. We never discussed a second tower, Ian. There beno plans fer a second tower."

Eggar was unabashed as he planted his feet wide and crossed his arms over his chest. He gave Ian a look that asked, *should ye tell him or shall I?*

Taking a fortifying breath, Ian replied. "There are no' only plans fer a second tower, but a third and fourth as well. I gave those plans to ye upon me arrival."

Ingerame's face turned an impossible shade of deep red. Anger flared in his eyes. "I can assure ye, there was nothin' on those plans about additional towers."

"And I can assure ye that there is," Ian ground out.

Ingerame began to argue again, but Ian stopped him with a raised palm. "To the tent," he ordered. Spinning on his heels, he headed toward his work tent. He had had it erected weeks ago, as a place where he could work without disturbing his wife. It sat at the far edge of the yard, in a quiet corner next to the forest.

The two men followed him inside. Ingerame was mad enough to bite his hammer in half, while Eggar looked victorious. But unlike his lead carpenter, Eggar kept his thoughts on the matter to himself.

Ian went around the table and looked down at the plans spread across it. Small rocks had been placed in each corner to keep the scroll flat.

"There," Ian said, tapping the plans with his index finger.

Hesitantly, Ingerame stepped forward. He studied the plans closely, all the while his countenance changing. He went from being bloody angry to being furious. "I was no' given these plans," he said as he stepped away. "'Tis no' me fault no one saw fit to give them to me."

Ian stood to his full height. "Are ye callin' me a liar?"

Ingerame balked at the accusation. "N-nay," he stammered. "I am merely sayin' I do no' have these plans. I have the plans Frederick gave me in Inverness."

Ian rolled his eyes and gave a frustrated shake of his noggin. His lead carpenter had been building off plans that were ages old. 'Twas no wonder he'd ordered the latrines built next to the granary. "Upon me arrival, I gave ye new plans." Ian's level of frustration was growing by leaps and bounds. "We talked about those new plans fer hours. I showed them to ye. I gave ye yer own copy."

Try as he might, Ingerame could not come up with a logical sounding response. "I must have misplaced those," he said rather sheepishly.

'Twas all Ian could do no' to wrap his hands around the man's neck.

"Then I suggest ye find them," he said through gritted teeth. "Before we build the kitchens next to the latrine, or plant the gardens on the top of the north tower."

Without apology, Ingerame simply inclined his head toward his laird and fled the tent as if his arse was on fire.

Eggar and Ian watched his hasty retreat. When the flap of the tent closed, Eggar turned to face his laird. "I thought somethin' was amiss," he said. "But every time I tried to get a look at the plans he was usin', he bit me head off. I did no' think 'twas me place to say anythin'. I be sorry, Ian."

Raking a hand through his blond hair, Ian sat down in his chair in exasperation. "I do no' ken *why me* brother hired him. Truly, I do no'."

"To hear Ingerame tell it, he was the best bloody carpenter in all of Scotia, if no' the world."

Ian was beginning to wonder if the reputation Frederick had heard of was from people who had actually used the man or from the man himself. He also wondered if that was why it had been so easy for him to hire such a talented, well-known carpenter so easily. Keeping those thoughts to himself, he offered Eggar a whisky.

Waggling his eyebrows happily, Eggar licked his lips before taking the chair across from Ian. "I admit, I be a bit parched, even though it be early in the morn."

Ian laughed raucously as he poured the amber liquid into two mugs. "The man does drive me to drink at times," he admitted as he offered a mug to Eggar. "I feel sorry fer his daughter."

"Leona?" Eggar asked before taking a gulp.

"Aye, Leona."

"She be an odd one, that lass," Eggar said. "A hard one to get to ken."

"My wife adores her, but detests her father."

Eggar waggled his brows again and lifted his mug. "I'll drink to that!"

The following afternoon, Leona appeared at the quarry, seeking out Ian. He'd been down in the pits with five of his men, chipping away at rocks. They had stripped down to their trews, sweat pouring down their backs and into their eyes. Because of Ingerame's *misplacement* of plans, Ian had to double the work in the quarry in order to make up for lost time.

'Twas Andrew the Red who came to tell him Leona was there. "Ian," Andrew called down. "Leona Macdowall is here. I think ye should see her. She seems verra upset."

Perturbed with the interruption, Ian splashed water from a bucket across his face and arms, thrust his sleeves into his tunic, all the while cursing under his breath.

"Keep at it," he told his brother Brogan. "Hopefully this will no' take long.

Brogan grunted in understanding as he hammered away at the hefty chisel Eggar was holding against a large piece of rock.

Ian shot up the rope ladder and into the warm afternoon sun. *It had better be a matter of life and death*, he cursed to himself as he crossed the open space and into his tent.

"What do ye want?" He hadn't intended on sounding so infuriated. But as soon as she spun around to face him, guilt assaulted his senses.

She stood near the table, looking for all the world like a very lost and embarrassed young woman. Around her left eye was the makings of a horrible bruise.

"What happened to yer eye?" he asked as he approached.

Startled by his change in tone and demeanor, she took a step back and away. "I-I tripped over me own two feet and landed on a felled log, m'laird."

He didn't believe that for one bloody moment. He decided, for the moment at least, to allow her this one tiny lie.

From where he stood, he could see her tremble. Twisting her fingers, she gazed at the floor. "I came to apologize, m'laird," she all but whispered. "And to take whatever punishment ye seek to give me."

He raised a curious brow. "Apologize fer what, lass?"

"'Tis me fault da was workin' off the wrong plans."

There was something in her tone that made her words sound forced. "Yer fault?"

She nodded her head rapidly as she swiped away a tear. "'Tis me job, ye see, to help him with his papers. I-I must have misplaced the new plans ye had given him."

He knew 'twas another bald-faced lie and it angered him no end. Not with her, but with her father. The man was forcing her to take the blame for his own stupidity.

"Da says ye'll be right angry with me. I will no' beg ye fer mercy." Her voice was but a mere whisper.

Brogan entered the tent then. "Ian, Andrew told me what was—" He stopped short when Leona looked up at him. "What happened to ye?" he asked.

"I tripped over me own two feet and landed against a table."

Odd, Ian thought. A moment ago 'twas a felled log. "She has come to confess that 'twas she who misplaced the plans I gave to Ingerame when I arrived."

Brogan cast him a wary glance. He didn't believe her lie anymore than Ian did.

"And to take me punishment fer it," she added, fixing her gaze on the floor once again. "I ken it caused ye a great deal of trouble."

Ian's fury increased tenfold, but he kept it well hidden. "What punishment do ye think we should mete out fer such a mistake?" he asked her.

Without flinching, she looked up at the two of them. "A beatin' I reckon. 'Tis what the last laird did."

The tick in Ian's jaw returned with a vengeance. "The last laird?"

"Aye," she replied. "I did this once before, a few years back."

Another wary exchange betwixt brothers. "I see," Ian said, taking a step toward her. "Do ye think ye have learned yer lesson about misplacin' important documents? Or do ye think this will happen again?"

Her brow drew into a thin line. "I do no' ken, m'laird. I tend to be a bit scatter-minded at times."

Ian thought on that for a time before responding. "Well, in the future, if ye misplace somethin', come to me at once, lass, and we'll help ye find it."

The line in her forehead grew tighter. "I will, m'laird," she said with a hint of confusion.

"Verra well then, ye may leave. I ken me wife will be glad to see ye this day."

"But me punishment," she said. "Would ye no' like to beat me now?"

Brogan grunted in disgust.

"Nay, I think no'," Ian answered.

Before he could go on, she stepped forward, her shoulders back and chin up. "M'laird, I would prefer the beatin' now, if ye do no' mind. I ken what I did was somethin' terrible, but I'd rather no' take me beatin' in front of the entire clan."

He knew 'twas common practice among some clans to make such public displays of punishment as the one she spoke of. 'Twas meant to set an example to everyone. He deplored such displays.

"Lass, I'll no' be beatin' ye now, nor will I be beatin' ye later, and neither will I be beatin' ye in front of the clan."

Suspicion set into her eyes.

"I can tell ye be awfully sorry fer what happened. I think ye've suffered enough."

It took a moment for understanding to set in, but there was no sign of relief. "M'laird, I hate to ask ye, but could *ye* please tell me da yer decision?" she asked with a good deal of trepidation. "I fear he might no' believe me."

Ian offered the warmest smile he could under the circumstances. "Aye, I shall have a verra long talk with yer da."

'Twas only then that her shoulders sagged in relief as she let out the breath she'd been holding. "I thank ye, m'laird, I kindly do!"

"Be gone with ye now," he said with a wave of his hand. "Go see me wife. I be certain she would be glad for yer help in preparin' the evenin' meal."

Leona returned his smile with one of her own, bobbed a curtsey to him, then to Brogan, before she fled the tent.

Once she was gone, Ian looked at his brother. "I am beginnin' to despise Ingerame Macdowall."

Brogan grunted in agreement. "I would like to be present when ye *talk* to him about his *daughter's* transgression."

By the time Ian and Brogan finished *talking* with Ingerame Macdowall, the man was sporting a black eye and bloodied lip.

"And if ye ever think to make yer daughter confess on yer behalf," Ian said as he shoved Ingerame onto the chair, "I shall make yer punishment a public one."

"And if ye think to take yer anger fer us out on yer daughter, ye may no' live to regret it," Brogan added as he pulled the man from the chair.

"This will remain betwixt us, Ingerame," Ian said, as he shoved the man toward the opening in the tent. "But never ferget our warnin' to ye."

With that, he shoved Ingerame Macdowall out of the tent and into the cool evening air.

The two brothers stood at the entrance, watching the foul man scurry away.

"Do ye think we went too far, brother?" Brogan asked, planting his hands on his hips.

Ian pondered the question for only a brief moment. "Nay," he replied. "I fear we may no' have gone far enough."

When Ian told his wife all that had transpired with Leona and Ingerame, 'twas all he could do to keep her from going after the man with a skillet.

"How dare he?" she fumed as she paced the small confines of their newly built hut.

"Some men do no' look at their wives and daughters with the same fondness I look upon ye." He said as he kissed the base of her neck. "They look at them as nothin' more than chattel."

"Do ye think he will be foolish enough to hurt her again?" Too angry to pay attention to the tender ministrations he was showing her neck, she stood looking out the small window toward Leona's hut.

Ian decided to take another route to wooing his wife into their bed. Tenderly, he rubbed a palm across her stomach, making a slow northerly progression toward the breasts he took such delight in. "Nay," he murmured against her neck. "Brogan and I made certain he understood clearly what the consequences of that action might be."

"I detest that man," she said with a huff.

"I am beginnin' to despise him even more," Ian said as he spun her around to face him. "Fer he's got me beautiful wife's full attention at the moment. Attention I very much desire to have all to meself fer the next hour or so."

"Ye are insatiable," she said with a beguiling smile. "I find I like that about ye."

One hour turned into nearly two as he made slow, languid yet passionate love to his wife. His wife surprised him mid-way through with something Ian was certain only Inverness whore's knew how to do with their mouths. Certainly not good, decent wives. Nay, he complained not once during nor after. Instead he relished her tender, seductive ministrations to his staff. Still, when they lay panting for breath afterward, sweat glistening on his brow, he felt the urge to ask how she had come up with the idea.

"We women talk about more than bairns and meals, Ian," she giggled against his chest.

He was not so certain that was a good idea or bad, but kept the thought to himself.

"Did ye no' like it?" she asked sleepily.

He chuckled as he pulled her closer. "If I *liked* it any better, me eyes would have bulged from me sockets."

A soft laugh, bordering on pride, formed in her throat. "Then I did it correctly."

Correctly? She did it with such finesse and expertise, one would have thought she'd spent years honing the craft.

They fell asleep, replete and content in each other's arms, and did not wake until long after dawn.

FIFTEEN

The following sennight passed without incident. According to Rose, Leona seemed far happier, her spirits lifted immeasurably. Though she still insisted 'twas her own fault for misplacing the plans. The story about how she got the black-eye varied, depending on who she told the story to. Very few people, however, had asked what happened. Most of the clan still treated her with indifference. However Ronna and Angrabraid, their auld healer, grew more and more fond of the young woman.

Now that those with families, and the widowed and unmarried women, had huts to call their very own, the mood across the clan seemed even lighter. With the completion of these temporary homes, Ian could focus more on building the tower and training with his men.

Because he could not be two places at once, the training of the men fell primarily to Brogan and Andrew the Red. Diligently, the two men spent the morning hours in an empty field next to the keep, training with the Mackintoshes, whilst also trying to teach the McLaren men.

Ian also felt it necessary to train the numerous laborers. That was when things grew more difficult, slowly chipping away at the calm, brotherly atmosphere of the clan.

They were standing in the courtyard on this misty morn. While women went about their daily chores and cleaned up after the morning meal, Andrew the Red faced off against eight of the laborers. One in particular was a thorn in his arse.

"Ye pay me to be a laborer, no' a warrior." 'Twas Robert Macelvy who first voiced his displeasure.

Andrew rolled his eyes and ran a hand across his chin. "Aye, Ian pays ye fer that, and pays ye quite well," he said. "But ye also need to learn to defend the keep."

The slender man with dark hair and even darker eyes, gave a slow shake of his head. "'Tis no' me job to defend the keep." The others standing behind him nodded their heads in agreement.

"And what do ye intend to do should we ever fall under attack?"

He answered with a shrug. "Surrender, I reckon."

Andrew's eyes grew so wide and round he looked as though he were on the verge of an apoplexy. "Surrender?" he asked, exasperatedly. "Have ye no ballocks man? No pride?" The thought of surrender to anyone was appalling.

"Better to surrender and live another day, than to die," Robert answered calmly. His cohorts readily agreed with more nods and a few murmured 'ayes'.

Someone had sent word to Ian that some of the laborers were refusing to train. Angry that he was once again pulled from the quarry, he thundered into the keep and toward the object of his ire.

"Andrew," he called out loudly as he approached. "Please tell me the rumors that there be cowards amongst us are false."

Seeing their laird in such a state of fury caused every one of the objectors to take tentative steps back.

"Aye, they be true, Ian," Andrew said, his voice filled with disgust.

Ian faced the cowards head-on, while speaking over his shoulder to Andrew. "Who be the one objectin' most?"

"That one," Andrew said with a nod toward the man. "Robert Macelvey."

Not wanting to appear any more the coward than he already did, the man lifted his chin and stepped forward. "Ye pay us to build yer keep, no' to guard it."

Bracing his feet apart, Ian crossed his arms over his chest and leaned ever so slightly toward the man. He towered over him and used that to his advantage. "Do ye no' also *live* amongst us?" he asked. "Do ye no' partake of our food? Our ale and wine? Does our healer no' tend to yer wounds? Do the rest of us no' work alongside ye, day after day?"

Flummoxed, the man gave a rapid nod of his head.

"And do I ask ye to pay fer any of those things?"

The man paled visibly.

"Yet ye refuse to train with the others?" Ian asked, rhetorically of course. "Verra well then, ye shall no' train with us. But ye can pack yer things now and leave. I will allow ye to live *outside* the protection of our walls. Ye will pay fer every meal, every cup of ale, every time ye see the healer." Done arguing, he turned to leave.

"Ye can no' do that!" Robert argued.

Ian had his sword drawn before he turned around completely. Using his fist, he hit the coward in the center of his chest and sent him flying hard to the ground. One heartbeat later, he stood over the man, one foot on his chest, pinning him to the damp earth. The tip of his sword stopped just a hair's breadth away from his jugular. "Think ye now that I can no'?"

The man gulped for air as he clawed at Ian's booted foot.

Ian looked up to the rest of the men. "If we were by chance attacked, do ye think the men attackin' will take the time to sort out coward from warrior?" he asked them in a demanding, firm tone. "Do ye think they will stop to ask ye anythin' before they gut ye?"

The small group of men looked as stunned as they did terrified. None was brave enough to answer his questions.

"I be no' askin' ye any more than I ask any other man amongst us," Ian said. "We all work hard every day. Besides the lot of ye, no' one man has refused to train. Men far aulder than *ye* are out on that trainin' field right now. They may no' be the fastest, they may no' be the best or the strongest. But I'd put the lot of them against any of ye any day of the week." He stopped long enough to draw a breath. "All of ye will be out of me camp within the hour. If ye wish to work, then ye *will* train. If ye refuse to train, ye can find yer own bloody way back to Inverness or whatever rock ye crawled out from under."

With much force and a look of utter disdain, he pressed his foot more firmly against Robert Macelvey's chest before turning away. "Andrew, make sure they are packed and out of here within the hour."

Andrew nodded quite happily. "'Twill be me pleasure, Ian."

Amazingly enough, six of the nine protestors opted to stay with the clan. Robert Macelvey and two others were the only ones to pack their bags that day and leave. The remaining men decided 'twas safer *inside* the keep than without, and although 'twas reluctantly, they did begin their training.

Though most of the McLaren men were aulder, there were one or two closer to Ian's own age. They trained just as hard and with as much dedication as the Mackintosh men, even if their skills were not nearly as good.

Rains came and went and came back again. In the space of any given day, it could be bright and sunny, then moments later, everyone would be soaked by a deluge. Such was the weather in October in these western Highlands.

On this cool yet sunny morning, a sennight before *Samhuinn,* Ian was training in the yard with the McLarens. More specifically with a lad of fifteen named Robby McLaren. Though he was young and inexperienced, Ian had to give him credit for his determination.

"Nay, lad!" Ian exclaimed. "Ye keep lettin' yer shield down!"

Sweat poured into the lad's dark blue eyes. Using his sword hand, he wiped it away. Dark brown ringlets were plastered to his forehead, his tunic sticking to his skinny torso. Listening intently, he lifted his shield up as he'd been instructed repeatedly over the past weeks.

Ian thrust his sword forward, tapping the center of the shield. "Never let yer guard down, else ye'll never get to bed yer first woman," he teased.

Robby took the taunt for what it was: simply a means to catch him off balance, to infuriate him to the point he'd do something reckless. He'd learned that lesson the hard way just a sennight ago. It took his arse three days before it quit throbbing from where the tip of Ian's sword had landed.

Once again, Ian thrust his sword forward, this time with such force against the shield, it made his own teeth rattle. Robby landed on his arse with a thud.

Scrambling back to his feet, he tried to return the favor, but his sword glanced off Ian's shield, barely touching it.

So intent was his focus on Ian, he was not paying any attention to the man behind him. Andrew the Red took the tip of his sword and thwacked his arse.

"Bloody hell!" Robby cried out, spinning around to see who the culprit was.

Andrew the Red burst into riotous laughter. Throwing his head back, consumed by his own cleverness, he did not see the blow coming. Robby thrust his own wooden sword against Andrew's stomach. But before he could let out a cheer of victory, Ian kicked his feet out from under him.

"Well played, laddie," Ian said with a proud smile. "But ye fergot yer back once again."

Andrew was appalled, and also a bit proud of the boy.

Ian hauled the red-faced lad to his feet. "Let us try again," he said as he righted the boy's tunic and gave him an affectionate pat on the cheek.

"Ye do no' have to treat me like a bairn," Robby ground out as he planted his left leg firmly behind his right, taking the appropriate stance.

Ian smiled deviously. "I treat ye no different than I would one of me own brothers," he said. "One of me *younger* brothers."

Fiercely, the lad scowled at Ian. Swiping more sweat from his brow, he noticed Ian had barely broken a sweat. And neither was he out of breath. He wanted to be *that* kind of warrior someday. One who could train for hours without his arms and legs feeling as weak as warm butter.

Just then, Rose appeared on the small mound. With his back to her, Ian didn't know she was there until she called out his name. "Ian! Come quick!"

So surprised he was to hear his wife call out, Ian spun, giving his back to Robby. Before he could form his next thought, young Robby McLaren kicked his laird's feet out from under him. Ian landed on his back, the air knocked clean from his lungs. Robby was over him in a heartbeat, with his wooden sword pressed against his throat.

"Be *that* how it is done, m'laird?" he asked cheekily.

Ian gave a quick nod. "Almost, laddie, almost."

As the boy's expression turned to confusion, Ian kicked against his arse once, with enough force to send the boy flying.

"Ian!" Rose was screaming and she sounded very distressed. "Please, come quick!"

"Andrew," Ian said with a smirk, "will ye teach young Robby here that last move? After he pulls his ballocks out of his arse."

The nearer he drew to Rose the more his gut told him something was horribly wrong. Her face was contorted and he could see that she had been crying. Hurriedly, she rushed into his arms. "Och, Ian!" she cried as she hugged him close.

"What be the matter?" he asked. She would never have interrupted the training session were it not important.

"'Tis Eggar," she said between sobs. "They found him in the pit at the quarry." She turned her face up, her eyes red from crying. After taking a deep breath, she blurted out the rest. "He be dead."

An overwhelming sadness fell over him. Eggar was one of the very few, if not the only, McLaren he had learned to trust when he had first arrived with his brother at the auld McLaren keep. Eggar Wardwin was a good, hard-working man.

His distraught wife cried against his chest as she told him what she knew. "I do no' ken how it happened, Ian. But they be bringin' him back now on a litter."

He squeezed his wife gently and kissed the top of her head. "I be so sorry, Rose. Let us go now and see what we can learn."

THEY RUSHED BACK TO THE CAMP just as two McLaren men were bringing Eggar. With great care, they placed the litter on the long table;

their crestfallen expressions were enough to bring tears to even the most hardened man.

Sniffing back a tear, Albert McLaren stepped away from the table. "His neck be broken, m'laird," he said in a low, hushed tone. "It looks as though he tripped and fell in."

Ian scanned the crowd for a brief moment before giving a quick examination of Eggar's cold, lifeless body. His clothing was soaked clear to his skin. It hadn't rained since last night, not long after the midnight hour. He must have gone back to the quarry sometime after the evening meal the night before.

What in the bloody hell was he doing at the quarry at that late hour? Suspicion began to form in his mind. Eggar was neither a drunkard nor a fool. Something had to have drawn him to the quarry at such an hour.

"His clothes are still soaked through. It did no' rain until after the midnight hour last night, and stopped well before dawn," Ian spoke to the crowd who had begun to form. "Does anyone ken why Eggar was at the quarry so late?"

No one answered his question. Each of them looked just as confused as Ian felt.

He did not enjoy where his thoughts led him. There had been much animosity of late betwixt Eggar and Ingerame. Had it gotten to the point that one would kill the other?

Ian knew Ingerame was not above hitting his own daughter, black eyes be-damned. Mayhap, just mayhap the man was angry enough or mad enough to take Eggar's life.

ALL WORK AND TRAINING WAS BROUGHT to a halt while Ian and Brogan began to question the members of the clan. Without fanfare, Ian sent someone to find Ingerame posthaste.

They had just finished interrogating a third clansmen, when Ingerame came rushing into the tent. His face was ashen, his jaw slack. Ian took one look at the man and knew 'twas not born of fear, but of great despair.

"Be it true, m'laird?" he asked breathlessly. "Be he really dead?"

So genuine was the man's anguish that Ian was hard pressed to remain suspicious of him. No one was that good at portraying an innocent man.

"Aye, Ingerame, it be true," Ian said as he left his chair.

"They said he was at the quarry long after midnight." Ingerame repeated what he'd been told. "What the bloody hell was he doin' out there? Alone?"

"I wish I kent the answer to that question," Ian replied.

Only three days ago, Ingerame and Eggar had been at odds once again, over something Ian could not recall at this moment. The way the two men got on, one would have sworn they were life-long enemies. It begged the question. "Ye and he were always arguin' with one another. Yet ye stand here lookin' like a man who just lost his dearest friend."

Ingerame swallowed back what Ian assumed were tears. "Aye, we quarreled all the time, m'laird, but that does no' mean I did no' consider him a friend. He was a good man."

Had he not witnessed the man's grief with his own eyes, had not heard with his own ears the tremor in his voice, Ian would never have believed it. Ingerame Macdowall possessed a heart after all.

Ian offered his condolences and a gentle hand on the man's back. Ingerame left the tent to be alone with his grief.

"Well that quells me suspicion that Ingerame was involved," Brogan admitted.

Andrew the Red had to agree as well. "If I hadn't seen it with me own eyes, I would never have believed it."

Ian nodded in agreement. "I can no' believe Eggar would go to the quarry in the middle of the night."

"Nay," Andrew said. "We did find a cold torch lyin' at his feet. Do ye suppose the rain was heavy near the quarry?"

Brogan thought on that for a long moment. "I'll no' say 'tis impossible, but I will say 'tis highly unlikely."

Ian had to agree. "I can no' help but feel someone kens somethin' about how Eggar Wardwin came to be dead at the bottom of the quarry. 'Tis no' too great a fall. Seven? Eight feet?

"I myself have slipped once or twice when the rope was wet. Fell halfway down it just a few days ago. I landed on me backside."

Ian pondered that for a moment. "What if he was pushed, with great force?"

"That might do it, but 'twould be like fallin' off a horse. About the same distance, would ye no' agree?" Brogan interjected.

"The earth at the bottom of the quarry is covered in dirt and mud from all the rain," Ian offered. "We often have to scoop out buckets of mud before we can get to the rock underneath."

The three men stared at one another for a long while. In the end, they had more questions than answers.

SIXTEEN

T was nearing Christmas tide, the land blanketed in heavy white snow that glistened and twinkled in the sunlight by day, and at night, as far as the eye could see 'twere magnificent colors ranging from indigo to silver. The trees popped and cracked, their branches and limbs weighed down from yet another heavy snowfall.

The little cottage Ian had built for his wife was warm and cozy. A fire burned brightly in the hearth, furs were stretched taught over the tiny windows. Everything was as it should be, save for Rose.

A week ago, she had grown quite ill. No matter what she tried, her stomach would not settle. She could keep nothing down, not even the tiniest morsels of bread. She threw up morning, noon, and night. Dark circles had formed around her sunken eyes, her skin was pale and often damp.

Ian grew more and more concerned as the days passed. On the morning of the sixth day of her ailment, he dressed quickly, throwing on a thick fur and declared, "I am fetchin' the healer." He would brook no argument even if she had the energy to give him one.

He stepped out into the cold, winter air. The sun was just coming up, the sky painted in brilliant shades of red, orange and lavender. Nary a soul was out, and who could blame them. On a morn like this, a man should be abed, under warm furs, and if he was lucky, under a warm wife.

The snow crunched under his heavy boots as he fought his way across the yard and toward the healer's hut. Though she was an aulder woman of indiscernible age, she was his only option. If he had to carry her back to his hut so she could tend to his wife, he would.

Reaching Angrabraid MacConnell's door, he pounded loudly, not caring if he disturbed her slumber. The door opened almost at once. "I be auld, no' deaf!" she shouted. Gray hair, braided and twisted around her head like a silver crown framed her weathered and worn skin, which resembled an auld piece of tanned leather. For a long moment she eyed him scrupulously with a pair of pale blue eyes. "Well? What do ye want? Or are ye just fond of poundin' on an auld woman's door at ungodly hours?"

"'Tis Rose," he managed to say. "She be quite ill. Can no' keep anythin' down."

"Fer how long now?" she asked with one quirked brow and a squinting eye.

"Six days," he answered. "Her skin be clammy. She throws up all day and night now. Can no' even keep down a tiny bit of bread."

With a nod of her head, she bade him wait. "I will get me bag," she said before closing the door.

As patiently as a man of his stubbornness and current distress could manage, he waited. And he waited. And he waited.

Had she forgotten he was here? Had she fallen or taken suddenly ill?

Just as he was about to raise his hand to pound on the door yet again, it flew open. With a walking stick in one hand and a large pouch slung over her shoulder, she stared at his upraised arm and massive fist. "Bah! Ye plan to beat me fer no' hurryin' as fast as ye like?"

Ian was unable to find an appropriate response. Desperate to have his wife well again, he changed the subject. "Can ye make it through the snow?"

Tapping her stick once, she said, "I be auld, no' dead!"

Ian sent a silent prayer for patience up to the heavens. Left to hope her bedside manner was kinder to his wife than it had been to him, he followed her through the snow.

While Ian paced like a caged animal just outside the door to the cottage, he was left alone with his fearful mind and heart. The healer had threatened to beat him senseless if he didn't leave her and his wife alone. Reluctantly, and at Rose's request, he had excused himself to wait out of doors.

Before long, he had beaten down the snow, wearing a path as wide as their little home. Ian Mackintosh was as pious as an Edinburgh whore, but he was not above tossing a prayer God's way every now and again. Today, he was in full-blown negotiations with Him. Making every bargain he could think of in the hope his wife would be well again.

I can no' lose her, he thought as he trampled down more of the snow. *I can no' live without her.*

With his mind and heart otherwise engaged, he had not heard Brogan approach.

His brother stood only a few feet away, observing Ian's agitated state. From the worrisome manner in which his younger brother paced, with his head down, hands clasped behind his back, he knew 'twas no time for playful jests. "Ian, what be the matter?"

When Ian glanced up, Brogan's stomach tightened. He recognized that look of fear and dread.

"'Tis Rose," Ian said, his voice cracking. "She is quite ill. Can no' keep even the tiniest morsel of food down." He went on to explain how she had been ill off and on for more than a fortnight. "It has only grown worse this past sennight."

There was no way for Brogan to mask his crestfallen expression.

"What?" Ian ground out.

"Nothin'."

He lied and Ian knew he lied. Ian studied him closely, taking note that his brother could not look him in the eye. The longer they stood in the cold morning air, the heavier his heart felt. "Is this how it began with yer wife? With the wastin' disease?" Ian asked, terrified to hear his answer. Brogan's lovely young wife had died from that horrible disease more than three years ago. He still had not recovered from his loss.

"It could be anythin' that ails her," Brogan offered. "She could have eaten somethin' that did no' agree with her."

Ian could appreciate his brother's attempt to offer the smallest glimmer of hope, but it did nothing to ease the deep ache and worry over Rose. Guilt tugged at his heart.

"I should never have brought her here," he whispered. "'Tis too rough and hard a life fer someone as wee as Rose."

A weak smile came to Brogan's lips. "She be much stronger than ye're givin' her credit fer."

Ian ignored him and went back to his pacing.

"Do no' bury her yet, Ian," Brogan said. "Ye have no idea what be the matter with her. Hold on to yer sanity and yer patience until ye hear from the healer."

"THAT CAN NO' BE," Rose whispered in stunned disbelief. "'Tis impossible."

Angrabraid clucked her tongue as she wiped a cool cloth across Rose's forehead. "Impossible? Ye be married, ain't ye?"

Rose could barely nod in affirmation.

"Be it a marriage in name only then?"

A slow shake of her head was the only answer Rose could manage.

Chuckling, the auld woman patted her hand. "I imagine if I were as bonny and young as ye, and had me a fine, braw husband like Ian, I'd be liftin' me skirts as easily as an Inverness bar wench would fer a groat!"

Rose found no humor in her jest. A heavy sense of despair draped over her heart. "But we were takin' precautions," she murmured.

Angrabraid threw back her head and laughed. "The only *precaution* to no' gettin' with child is to stay as far away from a man as ye can, lass. Especially a man like yers."

Removing the cloth from Rose's forehead, she dipped it into the bowl of cool water. "When was the last time ye bled?"

In truth, she had no earthly idea. "I have never been regular in that regard," Rose answered. "Sometimes I go two or three months, only bleed a day or two. Then other times, it lasts fer two weeks."

Squeezing out the excess water, Angrabraid drew the cool cloth over Rose's arms and neck. "'Tis more common an occurrence than most think."

Too weak and ill to hold them back, Rose let the tears stream down her cheeks. *This can no' be.*

"Lass, why is this no' good news fer ye? Do ye no' want children?" The healer's smile had faded, replaced with a genuine look of concern.

Taking in a slow, deep breath, she swiped away at her tears. "I was married before. I could no' carry past me third month." *I can no' bear the thought of losin' another child.*

As comforting as a kind grandmother, Angrabraid gave her hands another gentle pat. "Wheest, lass. I ken many a woman who lost more than one babe before one finally took. Who kens why one babe survives and another does no'?"

"I could no' bear it, Angrabraid, to lose Ian's babe." She admitted aloud her deepest worry.

"There be nothin' to say ye will lose it, lass. Ye must no' fash yerself over it. Ye need to keep good thoughts in yer head and heart. 'Twill do yer babe more good than worry ever will."

How was she going to tell Ian? They had taken every measure either of them knew of, to ensure she did not get with child. Together, they had made that most difficult decision. This was one more worry he did not need right now. There was too much important work to be done.

"Please," Rose pleaded, "do no' tell Ian."

From the doorway, she heard her husband's voice, filled with so much concern and worry it nearly broke her heart in twain. "Do no' tell Ian *what?*"

Before Rose could stop her, Angrabraid said, "She be carryin' yer babe."

CARRYIN' ME BABE? NAY, he could not have heard the auld woman correctly. "What did ye say?" he asked.

Angrabraid stood, smiling fondly up at him. "She be carryin' yer babe."

Had Brogan not been standing behind him and placed a palm on his shoulder, he would have fallen to his knees from the shock.

Nay, this can no' be, he cried silently. Only moments ago, he had been fully prepared to hear the healer tell him his wife was dying from the wasting disease or some other horrible illness. Not once did his mind ever allow him to think she might be with child.

A thousand thoughts and worries collided in his mind. When he stepped forward and looked into his wife's pain-filled eyes, he nearly came undone. Frantically, he searched for the right words, for a way to express to her his utter sorrow.

'Twas his own fault. Every day, like a rutting roebuck, he sought his pleasures with Rose. Morning and night, he loved her. Hell, he'd even forgone his noonin' meal in exchange for the chance to love her.

Desperately, he wanted to go to her on bended knee and beg her forgiveness. Suddenly, he understood why her first husband had kept away from her. It hadn't been his age, as Ian had previously thought. Nay, 'twas his love for her. He'd rather suffer a disembowlment than to have his wife suffer even the smallest of anguish.

"I be so sorry, Rose," he stammered.

"Bah!" Angrabraid said. "Ye both be actin' as though the world be at an end."

Anger flared inside his heart. "Ye do no' understand, auld woman! She can no' carry a babe to term!"

The auld woman stepped forward, eyes filled with fury. "I do no' care if ye be the king of Scotia, ye wee fool, ye do no' call me auld!"

Ian leaned down so he could look her squarely in her auld, yellow eyes. "That be me wife lyin' abed, her heart breakin' into a thousand pieces because I got her with child and she can no' carry past her third month!"

Squinting her eyes, Angrabaid shoved her bony hands onto her hips, undaunted and unafraid of the man standing before her. "That shows how much ye ken, ye troll-eyed eejit! She already be in her fourth month!"

ASTONISHED GASPS FILLED THE SMALL cottage. Feeling proud that she had set young Ian Mackintosh in his place, Angrabraid returned to Rose's side.

Slowly, she sat on the edge of the bed again. "Aye, lass, ye be in yer fourth month already. Come May, ye're goin' to be a mum. A right good one at that," she reassured her with a warm smile. "Yer husband, however," she tossed her words over her shoulder with as much disdain as she could muster, "as to what kind of father he'll be, 'twill be up to the Gods, new and auld. He'll need to practice a wee bit more kindness and patience."

"Four months?" Rose asked, uncertainty tumbling in her belly.

"Aye, lass," she said. "Now, because ye both be half scared out of yer minds, I am goin' to order ye to stay abed fer the next two months. Ye're no' to so much as lift a finger to peel a leek, do ye hear me?"

Still too stunned to string a coherent thought together, Rose nodded numbly.

Angrabraid patted her hand before taking away the cloth. "I shall leave some herbs that should help settle yer stomach. Ye might feel better in a few weeks, and then ye might no'. Me sister, och! She was still losin' her stomach fer two weeks after she had her third babe. 'Twas a boy, ye ken. Boy babes are always far more trouble than the lasses."

She stood once again, turning her attention back to Ian. "She is to stay abed, do ye hear?"

Stunned into muteness, Ian gave a curt nod.

"She's no' to do a thing, do ye hear? There'll be no cookin', no cleanin', and especially no ruttin' around like a bull in need, do ye hear?"

His face burned crimson. Joinin' with his wife was not a topic he wished to discuss with anyone, least of all this auld woman.

"Ye have me word," he promised. "I'll tie her to the bed if I must."

If Rose hadn't been so god-awful queasy and tired, the thought of being tied to the bed might have sounded enticing. Instead, Ian's comment angered her. "I am no' a bairn," she bit out. "Ye needn't treat me as such."

Ignoring her protest, Brogan stepped forward with a wide, beaming smile. "'Tis good news!" he declared happily. "I will enjoy bein' an uncle again."

Ian went to his wife and knelt down on one knee. Without taking his eyes from hers, he spoke to Brogan. "Mayhap it be best if we do no' say anythin' just yet, brother."

Angrabraid huffed as she stuffed the last of her things into her pack. "Och! The two of ye! I tell ye there be nothin' to worry over."

Anger flashed in Ian's eyes. If looks were weapons, the auld healer would have been pinned to the wall with a thousand daggers. "No' worry?" he growled. "She has already lost three babes. And just look at her," he demanded as he turned sorrowful eyes to his wife. "I have never seen anyone as sick as she unless they were dyin'."

Whether it was her age or the ache in her bones, the auld woman threw her hands up in defeat. "'Tis as if I be talkin' to a donkey," she said with more than a hint of disgust in her voice. After a long moment, her face softened, as did her tone. "Just as each woman be different, so be the way she carries each babe. Some are no' sick at all, some are only sick the first weeks, whilst others are sick all the while. And it varies from babe to babe." She began to wonder if her argument wasn't falling on deaf ears. "Did ye ever think that *yer* seed be stronger than her last husband's?"

Ian blinked once, then twice as he turned to look at Angrabraid.

A knowing smile came to her eyes, giving a twinkle to her aged eyes. "I see neither of ye did."

In truth, Ian hadn't given a moment's thought to such a prospect. He'd been too focused on *not* getting Rose with child to worry over what might happen if, by God's grace, she did conceive. Turning back to his wife, the heavy sadness remained in her eyes. He doubted anyone could say anything to brighten her spirit or ease her worry.

"Leave us," Ian said.

Silence stretched over the small hut. "I will escort ye back to yer hut," Brogan offered.

"At least one of ye Mackintosh brothers possesses more manners than a goat," Angrabraid said. Her voice sounded sweet, belying the fierce and oft hard-nosed woman Ian thought her to be.

Finally alone, he pressed a tender kiss to his wife's fingers. "I be so sorry, Rose," he said. "Mayhap it be God's will."

Rose scoffed. "Since when did *ye* become a God-fearin' believer in the all-mighty?"

A warm smile came to his face. "A heartbeat after I learned ye were carryin'."

THEY SPENT THE REMAINDER OF the morning talking about all the 'what if's' they could imagine.

"What if I lose this babe?" Rose asked, more than once.

To which Ian responded, "What if ye do no'?"

"But what if I do?"

"Think of it, Rose," he said as he gently tucked a strand of hair behind her ear. "I'd wager that if the babe be a girl, she'll be just as bonny as ye. I will have to have ten men guardin' her at all times. Mayhap I should add extra floors to the tower and keep her locked away?"

His jest could not break through her heartache. "Rose, what if Angrabraid be right? And me seed be stronger that Almer's? Could ye think of it fer just a moment?"

This was not her first time with child. Rose knew the dangers of getting her hopes up, only to have them torn asunder, shredded and tossed into the wind like tiny bits of dust. As she looked into her husband's eyes, she saw only hope. No worry, no trepidation. Silently, she cursed Angrabraid for telling him and for giving him false hope. 'Twas a cruel thing for anyone to do. To allow a man such as Ian to hope and dream of something he would never have was heartless. Oh, how she worried over his heart when the day came that she lost this babe as she had lost the others.

Deciding it best to keep her worry and despair to herself, she forced a smile. But she refused to play the 'what if' game with her husband any longer. "I will try," she told him. "I fear I be awfully tired, Ian. I would like to rest now."

Smiling, he kissed her forehead, and the smile never left his face. "I will leave ye to rest then. I shall go and ask the womenfolk to check on ye durin' the day when I be workin'."

She wanted very much to scream *Twill do no good fer me to lay abed!* But the love she felt for her husband prohibited such an outburst.

SEVENTEEN

The next weeks passed at a snail's pace, with Rose abed and Ian and the clanswomen hovering over her like midges. 'Twas enough to make the strongest Highland woman insane, what with all their fussing and fretting.

As one day passed into the next, Rose's worries lessened and before she realized it, her heart was lighter and her belly growing bigger. No longer as ill as she had been, she still had to be careful with what she ate. Sweets stayed down about as long as a Highland warrior thrown from his horse. Fish was no better. However, anything savory, such as meat pies, would oft calm her unpredictable stomach.

Their babe grew, as did her hope.

When she felt him kick for the very first time, she cried for hours after. "'Twas somethin' I never thought I'd feel," she confessed to Ian as he dried her tears of relief and joy. His smile was as warm and bright as the sun.

"Angrabraid was right, aye?" he asked as he held her head against his chest.

Now in her sixth month, 'twas easier for her to let go of some of her worry. There was still a chance she could lose the babe. However, she had made it farther than she had with any previous pregnancy. That alone was something to celebrate, albeit quietly.

"Aye," she told him. "She was right."

"I DO NO' SEE IT," LEONA said with a shake of her head. "Rose be far prettier than I."

'Twas her turn to keep Rose company this day. Ronna had joined them, bringing meat pies to the expectant mother. 'Twas she who remarked over the resemblance betwixt the two women.

"Och!" Rose exclaimed from her chair by the fire. "'Tis ye who be the pretty one." She had finally been allowed out of bed the day before, but was still restricted to her hut, per her husband's orders. And he still demanded she not be left alone for even the tiniest of moments.

Ronna clucked her tongue as she brought Rose a meat pie. "Ye're both daft," she declared. "Had I been half as pretty as either of ye in me youth, I could have married the king."

Rose and Leona giggled. "I have kent ye me whole life, Ronna," Rose said with a warm smile. "Ye were always beautiful." She took the pie in both hands and inhaled deeply. Her mouth watered as her stomach growled.

"Bah!" Ronna argued, doing her best to suppress a smile. "Ye only say that because I bring ye meat pies."

"Ye are still beautiful," Rose told her. "And I would think that even if ye did no' make such delicious meat pies." After taking a bite, she closed her eyes and sighed contentedly. "The best I ever had, I swear it."

Ronna smiled proudly. "Ye both be bonny women. Everyone says as much."

Leona cast her a doubtful glance. "Everyone?" she challenged. Not since her mother passed fifteen years ago had anyone referred to her as *bonny*. Tetched? Bedeviled? Strange? Aye, they'd called her all those things and more. But never bonny. They might say such nice things about Rose, but in her heart, Leona knew no such words were ever spoken about her.

"Mayhap no' *everyone*," Ronna admitted. "But even Ian and Brogan have remarked on how ye resemble one another. From behind, we can no' tell the two of ye apart. Ye could pass fer sisters."

"The closest thing to a sister I ever had was Aggie," Rose said, her mood suddenly shifting from light and happy to sorrowful. "I miss her somethin' terrible."

Ronna looked up from the sewing she'd brought with her and offered a warm smile. "Ye'll see her again, I be certain of it."

"But when?" Rose said, swiping at a tear. "Next year? The year after?" Though Aggie's letters had promised they'd be here before the end of spring, doubts lingered. What if Ada was not strong enough to make the journey? What if Aggie got with child again? There were too many things that could delay their travel.

Although Leona had never known anyone she could call her true friend until she met Rose, she could well understand her pain. Rose had shared many a story regarding all they, and Aggie in particular, endured over the years. Rising quickly, she went and wrapped an arm around her friend. "Wheest, Rose," she whispered tenderly.

Rose took a deep, cleansing breath and patted Leona's hand. "Thank ye, Leona. I fear me emotions sometimes run away with me."

"'Tis the babe," Ronna said. "One minute ye be as happy as a pig in mud, the next, ye be cryin' and betimes fer no reason at all."

Rose swiped away an errant tear. "I fear ye're right. 'Tis an odd thing that happens to us when we're with child, aye?"

Ronna gave her a knowing nod. "Aye, 'tis," she said in a low, mournful tone. She had been blessed with three children, two boys and a girl, but all had died before they reached the age of five.

"I fear I'll never ken such a feelin'," Leona admitted.

"Och! Do no' be daft. Of course ye will," Rose argued.

Leona sat on the floor in front of her friend and was quiet for a long while. "I be nearin' three and twenty. Me days of findin' a husband or bearin' a child are long past."

Rose could well understand Leona's plight and anguish. "I used to think the same," she told her. "But look at me now."

"But we are different, aye? Ye be beautiful and strong. Everyone looks up to ye," Leona said.

Rose started to object. "But—"

"But nothin'," Leona said. "Ye be Ian's Rose. I be Leona Two-eyes."

Aye, Rose had heard people whisper that horrible name behind Leona's back. 'Twas a reference to her oddly colored eyes. More than once, she had set the person to rights and threatened to put them on latrine duty for the remainder of the year should she hear them use it in reference to her friend again.

Her heart felt heavy for this young woman whom she had begun to consider a true friend.

"Do no' fash over it, Rose," Leona said, offering up a warm smile. "I be a free woman, ye ken. I can come and go as I please. I do no' have to answer to anyone, save fer me da."

Ingerame. Rose did not like that man, not one bit. Were he even the slightest bit kind to his daughter, mayhap she would have been married by now with a dozen bairns of her own.

"I like me life the way it is," Leona said. "So do no' worry over it or me."

Convincing as her tone might be, Rose did not believe one word of it.

BEFORE WINTER HAD SET IN, the men had erected a large tent in what would, in the future, be the central courtyard. On days when they were not plagued with snow or bitter winds, they would gather there to spend the hours discussing plans for the future, tell tall tales over mugs of ale, and otherwise do their best to stay out from under the feet of their wives.

On this particularly sunny day in February, the men gathered together to once again discuss the plans for construction that would begin in the spring.

Two large braziers sat in the center of the tent with tables on either side. Ian sat at a long table with Brogan, Andrew the Red, and Charles McFarland.

"We'll need men workin' day and night in the quarry," Andrew said as he played with the rim of his mug. "The work would go faster if we had more horses to pull wagons."

"Aye," Ian agreed. "I hear the Mactavishes breed fine stock. Mayhap we could barter with them."

"Now there is an odd lot of people," Charles said before pulling on his mug.

"What do ye mean?" Andrew asked, studying the man closely.

Charles gave a slight shrug. "They do no' have a chief."

Ian and Brogan exchanged glances with one another. "No chief?" Ian asked with a good measure of disbelief.

"Aye, 'tis true," Charles said. "I do no' ken the whole of the story, but their chief was murdered, along with his babe, more than two years ago."

"And no one stepped in to be chief?" Andrew asked.

Charles leaned over the table, drawing the men with him. "I hear tell that their mistress, Mairghread Mactavish, killed them. That she lost her mind one night and killed her husband and babe. Now her uncle, I can no' remember his name, he acts as chief of sorts. All the land, those are all Mairghread's. Her clan will no' let her rule or act as chief, so she must find a husband. Unless she dies, then everything will go to the uncle. As I said, 'tis an odd lot of people that border us to our north."

"Bah!" Brogan exclaimed in disbelief. "Women do no' kill their own bairns."

Charles leaned back in his chair and offered another indifferent shrug. "I only tell ye what I've heard."

"Rumors and lies," Ian began with a tone of warning, "have brought down more good men than truths ever have."

"Have ye met this Mairghread?" Brogan asked Charles.

"Nay," he admitted.

"Then ye might want to keep *what ye heard* to yerself until ye ken the whole of the story," Brogan warned him.

Deciding 'twas best to change the topic at hand, Andrew chimed in. "I kent a Mairghread once. She was a bar wench in Inverness. A comely thing she was, too!"

Ian and Brogan had heard Andrew's stories so often, they knew them by heart. They turned their attention away from his ribald tale and spoke to one another.

"So would ye like me to reach out to the Mactavishes about horses?" Brogan asked.

Ian gave a nod of affirmation. "Aye, I would. Take Rodrick the Bold and Andrew with ye on the morrow."

Brogan nodded before taking a pull of his ale.

As an afterthought, Ian added. "And see what ye can learn about their lack of a chief. I would like to ken if we should think them allies or enemies."

LESS THAN A SENNIGHT LATER, Brogan, Andrew and Rodrick returned with a dozen large highland ponies. The Mactavish keep was a solid two-day ride from the McLarens. Ian was surprised to see them back so soon, but mightily glad for the horses.

After putting their new purchases into the corral, the men headed into the large tent. They quenched their thirst on ale and cider and filled their bellies with a good hearty rabbit stew and bread.

Full of gratitude, Ian let them quench their thirst and fill their bellies before he asked for details of their trip.

"I got only a glimpse of Mairghread," Rodrick told him. "A right bonny woman she is, too."

Andrew scoffed at Rodrick's assessment. "I thought she looked quite odd. A wee bit tetched."

Brogan rolled his eyes at Andrew. "Ye only say that because of the rumors."

They argued back and forth about whether or not Mairghread Mactavish was tetched or beautiful or both. Ian had heard enough. "Lads, can we get to the matter at hand?" he asked, bringing their conversation to a halt. "Should we think them allies or no'?" He directed his question at his brother.

Brogan took a drink of cider before responding. "In truth? I do no' rightly ken if we can think them allies. But I do no' think we need to worry they be our enemies."

"That is as clear as mud," Ian said.

Brogan smiled. "They be a rather small clan. And no' well organized. It took them four hours just to decide who we should speak to in the matter of horses. Cainnech Mactavish— he be the uncle to Mairghread — had just left the day before we arrived. Apparently, he did no' leave clear instructions as to who was in charge, or fer anything else."

Ian mulled it over for a moment. "So they be too disorganized to be either a help or a hindrance?"

Brogan smiled wryly. "Aye. So I do no' worry over them." He took another drink of cool cider. "Now, what they lack in organization, they more than make up fer in horseflesh. 'Tis the finest I have ever seen."

On that, Andrew and Rodrick could both agree. "Aye. I would no' mind goin' back to deal fer a horse of me own," Rodrick said with a smile. 'Twas the second time since Ian had met the man that he'd seen him smile for any reason. He wasn't sure if he should be glad or frightened. But 'twas good to know the man had an interest in something.

.

EIGHTEEN

On his belly, the night raider looked down from the top of the hill. Smoke rose in swirls and whispers from the tiny huts that dotted the land. Nary a light burned from within them, for all were abed and sound asleep.

Torches lit the upper wood wall, to give the appearance they possessed more guards than they actually did. Thanks to his own keen intellect as well as the spy that lived among the Mackintoshes and McLarens, he knew every secret Ian Mackintosh had. Some were, by far, more important than others.

For instance, he knew that someone, more likely than not Frederick Mackintosh, had found the treasure hidden in the auld McLaren keep. 'Twas the only way to explain the influx of capital that allowed the construction of an entirely new keep. While the Mackintoshes were one of the richest and most powerful clans in all of Scotia, not even they possessed the ability to build everything from new and at their current pace.

He also knew that Ian and many of his men were off hunting for game. That information he had gleaned from his carefully placed spy. 'Twas amazing what one could purchase with just a few pieces of coin. They would be gone for days. They had left behind a decent enough contingent of men to guard what Ian held most precious: his wife.

'Twas all for naught, for his own party of warriors outnumbered them three to one.

Quietly, he slid back the way he'd come. Amongst the thirty men, mounted and on foot, stood his own gray speckled steed. Without a word to the others, he grabbed the reins and swung himself into the saddle. They'd gone over their plan until 'twas burned into their minds. Their mission was simple — kidnap Rose Mackintosh.

The execution of that simple mission would not be nearly as easy. He might be as arrogant as the day was long, but that did not mean he was a stupid man. The Mackintoshes were some of the best-trained warriors in all of Scotland, if not the world. His men, vicious and ruthless beasts every one of them, may not have been as well trained. But on this night, they possessed something the Mackintoshes didn't: greed and the blood of generations of greedy, ruthless bastards that ran through their veins. And a spy within who would soon open the gates to the McLaren keep.

ROSE WAS FAST ASLEEP, DREAMING pleasantly about her husband and the babe she carried. The dream was much the same from night to night. She and Ian were cooing over their babe, remarking over how beautiful a bairn he or she was. Betimes she dreamt she'd birthed a boy, others, 'twas a girl child. While the sex of the babe may have changed from night to night, the underlying tone of the dream was always the same: peace and contentment.

Della Mackintosh slept on a pallet next to her bed this night. The woman had insisted she did not wish to be sleeping alone whilst her husband was with Ian and the others. Rose knew 'twas mostly a falsehood, for she had three sons to care for. More likely than not, 'twas Ian's idea, for he worried over his wife being alone for even the shortest amount of time.

Either way, Rose did find some comfort in knowing Della was there should any emergency arise. Knowing Ian would be home in a matter of a few short days did nothing to stop her from missing him.

Whether 'twas her memory of the time Frederick had gone hunting and subsequently been kidnapped by Eduard Bowie or her ever-changing emotions brought on by being with child, tonight's dream suddenly turned dark. Ominous, misshapen shadows were pulling at her with black fingers. They screamed and screeched like banshees, turning her blood to ice. In the next moment, Della was standing in the doorway to Rose's hut, covered in blood and screaming for her to run. But she felt paralyzed, unable to blink, let alone will her body to move.

Terrified, Rose shot upright in her bed, out of breath and covered with sweat.

It only took a frantic heartbeat to realize 'twas not a dream.

DELLA WAS ON HER FEET, A *sgian dubh* in one hand and a stool in the other, fending off the dark stranger who stood just inside the doorway. "Rose!" she shouted. "Run!"

Seven months ago, 'twould have taken little time or effort for Rose to jump from the bed and help fend off the attacker. Heavy now with child, she could not move as fast as she needed to. The instinct to stand and fight fought hard against the battle to save her babe.

Outside, she could hear the sounds of battle, of metal clanging against metal, horses screaming, people shouting, and the loud peal of the warning bell calling all to arms.

Scurrying to her feet, she stood in stunned horror as the tall, dark figure lifted his sword in both hands and swung out in a wide arc.

In the small confines of Rose's home, there was nowhere to go nor any time to move out of the way. His sword sliced across Della's side, sending her to her knees. The stool fell from her hand and rolled away, the *sgian dubh* fell to the stone floor with a soft clink. A frantic heartbeat later, Della McLaren fell into a bloody heap on Rose's floor.

Rose let loose a blood-curdling scream. There was no time to ponder who this man was, nor what his intentions might be. Trapped, terrified for her unborn child, sickened that he had just killed one of her dearest friends, Rose backed away. Two steps later, she was pinned against the wall and he was hovering over her.

"Rose!" A shout came from the doorway. 'Twas Andrew the Red, sword drawn in one hand, his other holding a shield.

The stranger spun around just as Andrew lunged forward. Rose jumped out of the way and fell sideways onto her bed. Fear, panic and sheer terror enveloped her. *Run! Run! Run!* 'Twas the only thing she could think to do.

While Andrew and the stranger fought, Rose scurried across the bed and raced for the door.

Outside, chaos reigned supreme. Everywhere she turned, fires roared from the rooftops of huts, the flames stabbing at the cold winter's night. Men on horseback charged through the yard, slicing through anyone or anything in their paths. On the ground, men fought one on one, women holding bairns in their arms or pulling weans behind them, ran, trying to find a safe place to hide. But there was none.

There was no place to take refuge. No sturdy building in which to seek shelter from the slaughter playing out before her eyes. Rose could barely hear the din of battle over the blood coursing through her veins as her heart pounded rapidly against her breast.

Picking up her skirts, she ran as fast as she could, uncertain where she should go. The only thing that came to mind was to seek the cover of darkness within the forest.

She hadn't taken more than a few steps when she felt an arm wrap around her waist. A frantic moment later, she was lifted off her feet.

"I have her!" the voice called out. "I have Rose Mackintosh!"

Kicking, screaming, she clawed at his arms, struggling with all her might to be free. But 'twas all for naught. Moments later, she was being hoisted upward and onto a horse. Two arms wound their way around her waist, holding her tightly.

"Our laird wants ye alive, lass," the man shouted as she struggled against his tight hold. "But truth be told, I do no' care one way or the other. Resist me and ye will die this night."

Fighting was pointless; in her heart she knew it. She had two choices. She could fight to her own death or she could do whatever she could to save her babe.

The motherly instinct to protect her babe took hold. She would not fight. Instead, she would do whatever she must in order to keep her babe safe.

NINETEEN

Upon hearing the news about the raid where he and the other hunters were camped, Ian Mackintosh felt sick to his stomach with worry and regret. One of his closest friends since childhood, Andrew the Red, was dead, as were dozens of the men he'd left behind to guard the keep.

'Twas an odd blend of trepidation and sorrow that draped over his heart as Della Mackintosh's youngest son stood before him. Imparting the facts as best as he could, considering he was only eleven summers old, the boy fought gallantly to hold back his tears and personal anguish. Ian held his temper in check, along with his breath, while the lad frantically relayed the story.

When Ian learned his wife had been kidnapped, he experienced a level of fury and heartache unlike anything he'd ever felt before. 'Twas far worse than the worry he'd experienced when he thought he'd lost her to the fire.

Worse yet than when she'd gone back to the auld keep months ago. And worse even still than when he'd convinced himself she was dying from the wasting disease.

Nay, those were all nothing more than the wild imaginings of a man fraught with worry.

This? This was real. There was no uncertainty as to what had happened. She'd been taken.

"I was hidin' under a wagon, m'laird," the boy sniffled. "I heard a man shout "*I have Rose Mackintosh!*" Then he tossed her to a man on horseback. As soon as they had our lady, they left as quickly as they'd come. We had no warnin', m'laird. They killed so many people." His voice cracked. "Includin' me mum."

Tears streamed down the lad's dirty face. "They killed me mum, m'laird, while I hid under a wagon like a coward," he cried as he broke down into sobs.

'Twas Brogan who pulled the lad in and held onto him whilst he wept. "Wheest, lad," he whispered. "Ye did the right thing. Yer mum would agree. She'd want naught any harm to come to ye."

While Brogan did his best to comfort the boy, Ian stood in stunned silence while his fury built. The men he'd brought with him on the hunt had encircled him and waited. Many of them were husbands who had left their wives behind. Their expressions held a blend of outrage and grief. Either too shocked to ask or too afraid to know the answers, none asked after their own. Mayhap they already knew the answers but were not quite ready to hear the truth.

Ian looked at each of these brave men. Men who had sworn their fealty to him. Men — Mackintoshes and McLarens, as well as a few of the laborers — who looked up to him, who worked side by side with him every day. A few looked at him with tear-filled eyes. But each and every man looked him straight in the eye, as if to say, *what now?*

"M'laird," Thomas McLaren said, taking a step forward. "I'd like yer permission to leave as soon as possible. I have a wife and two weans at home."

They would get no argument from Ian.

IAN AND HIS MEN RODE THROUGH the night to return to the keep. The swathe of destruction left behind by the midnight raid was horrific. The scent of blood, smoke, and death filled the air, stealing the breath away from even the most experienced warrior.

This was not a raid, but a bloodbath.

Littered across the yard were countless bodies. Men and women who died for reasons Ian could not quite grasp. Aye, they fought to protect their families, their keep, and as in the case of Della and Andrew the Red, they fought to protect Rose.

But why?

Why did they have to die? For what cause? There was none, save for greed. 'Twas for greed and greed alone that these people were dead. Someone had taken his wife to hold her for ransom. 'Twas the only plausible explanation.

Thankfully, the death toll was not nearly as high as it might have been. His men had done a good job at defending the keep and their people. But one death was too many as far as Ian was concerened. 'Twas the bloody fires that did the most damage.

As Ian stood in the middle of it all, he could not help but feel an overwhelming sense of guilt. He hadn't listened to Rodrick the Bold's concerns about raids from other clans. Nay, he'd let his foolish pride stand in the way of protecting his people and his wife.

Brogan approached him, his face alight with anger and fury. "The gate was left open."

"What do ye mean?" Ian demanded.

"I've inspected the walls, the gates, and the area around us. There be no damage to the gate, no signs anyone scaled the walls. All the tracks lead straight through our front gate."

Irrepressible anger washed over Ian when he realized what Brogan was saying. "Someone let them in."

Brogan's jaw clenched tightly. "Aye."

"There is a traitor amongst us." 'Twas an undeniable statement of fact.

CHARLES MCFARLAND AND RODRICK the Bold had been injured in the attack. Though Rodrick's injuries were far more serious than Charles's.

Brogan and a group of men reassembled the main tent and began to help wounded inside. Two men carried an unconscious Rodrick in and laid him upon a long table. "Where be our healer?" One of the men asked.

"I do no' ken," Charles answered from a stool near the brazier. Brogan thought the man looked more stunned than wounded. A bandage was wrapped around his left arm, a small bit of blood seething through. But 'twas the only outward sign of injury. Brogan knew from personal experience, that a battle could oft leave a man's mind more injured than a blade ever could.

"What happened?" he asked as he stood next to Charles.

"I do no' ken. I was asleep in the armory with Rodrick. I woke up to the sounds of battle and the call to arms. I grabbed me sword and ran outside. 'Twas total chaos. Huts were burnin', people were screamin'…"

"We need bandages!" one of the men called out. Brogan looked up to find men surrounding Rodrick. "I can no' stop the bleedin'."

One of the surviving women rushed over with an arm full of bandages and set about offering what assistance she could. The men took a few steps away and watched.

Turning his attention back to Charles, Brogan asked. "Do ye ken who they were?"

Charles ran a frustrated hand through is hair. "Nay, I do no'. It all happened so fast."

Though Charles may have fancied himself a warrior, Brogan was not inclined to agree. Any good warrior would have paid attention, would have listened and looked for any sign of who was attacking. For the moment, he would not fault the man, for he knew he didn't possess the same level of experience as Brogan himself did.

"There were no banners waved?" Brogan asked, ever hopeful they could get to the bottom of things. He needed to know who had done this. The why of it didn't matter at the moment. Only the who.

"Nay," Charles said with a grimace. His arm was paining him something terrible. "I saw no banners, heard no names called out. I saw no plaids, nothin' to tell me who they were."

Brogan glanced back toward Rodrick. Though the man was not exactly the friendly sort, Brogan felt he was as good a warrior as his Mackintosh men. Rodrick, should he live, would be able to give him more information than the visibly shaken and terrified Charles.

'Twas then that he noticed Charles kept glancing toward Rodrick. Thinking he was worried about his friend, Brogan said, "He's a strong man. I am certain he's suffered worse injuries."

"Ye think he'll live?" Charles asked.

"I certainly hope so," Brogan answered.

Charles swallowed hard. Brogan sensed there was something the young man wanted to say but was afraid to say it. "Charles. If there is somethin' ye need to tell me, I suggest ye no' beat around the bush about it."

Looking away and back to Brogan, he said, "He was no' there when I awoke. He was already outside. Why did he no' wake me to help fight?"

An overpowering sense of dread draped over Brogan's heart. Was Rodrick their traitor? His first inclination was to think *Nay, that be impossible.* But if life had taught him anything, 'twas that people were not always as they appeared to be. Spies and traitors walked among the unsuspecting on a daily basis.

Fer yer sake, Rodrick, I hope ye do no' survive yer injuries. Fer if ye do, Ian and I will tear ye limb from limb.

Leaving Brogan in charge of the keep and taking care of the dead and injured, Ian set off with ten men in search of Rose.

There was no priest in attendance to either offer last rites or speak over the dead. The task fell on Brogan. For two solid days, he worked along side his clansmen to help bury the dead and tend to the injured, while Ian searched for Rose. When the final count was tallied, seven men and two women had lost their lives. Countless others had been wounded, some far more seriously than others.

While a team of men worked to bury the dead, other teams set about repairing the damage. From sunup to sunset, they worked harder than they ever had. Brogan decided 'twas best to repair the armory first. Its walls had withstood the attack quite well. The only real damage had been done to the thatched roof and a few of its beams.

He was unable to glean anything useful from the survivors. They all said the same thing; it all happened so fast that no one had time to respond.

The guards who had been posted along the walls had seemingly been killed before they could call out any warning. All six had had their throats cut, either from the enemies without or the one within.

Rodrick was the only logical suspect. Brogan doubted anyone else would have possessed the ability and stealth to kill six men in such a manner.

On the morning of the third day, Leona, Ingerame and the healer appeared at the gates. Leona and Angrabraid looked mad enough to kill. Ingerame, however, looked positively ashamed.

"Where have ye been?" Brogan demanded as he met the three at the gate.

Leona and Angrabraid cast hate-filled looks toward Ingerame. 'Twas the auld healer who answered the question. "Hidin' in the quarry. Like cowards."

Releasing a frustrated sigh, Brogan had the distinct feeling he was not going to like anything else she or the quiet young woman had to say.

"And how did ye come to be in the quarry?"

Angrabraid glowered at Ingerame. "When the raid came, *this one*," she nodded toward Leona's father, "was the first to flee." She tugged at a rope, jerking Ingerame in the process.

'Twas then Brogan noticed the man's wrists were bound and tied to a length of rope, the end of it in the auld woman's hands.

"I cannot always sleep at night, so I walk. Leona often walks with me. We were no' far from the wall when we heard horses. They were movin' far too quiet-like, ye ken? We — Leona and I — we felt somethin' was wrong. We hurried as best we could, when we saw the fires and heard the commotion."

"The gate was standin' open," Leona added. "While everyone inside was fightin', me father was fleein'."

"Like the rat he is," Angrabraid offered.

A dull ache began to form in Brogan's skull.

"Do no' listen to them!" Ingerame seethed. "I was no' fleein', I was goin' fer help."

"Then why, pray tell, were ye headin' north, when ye kent the men were huntin' to the west? And why, pray tell, did ye hie off to the quarry and hide like a coward?" Angrabraid demanded in accusation.

"I told ye I was waitin' until the raiders left. 'Twas the only safe place to hide!"

Angrabraid gave a good yank on the rope. For an auld woman, she was strong enough to pull the man to his knees. "Bah! Then why have ye held me and yer own flesh and blood at sword point fer nearly three days, refusin' to allow us to leave the cave?"

"'Twas fer yer own safety!" he shouted before pulling himself back to his feet. "Brogan, I be no' a warrior. I be a carpenter! I could no' fight against all those men!"

"Because ye be a coward," Angrabraid said.

"Enough!" Brogan shouted. Taking a deep breath, he eyed the trio closely for a moment. "When ye two left the keep, did ye by chance ferget to close the gate behind ye?"

Confused, the two women looked at one another before answering. "Of course no'," Leona answered. "The men on the wall opened it fer us and closed it when we left."

"When ye returned, was the gate open or closed?"

"'Twas open," Leona said, uncertain why 'twas so important. "That is how me father escaped. Through the open gate."

Brogan glared at the man standing before him. Could it be that Ingerame had left the gate open to allow murderers in? "Pray tell me, Ingerame, was it ye that opened the gate?" He did not want to believe his friend and fellow warrior, Rodrick the Bold, was a traitor. He'd been battling with his conscious for days now. He would much rather believe 'twas Ingerame who had betrayed them.

The man's brow furrowed into a line of confusion. "Nay. The gate was already open when I heard the warning bells go off."

As much as he disliked Ingerame Macdowall, Brogan could not believe the man was their spy and traitor. Nay, the fool was too much of a coward. So he was back to where he began, left to believe 'twas Rodrick the Bold who had betrayed them.

TWENTY

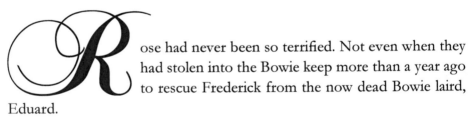ose had never been so terrified. Not even when they had stolen into the Bowie keep more than a year ago to rescue Frederick from the now dead Bowie laird, Eduard.

They had ridden nonstop all the night long. Her heart ached with fear and longing for her home and husband. Every muscle seemed to burn with a blend of exhaustion and worry.

With the repugnant man having such a tight hold on her, 'twas next to impossible to place a hand on her belly. Her babe had grown awfully quiet. He did not kick or turn as he had been doing so often of late. Dread set in as she worried she might lose her babe.

At dawn, they paused only long enough to relieve their bladders. "I need a moment of privacy," she told her captor.

"If ye think I will be givin' ye the chance to escape, ye're sadly mistaken," he told her gruffly.

If she had not been with child, she might have been tempted to hold her bladder. Instead, she found a tree, turned her back to him, and relieved herself. All the while he watched. 'Twas as humiliating a moment as she could ever remember experiencing.

They soon mounted and were off again. With each step away from her home, from her husband, her heart filled with despair. How long would it take before Ian learned about the raid? How many of her clansmen had died? How had these men gained entry into the keep?

A hundred unanswered questions that she could only pray she lived long enough to ask Ian. Lord, did she pity the man behind this raid. Once Ian found out, he would not rest a moment until he had her back and avenged the deaths of their people.

That thought quelled some of her trepidation. While it could be said Rose Mackintosh was the least vengeful person on God's earth, the only thing that kept her from breaking down into a heap of sobs was knowing Ian would come for her.

She began to imagine the ways in which he would procure her inevitable rescue. 'Twas doubtful he'd sneak in and whisk her away in secret. Nay, knowing her husband as she did, a full out attack was a more likely scenario.

She thought about asking her captor who he was, thought to demand an explanation and to know where they were going. But he was such a foul man, both in odor and countenance, she doubted she'd gain any reasonable or truthful answer.

More hours passed by before they stopped again. Her back ached, every muscle in her body felt afire. She was unaccustomed to such harsh treatment, to riding so hard or so long. When they stopped, her captor swung down from the mount first, then pulled her down without a care to her person or her babe.

Sharp needles of pain stung at her tired feet. She had to cling to the horse for balance lest she fall to the ground. Leaning her head against the saddle and gripping the stirrup, she prayed for strength. *God, please send Ian to me soon. Please protect me babe.*

As she prayed quietly, she heard a commotion build.

"Who goes there?" a booming voice shouted into the night air.

"Haud yer wheest, ye eejit!" came the reply. "It be me, Alec, brother to yer laird, Rutger Bowie."

Well, that answered one of her questions.

The Bowies.

Clinging to the stirrup with both hands, Rose began to pray more urgently. The Bowies were a ruthless lot of savages. While Eduard might very well be long dead, who knew what kind of man now stood as their chief? Was it possible this Rutger Bowie was even more ruthless, more evil than his predecessor? She began to pray she would never learn the answer.

For a long while, the men spoke in hushed yet angry tones, as if they did not want her to hear what their plans for her were. An overwhelming sense of trepidation fell over her. If Rutger was anything at all like Eduard, she was as good as dead.

"PARDON ME, M'LADY," CAME a voice from behind her. Willing herself not to show the deep fear coursing through her veins, she pulled her shoulders back and turned to face him.

He was not at all what she expected. Tall, with dark hair that fell just past his shoulders, big brown eyes, and a warm smile, he looked every bit a gentleman. But Rose was no fool. She knew looks could be deceiving.

"I will apologize to ye fer the men's harsh treatment of ye," he said with a formal bow. When he stood, he looked to the man who she'd been riding with since late last night. "I can assure ye that Horace will no' get the opportunity again to act like such an arse."

Horace. She burned his name into her memory. If given the chance, she would kill the man with her own hands.

Horace didn't look at all remorseful for his mistreatment. Instead, he simply rolled his eyes at Alec and walked away.

"How do ye fare, lass?" Alec asked in a low tone.

Was the man serious? "How do I fare?" she asked. "How do ye think I fare? Ye attacked our keep in the middle of the night. Ye killed I don't know how many innocent people. Ye burned our homes. And ye kidnapped me!"

Even in the pale evening light, she could see something akin to guilt flash behind his dark eyes. And for the briefest moment, she thought he resembled a child who'd just been chastised by his mother. But 'twas gone in a flash.

In one long stride, he towered over her, the guilt replaced with anger. "Ye will be comin' with me," he said as he grabbed her arm and pulled her away forcefully.

"She rides with me now!" he shouted to the men standing in his path.

Good lord, was he serious? "Wait!" she pleaded with him as she tried to keep her footing.

Her pleas to stop fell on deaf ears.

Moments later, he was tossing her into a saddle and pulling himself up behind her. Tears welled in her eyes, and damnation, she could not stop the flow. He kicked the flanks of his mount, let out a shrill whistle, and soon they were off.

They had ridden a good distance before he leaned in and whispered in her ear. "M'lady, I ken ye be with child and verra upset at yer circumstances. I do apologize for our hasty retreat, but I had no other choice."

The cold night air stung at her cheeks as they trod through fresh, wet snow. "Ye had no choice?" she asked sarcastically. "Ye could have chosen no' to attack us. Ye could have chosen no' to steal me away from hearth and home in the middle of the night. Ye could have chosen no' to kill me people."

She could feel him grow tense. "M'lady, none of those actions were me choice. Had me foolish brother listened to me, ye'd be in yer own bed right now, dreamin' peacefully."

Confusion set in as she wondered if she could believe a word he said.

"I want peace fer our clans. Me brother wants war and gold. The two yearnings oft collide. And since me brother be chief, what I want doesn't matter at all."

Was that really sincerity she heard in his tone? Or was this nothing more than a ploy to gain her acceptance and cooperation? Swiping at her cheeks, she remained silent.

"I foolishly believed I had talked me brother out of this ridiculous raid. I learned too late what his plans were. I have come to insure that ye arrive at our keep unharmed and remain that way durin; yer stay."

Openly scoffing at his choice of words, she said, "My stay? Ye make it sound as if I be on a holiday visit with family."

"I ken ye might no' believe me, but I swear to ye that I mean ye no harm. I will do everythin' within me power to keep ye safe."

"Why should I believe ye?"

"Because I am no' me brother. Unlike him, I do possess some honor and even a heart. But if ye ever tell a livin' soul I said so, I shall deny it."

TWENTY-ONE

ays passed before Ian and the men returned. It only took a glimpse of his brother for Brogan to know he was a broken man. Ian was covered with sweat and mud, his boots snow-encrusted. Dark circles had formed under his eyes. Brogan doubted the man had slept much at all, and who could blame him? His entire world had been taken from him, by faceless, nameless men.

They dismounted just inside the gate, handing their worn and haggard horses off to young stable boys.

Before Brogan could tell the men that a fine stew awaited them inside one of the tents, Ian spoke. "'Twas the Bowies." A tic had formed in his jaw, his haggard face taught with fury. *Rodrick had been right.*

"Rodrick tried to warn me an attack from them was no' a matter of *if* but when. But I did no' listen." He ground his teeth together, his muscles coiled, ready to explode.

"Are ye certain 'twas them?" Brogan asked. Why would Rodrick have warned them about the Bowies only to turn around and allow them entry to raid?

"We followed their trail all the way to Bowie lands," Ian ground out. "If it be no' the Bowies, it be someone workin' with them. Since I ken no' of any allies they might have, I am left to conclude 'twas them."

Brogan knew all about the Bowies, their reputations as ruthless savages was nearly legendary. To know his sister-by-law was in their hands made him want to retch. And kill.

It would fall upon upon Brogan to tell his brother and laird all that had transpired in his absence. 'Twas not a task he took lightly. He placed a hand on Ian's back and guided him toward a small tent he had ordered erected for Ian's return. "Come, eat and rest while I tell ye all that I ken."

Furious, Ian stood over Rodrick the Bold, debating on whether he should kill the man outright or wait to see if he recovered from his injuries. The tick that had formed in his jaw earlier now seemed to be a permanent part of his countenance. Seething, he clenched and unclenched his hands.

"He has no' awakened since the attack," Angrabraid explained as she sat on a stool next to the injured man. "He lost a good deal of blood. A fever has set in now, and I fear he might no' ever wake."

"Fer his sake, he best pray he does no'," Ian ground out.

Brogan placed a palm on his brother's shoulder. "Ian, ye need to rest. Ye'll be no good to anyone if ye die from exhaustion and lack of food."

As soon as Brogan began to divulge what he knew about the raid and the possibility a traitor was among them, Ian had stormed out of his tent in search of the wounded Rodrick the Bold.

"I do no' care about me own comfort," he said angrily. "No' while Rose is sufferin' at the hands of the Bowies."

He'd not rest until he had his wife back.

"I understand how ye feel," Brogan said. "I would feel verra much the same way were I wearin' yer boots."

His words did nothing to quash the ache in Ian's heart.

"Come, let us leave Angrabraid to her work. We have more to discuss."

Crestfallen yet ready to kill, he followed his brother back to his tent. Once they were back inside, Ian refused the offer of food, for he doubted it would stay down long. Sick with worry, his stomach felt as though he'd swallowed a bucket of dead fish. He did, however, accept the offer of whisky. He needed something to ease his worry.

"So what do we do, Ian?" Brogan asked. "Carpenters and laborers be no match fer the likes of the Bowie."

"As much as it pains me to admit it, ye're right. While I would like nothin' more than to lay siege to the Bowie keep, I can no' risk any harm comin' to Rose." *Rose.* Even saying her name was enough to make him want to break down. But he had to keep a brave face as well as a level head.

"Do we send a messenger to the Bowie, askin' him what the bloody hell his intentions are?"

Ian thought long and hard on that idea. "The only explanation fer takin' her is ransom. Nothin' else makes much sense."

'Twas Brogan's line of thinking as well. "I've asked everyone here what they ken of the Bowie clan. They all say the same thing. They be ruthless and above no crime."

Ian nodded slowly. "As evidenced by the dead bodies the whoresons left behind."

When Brogan gave him the final death toll, Ian gave a long, slow shake of his head. "Why? Why would they kill innocent people?"

Brogan had no answer. "I do no' ken, Ian. But what do we do now? Do we send a messenger or wait until they contact us?"

Ian let out a long, exasperated sigh. "I will no' wait fer them to decide. Send messengers in the morn."

"If they ride hard, they can be there and back in five days."

Ian snorted derisively. "That is if the Bowie cooperates."

Knowing what he did of the Bowie's former laird, of the sick and demented pleasure he took in torturing people, Ian could only pray their new laird was not thusly inclined.

THE FOLLOWING MORNING, WHILE THE messengers prepared to leave, Ian went to the tent where the injured were recovering. He found Leona tending to Rodrick. Seeing her offering such tender care to their traitor was enough to make his blood boil.

"Why do ye tend to him?" he asked her as he stood over the sickly Rodrick. She was wiping the man's brow with a cool cloth.

"Why do ye believe he be a traitor?" she asked without taking her eyes away from the sleeping man.

Ian glowered at her. "There be no other explanation fer how the gate was opened," Ian replied.

Looking up at him from her seat, she studied him closely for a moment. "Are ye certain Rodrick be the one who left it open?"

Ian glowered at her. "Do ye doubt me judgment?"

"Nay, m'laird," she answered softly. "But in truth, I would like to hear from the man's own lips before I judge and convict him."

"Can ye tell me any other way it happened?" he asked through gritted teeth.

"I have no answer fer that at all, m'laird. I wish I did."

Ian was just about to respond when Brogan rushed into the tent. "Ian!" he called out. "Come quick! We have word of Rose."

Racing from the tent, Ian followed his brother to the armory. Inside the newly repaired stone building, stood a group of men huddled around a long table. Something had their full attention.

Making his way through, Ian stopped dead in his tracks. There upon the table was an arrow, a parchment, and a blood-stained piece of linen.

"Gunter and Able were mannin' the walls when a man on horse appeared," Brogan explained. "He called out that he had a message fer our laird, then knocked an arrow. It landed on our gate, and these things were attached."

Numb and mute, all Ian could do was stare at the objects.

"We did no' read the parchment," Brogan said as he picked up the scroll and tried handing it to his brother. Realizing he could not tear his eyes away from the bloody cloth, Brogan broke the seal and began to read it.

"'Tis from Rutger Bowie," he said, pausing to read silently what the rest of the missive said.

"She is alive," Brogan said breathlessly, with much relief.

Ian closed his eyes, wanting with all his heart to believe 'twas the truth. A dull ache had formed in his skull days ago. There was no amount of sleep, no special herb, no amount of ale that would diminish it. The only cure for it would be to get his wife back.

"This can no' be," Brogan said. He'd read and re-read the demands three times.

"What is it?" Charles McFarland asked from his position behind Brogan.

Brogan looked up from the parchment. "Ian, ye need to read his demands."

Shaking away images of his possibly dead wife, he finally took the parchment in hand. When he finished, he slowly raised his head to look at his brother. Though they looked nothing alike, their expressions were mirror images of one another: sheer fury.

"He wants thirty-thousand groats fer Rose's return," Brogan said.

"We do no' have thirty-thousand groats," Ian replied.

"He wants it in seven days time."

"We do no' have seven days."

Brogan swallowed hard. "I've already sent word to our father."

"He does no' have that kind of coin either."

"And to Frederick."

Ian raised one angry brow. "Neither does Frederick. And neither of them can get here in time."

Not ready to give up hope just yet, Brogan looked from his brother to the men. "I need ten men mounted and ready to leave within the hour. Pack enough supplies fer a sennight."

"Where are we goin'?" someone from the back of the room asked.

"To have a wee chat with Rutger Bowie," Brogan answered over the growing din of conversation. Turning back to his brother, he said, "I will no' give up hope that she is alive and well, as his missive states. I will also no' give up hope that we can get her back."

"Ye be too furious, Ian. Ye'll serve none of us, includin' Rose, by goin' along," Brogan said firmly.

The courtyard was a flurry of activity. Food and supplies were packed and the horses readied. A young lad held the reins to Brogan's gray speckled gelding, while he adjusted the straps to the saddle and tried to get his brother to see reason.

"She is me wife, Brogan," Ian argued. "I should be the one to kill Rutger Bowie." He glared at the back of his brother's head. "And might I also remind ye that I be chief of this clan, no' ye?"

"And that is why ye should no' go. I have no intention to kill the man," he said, giving one hard tug on the leather strap. "But I can promise ye that when the time comes to take his life, I will leave the blood lettin' to ye. Fer now, we must try to convince him to agree to different terms."

Ian had no interest in *terms*. All he wanted was to get his wife back and kill Rugter for taking her. Sick with worry over her safety, as well as the babe she carried, he knew he was not thinking with the clearest of minds. "I will look a coward to everyone if I stay behind and hide."

Brogan spun around to face him. "Ye? A coward? Nay, none could ever say that about ye. If ye'll set yer anger aside, ye'll see this makes more sense. I shall ask fer a meetin' with the Bowie, no' only to gauge the man's character, but to gain knowledge of his men and the inside of his keep. And, 'twill give us time."

"Time?" Ian ground out. "Time is no' a luxury me wife possesses at the moment. Might I remind ye she is heavy with child? A child we thought we'd never be blessed with?"

"Ye need no' remind me," Brogan answered. "'Tis one more reason ye should no' go. We have never met this man. We do no' ken if he is simply a man motivated by greed or somethin' more." He regretted the last part as soon as it left his lips.

Fury blazed brightly in Ian's eyes. "Like his predecessor?" he asked, referring to Eduard Bowie.

"Aye, like his predecessor," Brogan answered ashamedly. "But I make ye this promise. If he will no' allow me to see Rose with me own eyes, I will drag the bloody bastard back here and allow ye to do to him what ye will."

Aside from having his wife back in his arms, killing Rutger Bowie was the only thing that kept him moving forward.

IAN HAD NOT SLEPT IN DAYS; his worry and grief over the raid and Rose's kidnapping plagued him. His best friend since childhood, Andrew the Red, had died protecting her.

No matter where he turned, where he looked, there was a reminder of that God-forsaken night. Huts with charred walls and no roofs, the cloying scent of blood that he swore still permeated the air. The sorrowful and forlorn faces of those left behind.

If he did not gain some semblance of control over his emotions, madness would most assuredly set in. To keep his sanity, he dedicated himself to directing the men and women in repairing the huts and the others parts of the keep that had been destroyed in the raid. The hard work distracted him a little; it was good to be working, to be doing something constructive. The clanspeople appreciated it as well. It showed them he had not given up on the future; he was still their leader, even in the worst of times.

At the end of each day, when he finally allowed himself the time to rest, 'twas to no avail. Whenever he closed his eyes, he saw his beautiful wife's face. And on those rare occasions when he managed to sleep, his dreams haunted him. In them, Rose was afraid, calling out his name, pleading with unknown enemies for mercy — never for herself, but always for her babe.

Visions haunted him of Rose being trapped in some hell-hole of a dungeon, or imprisoned in a tower, of her being tortured, set afire, hanged. No matter the dream, the outcome was the same; she and their babe would die.

Guilt was the heavy cross he bore. Guilt because he had not been there that fateful night. He had let his wife and babe down. He had let the clan down. Even Frederick and Aggie who had entrusted this most important project to him. He was no chief. He was an utter failure.

Fury was the one thing that kept him taking one breath after another, kept his heart beating, kept him upright and moving throughout the day.

Revenge was his motivation to push his men harder than he'd ever pushed before. If they were not rebuilding the lost huts, they were training for a battle that would most assuredly come. Though he did not know the day nor hour of that future battle, in his heart, he knew 'twas inevitable.

Even if Rose and their babe survived and he somehow managed to gain their freedom, he would exact his revenge on Rutger Bowie. Even if it killed him.

TWENTY-TWO

Alec Bowie badly wanted peace for his clan. But with his older brother Rutger as its chief, peace would be a long time coming.

They sat across from one another in ornately carved, padded chairs in front of the hearth in Rutger's study. 'Twas long after the midnight hour and most of the inhabitants were abed, save for a few men still drinking ale in the gathering room. Occasionally, Alec could hear laughter floating down the hallway.

So 'twas just he and his brother now, sipping fine whisky and enjoying the warmth of the fire. He knew he must tread softly when broaching nearly any topic with his brother. Rutger was by far the most impatient man he'd ever known.

"How fares our hostage?" Rutger asked with an air of indifference.

Alec took a slow sip of *uisage beatha* before answering. "As well as we could expect under the circumstances."

"I am told ye went against me orders to have her put in the dungeon."

"Aye, I did defy yer order," Alec answered coolly. "I felt it best we keep her and her babe alive, else we'll never see one sillar from Ian Mackintosh." *Or if we want to get out of this mess ye've created with our skulls still attached to our bodies and our hearts still beatin.*

Rutger drew his gaze away from the fire to study his brother. "We outnumber the McLarens ten to one," he reminded him. "They'll no' attack. He'll pay. And gladly to have his pretty wife back."

Alec knew 'twas more like five to one, but he'd felt it best not to be irksome. He had to remain on Rutger's good side in order to keep Rose Mackintosh alive.

"Ye still feel this was a mistake? Our takin' the McLaren's wife?" Downing the rest of his whisky, he set the empty cup on the table beside his chair.

"Nay." 'Twas an outright lie. One he prayed his brother was too drunk or too arrogant to see through.

"But ye still want peace?" Rugter asked.

With a nonchalant shrug, Alec said, "I no longer ken if peace is possible or just a dream of a naive young man." *But one can always hope.*

Rutger laughed loudly. "Och, brother o' mine! I'll have peace. Peace of mind and freedom from worry once Ian Mackintosh pays the ransom fer his wife!" He slapped a hand on his knee, delighted with his own jest.

Alec offered him a smile, downed the rest of his whisky and pulled himself to his feet. "While ye dream of peace of mind, I shall go seek me peace elsewhere," he jested.

Rutger laughed again. "Anyone I ken?"

"I have several to choose from. Mayhap I shall choose more than one this night?"

"Of course ye will," Rutger said with just a hint of jealousy. Alec was by far the more handsome of the two brothers. There was always a young lass all too willing to share his younger brother's bed. "But do me a favor and leave Patrice be."

Quirking a curious brow, Alec asked, "Ye have yer heart set on her then?"

"I might. Then again, I might no'."

'Twas as close an admission of admiration for any woman Alec had ever heard from his brother. "Verra well, I shall leave Patrice to ye."

With a bow, he left his brother alone in the empty room. The last thing on his mind was bedding anyone, no matter how pretty or amiable. Nay, his mind was solely focused on how he could keep Rose Mackintosh alive and his brother's head attached to its shoulders.

TWENTY-THREE

The snow had begun to melt days ago, leaving the ground a muddy mess. By the time they reached the Bowie keep, Brogan and his men were covered from head to toe in muck. He was cold, soaked to the bone, and furious.

Rutger Bowie had kept them waiting outside the gates for hours, until the sun had set and the sky grew dark, filled with more promise of rain. In war, some of the hardest fought battles were those of the mind and heart. Rutger was making them wait on purpose, as was oft done in times of battle or negotiation. He and his men built a small fire and ate in silence as they waited for word from within.

'Twas as formidable a keep as any, Brogan supposed. Three stories tall, surrounded by a moat, four towers on each corner. Large fires burned in braziers all along the upper wall. Dozens of men stood at the ready, as if an attack were imminent. 'Twas meant to instill fear into the heart of any man who even thought of such a folly. But as Brogan knew, no keep, no castle, was completely safe or fortified.

By the time the order to lower the drawbridge was given, Brogan was fighting mad. Tamping down his ire and setting his anger aside, he gave the order to proceed. He'd take half his men inside the keep with him. The others would remain a safe distance away in case Rutger decided to do something foolish, such as ignore the white banner of peace they carried.

Slowly, they crossed over the drawbridge, the sounds of clopping hooves against the wood echoing into the quiet night. The courtyard was lit with torches and more large fires. The moment he entered the large, cobblestone yard, men began spilling out like roaches. They were not here to attack, but to guard them.

Men took their horses in hand, stopping them just shy of another small wall that surrounded the fortress. They dismounted in silence, surreptitiously scanning the space. Each taking mental notes of the number of men, the size of the walls, dark spaces where light from torches did not touch.

Through a large gate in the smaller wall, they entered another courtyard. Silently, they were led up the stone steps and into the keep.

What fate awaited them inside, none of them knew. Brogan only cared about two things: setting eyes on Rose and meeting Rutger Bowie.

Brogan sat at a long table, across from the Bowie. He was unimpressed. Average in height and looks, with a well-fed belly, he was dressed regally, in a heavily brocaded jerkin over a fine silk tunic. Gold rings with ruby and emerald insets covered nearly all his fingers. A diamond encrusted pin held his plaid in place and thick chains of gold hung from his neck.

Before them lay a feast. Duck, pheasant, venison, sweetmeats, roasted vegetables, and countless flagons of wine.

At each entrance to the room, men stood in the shadows. Brogan could not make out any of their faces, but had no doubt they were there to protect their laird. He counted nine in all.

'Twas no wonder he'd kidnapped Rose. The fool spent lavishly on a lifestyle he could ill afford.

"Eat up!" Rugter said joyfully as he poured himself a cup of red wine. "'Tis no' often we receive guests such as ye."

A servant girl appeared beside Brogan, a heavy platter of venison in her hands. Brogan waved away the offering. "Had I kent we were feastin' this night, I would no' have eaten with me men. But thank ye, laird."

Indifferent, Rutger piled his own trencher with various foods and set about eating. "So to what do we owe the honor of yer visit?" he asked with a mouthful of venison.

"I think ye ken why I be here," Brogan replied before taking a sip of ale.

"The McLaren's wife," Bowie said before plopping a large fig into his mouth. "I can assure ye, she fares well. She be in one of me finest rooms above stairs."

"I should like to see fer meself how she fares."

Wiping greasy hands on the tablecloth, Rutger eyed him suspiciously for a long moment. "Ye do no' trust me?"

"Ye seem an intelligent man, Bowie. I doubt ye'd do anythin' to harm me sister-by-law. After all, she be worth a fair amount of gold, aye?"

Rutger laughed boldly, probably more than was necessary. "Callum!" he shouted over his shoulder. "Bring down the wench."

A young man, tall and slender of build, with dark hair, did his master's bidding. He bounded up the stairs and disappeared down a dark corridor.

"Have ye brought the ransom with ye?" Rutger asked, his tone hopeful.

Brogan gave a slow shake of his head. "We do no' have that kind of coin."

Anger flashed briefly behind the Bowie's eyes. "Then why are ye here?"

"To negotiate. It would take ten lifetimes fer us to obtain the vast amount ye be askin' fer. We are hopin' ye'd settle fer less."

Rutger leaned back in his chair, suspicion filling his eyes. "Less?" he asked. "How much *less*?"

"We be a verra poor clan," Brogan began. "I fear we can only gather two-hundred and thirty-seven groats."

Rutger was silent for a long while before bursting forth into a fit of laughter. "Ye had me believin' ye fer a moment, Mackintosh!" Greedily, he drank from his cup of wine before plunking it down on the table. "I ken ye have far, far more than that."

Movement from the staircase caught Brogan's eye. Rose was gradually descending the stairs with one hand on the young lad's arm. Slowly, he stood, quietly masking the relief at seeing her. As far as he could tell, she appeared uninjured. And from her angry expression, she was faring quite well.

Dressed in a fine wine colored gown, her blond locks coiled around her head, she looked as regal and ladylike as ever he'd seen her. "Rose," he said as she approached.

"Brogan," she replied through clenched teeth. Turning to glower at Rutger, she said, "I hope ye are here to tell this son of a whore where he can put his ransom demands."

Aye, she was doing verra well.

"Blast it woman!" Rutger shouted. "I told ye to keep yer mouth shut!"

"And I told ye, ye could burn in hell, Bowie!" she shouted back.

Ignoring her, Rutger turned back to speak to Brogan. "I be nearly tempted to pay yer brother to take her back!"

Brogan could not resist a chuckle as he stepped around the table to embrace his sister-by-law. "How do ye fare?"

"How do ye think I fare?" she asked. He could see the relief in her eyes, could feel it in her embrace. "How fares Ian?"

Holding her at arms length, "He be well," he answered. "He misses ye. How fares the babe?"

Rose placed a hand on her belly and smiled. "Kickin' me day and night, he is."

"Enough!" Rutger bellowed as he shot to his feet. "I fear this display of family adoration is enough to make me lose me supper."

Brogan took Rose's hand in his and gave it a gentle squeeze. With great tenderness, he helped her into a chair next to his.

"Now, let us sit and discuss the thirty-thousand groats ye're goin' to pay me fer the wench's safe return."

Rose rolled her eyes. "I've told ye and I've told ye and I've told ye, we do no' have that kind of coin!"

"And I've told ye and told ye and told ye that I do no' believe ye!" Rutger shot back.

"Careful with yer tongue, m'laird, else I set a curse upon ye so vile, so horrible, that 'twill make yer ballocks shrivel up and turn to dust," Rose seethed.

From the pained expression on Rutger Bowie's face, he believed every word she said.

Brogan leaned forward in his chair. "I would advise ye, m'laird, to quit shoutin' at me sister-by-law." His tone dripped with warning.

Waving Brogan's veiled threat away, Rutger poured another cup of wine and took a long swig. "The ransom is thirty-thousand groats. No' one siller less. And Ian will pay it unless he wants to see his witch of a wife burned at the stake."

"Ye're mad," Rose said, throwing her hands in the air. "Completely mad. And ye'll no' kill me. I be the only one who can lift the curse I've set upon ye."

Brogan was taken aback by what Rose was saying. She was the furthest thing from a witch as Rutger was from a priest. Still, he had to give her silent praise for thinking up such a ploy.

"Might I remind ye that it be by me good grace alone that ye be no' locked in the dungeon at this verra moment?"

Rose leaned forward. "'Twas by yer brother's good grace, no' yers."

His nostrils flared, his eyes turned to slits. "Were I no' assured of me reward, lass, I'd hang ye."

His sister-by-law was either too brave or too angry for her own good. Brogan stayed her next verbal assault by placing a hand on hers. Silently, he pleaded with her not to anger her captor any more than she already had.

To Rutger, he said, "M'laird, I do no' ken where ye have come up with the notion that the McLarens and Mackintoshes possess such a vast amount of gold or coin."

Quirking one brow, Rutger Bowie smiled at each of them. 'Twas the most menacing smile Brogan had ever witnessed. He waved his hand toward someone standing behind Brogan and Rose. "Ye have no idea?" he asked. "Mayhap me good friend here can explain it to ye."

A figure came around the table to stand next to Rutger. Brogan hadn't the slightest idea who the man was. But from Rose's astonished expression, she did.

"Ye!" she shouted as she jumped to her feet. Searching the table, she found a knife and grabbed it. Pointing it at the man, she seethed. "Frederick and Ian should have killed ye when they had the chance!"

Brogan stood and twisted the knife from her grasp. "Rose," he pleaded. "What has come over ye?" Whoever this man was, he had the feeling Rose knew him all too well. Standing beside the Bowie, the man appeared to be unbothered by Rose's outburst. He was dressed almost as regally as the Bowie, sans the expensive rings. There was something about the way he smiled at Rose that was more than off-putting. 'Twas downright sinister.

"I take it ye have no' yet been introduced to me friend," Rutger said. "Allow me to introduce ye to Donnel McLaren, former second in command to Mermadak McLaren. Donnel, this be Brogan Mackintosh, older brother to Ian."

Brogan knew the name from the many stories Ian and Rose had shared with him these past months. They had been under the misguided notion the man was dead.

"What stories has he been fillin' yer head with?" Rose asked Rutger. "I can assure ye this man can no' be trusted. He was just as vile as our former laird. Just as mean, just as vicious. And every bit the liar Mermadak was."

"Ye wound me, lass," Donnel said as he took a seat next to Rutger. "Ye wound me deeply."

"Bah!" she spat at him. "Ye canna wound someone without a heart."

Brogan was witnessing a side of his sister-by-law that he'd never seen before. Fury, contempt, unadulterated hatred. If she did not rein her temper in, she could very well get herself killed, and he in the process.

"Rose," Brogan said as he helped her back into her seat. "I do no' think all this anger ye be feelin' is good fer yer babe."

She shot him a look that said she thought him insane. "Neither is bein' torn away from me family. And neither is bein' in the presence of a liar and traitor. But here I am, me brother-by-law. What would ye have me do? Sing like a lark about the joys of bein' a captive?"

Taking a deep, cleansing breath, he leaned in to whisper in her ear. "If ye do no' control yerself, ye will get us all killed. I warn ye lass, do no' poke these madmen. Do no' tempt them into cuttin' yer throat. Or mine."

Understanding of sorts began to settle in. Her shoulders relaxed as tears threatened to spill from her eyes. With some of the fight gone out of her, she placed her hands in her lap and gazed at them.

"M'laird, I do no' ken the man beside ye. But I have heard many a tale about him. I do no' ken what he has told ye, but I can assure ye, 'twas probably as far from the truth as ye can get."

The Bowie cast a sideways glance at Donnel, who sat unflinching, piling a trencher with food. He stuffed a huge chunk of goose into his mouth and chewed slowly.

"Would it surprise ye to ken, Mackintosh, that I ken all about Mermadak's treasure?"

Brogan remained silent with his elbow on the table, his index finger resting on his temple.

"Would it also surprise ye to ken that *I* was one of only three other men who kent about it? The other two are dead, now. And I wish to collect me reward for all me hard work and years of dedication to Mermadak."

Rose refused to look up at the man. Brogan and the Bowie remained silent as Donnel stuffed his mouth and spoke. "'Twas *I* who collected all the gold, silver, and coin from the countless men he blackmailed over the years. I ken how much he had accumulated. I ken he hid it in his office. I ken he hid it in the mantle."

Brogan knew all about Ian and Rose finding the treasure in the mantle. 'Twas what they had been using to rebuild the keep and clan. Outwardly, he might have appeared unimpressed, but his insides were turning into knots.

"I also happen to ken 'twas Rose and Ian who stumbled upon it by accident. They took what by rights belonged to me and I want it back."

Bloody hell! This was not going as he had planned or even hoped. A dozen questions burned and begged to be asked, but now was not the time. "I do no' ken from where ye gained yer information," Brogan said as he leaned back in his chair. "But it be wrong."

Undeterred, Donnel took a long pull of wine. "Would it surprise ye to learn I have a spy amongst yer people?"

"Nay," Brogan answered with a shrug of indifference. "We ken all about yer spy. He was grievously wounded the night the Bowie's attacked.

He still has no' awakened, and might never wake."

Donnel threw his head back and laughed. "Och! Ye think Rodrick the Bold be me spy?"

The question sent a chill down Brogan's spine. How did he know he was referring to Rodrick? And if Rodrick was not the spy, then who was?

His question was answered a moment later when Charles McFarland stepped from the shadows.

Brogan was able to hide his contempt, anger and surprise far better than Rose. She gasped as her hands went to her mouth in horror.

"Nay!" she whispered. "No' ye, Charles." She was far too stunned to utter much more.

Donnel and Rutger laughed boisterously at their astonishment. But the expression on Charles's face? 'Twas not the look of a man proud of his actions. Nay, he looked positively ashamed.

"'Tis amazin'," Donnel said as the laughter subsided. "The loyalty one can buy with a few pieces of gold."

Brogan shot an angry glare at Donnel. "That be the funny thing about Charles's kind of loyalty. It can be bought again and again."

Charles's face burned a deep red and he could not maintain eye contact with either Rose or Brogan. Donnel and Rutger either did not understand or they chose to ignore Brogan's words of wisdom.

"And his isn't the only loyalty we own," Rutger said. "Ye have more than one traitor amongst ye, Mackintosh."

More than one? There would be time to sort that out later. For now, he must do everything he could to insure Rose's safety.

"Be that as it may," Brogan said cautiously. "There is much we need to discuss."

"Indeed we do!" Rutger exclaimed happily. Raising his cup to Donnel, he said, "To ransoms!"

After saying goodbye to Brogan, Rose returned to her room. With a heavy heart, she removed her dress and slipped back into her own chemise. She wanted nothing Rutger Bowie had to offer, least of all dresses.

Wadding the ensemble up, she tossed it into the hallway and slammed the door shut. She'd only worn the dress because she wanted to show her brother-by-law that she was faring far better than she in truth was.

The room was well appointed but frigidly cold, no matter how high she stoked the fire. She supposed 'twas more her current condition and circumstance that kept her bone-cold all the day long. Grabbing the iron, she poked at the fire, bringing it to high flames before tossing another small log onto it.

With a sigh of resignation, she crawled back into the bed and pulled the heavy blankets up to her chin.

Her thoughts were never far from Ian. She knew beyond a shadow of a doubt that he was miserable with worry. Hopefully, Brogan would report back to him that she was hale and hearty, filled with piss and vinegar, and holding her own against Rutger Bowie. 'Twas all a lie of course, but no one need know that but her.

What she would not give at the moment to be back in the waddle and daub hut, in her own bed, with Ian sleeping beside her. His strong, warm arms wrapped around her in a protective embrace. His hot breath caressing her skin. Or watching him as he pressed a kiss to her growing belly and hearing him speak to their unborn babe.

Tears streamed down her cheeks, dripping onto her pillow. She imagined she had cried an ocean of tears since that awful, dark ugly night of the attack. She reckoned she'd not stop crying until this ordeal was over.

Daily, continually, and fervently, she prayed she would live long enough to give birth to their child. After that, she cared not what happened to her, as long as her babe was healthy. She also prayed her stubborn husband would not do anything foolish that would keep him from watching their babe grow and thrive and live a good long life.

She supposed it odd that she did not pray for a means of escape or rescue. All she wanted was her wee babe to live, as well as her husband. There was nothing more she could ask God for. 'Twas all she wanted.

Brogan and his men returned to the McLaren keep as quickly as they could. They made the normally three-day ride in two.

He returned to a brother on the verge of madness.

'Twas just before the evening meal when he entered his brother's tent. A bed sat in one corner, an empty brazier in the center. A long table filled with scrolls and maps took up the entire eastern wall of the small tent.

He took note of the dark circles that had formed under Ian's eyes. The man had not slept in days.

Hope alight in his dark blue eyes, Ian jumped to his feet when he saw Brogan. "Well?" he asked as he made his way around the table. "Do ye have her?"

Brogan let loose a heavy sigh. "Nay brother, I do no'."

Ian's shoulders fell along with the hopeful expression.

Searching the room for a stool, Brogan found one under a pile of dirty clothes. Grabbing one of the legs, he righted it, kicked clear a space with the toe of his boot, and sat down.

"Ye'll want to sit when I tell what I have learned."

Ian retrieved the chair from behind his desk and sat in front of his brother.

"I saw Rose and she is well."

Ian's spirits lifted with the news. His eyes filled with hope as well as relief. He ran a hand through his dirty hair and let out the breath he'd been holding. "Thank God!"

"She was as mad as a swarm of hornets," Brogan said with a smile. "I think Rutger Bowie is a wee bit afraid of her."

Ian attempted to shake the confusion from his mind. "Afraid of her? She be a slip of a woman. Defenseless and unarmed and with child."

"I take it then ye've never met yer wife?"

Ian could not help smiling, just a little bit. He should have known his wife would not take lightly to being kidnapped.

"Ian, yer wife may be a wee woman. But I do no' fear fer her safety as much as before. She is well, yer babe is well, and she is drivin' Rutger Bowie to madness."

"I sometimes forget just how strong me wife is," Ian admitted. "'Tis only me worry over her safety and that of our child that makes me half-mad."

Brogan chuckled. "I fear I would feel much the same way," he admitted. "Somehow, she has managed to convince Rutger Bowie that she is a witch and has cast a spell upon him. He takes her verbal insults, her fury out of sheer fear she speaks the truth. Ye should be verra proud of yer wife."

The realization that Rose was well began to settle in. And hearing she was making Rutger Bowie's life a living hell made him laugh. "I should have kent it," Ian said as he rubbed his face with the palms of his hands. "Rose is no' a woman to lie down weakly. Nay, she would fight tooth and nail to keep herself and our babe safe."

Seeing his brother so relieved and nearly happy, Brogan kept his worries to himself. Hopefully, Rose would not push Rutger too hard or too far.

"There is more," Brogan said. "Much more that ye need to ken."

Pushing himself to his feet, Ian searched his desk for a flagon of ale. "What else have ye learned?" he asked. Finding two semi-clean cups, he asked, "Would ye like some ale?"

Brogan shook his head. "Nay, I have cider," he said, pulling a flagon from his belt.

"I apologize fer me momentary lapse of memory," Ian said. Brogan had given up drink a year ago, after falling into the abyss of drunkenness for two solid years after his wife's death. Ian knew not all the details, only that it had been a long and difficult journey.

"Yer old friend, Donnel McLaren, is alive and well."

Ian grimaced at hearing that old and familiar name.

"He kens all about the treasure, Ian. Apparently he helped amass it." Brogan explained in detail his meeting with the Bowie and his new friend, Donnel McLaren. When he finished, he said, "I fear we can no longer make the Bowie believe we are penniless."

The thought sickened Ian. The treasure was rightfully Aggie's, not his. He could no more ask her to hand over thirty-thousand groats than he could ask a horse to give birth to a cow. "I can no' ask Aggie fer the ransom," he said.

"I ken that. Which is why I told Rutger most of the money has already been spent. I was able to barter him down to ten-thousand groats."

Ian scoffed. "We do no' have five hundred groats to all our names," Ian reminded him. "Why in the bloody hell did ye promise ten-thousand?" Once again he was overcome by anger. Had his brother lost his mind?

"To buy us time. I explained how most of the coin had been spent. I also explained the rest of it was on Mackintosh lands. I gained us four more weeks, Ian. Our father and his warriors should be here by then."

"Ye plan to attack?" Ian asked, appalled at the idea. "We can no' risk Rose's life! I will no' do it until she's safe! There has to be another way."

"Well, if ye think of another way, let me ken, because I have been unable to come up with anythin'."

Ian sat deflated. One moment Brogan filled him with hope, only to tear it to shreds the next.

"I ken how ye be hurtin', Ian. Mayhap between now and then we can come up with a plan to get yer wife back."

Ian looked somewhat hopeful. He had been too dazed to make plans since he'd returned to McLaren lands. It was time to start thinking like a leader again. "Did ye learn anythin' else?"

"Rodrick the Bold is no' our traitor," Brogan said as he sipped on cider.

Ian paused, taken aback by that bit of news. "Are ye certain?"

"Aye, I am," Brogan responded. "He be no' one of the traitors, of that, I am certain."

"Traitors?" Ian asked. 'Twas bad enough to think there was one traitor amongst them.

"Aye, there be two." He took another sip of cider. "Charles McFarland is our first."

Ian's eyes bulged in their sockets. "Nay!" The idea was preposterous.

"I saw him with me own eyes," Brogan told him, the anger still raw and real. "At the Bowie keep."

Ian could have fallen over with the slightest breeze. "He lied to us. Lied about Rodrick no' bein' there when he woke to the alarms that night."

"They found Rodrick between the armory and the wall. Mayhap Rodrick tried to stop Charles and Charles tried to kill him?"

Ian considered that for a moment. "Chances are better that Charles came upon him from behind. I can no' see him woundin', let alone killin' Rodrick otherwise."

"Has Rodrick awakened yet?" Brogan asked.

"Nay, but his fevers finally broke this morn," Ian informed him. "Angrabraid is hopeful he will recover."

Brogan was relieved to hear it. "But who could the other traitor be?"

"I do no' ken. I would guess it to be someone who comes and goes unnoticed. Someone we'd least expect." A thought formed in the back of his mind then. "Someone who disappears fer days at a time. Someone who is able to get in and out of the keep without suspicion." He did no' like where his mind was taking him, but take him there it did.

Brogan studied him closely for a moment, trying to ascertain who Ian suspected. "Who?" he asked in a low tone.

"Bloody hell!" Ian ground out. Jumping to his feet, he slammed his cup onto his desk and stormed out of the tent.

Brogan was fast on his heels.

Ian stormed into the large tent. He found her just where he knew he would, hovering over Rodrick the Bold. In the dim light of the tent, her resemblance to Rose was quite remarkable. His wife had considered this woman a friend, which made the betrayal all the harder to swallow.

Seething with fury, he crossed the tent in a few short strides. Her eyes grew wide with puzzlement as he approached. "M'laird?"

Grabbing an arm, he pulled her to her feet. "With me. *Now*."

Brogan watched in stunned horror as Ian pulled the confused and terrified Leona Macdowall outside. "Ian!" he called out after his brother. "What are ye doin'?"

Ian did not utter a single word. He all but dragged Leona across the yard and into the armory. "Out!" he barked a command. "Everyone out!"

Men scrambled to get out of their laird's way as he shoved Leona into a chair. The angry tick in his jaw returned with a vengeance as he paced back and forth. 'Twas all he could do to keep from wrapping his hands around her throat and squeezing the life right out of her.

Under normal circumstances he might not have been so bloody furious. But these were far from normal times. Brogan entered the armory, awash in uncertainty. Was Leona the other betrayer? Was she truly one of Donnel's spies? He found it exceedingly unlikely. Still, he would never have thought Charles a traitor either. Keeping his thoughts and opinions to himself, he stood back a ways and watched his brother and the accused carefully.

Rubbing the arm he'd used to yank her halfway across the keep, Leona sat perplexed and afraid. "M'laird, why are ye so angry? What have I done to upset ye so?"

Ian came to a dead stop and spun around. He fought for the right words. "How be yer friends, Rutger and Donnel?"

The brothers watched as confusion settled over her face. "Who?"

"Rutger Bowie and Donnel McLaren," Ian said through gritted teeth. "The men who hired ye to spy on me clan. The men who paid ye to open the gates of the keep the night of the raid."

She sat in abject horror, appalled he would think her capable of such an act. "I be no traitor," she exclaimed. "I do no' ken who those men are nor why ye'd even think such a thing of me!"

Ian leaned in, his face just inches away from hers. Staring into her eyes, he said, "Ye be verra good at portrayin' an innocent lass."

Her lips drew into a hard line, her nostrils flared, her eyes blazed with anger. "I do no' ken where ye have gained such a foolish notion. Rose is me friend. I would never betray her in such a manner. Who has told ye these lies about me?"

Standing to his full height, he crossed his arms over his chest. "Brogan has learned of two traitors amongst us. Charles McFarland is one of them."

Her eyes grew wide with stunned surprise. "Charles? A traitor?" She gave a slight shake of her head in the hope that the entire conversation would somehow begin to make sense.

"Aye, Charles is a traitor. Brogan saw him with his own eyes just two days past at the Bowie keep. We now ken that Rodrick was no' the traitor."

"I— " she was at a loss for words. "Is Charles the one who accuses me? If so, he is a liar!"

Ian gave a slow shake of his head. "Nay, Charles does no' accuse ye. I do."

She jumped to her feet, her hands drawn into tight fists. "On what grounds?" she demanded.

Forcefully, he pushed her back into the chair. "There be no one else among us who disappears fer days at a time, who leaves without so much as a word to anyone on where she is goin'," he said. "Ye disappear and reappear repeatedly."

Dumbfounded, she shook her head slowly. "On that fact and that fact alone ye accuse me?"

"Nay," he said. "Ye were the only one who felt certain Rodrick was no' our traitor. Why is that?"

Her shoulders fell ever so slightly. Pulling her gaze away from Ian, she looked instead at the floor.

"I ask ye again why ye felt so certain Rodrick was no' our traitor."

Silence stretched on for a long while before she answered. Finally, she looked up at him with damp eyes. "He was too nice a person to be a traitor or a spy."

'Twas Ian's turn to look stunned. "Ye think Rodrick the Bold *nice*?" 'Twould have been the last description Ian would have used when speaking of Rodrick. He was a hard, unyielding man.

"Aye, I do."

"I find that verra difficult to believe," he challenged her.

"Of all the people here, he be the only one besides Rose who did no' think me a witch or bedeviled. He never called me Leona Two-Eyes, or Leona the Witch, or that bedeviled Leona Macdowall. He was nice to me when no one else was."

The pain and hurt was plainly evidenced in her tear-filled eyes, the humiliation painted on her face and in her tone. Ian had wounded her deeply.

"Ye would no' understand that, m'laird, fer none have ever looked down upon ye before. Ye do no' ken what it be like to go the whole of yer life with people whisperin' harsh words behind yer back or to yer face." She wiped away her tears on the sleeve of her wool dress.

Guilt began to settle in. Either she was a very good actress or she was completely innocent. "Where do ye go when ye disappear?" he asked. This time, there was far less venom in his tone.

"'Tis personal and private," she replied.

"Lass, under our current circumstance, there be nothin' personal or private left. I must know."

Sniffling and wiping away more tears, she took in a deep, cleansing breath. "People are no' always nice to me. So I walk. Sometimes I walk fer miles, until I find a peaceful place. Then I sit and think."

Ian quirked a curious brow. "Sit and think?"

"Aye. Among other things," she answered reluctantly.

"Such as?"

Realizing he would not relent, she let out a sigh of resignation. "I write sonnets and such."

Ian cast a confused glance at his brother. Brogan shrugged as if to say it made no sense to him either. Turning back to Leona, Ian asked, "Sonnets?"

"Aye, sonnets and poems and such. I write me feelin's down in a journal I have."

Ian noticed she placed a protective hand on the large pouch draped over the belt of her dress. "Be yer journal in yer pouch?"

She answered with a nod.

"May I see it?"

"Nay, m'laird. It be me private thoughts and such. I would prefer no' to share them with anyone."

As much as he was beginning to doubt his previous suspicions, he needed to know, without a doubt, that she spoke nothing but the truth. "Lass, I swear to ye that I'll no' share yer journal with anyone. I need to see it."

With a great deal of hesitation and humiliation, she slowly untied the pouch. Reaching inside, she withdrew a small, leather-bound book and held it to her chest. "Ye promise ye'll no' tell anyone?"

"I do so promise, lass."

Reluctantly, she handed her journal over to him. Carefully, Ian opened it and began to thumb through. In tiny, delicate handwriting were poems and sonnets and journal entries, just as she had said. One entry caught his attention only because of a recognizable name. 'Twas dated four weeks ago.

I can add one more person to the short list of people who are nice to me. Brogan Mackintosh. He spotted me carrying a heavy bundle of firewood across the yard today and insisted on helping me. I be certain 'twas just a simple, friendly gesture on his part, but it meant the world to me. 'Tis not often anyone goes out of their way to be kind. On those rare occasions, I am often wary of such kind acts, for they are so very rare. me first inclination is to think 'are they being nice only to gain me trust for nefarious reasons.' It has happened to me in the past, where a person only pretended to be kind as some cruel jest, to make me look a fool later.

But I do no' think Brogan would behave in such a manner.

Ian immediately felt sorry for the young woman. And more than just a little guilty for accusing her and then forcing her to share something so personal. Slowly, he closed the book and handed it back to her.

"Leona, I have no words at the moment to express how sorry I am."

With an indifferent shrug, she returned her journal to her pouch. "Ye are wrought with worry over Rose, m'laird. There be traitors among us and ye would no' be a good laird or chief if ye did no' try to find out who the traitor be."

He could not understand how she was able to forgive him so easily. "I believe me wife has a verra good friend in ye, Leona."

"'Tis I who have a good friend in her. She is me only friend."

That knowledge made him feel a good deal of compassion toward her. What a hard life she must have lived thus far. He had heard the names people called her but had never stepped in to intervene on her behalf. Why? He had no good reason, but he knew 'twas a shameful way to treat another person. Especially when his wife held her in such high esteem.

"Leona, in the future, if ye feel the need to *walk,* please, tell me or Brogan, so we will no' worry over yer safety."

She eyed him suspiciously for a long moment. "Why should ye care about me safety? No one else does."

"That, lass, is no longer the case. I can assure ye that I do care. And once we get Rose back, there will be changes taking place around here. Many changes."

She was afraid to ask him what he meant.

RODRICK THE BOLD WOKE LATE THE following day. And he was angry enough to bite his own sword in half.

Leona offered him her warmest smile. "'Tis good to see ye back amongst the livin'."

When he struggled to sit up in the bed, Leona pushed him back down. "Ye be no' ready just yet to leave yer bed, Rodrick."

"We were under attack," he muttered. "We need to get word to Ian."

"The attack is over, Ian has returned, and ye need to lie back down," Leona told him.

Rubbing his eyes with his palms, he kicked at the covers. "I need to speak to Ian at once," he demanded.

Leona rolled her eyes at him and sighed. "Verra well. If I fetch Ian fer ye, will ye promise to stay abed until Angrabraid gives ye permission to leave it?"

Angrily he said, "I do no' need that auld woman's permission to do anythin'! I be a grown man fer the sake of Christ and I *have* to speak to Ian at once!"

"Ye be lucky Angrabraid is no' in this tent right now, or she'd box yer ears. Lie. Down!"

Weak from his injuries and days abed, he gave up and fell back against the pillow.

"Thank ye," Leona said. "Now, I shall fetch Ian fer ye." With a warm smile, she left the tent and returned a short time later with Ian.

"Thank God, ye've returned!" Rodrick exclaimed. "Charles, he be a traitor!"

Ian quirked a brow. "Tell me somethin' I do no' ken."

Puzzled, Rodrick stared up at him in disbelief.

"Ye've been asleep fer more than three weeks, Rodrick. Ye're verra lucky to be alive."

"No thanks to that son of a whore, Charles McFarland!"

Ian nodded his agreement as he pulled up a chair. For the next hour, he relayed everything he knew to Rodrick, who gratefully listened intently and quietly until he was finished.

"Now, ye tell me, what do ye remember the night of the raid?" Ian asked.

Rodrick sighed before answering. "I was just about asleep when I heard Charles creep from his bed. At first, I thought he was just sneakin' out to meet that widow woman, Bealraigh."

Ian hadn't been privy to that bit of information. "Bealraigh McLaren?" he asked.

"Aye. He'd been seein' her fer a few weeks, stealin' over to her hut whenever he could." He was growing tired again and was fighting to remain awake. Sensing his distress, Leona offered him a drink, lifting his head while he sipped from the cup. "Thank ye, lass."

She smiled at him and returned to the stool not far from his bed. Ian was beginning to wonder if the lass did not have feelings for the man, so attentive she was in her care for him.

"I did no' ken about Bealraigh," Ian admitted. He was not sure if she was among the living or dead and made a mental note to ask Brogan later. "What happened after he left?"

"I was just about asleep again, when I heard a 'thump'. Ye ken that sound as well as I," he told him.

"The sound of a dead man fallin' to the ground," Ian replied with a nod of understanding.

"Aye. *That* sound," Rodrick told him. "I immediately threw on me trews, grabbed me sword, and went outside. 'Twas verra late, ye ken. Verra dark, with only a wanin' moon. But even in the darkness, I could see the men on the wall were missin'. Then I heard the sound of the gate openin', verra slow like. I could hear horses on the other side." His anger began to return. With his lips pressed into a hard line, his forehead drawn into a hard knot, he went on to recount what had happened that night.

"I was just about to shout out fer help, when I was hit from behind. As I spun around, I felt the sword pierce me gut and I fell to me knees. Bloody hell it hurt!" He drew his hands into fists and slammed them hard onto the bed. "'Twas then I saw Charles McFarland standin' over me. I tried to get up to kill him, but he stepped away before me sword could hit him. I fell face first into the dirt, unable to move. Someone hit the back of me head again, but I do no' ken who. All I could do was lay there and watch as the bastards came through the gate before I passed out."

Ian could sense the guilt Rodrick felt. "Ye were one against dozens, Rodrick."

"Had he no' gutted me," he argued, "we could have saved more lives." As he tried to adjust himself in the bed, a bolt of pain shot through his side. He winced and immediately, Leona was at his side.

"Angrabraid left somethin' in case yer pain is too much to bear," she said as she began pouring a powdery substance into a cup of water.

"Bah!" Rodrick groused. "I do no' need nor do I want any of *that*."

Exasperated, Leona set the concoction on the table and placed her hands on her hips. "Well, what *do* ye want?"

"Besides Charles McFarland's head on a pike sittin' next to Rutger Bowie's?" he lashed out.

Leona's expression changed rapidly, looking slightly hurt at his outburst.

Ian did his best to lift her spirits. "Have ye ever been around a Highlander recoverin' from a battle wound before, lass?" he asked.

Leona gave a slight shake of her head. "Nay, m'laird."

"He will grumble and grouse and complain he does no' need a lick of help. He will sometimes lash out at those he cares about who are only tryin' to help him. But once he begins to feel better, his mood will change."

Rodrick grunted. "There be nothin' wrong with me mood that a little blood-lettin' and revenge will no' cure."

Ian leaned in to whisper into the man's ear. "Be kind to Leona. She has rarely left yer side, has tended to yer wounds, fretted when ye were feverish."

Duly chastised and more than a bit embarrassed, Rodrick shrugged.

"Be kind to her or I'll gut ye again and leave ye to rot."

TWENTY-FOUR

The only experience Alec Bowie had with women was through those he purchased to slake his lust. Growing up, he had spent very little time with his mother. The relationship she and his father shared had been tumultuous at best. They fought more than the Scots did with the English. He'd been primarily raised by his father, while seeing his mother only a few times a year.

As a very young boy, he had missed her a great deal. But as time went on, he found himself missing her less and less. Still, he did love her, as much as any boy could, he supposed.

Then she up and died on him when he was twelve years old and fostering with the MacGregor clan. The last time he'd seen her, he was all but nine, when she tearfully bid him goodbye the day he left for his new home with his foster family.

As a lad, he'd been far more interested in warring than in whoring. He believed his mother's death had very little affect on him. Still believed it to this day. He'd been surrounded by good people, had learned a great deal about battles and wars, had honed his skills with all manner of weapons, and had also learned about history and science.

At the age of fourteen, his father sent him to an Italian monastery in order to finish his education. His interest in women blossomed when he entered his first whorehouse in Rome when he was seventeen.

Were he a more intelligent and less self-indulgent man, he might have thought to pay more attention to the women who had entered his life over the years. He might have thought to glean a little insight into the tender feelings of women in general.

Such knowledge would certainly have been quite useful. Especially on this rainy afternoon, a day after Brogan Mackintosh's visit, when he stopped to check on his brother's hostage.

The young woman was a crying, sobbing mess. He could not recollect ever seeing a woman in such a state before, save for the times his mother and father fought.

He'd dared ask the poor creature what was wrong.

"What do ye think is wrong?" she cried into a square of linen.

He had no idea how to safely respond.

She had a long list of what ailed her and she saw no problem sharing her woes with him.

"I am a prisoner here, by yer brother's hand. me belly grows bigger each day as me time draws nearer, and I be no closer to getting home as I was yesterday or the day before. I be tired and lonely and missing me husband. Yer brother is an arrogant, witless fool!"

Silently he agreed with her.

"And *ye!* Ye pretend to care fer me safety and comfort, but all the while ye conspire with yer brother to keep me here! There is no way me husband can come up with the ransom in time to meet yer brother's demands. I am sure to die here. Alone and bereft, and fer what purpose? Greed!"

There was no way for her to know his own secrets, his plans to help procure her release. He certainly could not share those plans with her. Only three other men knew them. If Rutger so much as heard the tiniest whisper of what Alec wanted to do, they'd all be dead. 'Twas for her own safety that he not divulge anything to her. At least not yet.

"M'lady, I understand yer anguish," he began as he stepped forward. In a low hushed tone, he said, "I will do everythin' within me power to see that no harm comes to ye or yer babe." 'Twas the same promise he had made to her the night he'd taken her away from his brother's men and into his own charge.

"How?" she asked as more desperate tears streamed down her cheeks.

Leaning in to whisper in a low, hushed tone, he said, "Trust me."

She searched his eyes for some inkling, some sign that she should indeed trust him.

Alec knew 'twas a delicate line he now walked, wanting to keep this poor woman from going mad, and at the same time, keeping his plans safely guarded. A long moment passed between them before she collapsed into his arms.

Between sobs, she cried, "I want to go home. *Now.* I want to kill yer brother and Donnel McLaren with me bare hands. I want to run a dirk through each of the hearts of the men who destroyed me home and killed me people."

Stunned, he stood with her head pressed against his chest, and knew not what he should do or say. He tensed, his arms hanging at his sides, feeling more than just a bit befuddled. Slowly, some instinct he hadn't realized he possessed until then made him draw his arms around her in comfort. "Wheest now, lass. Ye'll be home before ye ken it."

Pulling away ever so slightly, she once again searched his eyes. "I do no' ken why, but I believe ye."

A warm smile crossed his face. "I be glad to hear it."

"But I swear to ye, if I learn ye played me false, Alec Bowie, I shall kill ye with me bare hands."

Somehow, he did not doubt a word she said.

So as not to draw attention to himself, Alec enlisted the help of three men he trusted beyond all others to visit Rose Mackintosh each day: Keyth, Gylys, and Dougal Bowie. Related distantly to one another, their families had been a part of the Bowie clan for five generations.

The meetings were held in secret, sometimes after the midnight hour. Since Alec's room was three doors down from hers, it was an easy enough feat to visit Rose.

However, he knew his brother had spies in every dark and shadowy corner of the keep and beyond. On guard at all times, he could not take too many chances of being seen entering or leaving her room.

Ten days had passed since Brogan Mackintosh visited. Ten very long days in which these four men did their best to make their captive feel better and to gain her trust. Without it, anything they might attempt in the future would most assuredly fail.

'Twas Alec's turn to visit with Rose. 'Twas long after the midnight hour, that time of night when the sky was at its darkest. Tonight, without any moon, and heavy rain clouds overhead, the hallways seemed even darker, far more ominous and mysterious.

When he entered Rose's room, he expected she would be fast asleep. Prepared only to make a cursory inspection and leave quickly, he instead found her at the only window in her room. Wrapped in a blanket she stood staring out at something only she could see.

She cast him a furtive glance over her shoulder before turning back to the blackness without. According to Gylys, she had seemed in good spirits earlier that morn. But now? Something bleak and untoward seemed to hang in the air.

"M'lady," he said as he slowly shut the door behind him. "Are ye well?" By now he had learned even the most innocuous seeming inquiries into her well-being brought forth a litany of either woes or curses. This night, however, he was met with neither.

"I have been havin' pains off and on all day," she informed him bleakly. "'Tis far too early to be experiencin' them."

Although he'd never been around an expectant woman, he was at least knowledgable enough to know this was cause for concern.

"I shall fetch a midwife to ye at once," he said.

"Do no' bother," she told him. "'Twill no' do any good."

Puzzled, he stepped forward in order to see her more clearly. "What do ye mean?"

One lonesome tear trailed down her cheek. "'Tis a miracle that I am as far along as I am. I was never able to carry beyond me third month. This time, 'twas different. Better. A stronger babe I carried." Wiping her cheeks on the blanket, she gave a shrug of indifference. "But I fear all the stress and worry of bein' here, of bein' so far from home…" She paused to take a steadying breath. "I be losin' me babe."

At once, he felt as though he'd been kicked in the gut by an angry mule. Anger crept in and 'twas all he could do not to seek out his brother and slice his throat. If this babe died, and worse yet if Rose did not survive, he knew beyond any doubt that the vengeance Ian Mackintosh would seek out would mean the end of his clan. There would not be a Bowie standing once he was done.

It might not happen immediately, but it would happen. Ian would call on his vast number of allies as well as his family, and in a matter of weeks, he would unleash a hell unlike anything the Bowie's had ever seen.

"I will no' allow ye to lose this babe, m'lady," he told her.

Without a clear idea of how exactly he could keep that promise, he left the room as swiftly and quietly as he had entered. Immediately, he went in search of the only three men he knew he could count on.

TWENTY-FIVE

His brother hadn't been home from the Bowie keep a full fortnight when another messenger arrived. As had been done the last time, the message was left via an arrow to the gate.

Just when he'd begun to feel better about his wife being held captive, just when he was able to sleep at night when he'd let the satisfaction of work well- done satisfy at least his basic needs, his world was once again turned upside down.

Ian stood now at the table in the armory, surrounded by his brother and men, and read Rutger Bowie's missive a third time.

I detest being the bearer of bad news. But late last eve, yer wife gave birth. The wee lad is faring as well as can be expected considering how small he is. Unfortunately, your wife did not survive the birthing. I submit to ye the clothing she wore whilst giving birth to your son as evidence.

I have enlisted the help of one of our womenfolk to act as wet-nurse for the boy. However, if ye continue to delay the payment of the ransom, I shall order the child not to be fed or cared for.

I am certain ye do not wish to be responsible for losing another life that is so precious to you. I expect the full ransom of ten-thousand groats to be paid on -or before- the first of April.

Rutger Bowie
Chief of Clan Bowie

Ian refused to believe it, even for a moment. *I would ken it in me own heart if she were dead.*

Brogan took the missive from his hands and read it. Horrified, he looked at his brother. He half expected him to fall apart, to fall to his knees with grief. Instead, Ian looked mad enough to bite his sword in half.

He waited in silence, closely watching to see what Ian would do or say next.

Deafening silence filled the space and seemed to stretch on interminably. Finally, Ian took in a deep breath and faced his brother.

"I refuse to believe me wife is dead," he told his brother.

"Ye do no' believe what the missive says?" Brogan asked.

Ian gritted his teeth. "Nay, I do no'. This is nothin' more than his way of tryin' to make me mad with grief, to do somethin' stupid. But I do believe we do no' have much time before he kills her."

Brogan had to agree that 'twas a strong possibility and he could only pray his brother was right.

"Brogan, I need messengers sent to the Mactavishes, the MacDougalls, the Grahams, and McDunnah. I need as many fightin' men as they can spare and I need them quickly."

The one thing Brogan had hoped to avoid was a battle against the Bowies. There would be no stopping it now, and he could not blame his brother for the call to arms. Knowing now was not the time to argue, he asked, "Have ye a plan?"

Ian looked at him as if he'd gone mad. "We will lay siege to the Bowie keep."

"And yer wife? What of her?"

"I fear we no longer have the luxury of waitin' fer the right time to perfect a rescue. If we do no' act now, 'twill be too late."

Brogan's meeting with the Bowie had been brief. Still, he was able to gain some sense of what kind of man they were dealing with. As much as he was loathe to admit it, his brother was probably right. The Bowie was a most dangerous man, for he was motivated entirely by greed.

With a nod, Brogan stepped away from the table and gathered what was left of their men.

As soon as the messengers left, Ian went to his tent. The fury he'd been tamping down for days finally erupted. A low, deep growl grew from deep within, building until he could no longer suppress it. Grabbing the table he used as his desk, he upended it, scattering the contents hither and yon.

He tossed chairs and stools against the fabric walls, picked up his bed and heaved it with all his might. It landed upside down on top of the table. The trunks that were stacked neatly near the bed, he kicked and clawed at before heaving them as well. The contents spilled out and tumbled to the floor.

Covered in sweat, his chest heaving more from heartbreak than exertion, he scanned the room for something else to destroy. 'Twas then he caught sight of something lying on the floor.

'Twas a wee bonnet that rested atop one of the sleeping gowns Rose had made for their babe. In nearly sent him to his knees.

Rose was his life, his soul, his heart. He would stop at nothing until he had her and their babe back.

The decision to lay siege to the keep was one of the most difficult decisions he had ever made. Rutger's missive was nothing more than a lie. He was as certain of that as he was the sun would rise on the morrow.

He was also certain Rutger Bowie was delusional. Much like his predecessor, he enjoyed toying with a person's mind and emotions. The kidnapping, the threats, the letter were all nothing more than a game. Oh, he had no doubt the man was motivated by greed. But there was much more at play here than avarice. Much more.

Rutger might believe he had the upper hand simply because he was in possession of the one thing Ian loved and valued above all else. To a certain extent, that was true.

But Ian had one thing Rutger didn't. Ian had allies.

Alone, the Mackintoshes were a mighty force. But add the Grahams and McDunnahs to their forces? They would be unstoppable.

Ian knew the Bowie's had no allies, at least not any who might be mad or stupid enough to go up against his.

Rutger would not harm Rose. He needed her alive. He needed the babe alive as well. The man might be mad, but Ian doubted he was mad enough to harm Rose. If he did, there was no way on God's earth Ian would give him a groat.

Ian had been too beset with worry half the time to get a true grasp on the situation. After he read the missive, he knew he had to stop worrying and start thinking. He needed to think like a Mackintosh. Like a laird and chief.

Rutger Bowie may have had the upper hand, but now? Oh, the tides of fortune were about to turn for the Bowie. And they'd turn now to Ian's favor.

THE FOLLOWING TWO DAYS WERE spent in preparation of battle. From dawn to dusk, he and his men trained hard and without restraint. The McLarens, the carpenters and laborers, all trained together, side by side with the Mackintosh men. They were just as determined as he to get their mistress back.

Weeks ago, when the Bowie's first attacked, it set the clan in turmoil. But now? Now that he had announced the attack on the Bowie keep, made his promise to get his wife back, his people had a mission. A purpose. And it was far bigger than simply building the McLaren keep. Along with it was the strong desire to return the McLaren clan to its former glory.

Generations ago, the McLarens were as strong a fighting force as any. They possessed hundreds of warriors. Warriors who protected their lands, their people, with a fierceness that resembled the Mackintoshes.

It took one man, Mermadak McLaren, to run it all into the ground. One man who all but destroyed it through greed and malice.

The warriors had left in droves. Unable and unwilling to be led by such a cold, brutal man. Their numbers dwindled to the point there was nothing left but old men and women, widows, and a handful of children.

For months, Ian fought an inner battle, disgusted with the thought of being *The* McLaren. He was a Mackintosh for the sake of Christ. Not some lowly, lazy, McLaren.

But now? At seeing these McLaren men and women in a new light, he could no longer call them lowly or lazy. They were anything but that.

While they might not have the same skills as the Mackintoshes, they did possess the same heart and determination.

Rose had been right when she said her people only needed a strong leader, a good example, a good man to look up to. Someone who would lead by example. Someone who could deliver them out of the depths of poverty given to them by their last laird.

One man.

One man who would lead them out of the darkness and poverty and into the light. Into a much brighter future. One man who would look upon them with pride. One man who could show them the way.

Ian Mackintosh was that man.

THREE DAYS AFTER RECEIVING THE MISSIVE, Ian was awakened by the sound of his brother's voice.

"What the bloody hell?" Ian growled. Last night was the first time in weeks where he actually slept, succumbing to exhaustion.

"We have a visitor," Brogan told him.

"Unless it be our father and a thousand battle-ready warriors, I do no' care." He grumbled into his pillow.

"Trust me when I say ye will want to meet this visitor."

Visitors were the last thing on his mind. He needed to sleep or he would be of no use to anyone.

"He be from the Bowies."

As HE WASHED HIS FACE WITH COLD water from the basin, Ian barraged his brother with questions. "Another arrow in the gate?"

Brogan handed him a drying cloth. "Nay, no arrow. This time, they came to the gate and asked to see ye."

Rubbing his face dry, he tossed the cloth on the back of his chair and began digging through the pile of clothes strewn on the floor. He knew Rose would be appalled by the current state of this space, but he knew she'd rather he be too busy planning her escape than keeping his makeshift home neat and tidy. "How many?" he asked as he gave a careful sniff to a tunic he found.

"Only one."

Deciding the tunic was not overly offensive in smell, he tugged it on. "One? What has he said?"

"Nothin' thus far. He refuses to speak to anyone but ye," Brogan replied as he handed Ian his boots.

"He be rather brave, aye?" Ian asked as he pulled the boots on.

Brogan chuckled. "Tell me that again *after* ye see him."

Grabbing his sword and belt, Ian led the way outside. A heavy mist hung in the air. The yard was dotted with puddles left over from last night's rain. The cool morning air did nothing to cool the anger building within Ian's gut. He strapped on his belt as they crossed the yard and headed toward the armory. "Do ye suppose the Bowie has learned we have sent word to our allies?"

"That be a distinct possibility," Brogan said as he stepped around a large puddle.

"It matters naught," Ian told him as they passed one of the cooking fires. "Either way, a war will be fought."

ENTERING THE ARMORY, IAN SCANNED the room quickly. His gaze immediately fell on a group of his men, standing in a close, tight circle and looking down at something. As he moved toward them, Ian soon realized 'twasn't something, but someone.

A young lad of no more than four and ten stood in the center of Ian's men. Scrawny, with shaggy light brown hair and visibly shaking legs, he looked as though he was ready to piss himself with fear. His head barely reached the shoulders of Ian's smallest man. Ian locked eyes with one of his men, and slowly, each man took a few steps back.

With a fierce glare, Ian approached the boy. Looking him up and down, he was unimpressed. "Who are ye?" Ian growled.

"Fenner Bowie," he stammered. "And I'll say nothin' else but to Ian Mackintosh himself."

One of Ian's men, Fergus Mackintosh, smacked the boy in the back of the head. "Show some respect, ye whelp. Ye *are* speakin' to him."

The boy rubbed the back of his head. "Ye be Ian Mackintosh?"

"Aye," Ian said as he crossed his arms over his chest and grunted with disgust. "I suppose the Bowie sent a young lad to do his talkin', thinkin' I would no' kill an innocent."

"'Twas no' the Bowie, but Alec Bowie who sent me. And aye, he said ye would no' harm me," he said cautiously.

Fergus smacked the boy's head again. "Ye shall show our laird the respect he's due, boy."

Flinching, the boy rubbed the back of his head again as he gave Fergus a fearful glance. "M'laird," he began once again. "I be here on Alec Bowie's behalf."

"And who be Alec Bowie?" Ian asked.

"Brother to the Bowie, m'laird. He be Rutger's younger brother."

Ian and Brogan exchanged curious glances. "And what, pray tell, does Alec Bowie want?"

The lad swallowed hard before answering. "A meetin' with ye, m'laird."

Quirking a brow and cocking his head to one side, Ian studied the boy closely for a long moment. "So Rutger sends his brother instead of himself? I kent the man was a coward."

"Rutger does no' ken we be here," the boy said.

Ian found that information curious and questionable. If he'd learned anything at all about the Bowies, 'twas that not a one of them could be trusted.

"Alec be a good man," the boy said. "He does no' support his brother kidnappin' yer wife."

Ian all but lunged at the boy. Grabbing him by the front of his tunic, he lifted him off the ground. "Ye are never to speak of me wife again, do ye understand? Lad or no, I'll cut yer throat and send ye back to yer laird in pieces."

"I be sorry, m'laird," the boy stammered. "I meant no disrespect."

Pushing the boy away, Ian saw he landed against Fergus, who tossed him toward Martin Mackintosh, his cousin. Martin righted the boy and grunted with a fair amount of disgust.

"M'laird, Alec awaits no' far from here. He asks to meet with ye in person, but he wants yer promise ye'll no' gut him. He will come here, alone and unarmed, to meet with ye."

Fergus chuckled. "That be either verra brave or verra stupid, considerin' he be the brother of the man who killed our laird's wife and bairn."

Unfortunately, some of Ian's men still held the belief that not only was Rose dead, but her babe as well.

The boy's face twisted in confusion. "Dead?" the boy replied. "She be no' dead. At least she was no' two days ago when we left."

"I received a letter from yer laird three days ago, sayin' me wife died in childbirth and he now holds me son hostage." Ian told him. Although he hadn't believed Rose was dead, his heart skipped a few beats learning he was right.

Fenner's eyes grew wide with fear. He gulped once, then again. "I swear, m'laird, she was alive and well two days ago when we left. I swear it!"

Ian took note of the surprised expressions on his men's faces as they worked through this bit of news. He had been right. Mayhap in the future they'd be more inclined to believe him, even if it didn't seem reasonable.

"It takes two days to travel between our keeps," Brogan said. "Rutger would have sent that letter out a sennight ago. If what the boy says is true, then ye were right. Rutger Bowie lied to ye."

"Boy, ye return to this Alec fellow, and ye tell him I will meet with him. He is to come unarmed and alone. And if I learn this is but a trick, I shall kill him and anyone else who might be with him. Do ye understand?"

The lad nodded his head violently. "Aye m'laird, I do!"

IN LESS THAN AN HOUR, IAN and Brogan met Alec Bowie for the first time. The man was not at all what he expected. To begin with, he was exceedingly clean. As tall as Ian and as well muscled, he did not at first glance appear to be a ruthless killer. Dark brown, nearly black hair, the top half pulled away from his face and tied back with a leather thong. The rest fell down his back, well past his shoulders. He had a strong jaw covered with a neatly trimmed beard and dark brown eyes that did not look like they belonged to a madman.

The dark green tunic he wore over brown leather trews was clean. A belt at his narrow waist, sans sword, proved he was not a glutton like his brother. He looked as though he could well hold his own in any battle.

Once the introductions were made, they sat at a table in the armory. Next to Ian sat his brother. Behind them, forming a wall of muscle and contempt, were fifteen of Ian's best men.

Alec read the last missive sent from his brother. With a disgusted shake of his head, he lay the parchment down. With a heavy sigh, he looked across the table at Ian. "I can assure ye that this is all lies. Rose is verra much alive and still carryin' yer child."

Ian studied him closely, looking for any tell-tell signs of deceit or treachery. Thus far, he hadn't found any. But 'twas still too early to make a judgment.

"I left behind one of me most trusted men, Dougal Bowie, to watch over yer wife. He will protect her as if he were protectin' one of his own. This I swear to ye."

"Ye can swear and vouch fer yer man all ye want," Ian said through clenched teeth. "I ken no' him nor ye. All I ken is that 'tis *yer* brother who has kidnapped me wife, killed over a dozen innocent people, and laid siege to our keep. Why the bloody hell should I trust *ye?*"

Alec rested his hands on top of the table. "A wise man would no'," he replied. "I ken I would no' trust ye were our roles reversed."

Ian raised a brow but remained quiet. He would listen to what this man had to say, but that didn't mean he'd believe a word of it.

"More than a year ago, Aggie McLaren killed our former laird, me cousin, Eduard Bowie."

The men standing behind Ian chuckled with amusement.

"I ken. I was there and saw it happen. 'Twas a grapplin' hook to his neck, I believe," Ian said with a bemused smile.

"Aye, 'twas. And if ever I get the chance to meet her in person, I shall thank her."

All eyes were on him then.

"Eduard was beyond ruthless," Alec began. "He was beyond savage, beyond nightmares. No one mourned his loss."

"No one?" Ian asked doubtfully.

"Nay, his people celebrated his death." He let the words sink in for a moment before continuing. "I was no' there. I had no' been home in a good number of years, but I had heard of Eduard's disgustin' ways through letters from me father and brother. I was in France when I received word of Eduard's death and me brother's claim to the title of chief. I came home at once."

"And ye say none grieve the loss of Eduard Bowie?" Ian asked again, only for clarification.

"Not one."

"Pray tell me, Alec. Will any mourn the loss of yer brother when I kill him?" Ian asked in a low, firm tone.

If he thought to garner any kind of reaction from Alec, he was wrong. "The only one who will mourn me brother's death is me. And 'tis only fer the fact that he is me brother."

They eyed each other suspiciously for a long moment. Ian knew were anything to happen to any of his brothers, he would not only mourn their loss he would seek justice if required. But then again, the Mackintoshes were as opposite the Bowies as dust was to water.

"My brother was no' always such a greedy bastard," Alec said. "There was a time when he was a good man. In his short time as laird, he's become a greedy fool. I pray daily that he comes to his senses and sees reason."

"Be that why ye're here?" Brogan asked. "To pray fer mercy fer yer brother?"

Alec gave a slight shrug before answering. "I doubt 'twould do any good."

Leona had entered the armory with a tray of bread, cheese, and meat. Quietly, she placed the tray on the table and stepped away. Alec's eyes grew wide when he noticed her. An action that did not go unnoticed by either Ian or Brogan.

"Do ye ken her?" Ian asked when she was out of earshot.

"Nay," Alec said. "Be she Rose's sister?"

Ian and Brogan chuckled slightly. "Nay," Ian answered.

When Leona appeared again, this time with a tray of mugs filled with ale, Alec could not help but stare at her. "The resemblance is uncanny."

Feeling all the eyes in the room were upon her, she looked up from the tray and into Alec Bowie's eyes. "Be there somethin' else ye want, m'laird?" she asked.

"I be sorry fer starin', lass," Alec said. He watched as her face turned a deep shade of red. "But yer resemblance to yer mistress is quite remarkable."

She started to say something, but apparently thought better of it. Quietly, she left the table and the men to their discussion.

"So why are ye here?" Brogan asked as he cut a hunk of cheese and popped it into his mouth.

"I want peace amongst our clans. I want the warrin' to stop."

Both Ian and Brogan found his claim surprising. "I have never kent a Bowie to want anythin' save those things that belong to someone else. Whether it be their cattle, sheep, coin or women." Brogan said.

"Aye, we do have a reputation fer thievin' and reivin'," Alec agreed.

"But ye want to change that?" Ian asked.

Taking a mug from the tray, Alec gave a curt nod. "Aye, I do."

"I take it yer brother does no' hold the same line of thinkin'?" Ian asked.

"Ye take it rightly, m'laird," Alec said with a slight chuckle.

Ian took a cup of ale and sipped it slowly. "And how, pray tell, do ye plan on gainin' peace fer yer clan?"

Looking him straight in the eye, Alec said, "By helpin' ye get yer wife back without ye havin' to pay the ransom."

His outward calm appearance belied the fact Ian was stunned. Could he really believe Alec Bowie? Did the man sincerely wish for peace? Did he honestly want to help him get Rose back?

"How do ye propose to do that?" Ian asked.

"With as little bloodshed as possible," Alec replied.

Ian was not sure what to make of this man. "Whilst I can applaud yer wish fer peace and wantin' to resolve our current conflict with as little blood as possible, I do no' see how it can be done."

"In truth?" Alec said as he set his mug down. "I do no' rightly ken how myself. That be why I am here. I want ye to ken that no' all of Rutger's people support what he has done."

"His people?" Brogan asked suspiciously. "Be they no' yer people too?"

Alec gave another slight shrug. "I suppose they are. But I have been away fer many years, ye ken. I fear I do no' recognize the clan I left. I barely recognize me brother, fer that matter."

"So ye want us to help *ye* get me wife back so that *ye* can take over as chief of Clan Bowie?" Ian asked.

Alec raised his hands. "Nay! I have no desire to be chief of Clan Bowie. Or any other clan. I only want to help ye get yer wife back. It is me hope that if we can do that, me brother will see the reason in it and accept a peace accord between our clans."

"Pardon me," Ian began, "but I find it verra difficult to believe a man would go against his own brother to help his sworn enemy, in order that his clan have *peace*."

Alec leaned back in his chair. "Most of the Bowies have never travelled more than a day's walk from their homes. Only the warriors have gone farther than that, and only to raid and steal. I have seen more of this world than me people could ever dream of seein'. I have seen war. *Real* war. I want no part of that."

Ian's brow furrowed into a hard line as he listened to Alec Bowie's talk of peace.

"I fostered with the MacGregors fer seven years. They are a good people. They are prosperous by their own hard work, no' by stealin. They are a happy, peaceful people. I want *that* kind of life fer the Bowies. If it means goin' against me brother to have it, then I shall."

Ian cast a questionable glance toward his brother, as if to ask, *do ye believe this man?*

"So ye want peace and are willin' to go against yer brother to have it, even though ye say ye have no desire to be chief," Ian recounted to be certain.

"Aye, I will and, nay, I do no' want to be chief."

Brogan was just as leery as his brother, but the most important question still went unanswered. "How do ye propose to get me sister-by-law out of the Bowie keep? The same way Aggie, Rose and Ian made their way in when Aggie killed Eduard?"

"Were those tunnels still open, I would have brought yer sister-by-law with me this day," Alec replied in frustration. "But me brother had all those passages and tunnels sealed off or destroyed when he learned how entry was made that night."

There went Brogan's plans for entering unseen into the Bowie keep.

"Then how?" Ian asked.

Another shrug from Alec, this time born of irritation. "I do no' ken. Rutger has men watchin' her day and night. He has an old woman to bring her food and check on her several times throughout the day. He has doubled the guard on our walls, has increased the men on patrol. He might be a greedy bastard, but he's no' foolish enough to let his guard down."

Ian and Brogan were as lost as Alec when it came to any viable plan to remove Rose unharmed.

From the back of the room, came Leona Macdowall's soft voice. "Can ye steal someone *inside* the keep?"

EVERYONE IN THE ENTIRE ROOM TURNED to look at Leona. She stood in the far corner, half in the shadows, half out. With her head held high and shoulders pulled back, she waited for Alec to answer her question. When the silence stretched on far too long, she nervously asked the question again. "Can ye get someone *inside* the keep?"

Ian stared at her as if she'd lost her mind. On Brogan's face was the same expression.

"What did ye have in mind, lass?" Alec was the only one brave enough to ask.

She took a tentative step forward as she fidgeted with her fingers. "Everyone is always remarkin' on how much Rose and I look alike. I volunteer to take her place."

Half the men in the room laughed while the others shook their heads derisively.

"Leave the plannin' to the men, lass," Fergus said as he turned his back to her.

Ian and Brogan stared at Alec Bowie. The three men were giving some strong consideration to her idea.

"Do ye think 'twould work?" Ian asked.

"It might," Alec replied.

"Until someone notices she is no' heavy with child. Or her eyes."

Leona made her way quickly to the table. "I ken me eyes be different!" she seethed at Brogan.

"Lass, I meant no offense. I am merely statin' a fact. Rose has bright green eyes and she is with child."

Undeterred, she argued on. "Aye, but we only need them to believe I am she long enough fer Alec to get her out of the keep and on her way back home."

"And what then, lass?" Alec asked. "What happens when me brother discovers Rose is gone?"

"I do no' ken, but ye must admit it be a good idea."

Fergus stepped forward. "Leona, 'tis madness ye speak." He looked to Ian for confirmation but did not find any. "Ian, ye can no' be thinkin' to agree with her?"

"Aye, Fergus, I am," he told him pointedly. "Unless ye can come up with somethin' better?"

Fergus clamped his jaw shut and walked away, shaking his head in disbelief.

Ian turned to his brother then. "Well?"

Brogan thought on it for a long moment. "Do ye think ye can get her into the keep unnoticed?"

Alec chuckled slightly. "I am ferever bringin' one whore or another into our keep—" he stopped abruptly to look at Leona. "I be no' sayin' ye are a wh-, that is I mean—"

"I ken what ye're meanin' m'laird," Leona said in a firm tone.

For the first time in years, Alec blushed like a lad who'd just been chastised by his mum.

THE REMAINDER OF THE MORNING WAS spent developing a plan whereby they could gain Leona's entrance into the Bowie keep without harm, and then the safe rescue of Rose.

While Ian, Brogan, Alec and Leona went over the plans, horses were readied and supplies packed for the two-day journey. Because he still did not know who the second traitor was, they kept the plans to themselves, save for the fifteen men who had heard the original idea to begin with. Those men, though well respected and trusted, were not allowed out of the armory.

The entire McLaren keep was on lockdown. No one would be allowed in or out until Ian's return. Brogan would be in charge of the keep during Ian's absence, something he was growing more and more used to doing.

Alec's men had been waiting for Ian a safe distance from the keep. A messenger was sent to retrieve his man Kyth, to join his friend and partner in crime inside the McLaren keep. Ian and Brogan were taken aback by the man's size. He stood well over six feet tall with shoulders that seemed nearly as broad as he was tall. He wore his dark hair in the same fashion as Alec, but his face was cleanly shaven. With dark brown eyes, he could very well have passed for Alec's brother. He was introduced as the man's cousin and most loyal ally.

As requested, he was as unarmed as Alec. Even the sheaths on the outside of his boots were empty. Alec quickly filled Kyth in on their plans for retrieving Rose. He listened quietly and intently with his arms crossed over his chest.

While the two men talked, Brogan leaned in to whisper to Ian, "If we had more men that looked like him, we could lay siege to the Bowie keep with great ease."

Ian gave a wry smile and nodded his agreement.

After a quick summary, Kyth looked about. "Where be this lass?" he asked, directing his question to Ian and Brogan.

Brogan cleared his throat before answering. "She is off tryin' to see if she has any clothes that will make her look like a common bar wench."

"The girl be far too bonny to be a bar wench," Alec pointed out. "But I think if we keep her face obscured, mayhap with a hooded cloak, she should do well enough."

"Bonny is she?" Kyth asked with a devious smile.

Brogan stepped forward. "Aye, she is. And she be a fine young woman and an innocent. We will thank ye kindly to make certain she remains so," he said in his most serious tone.

Kyth offered him a nod of understanding, taking the warning to heart. "Her virtue shall be safe with us. I give ye me word."

"I shall hold ye to that," Brogan and Ian said in unison.

A thought suddenly occurred to Brogan. "What if Ingerame does no' allow Leona to go?"

Ian had not given that a moment's thought either. "Do no' worry it," he said. "We all ken how he feels about his daughter. And after his shameful behavior the night of the raid, he will want to do everythin' he can to get himself back in me high regard."

"How old is the lass?" Alec asked.

"Three and twenty," Ian told him.

"Unmarried?"

"Aye," he said. "As far as I ken she has never married. Her father be me lead carpenter. While he is one hell of a man with a hammer, his parenting skills leave much to be desired."

Alec left the subject alone then. "Let us hope he will allow her to go."

"He will," Ian said. "He will."

TWENTY-SIX

Ian had been right in his assumption that he would get no argument from Ingerame Macdowall as it pertained to his daughter. He even went so far as to see them all off, though he had not one kind word for his daughter, nor did he offer her any words of encouragement. The more Ian got to know the man, the less he liked him. Carpentry skills be-damned. As soon as he could, he would write to Frederick and suggest seeking a replacement for the ill-mannered man.

Leona met them in front of the armory, somewhat excited about what lay ahead. Over a serviceable dark green gown, she wore a wide apron draped just so — in order to help hide her ample bosom — warm boots and a brown hooded cloak. Her ever-present pouch hung from a belt at her waist and on her back she carried a bundle filled with what Ian assumed were clean clothes and supplies.

She was given her own mount, a brown speckled, good-natured mare. 'Twas her first time ever riding. "I fear I be used to walkin' or ridin' in a cart or wagon," she said as Ian and Brogan gave her a quick lesson. "But I shall do me best to keep up and no' fall off."

Not long afterward, the Mackintoshes and McLarens headed out of the keep, where they picked up the rest of Alec's men: Gylys Bowie, the young lad named Fenner, and a man named Davy MacReynolds.

"This be *all* yer men?" Ian asked disappointedly.

"Aye," Alec said with a proud smile. "'They be all that I need at the moment.

Ian flinched inwardly. Hopefully the man's arrogance would not get them all killed.

They would ride until well after nightfall, using the moon to help guide their way. The contingency of men and one woman rode in relative silence, each one of them lost in their own thoughts and concerns.

For Leona, this was a chance to prove to herself and to those who thought they knew her, that she was neither tetched nor possessed by the devil. She wanted to prove to one and all that she was an intelligent young woman, completely worthy of anyone's respect. Mayhap, just mayhap, if this mission was successful, they would stop calling her Leona Two-Eyes or Leona the Witch.

Ian's thoughts went between the plan they had developed and worry over the possibility of its working. For once, he would not allow his mind to wander to all the conceivable horrible outcomes. Instead, he chose to do what Rose would do: concentrate on nothing but the positive outcome.

Feeling a good deal more hopeful than he had in weeks, he thought instead about his reunion with his wife. As soon as she was safely in his arms, she would be surrounded by no less than six men at all times. He would write to his father and brother, asking for more volunteers to help rebuild the clan. Never again would he take another chance on his wife being kidnapped or hurt. And never again would he be besieged with worry and dread over her well-being or that of their child. Nay, he would do whatever he could to ensure their safety, no matter the cost.

By the time they made camp, just a few hours before dawn, Leona was exhausted. Her back and legs hurt, as did her bottom. But she'd not utter one word of complaint. Rose's safe return was the only significantly important thing that mattered.

A fire was made and a pallet placed near the fire for her. She could not help but wonder if the men were silent because of her presence, or if they were always this quiet. Oftentimes she had helped serve the Mackintosh and McLaren men. Always boisterous and talkative, save for now. Mayhap the seriousness of this mission was what had them holding their normally wagging tongues. She was asleep before she pulled the covers over her shoulders.

As soon as the sun rose the following morning, Brogan gently woke her. "We need to be on our way, lass," he said with a sleepy smile.

Quickly — or as quickly as her sore muscles allowed — she tended to her morning ablutions and they were soon on their way. They ate while they rode, bread and dried meat, and again, silence fell in all around them.

It took two days to reach the border between Bowie and McLaren lands. With the increased patrols, the Mackintoshes and McLarens could not risk going farther onto Bowie lands. They would have to wait behind in the forest and avoid being seen by anyone. 'Twas not a position Ian relished.

'Twas early morning and a fine mist hung in the air, while gray skies overhead threatened more rain. "This is as far as we can go with ye, Leona," Ian said as they stood next to their mounts. His tone and countenance were both quite serious. "Ye can change yer mind if ye wish. No one will hold it against ye."

Leona offered him a wan smile. "Nay, m'laird, I will no' stop now. No' when we be so close to gettin' Rose back."

He admired her tenacity and was grateful for her devotion to his wife. "Rose has a good friend in ye, Leona Macdowall."

"As I have in her, m'laird."

Brogan appeared, looking just as serious as his brother. He too offered her the chance to back out and once again she refused.

"Do ye have a *sgian dubh*, lass?" Ian asked.

With wide eyes, she answered, "Nay, I was in such a hurry to pack, I did no' think to grab one of da's."

Almost in unison, Ian and Brogan each reached into their boots to retrieve hidden daggers. With hands extended and hopeful expressions, they presented the *sgian dubhs* to her.

"Keep one in yer pouch," Ian said. "The other in yer boot."

"Thank ye," she said breathlessly as she took both daggers. "I shall return these to ye in a matter of days."

"Nay," Ian said. "Keep them."

She looked at them in awe, as if they had just presented her with the crown of Scotland. 'Twas the first gift she had received since childhood, when her grandminny presented her with her first journal.

THEY'D LEFT THE MACKINTOSHES AND McLarens behind hours ago. Leona now travelled with four relatively complete strangers, heading toward heaven-only-knew what. Though she tried to keep a reserved facade, her insides were a jumbled knot of nerves and trepidation.

Riding on either side of her were Alec Bowie and Kyth, while Fenner and Davey took up the rear. They had just poured out of a small forest and onto a hilly, rock-covered area of land. The morning mist had abated and now the sun shone down brightly. 'Twas an altogether beautiful day, which would be made more beautiful if they were successful in their mission.

"Lass," Alec asked as they made their way around a large boulder. The sound of his voice startled her, for they had all been riding in silence for hours. "Why do ye do this?"

Leona cast him a sideways glance as she focused on guiding her horse through the rocky terrain. She thought it a rather odd question. "To help me friend."

Alec thought it a rather odd answer. "Do ye always risk yer neck fer friends?"

'Twas not an easy question to answer without looking like a downtrodden fool. Carefully, she chose her words. "Rose is me dearest friend," she told him. *And me only one.*

He was quiet for a long moment. "Do ye truly understand how dangerous this is?"

"I do," she replied.

"And yet ye take the risk in hopes of helpin' yer friend," he said with a hint of disbelief.

Deciding 'twas a statement and not a question, she fell silent. Her reasons were her own. Some of them were purely selfish. But her primary reason for risking life and limb was most sincere. She had to help Rose get back to her family and clan.

Slowly, they made their way up a small incline, winding their way around large rocks and small boulders. When they crested the top of the hill, he began his questioning again.

"Have ye thought of what will happen to ye, should we be found out?"

In truth, she had given that some thought. "It matters no'," she told him. "I must do everythin' I can to get Rose back to her family, to Ian. To the clan."

"And if me brother learns of our plans?"

Leona smiled wanly. "Me own neck is no' near as important as Rose's."

She took note of his furrowed brow and puzzled expression. "Ye see, m'laird," she continued to explain, "Rose is verra important to her people. If anythin' were to happen to her or her babe, the ramifications are most severe. 'Twould be a loss felt for many years by many people."

"And if they were to lose ye?"

Growing frustrated with the conversation, she answered as honestly as she could. "None would mourn me passin', m'laird."

THE PLAN WAS TO WAIT FOR NIGHT to fall before entering the keep. Darkness would be their precious ally this night.

An hour before reaching the keep, they stopped at a small thicket of trees and bramble. Alec helped Leona from her mount, setting her on the ground with great care. She thanked him politely, before stepping away with her bag. "I shall change me clothes now, m'laird."

He thought her a most comely lass and was beginning to doubt the success of their plan. Far too pretty and quiet to pretend she was a bar wench, he began to worry no one would believe it.

Surprise did not begin to describe how he felt when she stepped out of the thicket.

Gone was the sweet, innocent looking lass. Before him stood a beautiful young woman. She had pulled her chemise to rest seductively low on her shoulders. Over that, she wore a bright green dress, the laces of which were stretched taught over her large, round breasts. Breasts he hadn't noticed until then. The skirt was pulled up at different points, and tucked into a dark belt, exposing more of the chemise as well as her slender ankles than was right or proper.

And no longer was her hair tied into a simple braid. Nay, it was unbound, tossed loosely over her shoulders, where it cascaded down her back. Golden blonde, wavy locks that looked as soft as silk when the setting sun glinted off it.

Apparently his men were just as surprised as he, for he heard Kyth utter under his breath, "God's bones," while Gylys all but gasped.

"Well?" she asked as she rested one palm on a dainty hip. "Will I pass fer a bar wench?"

Before his men could answer, Alec removed his own cloak, stepped forward, and draped it around her shoulders. "Aye, lass, that will do."

'Twas then she smiled. A smile that very nearly stole his breath away. Proud as well as relieved, she allowed her lips to curve upward, exposing nearly perfect white teeth. Even her eyes sparkled with glee.

"I have a patch too," she said happily as she reached into her pouch. Carefully, she tied the patch around her head, taking great care to settle it just so. "To cover me blue eye."

Inexplicably, he found he did not care for the patch, but understood its importance. While he found her oddly colored eyes intriguing, they would surely bring unwanted attention. Then he chanced another glance at her beautiful bosom and realized she could have three eyes, all of a different color, and not a man on earth would notice.

SHARING A MOUNT, MUCH TO HIS unruly body's consternation, Leona and Alec rode up to the Bowie keep. Were the situation and circumstances different, he would have taken great pleasure in having her perched on his lap, watching her breasts bob up and down in time with the horse. Feeling a lecher and cad, he pushed those thoughts aside to focus on the mission at hand.

Before he could stop at the end of the path at the edge of the moat, a voice called out from above. "Who goes there?"

"'Tis me, Alec Bowie. Let me in Seamus!" Alec boomed his reply.

"Who be that with ye?" Seamus called back down.

Alec laughed raucously. "Me company fer the night!"

Laughter broke out along the upper wall. Moments later, they began to lower the drawbridge. Loud and aged, it creaked and groaned.

"Just follow me lead, lass, and all will be well," he whispered into her ear.

She could only offer a rapid nod for she was too afraid to speak.

Soon, they were traversing over the drawbridge and into the Bowie keep.

Someone came to take hold of his horse. Alec dismounted first then helped Leona down.

"Would ye like me to let Rutger ken ye're here?" the young man holding the reins asked.

Alec laughed loudly. "Nay, I'd prefer ye did no'. me new friend and I would much prefer no company this night."

The young man laughed before leading the horse away.

They made their way in through the gate in the second wall with relative ease. Once inside the keep, they realized the gathering room was still alive with men and women enjoying one another's company and the ale that poured freely. Too into their cups to notice much of anything.

Alec took her hand in his and quietly, they made their way up the dark stairs. Down the torchlit hallway, she clung to his hand with a deathlike grip.

As soon as he closed the door to his bedchamber, he leaned against it and let out a sigh of relief.

"That was easier than I thought," Leona remarked. She was standing with her back pressed against the wall that stood opposite his bed.

Running a hand across his jaw, he said, "Aye, but the night is far from over."

LEONA HAD NEVER BEEN ALONE with a man before, at least not in his bedchamber. Still pressed against the wall, she watched him as he checked the bar on the door. Watched still as he crossed the room and lifted the fur to peer out the window.

"Ye should rest," he said without turning around.

Rest? Nay, she doubted she'd be able to sleep this night. She was in the proverbial lion's den, amongst hundreds of Bowies. They were sworn enemies of the Mackintoshes and McLarens. Though she didn't truly belong to either clan, she still felt a tremendous sense of duty and fealty to them.

Uncertain as to where exactly she should rest — the bed was completely out of the question — she took a seat at the small table that sat in the corner of the room.

"Lass, ye can have the bed," he told her as if he could read her thoughts.

Furtively, she glanced at the bed then at Alec.

Finally, he turned to face her. "I promised yer laird yer life as well as yer innocence, would be safely guarded."

Why that bothered her, irritated her no end, she couldn't rightly say. Deep down, she wished he would at least make the attempt at defiling her. Even something as simple as a kiss. But nay, he just stood there at the window, being a gentleman. Three and twenty years old and she'd never been kissed. Not even a drunken lout had tried.

Mayhap she was exhausted from all the travel. Mayhap she was simply *tired*. Tired of men running in the opposite direction. Tired of being called names by complete strangers and those people who should have known better.

Pushing her ire aside, she threw off her cloak, hung it on a hook by the door, and climbed into the bed. Either way, it simply didn't matter. There were more important things to worry about at the moment. Such as what would transpire on the following morning, just before dawn broke over the horizon.

Thus far, it appeared as though God were in favor of this devious plan. Hopefully, He would continue to bless them and Rose would soon be back in the loving arms of her husband.

"Are ye warm enough?" Alec asked in a low, hushed tone.

His voice felt as warm as sunlight. She heard his soft footfalls as he walked across the floor, drawing nearer to the bed. Panic slowly crept in as a hundred different scenarios bombarded her mind.

"Aye, I am," she whispered.

Just when she thought he meant to climb into the bed with her, she felt him drape a fur over her and pull it up over her shoulders. She tensed, holding her breath, wondering what on earth she should say or do.

Quietly, he stepped away. She could hear him building a fire in the hearth, all the while she lay unmoving in the bed. What would her father think, should he ever find out she was alone in a man's bedchamber? What did it really matter? The only time he cared one whit about her safety or well-being was when it came to men. In truth, she really didn't think he cared one way or another.

Once Alec was finished with the fire, she heard his light footfalls as he walked back toward the bed. The chair scraped quietly across the floor when he pulled it away from the table. It creaked ever so slightly when he sat down.

"Go to sleep, lass. We've a very big day on the morrow."

She remained mute and as still as a rabbit hiding from a fox. Aye, whatever happened on the morrow would determine her future destiny. 'Twas a rather unsettling feeling.

TWENTY-SEVEN

*D*awn had yet to caress the sky when Leona felt a gentle hand on her shoulder. Startled, she shot up in bed, forgetting for a moment just where she was.

Alec was sitting on the bed next to her, a warm smile on his lips. "Wheest, lass. 'Tis only me. 'Tis time."

Wiping the sleep from her eyes with her fingertips, she swung her legs over the side of the bed. Her heart pounded against her breast. *Tis time.*

Unease settled in like a waterlogged fur. Suppressing the urge to cry, she took slow, steady breaths. Alec placed her slippers on the floor at her feet and helped her to stand.

"'Twill all be over soon, lass. I promise."

That was what terrified her most. That her whole life would be over soon if they were discovered.

Quietly, she tugged on her slippers, grabbed her cloak from the peg and waited while Alec checked the hallway for any of his brother's spies.

Once he felt certain 'twas safe to move, he took her hand in his and led the way. Her palms were sweaty and her heart raced rapidly. Deftly, almost silently, they made their way down the hall. Leona did not breathe again until they were safely inside a second chamber.

Rose was fast asleep on her side, covered in heavy furs and blankets. Leona was much relieved to see her friend and went to her at once. Crouching low, she whispered, "Rose, wake up. 'Tis me, Leona."

Rose grumbled incoherently and pulled the covers more tightly around her neck.

Alec came to them then. Crouching beside Leona, he placed a hand over Rose's mouth and whispered her name.

Her eyes flew open at once, filled with fear until she saw his face.

"Wheest, Rose," he whispered. "We're here to take ye home."

Confused, her brow furrowed as she gave a nod of understanding. Slowly, Alec withdrew his hand and stood to his full height.

"Rose," Leona whispered again, her smile bright and beaming.

Stunned, Rose sat up in utter disbelief. "Leona!" she exclaimed.

"Wheest, ladies!" Alec admonished. "We must be verra quiet."

Leona wrapped her arms around her friend and held her tight. "Och! 'Tis glad and relieved I am at seein' ye."

"Why are ye here? How? What is goin' on?" Rose asked as she pulled away.

Alec helped her to stand and quickly set about explaining their plan. When he finished, she looked up at him and asked, "Are ye both mad?"

"Aye," Leona and Alec answered in unison.

"Does Ian ken of this plan?"

Still smiling, Leona answered. "Aye, he does. He is no' far from here. Soon, ye will be with him and returnin' to McLaren lands."

"But what of ye?" Rose demanded to know.

"As soon as I have ye safely back with yer husband, I shall return to retrieve Leona."

Rose shook her head, hopeful the motion would bring some sense to the matter. "What if ye're caught?"

Leona hugged her once again. "Do no' worry it, Rose. I will be fine. Please, just do everythin' Alec says and ye'll soon be out of here."

From the look on her face, Rose was not nearly as hopeful as she.

In short order, Leona removed her gown for Rose to wear. She also gave her the eyepatch and cloak.

"Do no' worry and do no' be afraid," Leona told her. "'Twill all be over verra soon. Trust us."

Worry was etched on Rose's face. "I'll no' be able to rest until ye are back with us, Leona."

They shared one last, teary-eyed embrace. "Be gone with ye now, and take care of that bairn," Leona told her as she bid the two of them goodbye.

As soon as they were out of the room, her own worry bubbled up. Kneeling at the foot of the bed, she prayed fervently for her friend's safe return to her husband.

#

Their retreat from the keep was as easy as their entry. With Rose perched atop his lap, the eyepatch carefully placed, the cloak drawn around to cover her large belly, they were soon out of the keep and on their way to her husband.

Once they were out of eyesight of the keep, Alec kicked his mount into a full gallop. "I be sorry to have to go so fast, but we must get ye to Ian before anyone discovers ye're missin'."

"What will happen to Leona should yer brother discover I be gone?" She dreaded learning the answer to that question.

"She will be fine. Dougall is there to watch over her. He will make certain she is unharmed."

Wiping tears from her eyes, she asked, "And who is there to protect Dougall?"

Alec refused to answer that question.

TWENTY-EIGHT

It had been too risky to build a fire, so Ian and his men hunkered down inside a small forest. While his men kept themselves busy by sharpening their weapons or discussing the different ways they would like to kill Rutger Bowie and Charles McFarland, Ian paced.

Like a wild animal in a cage, every nerve, every muscle was coiled, ready to spring at the slightest provocation.

For the most part, his men left him alone. Occasionally, however, they would offer an encouraging word. "'Twill no' be long now, Ian, and we'll have our Rose back."

Their Rose. Mackintosh and McLaren alike loved and respected his wife. They thought of her more as a beloved sister than simply their mistress. It did lift his spirits to know how fondly they thought of her.

Dawn broke out over the horizon, painting the sky in lavender and wine. As he stood watching the sun come up, he could not help but wish his wife was there to enjoy it with him. Never again would he take for granted the majesty of a rising sun or the blessing he had in Rose.

His attention was drawn away by the sound of very distant thunder. He scanned the sky, looking for rainclouds, but could not find any. Soon, he caught a glimpse of something in the distance, far to the east. Something glimmered in the morning light.

As soon as he realized 'twas the sun glinting off steel, his stomach turned and his heart all but seized. 'Twas not thunder, but men on horseback. Hundreds of them.

He let loose with a shrill whistle, an alarm call to his men. Jumping to their feet, they came to see for themselves what had brought forth the alarm. It took only a glimpse to realize hundreds of men were heading their way.

"Has the Bowie come around to attack us from behind?" one of his men asked. All eyes turned then to Gylys, Fenner and Davy.

The three men backed away slowly. "I do no' ken who those men be," Kyth said. "It can no' be the Bowie."

Three of Ian's men had swords on the Bowie's in the blink of an eye. "If ye have played us false," one of them warned, "we will gut ye before they arrive!"

None of the Bowies made the slightest attempt to either flee or fight. "We have no' played ye false. If it be the Bowie, 'tis only because somethin' happened at the keep," Gylys said, holding his hands in the air.

From the expressions on the three Bowie men standing nervously before them, Ian knew their confusion was as real as his own. "Mayhap yer *leader,* Alec, has played us all false?" he asked, his voice filled with anger.

The Bowies were insulted. "Alec would never play anyone false!" Gylys ground out harshly. "If it be the Bowie, 'tis only because Alec's plan did no' work."

"What do ye want us to do, Ian?" Fergus called out as he watched the army of men fast approaching.

Ian's mind raced for a plan. "We can no' go to the west, fer that be Bowie lands," he said as he headed toward his horse. "Mount up!" he called out. "We shall head north and east and see if we can no' circle back toward our keep."

"What about these unholy bastards?" Seamus asked in reference to the three Bowie men.

Ian clenched his jaws together as he stared at the men who could very well have betrayed them. "Go back to yer leader. If what ye say is true, he needs yer help. If what ye say be false?" he said as he grabbed the reins of his horse and mounted. "Then I'll meet all of ye in hell."

As EVERYONE SCRAMBLED TO MOUNT, the sound of horses grew louder and louder. Nearly all eyes were on the three Bowie men as they carefully watched them take to their own horses.

"I shall keep an eye on them," Ian told Seamus, "while the rest of ye hie off to the west."

"Nay!" Fergus protested. "What if they turn back? Ye can no' fight them all alone."

Ian pulled his own sword from its sheath. "Then tell me brother and father I died gallantly! Now be gone with ye!"

"We fight with ye, Ian." Fergus argued again. "We'll no' leave ye here to die alone!"

While he admired the man's loyalty, he knew someone had to get word back to the people left at the keep. "Damn ye, Fergus!" Ian yelled as the sound of approaching horses grew louder. "I need someone to get word to the keep!"

Suddenly, Seamus called out from atop his horse. "Wait!"

Quickly, Ian and the rest of his men spun their horses around.

"It be no' the Bowies!" Seamus said, sounding much relieved. "Look! That be a Mackintosh banner!"

Squinting his eyes to get a clearer look, Ian stared at the approaching army. His horse snickered and stomped at the ground, gave a great shake of its head. Ian reined the horse in, whispering to quell its nervous anticipation.

There, riding in front of the army of men, was the red Mackintosh banner. In the center was the gold emblem of a cat with its claws extended.

Relief washed over him. His shoulders and muscles relaxed. It mattered not how they were here this day of all days; he was mightily glad to see them. Another banner soon came into view, one that belonged to Clan Graham.

"Seamus, come with me," Ian said. "The rest of ye, keep an eye on the Bowies."

IAN AND SEAMUS RODE OUT TO meet the Mackintosh army. Ian soon caught sight of his brother, Frederick, and their long-time friend, Rowan Graham, riding at the front of the pack.

With a much-relieved heart, Ian raced to meet his brother. It had been nearly a year since last he'd seen him. Frederick was sporting an unshaved face and his hair was much longer.

"Ian!" Frederick called out as they drew nearer. Pulling rein, he slid from his horse, as did Ian. Frederick pulled his brother into a firm hug, slapping his back. "'Tis much reassured I am to see ye with yer head still attached to yer shoulders!"

"And ye as well, me brother!"

Rowan dismounted and came to offer the same greeting, pulling Ian in and slapping his back. "It has been far too long, Ian," he said with a devilish smile. "We really must try to get our clans together at times other than war."

"I do no' ken how ye are here this day, but I am verra happy ye are," Ian said with a smile that didn't quite reach his eyes.

Frederick stood with his feet spread, his arms crossed over his massive chest, and took a more serious tone. "We left on the first of March, at me wife's insistence," Frederick told him. "A week ago, we met the messenger ye were sendin' to us. We changed course and went to Rowan, who was all too happy to offer his aid."

Rowan chuckled at Frederick. "Yer lovely wife was fit to be tied, Frederick. I feared had I refused her request, she would have had me head on a pike. And me own lovely wife would have fed me entrails to our pigs."

Ian could imagine all too well how Aggie had taken the news of Rose's kidnapping. The image of her angry, threatening to kill anyone involved brought an amused smile to his lips. And Lady Arline? She was never one to turn a blind eye to an injustice. "'Tis glad I am then that ye both married such stubborn women!"

They could do nothing but laugh in agreement.

"And ye?" Rowan asked. "I hear yer wife is just as stubborn as ours."

Ian's smile faded at the mention of Rose. "Aye, she is. In truth, knowin' how stubborn she is has been the one thing to help me survive this ordeal."

"Mayhap she has already gutted Rutger Bowie and is draggin' his carcass to us now," Rowan said in an attempt to lighten Ian's mood.

Ian could only pray he was right.

TWENTY-NINE

lood filled her mouth, her skin burned from the multiple strikes against her cheek. Rutger Bowie was furious and not afraid to let her know it. Repeatedly over the past half hour, he had back-handed her, kicked her in her legs when she fell to the floor, screamed, ranted and raved. Still, she refused to tell him what she knew.

"Tell me *where she is!*" he yelled, hovering over Leona.

Gripped with fear, her cheek and eye swelling to the point she could barely see out of it, Leona shook her head. "I tell ye, I do no' ken who ye be askin' after," she told him.

"Ye lie, ye stupid wench!" His voice boomed and echoed off the gathering room walls.

"Nay!" she whispered harshly. "I tell ye true. I have told ye everythin' I ken, m'laird."

Rutger began to pace while he thought on what this young wench had told him thus far. "So me brother picks ye up at a tavern, brings ye here and spends half the night swivin' with ye, only to wake ye before dawn to put ye in the room where me hostage was kept?"

Leona gave a slow, exhausted shrug. I ken nothin' about a hostage, only that he told me he'd pay me well if I stayed there." Every muscle hurt, her face burned, her eye throbbed painfully. "Aye, m'laird. 'Tis the truth. I swear it."

Donnel McLaren had been watching from the long table as Rutger beat and interrogated the wench. As far as he was concerned, Rutger could kill the hapless creature, for she was the only thing standing between him and what rightfully belonged to him. "Seems too much of a coincidence, if ye ask me."

Rutger spun to look at him. "What do ye mean?" he demanded loudly.

Donnel let out a long, heavy sigh. "I mean, she looks a bit too much like Rose Mackintosh," he said. "If I hadn't kent Rose the whole of her life, and her family, I would swear the wench before ye is her sister."

"I have no sisters," Leona whispered. *At least no' by blood.*

A swift, hard boot to her thigh was Rutger's response. His chest heaved with fury; sweat dripped from his forehead into his eyes. He'd been beating the wench for nearly an hour and she'd yet to confess.

Turning his attention back to Donnel, he said, "Ye be certain Rose's da never strayed?" He could not quite comprehend what could have caused the striking resemblance between the two women.

"Well I can no' say that with a certainty, m'laird," Donnel replied. "All I ken is there be no sister that I've heard about."

Rutger turned back to Leona. She was curled into a protective ball, her knees drawn up to her chest, her hands covering her head. He was by no means nearly as ruthless as his cousin, Eduard Bowie, had been. In truth, the man's actions had often sickened him. But right now? He was not above beating this wench in order to learn all that she knew. A fortune was at stake.

Worn out from beating her, covered in sweat, he needed to rest and think on what his next course of action should be. He'd already sent out seventy-five of his best men to track down Rose and whoever had taken her. If his sentry was correct, Alec had been gone for four hours before it was discovered that Rose was missing, and this whore had taken her place. Loathe as he was to admit it, his brother was probably the one who had taken her.

"Take her to the dungeon!" he barked the command.

Two men appeared from the shadows to do their laird's bidding. Without any care toward her, they pulled her up by her arms and dragged her away.

DONNEL WAS ANGRIER THAN HE could ever remember being. If it was the last thing he did on this earth, he would have the head on a pike of whoever 'twas that betrayed them.

He and Rutger had planned for every contingency. Or so they'd thought. What they hadn't planned on was a traitor.

'Twas all beginning to slip from his grasp once again. The treasure, his future, his plan of living out the rest of his days in comfort.

If he could not get Rose back, 'twould all be lost.

Infuriated, he jumped to his feet, pounding his fist on the table before him. "We must attack them at once!" he shouted. "We can no' let them get away with this!"

Rutger glowered at him. "Do ye think I do no' realize that?" he ground out. "I want that bloody ransom as much as ye do, ye fool."

Donnel didn't think it very likely that anyone could want the ransom paid as much as he. "Then call yer men to arms. We must attack before the McLarens have time to call on their allies!"

Rutger sprang forward, stood only inches away from Donnel. "If ye *dare* order me about again, I will have ye hanged."

Donnel did not so much as bat an eye at the man's threat. He'd lived and worked for Mermadak McLaren for far too many years to be afraid of *this* man. Still, he was no fool. "Fergive me, m'laird," he said with a nod of respect. "I fear where me treasure is involved, I lose all patience."

"Ye best pray I do no' lose mine," Rutger warned before stepping away.

He paced for a few moments, his own fury rising. Though he had no sure proof of it yet, he was all but certain his brother Alec was responsible for Rose's escape. As soon as they learned Rose was missing and that whore had been left in her place, he ordered the drawbridge raised and men sent to investigate. That was nearly two hours ago.

Just as he was prepared to send more men out to bring everyone into the keep for questioning, two of his men came rushing into the gathering room.

"M'laird!" Adam Bowie shouted. He was a younger lad, tall and skinny in build. "I spoke with the men mannin' the walls and gates."

"And?" Rutger asked through gritted teeth.

The young man was reluctant to share what he'd learned. He swallowed hard before answering. "The only one in or out of the keep since last night was yer brother. He left at just before dawn with a whore."

'Twas exactly what he'd suspected. Alec had betrayed him. Of that, there was no longer any doubt. Were his brother any other man, Rutger would have believed he had taken the woman to ransom her himself. But his brother was not cut from the same cloth as himself. Nay, somewhere, somehow the bloody bastard had inherited a streak of honor, a lust for peace. There were times, just as now, where he would have sworn they were not related, that mayhap their pious mother had strayed from her marital bed.

"Raise the drawbridge," he said in a manner so calm it made even Donnel afraid. "Gather every available man. No one leaves or enters this keep without me order. Let our men ken we leave at dawn."

The young man appeared confused. "Shall I tell them where we be goin' and what to prepare fer, m'laird?"

Pinning the young man in place with a terrifying glower, Rutger answered. "We shall be raidin' the McLaren keep. Tell them to bloody ready themselves fer war!"

FROM THE SHADOWS OF THE hallway, Dougall Bowie heard his laird's orders. Heard the call to war that sent a shiver down his spine.

As quickly as he could, he left the hallway and the keep. When he was stopped at the drawbridge, the young man in charge at first refused to lower it.

"Yer laird has just called fer war against the McLarens, ye whelp! I need to get to me wife and bairns. Ye lower this drawbridge or I'll bloody well gut ye where ye stand."

The young man hesitated only briefly, for he knew Dougall Bowie had a reputation for never backing down from a fight and for almost always keeping his word. Not wanting to test the man, he ordered the drawbridge lowered so Dougall could get to his family.

Before he'd even reached the edge of the bridge, the order to raise it was given. Jumping a few feet, he landed safely on the other side and raced down the path and to his cottage. He had to get his wife and bairns to safety before the McLarens attacked. Last night, Alec had come to him after the lass with the odd eyes had fallen asleep. He had filled him in on his plan as well as his worry the McLarens would attack once they had Rose back. Regardless of who now attacked first, be it Bowie or McLaren, war was inevitable.

And the poor young woman Rutger had beaten the bloody hell out of? If the McLarens attacked first, then the young woman was sure to die. Rutger would make certain of it.

Just before he opened the door to his cottage, the battle horn sounded from the wall. Were the circumstance different, he would gladly have rushed to that call. But he was older now, wiser, and with far more at stake. Peace was within their grasp, even if his foolish laird could not or would not see it.

As much as he would have liked taking his time to get Rose back to her husband — for her own comfort — Alec could not take the risk. Who knew how much time they had before 'twas discovered she was missing? Nay, 'twas best to ride hard and fast, away from his brother's keep and toward the spot where he'd left the McLaren and his own men.

Not once did Rose complain of the hard riding. For a change, she was quiet and composed while she perched in front of him.

Over hills and through glens, he raced as fast as his mount could go. He had to get Rose to her husband, away from the danger behind them. And the sooner he could return her, the sooner he could go back and fetch Leona.

Hours passed and they stopped only twice and but briefly. By the time he crossed out of Bowie lands and onto McLaren, his heart was pounding in his chest, sweat covered his brow, and his worry and concern for Leona grew.

'Twas late afternoon before he caught a glimpse of the spot where he'd left Ian and the others. As they drew nearer, his heart seized at the sight before him. Hundreds upon hundreds of men and horses filled the open field. Banners waved in the afternoon breeze. Banners of war.

As soon as Ian received word from the sentry that someone was approaching, he mounted his horse and headed toward the riders. When he caught sight of his wife's golden blonde hair waving in the wind, his heart nearly leapt from his chest.

Overwhelmed with joy and relief, he kicked his horse into a full gallop and raced toward her. His heart skipped so many beats he worried it would stop before he had a chance to hold her.

Moments later, Ian was pulling rein on his horse, sliding down and running toward her. Alec Bowie followed suit and helped Rose. With great care, he helped her to her feet. He tried to steady her so she would not fall, but she was having none of it. She only wanted her husband.

As fast as her legs could carry her, she ran to Ian and flung herself into his arms, an explosion of relief filling her chest, her stomach, her very core.

There was no holding back tears for either Rose or Ian.

Collapsing to the ground, he pulled her into his lap and held her as tightly as he could. "I missed ye!" they exclaimed to each other between kisses and hugs.

"Do no' ever leave me again," Rose begged. "Never, ever again!"

"I will no'," he promised her. "Even if it means we have to eat leeks fer the rest of our lives."

Rose fell against his chest with her arms wrapped around his neck, holding on for dear life. "I thought I'd never see ye again."

"Och! Ye did no' think I would leave ye to rot with the Bowies, did ye?" he asked.

Rose wiped her tears onto her cloak. "Nay, I thought ye'd do somethin' foolish and try to attack."

So they sat for a long while, alone in the field, making promises that were probably impossible to keep. But they made them nonetheless. It took some time before Rose's tears subsided and even longer before she could let go of her husband. Beyond all reason and measure, she loved this man with all that she was.

Ian felt the same toward her. The relief at having her back in his arms would have been impossible to describe to another living soul. For weeks he had worried, almost to the point of madness. What hell she must have endured at Rutger's hands. Now, he decided, was not the time to ask those ugly questions. Nay, for now, he would rejoice in simply having her in his arms once again.

ALEC BOWIE WATCHED THE REUNION between husband and wife. Other men might have been jealous of the undeniable love these two people shared, but not he. Nay, Alec did not understand such emotions as love. Love was a weakness, an emotion that lead to a man's downfall. He knew this unequivocally because he'd witnessed his father suffer the torment of loving a woman.

Tired to his bones for a number of good reasons, he could no longer watch as Ian and Rose professed their undying love for one another. Quietly, he grabbed the reins to his horse and walked away to find his men.

IAN TENDERLY SMOOTHED HIS WIFE'S hair while he placed tender kisses on her cheeks, then lips. He'd realized days ago that he could not live on this earth without her. His worry over how harshly she was being treated, his worry over their babe, had consumed him. Now he felt ashamed for having doubted just how strong his wife truly was. Still, there was much to be done before he could rest easy again.

"Rose?" he whispered against the top of her head. "I must get ye away from here at once."

"Ye'll get no argument from me." Her voice was low and scratchy from crying. "I want to go home."

Without a fortified keep or anything stronger than a wood wall, *home* was not safe. He could not protect her there. "As do I, but ye will no' be goin' home just yet."

Pulling away, she stared into his eyes. "Are we goin' back to the Mackintosh castle?" she asked, her tone hopeful.

"Nay, lass, ye be goin' to Rowan Graham's keep. I have an escort waitin' fer ye."

Confusion set in first, but it was quickly replaced by anger. "I will *no'* be goin' to Rowan Graham's keep!" she all but shouted at him. "We be goin' *home*. Back to our keep."

"I can no' protect ye there. Rowan's keep is well fortified —"

She cut him off by scrambling to her feet. "I do no' care how well fortified it be. I have no' seen ye in weeks. I am tired and I want to go home with ye."

The last thing he wanted was to argue with her. Standing to his full height, he did his best to remain calm. "Rose, there be no time to argue it. The Bowie started this war and I aim to finish it."

She looked as though he'd just slapped her. "War? Why must there be war? Why can we no' just go home? I am here now, away from the Bowies. I be safe and with ye."

Raking a hand through his hair, he mumbled a curse under his breath. "The Bowie *will* come after ye again. And again. And again until he bloody well gets what he wants. I will no' risk yer safety or our babe's. Ye be goin' to Rowan Graham's keep and ye be goin' *now*."

Hurt, angry, and exhausted, she felt huge disappointment. The only thing that had kept her sane these past weeks was to think of being reunited with Ian. Of falling asleep in his arms and waking up in them. But now, he was sending her away to go fight some ridiculous war with a crazed man.

She could not bear it. "Nay, I will no' go. I will stay here with ye."

"I will no' be here, do ye no' understand?"

Swallowing back tears, deflated but not yet ready to give up her argument, she wrapped her arms around his waist. "Please, Ian, I beg ye no' to go. I need ye. I can no' bear the thought of losin' ye." 'Twas nothing but the truth of it.

"And I can no' bear the thought of losin' ye again, Rose. Or our babe. I need ye to go to Rowan's." He pressed another kiss to the top of her head.

From behind her, she heard an all too familiar voice speak her name. "Rose."

Releasing her hold on her husband, she spun to see her brother-by-law. Stunned, she could only stare in confusion for a long moment.

"If ye do no' go to Rowan's, I fear me wife will kill me."

"Frederick!" she exclaimed as she flung her arms around his neck. "What are ye doin' here?"

He chuckled as he returned her embrace. "We left weeks earlier than I planned. Ye can thank Aggie fer that when ye see her."

"Where is she? How is she? How are the children?" she blurted out one question after another.

"Wheest, lass," Frederick said with a smile. "She be verra well, as are our children. Aggie awaits ye at Rowan's keep."

Her head began to swim. "Aggie is at Rowan's?" She would not allow herself to believe it just yet.

"Aye, she is. There be little time to explain it now, lass. We must get ye away from here. But I swear to ye, I'll bring yer husband to ye as soon as we are done dealin' with the Bowies."

The Bowies. Oh, how she hated the sound of that name! Uncontainable anger hit her full on. Stepping away, she caught a better sight of all the men Frederick had brought with him. He could have brought ten thousand more and it would have done nothing to ease the ache in her heart.

No matter what promises her husband or his brother made to her, she knew there was a distinct possibility that neither of them would return. But they were hard-headed, stubborn men and there was nothing she could say or do to change their minds. They were determined to seek vengeance on Rutger Bowie.

"Ye look bloody awful," Gylys said as Alec approached his men. They were standing not far from the army of McLarens, Mackintoshes, and Grahams. Gylys held out a mug of ale for his friend.

"I feel bloody awful," Alec told him, accepting the offered mug. He downed the cool ale, wiped his lips on the sleeve of his tunic, and handed the mug back. "When did the army arrive?" he asked, inclining his head toward the massive group of men.

"A few hours ago," Gylys told him. "And they're bloody well angry."

Alec couldn't say that he blamed them. His brother was foolish for kidnapping Rose Mackintosh. Now 'twould be up to Alec to keep them from burning his keep to the ground.

"I will need a fresh horse," he told his men. "I have to go back and get Leona."

"Rest a bit first, then ye may take mine," Kyth told him.

He hadn't slept more than an hour here and there in the past several days. While very tempted to take his cousin's advice, he had a promise to keep. "I fear there be no time fer restin'," he said. "Who kens how long before Rutger discovers Rose is missin'." He dreaded to think what would happen to the young woman he'd left behind in Rose's place.

"We shall go with ye," Kyth declared.

"While I appreciate yer offer, cousin, I fear we will all soon be wanted men. Once Rutger discovers we be missin' along with Rose, he'll put a price on each of our heads."

His men, including young Davy, lined up before him. They cared not about Rutger or being considered traitors by their clan.

"We would follow ye anywhere, Alec." Gylys spoke on behalf of the others. "We did no' help ye get Rose out only to leave ye alone to accept whatever fate Rutger has in store for ye."

"And I can no' go to me grave knowin' I took ye with me," he told them. "Nay, ye need to leave this place until I can get me brother to see reason."

Kyth scoffed openly. "If ye were able to get yer brother to see reason, none of us would be here this day. He would never have taken Rose Mackintosh."

In his heart of hearts he knew 'twas the truth his cousin spoke. "I can no' give up yet," he replied. "There is still a chance I can stop this war. We could finally have peace, once and fer all, fer our clan."

Peace. That was why these men had followed him. They were just as tired of thieving and warring as he was. Each of them, including Dougall, who was in great danger, wanted the same as he. Peace for their clan.

"Ye'll nay have peace until Rutger Bowie is dead." The words came from Ian Mackintosh.

Slowly, Alec turned to face him. "I ken ye want revenge fer him takin' yer wife," Alec said in a low, calm tone. "But would we rather no' have peace without bloodshed?"

Rowan Graham and Frederick Mackintosh stood on either side of Ian. They looked just as angry and as determined as he. "I would rather ye and I had never met," Ian said. "I would rather me wife was never taken. I would rather I was at home, buildin' me own keep and happily awaitin' the arrival of me first bairn. But yer brother has started this war. He does no' want peace."

A shiver of dread traced up and down Alec's spine. He knew the McLaren spoke the truth. The last thing Rutger wanted was to give up the only way of life he'd ever known. And now that he was chief, the power he yielded was almost as important to him as gold. Still, Alec could not give up hope that he could get his brother to see the folly of his ways.

"Were it yer brother who had made such a terrible mistake—" Alec was cut off by Ian stepping forward.

"Ye think this a wee *mistake*?" he asked, seething with anger. "We be no' speakin' of a bairn who was caught stealin' sweet cakes from the larder."

Poor choice of words, he knew it. "I apologize, m'laird. Me point bein' that were it one of yer brothers who had done somethin' so foolish, would ye no' be arguin' fer at least the chance to set things right?"

Ian's jaw twitched. "First of all, none of me brothers would be stupid enough to kidnap another man's wife, let alone one with child."

"Be that as it may, m'laird, I think ye're fergettin' one verra important thing," Alec said.

"Pray tell, what is that I am fergettin'?" Ian ground out.

Alec cocked his head to one side. "Leona."

LEONA MACDOWALL WAS THE ONLY thing standing between war and peace. Ian knew it as well as Alec.

"If ye lay siege to me brother's keep, the first thing he will do is kill anyone who he believes betrayed him. Leona would be the first to die."

Alec let the words sink into Ian's mind before continuing. "The only hope that lass has of survivin' is fer ye no' to attack."

Ian mulled it over for a short moment. His wife would never forgive him if anything happened to Leona. Hell, he wouldn't be able to forgive himself. Their original plan was for Alec to return to the keep and bring Leona back. God willing, she was still safe and had yet to be found out.

"Verra well," Ian said, pulling his shoulders back. "We will no' attack until ye have retrieved Leona."

"And if I can get me brother to agree to peace amongst our clans?" Alec asked with a raised brow.

"Then we shall have peace," Ian replied.

What he left unsaid could have filled a large tome.

THIRTY

Will Bowie had never been on such an important mission before. 'Twas a mission he aimed to complete, for as his father had explained it, countless lives were at stake.

The eleven-year-old boy held on tightly to the mane of his 'borrowed' mount, his knees digging into its sides. There'd been no time for saddle nor bridle, for auld Harry Bowie might have objected to the necessity of borrowing his gray speckled gelding.

His father was adamantly opposed to stealing, but in times of war 'twas often a necessary deed. Deciding he would return the horse as soon as he was done using it, Will reasoned 'twasn't really stealing but borrowing. Hopefully his father would agree.

And never had he been this far from home alone without any of his kin. 'Twas as exhilarating as it was terrifying.

Over hill and glen he rode as fast as he could, running over and over in his mind the message his father had given him to relay to Alec.

Just exactly what the message meant, he could only guess. He knew it had something to do with his uncle, a woman whose name he'd never heard before, and war.

He'd been riding for hours now, the sun just beginning to set behind him. Riding into darkness, alone, with only a *sgian dubh* and his grandsire's old sword, was becoming less and less appealing.

Worry and unease began to play with his courage as well as his mind. Who knew what ne'er-do-wells or brigands hid under the cover of darkness.

Nay! He told himself. *Ye be neither bairn nor wean, Will Bowie. That's what yer da told yer mum just before he sent ye off on this mission. If yer da did no' think ye could get to Alec in time, he never would have sent ye.*

Rebuilding his wavering courage was not easy, but 'twas necessary. No matter what lay ahead that might stop him, be it man or beast, he must get to his uncle Alec.

'TWAS A BRILLIANT SUNSET, THE sky splattered in shades of crimson, burgundy, and yellow. But to the east of their encampment, the sky was as black as pitch. Great thunderclouds blocked the stars and moon. Rain would be upon them soon.

"Ye will be safe with Rowan's men," Ian told his wee wife. In truth, he was trying to convince her as much as himself.

She clung to him, unable yet to let go. Ten of Rowan's best men and a few of Frederick's were mounted and waiting patiently as the couple said their goodbyes.

"I swear to ye, Ian Mackintosh, if ye do no' come back to me, I'll never fergive ye," she murmured against his chest.

"I will come back," he said, squeezing her more tightly.

"If ye do no', I will marry a man far richer, far braver, and far more handsome than ye, just to torment ye."

While meant in jest, her threat was enough to raise his ire. "Ye would no' dare."

"I would," she said before looking up into his eyes. Hers were damp with unshed tears and 'twas enough to take his breath away.

Wanting desperately to keep the mood between them as light as possible, he said, "Impossible. There be no man braver, nor more handsome than I."

"Ye fergot about 'richer'," she politely reminded him.

"What are riches without love to share them with?"

They both knew her threat was a lie. But for now, they would pretend it was as real as the sunset or the beating of their hearts.

"No matter what happens, Rose, remember, none has ever loved ye as fiercely, as deeply, nor as passionately as I."

Choking back a sob, Rose took a deep breath before kissing her husband goodbye. Gently, with great care, he lifted her onto Aric Graham's steed, setting her on his lap.

"I shall guard her as if she were me own, Ian," the dark-haired man promised.

Without another word, Ian Mackintosh watched as the horses turned and headed away. He stood for a long while, watching them ride to the east, until they turned into tiny black dots on the horizon.

TOGETHER WITH FREDERICK, ROWAN, and Alec, they went over their plans one last time. Ian and his newly obtained army would camp where they were for the night. But if Alec did not return before noonin' time on the morrow, they would attack the Bowie keep without waiting for him or Leona. If they didn't return 'twould mean only one thing: they were both dead.

Just as Ian was about to give the order to mount, a sentry called out. "Rider approachin'!"

Ian and Alec mounted immediately to stand with the sentry. Whoever 'twas that rode toward them was riding like the hounds of hell were chasing him.

"Alec!" a young lad called. "Uncle Alec!"

Ian watched as Alec's face contorted into confusion and worry.

"Shite," Alec ground out under his breath. Kicking the flanks of his horse, he rode out to meet his nephew.

"Will!" he shouted. "Slow the bloody hell down!"

Stunned, the lad pulled on the gelding's mane and very nearly crashed into Alec's mount. Alec soon realized there were no reins with which to settle the horse or gain control. Quickly, he grabbed his nephew by the waist and pulled him onto his own horse.

"What the bloody hell are ye doin' here?" he asked gruffly, although he was certain he already knew the answer.

Out of breath, the boy could only shake his head and say, "Thirsty!"

Letting loose an exasperated sigh, Alec took the boy back to their camp while Ian followed. Once they were off the horse, Alec sat the boy on a felled log and called out for ale.

Placing his palms on Will's shoulders, he began looking for injuries. Someone handed the boy a mug of ale while Alec questioned him. "What happened? How are ye here? Where be yer da?"

Soon they were surrounded by curious men. Will drank down the ale, willing his nerves to settle as he fought hard to catch his breath.

"I have a message," he stammered out as he gasped for air. "From da."

Alec waited as patiently as he was able for his nephew to speak. The others with him were not thusly inclined.

"Who is this boy?" Rowan Graham asked.

"Me god-nephew, Will Bowie," Alec answered over his shoulder.

Kyth, Gylys, and Davy came to join the crowd of men. At seeing Will, they pushed their way through. "What in the hell?" Gylys muttered.

"Good eve, Uncle Gylys," Will said before finishing the last of the ale.

"Will," Alec said as he took the empty mug away. "What is yer da's message?"

In wide-eyed awe at all the attention being shown to him at that moment, the lad stiffened his spine and pulled back his shoulders. "Da says to tell ye that Rutger kens about Rose bein' gone and Lenora takin' her place."

"I think ye mean Leona," Alec corrected him.

Will gave a curt nod. "Leona," he repeated the name. "He says to let ye ken that he — Rutger no' da — beat the poor woman then tossed her into the dungeon. He also says to tell ye that Rutger has sounded the alarm fer war. They will soon be headin' this way."

Ian let loose the breath he'd been holding. "Bloody hell."

THIRTY-ONE

This new turn of events changed Ian's plans significantly. While he had been prepared to wait for the break of day before attacking the keep, they had to push their plans up by several hours.

There was no moon overhead this night, but the stars twinkled and shone brightly. Ian was thankful for the cover of darkness, for he and his army could approach the Bowie keep unseen. Unease filled his gut as he and his men waited deep within the forest, some two hundred yards from the fortress. If Alec could not gain entry, or worse yet did and was killed by his own brother, there was a distinct possibility that Leona would die this night as well.

Dawn would soon be upon them, another factor he did not relish. Hopefully, Alec was able to get word to those people sleeping soundly in their cottages, to remain hidden and indoors until this was all over.

Alec had all but begged on behalf of those folks, doing his best to reassure Ian that none of them would sound any alarms. They were just as beleaguered as his own men by the way Rutger ran his keep. Ian could only pray the man was correct in his assumption. Fear oft made people do the strangest things.

"WHO GOES THERE?" A voice cried out from the upper wall, breaking the stillness of the late hour.

"It be me, Alec Bowie," Alec replied in a loud voice.

There was much commotion and scrambling overhead. Alec knew at least one of the men manning the wall had been sent inside to give word to his brother that he had returned.

With much aplomb, he waited patiently for the order to lower the drawbridge. A great deal of time passed before the sound of creaking gears kicked in, signifying he was being granted entry.

'Twasn't so much that they let him in which surprised him, but the fact that he was not immediately put into chains made him wonder. What was his brother up to?

What the men manning the wall did not see was that Dougall Bowie slipped in beside Alec when he crossed over the bridge. Dougall slipped into the shadows to observe. At the first sign of any trouble, he would sound the alarm, and the McLarens, Mackintoshes and Grahams would storm the keep. Alec prayed it would not come to that.

IN SHORT ORDER, HE ENTERED THE gathering room without incident, without having a dirk carefully placed into his back, and without being thrown into chains. Odd though it was that he would be allowed to walk about freely, he knew 'twas simply a game his brother played. Some feeble attempt to make him feel at ease and get him to let his guard down.

The gathering room was dimly lit, only a few torches flickering here and there, a few candles, and a low burning fire in the hearth. Alec knew all too well that his brother liked to keep his men hidden in the shadows, to be called upon with a simple gesture or glance.

His brother, sitting in his ornately carved chair at the high table, soon came into view. In an instant, Alec knew the man had not slept. Dark circles had formed around his eyes, his hair was disheveled and unkempt. Still, Rutger sat with a finger against his temple, affecting an air of nonchalance.

"So the prodigal brother returns," the Bowie said with a wave of his hand, directing Alec to stand before him.

"I was no' gone *that* long," Alec replied drolly.

Rutger smiled down at him, all smug and haughty. The power that came with being laird had gone to the man's head. Alec could only hope and pray he would be able to get through that thick skull of his.

"I take it Rose Mackintosh is now in the safe and lovin' arms of her husband?" Rutger asked dispassionately as he poured himself a cup of wine.

Alec's life depended on how carefully he responded. Apparently, he thought about it too long for his brother's liking. "Oh, do no' be coy," Rutger said through a veil of false calm. "I ken 'twas ye who helped her escape."

"Do ye ken *why* I did it?"

"Aye, I do. Ye did it fer peace."

Alec knew his brother must be itching to pound the life out of him. It must be taking great effort to remain so phlegmatic. A calm Rutger was as dangerous as an outraged one.

"The time fer warrin', fer thievin', needs to end. We must learn to—"

Rutger stopped the speech by slamming his mug of wine down hard onto the table. Shooting to his feet, spittle forming on his chin, he looked every bit the madman their former laird had been. "Since when did *ye* become chief of this clan?" he bellowed.

"I have no desire to be chief, ye ken that as well as anyone," Alec argued. 'Twas the God's honest truth.

"So ye say. But I fear I no longer believe ye." Rutger left the high table and stepped down from the dais. Standing but a few steps from his brother, he let loose a tirade. "We could have lived like kings! We could have owned a vast fortune. We could have instilled fear into the hearts of every man, woman, and child from here to France and back!"

Mayhap for the first time in his life, Alec was getting a true glimpse into his brother's heart. 'Twas more than simple greed that motivated him, more than a simple lust for power.

Each brother studied the other for a long while. 'Twas Rutger who finally broke the silence. "At dawn, me men and I will be heading to McLaren lands. We will kill any man who stands in the way of me having that blasted fortune. I imagine Ian's brother and father would pay handsomely fer his safe return, mayhap double fer Rose's life and that of her unborn babe."

"'Tis madness." Alec swallowed hard, fighting back the urge to bellow and thunder his thoughts on the matter.

"Nay, brother, 'twas madness fer ye to return that which belonged to me, to mine sworn enemy."

Alec scoffed openly. "Since when is Ian Mackintosh or the McLarens yer sworn enemies?"

"Since the moment ye took Rose back to them. I shall have ye ken I hold ye in the same regard now."

The tone he used sent a frisson of fear tracing up and down Alec's spine. Believing his brother was ready to do battle, he withdrew his sword. "Rutger, ye be me brother, me blood, me laird."

Fury flashed in Rutger's eyes. "A pity ye fergot that when ye climbed into bed with the McLarens."

Alec heard the soft scrape of boots against the floor behind him. He spun, ready to fend off his attackers. There were only two.

Never had he witnessed such evil in a man's eyes, as he did in Donnel McLaren's. The lad beside him, Charles McFarland, looked as confident as a newly born kitten.

"'Tis because of ye that we are forced to war against the McLarens," Rutger called out from behind. Alec moved ever so slowly to his left in order to keep an eye on his brother. Donnel and Charles followed him, never taking their eyes from him. He had to keep his eyes on these two men, his brother, and anyone else who might be lurking in the shadows.

Without looking away from Donnel or Charles, he spoke to Rutger. "There still be time to stop this. The McLarens have agreed to a peace accord. They'll even allow ye to live."

From his position on the dais, Rutger laughed maniacally. "Aye, there be time to stop ye from dyin', Alec. Admit yer treachery and accept yer fate. I might let ye live out the rest of yer days below stairs, with the whore ye brought with ye."

"Ye have cost me a fortune," Donnel ground out. "If I can no' have it in coin, I will only accept repayment by havin' yer head on a pike."

Alec made the first move. He feigned left, drawing Donnel forward. Their swords clanged together. Donnel pushed off with a grunt, stumbling only once before regaining his feet. Charles jumped backwards and watched as the two men fought.

Sword against sword, lunges, thrusts, they fought one another. In a tight circle one moment, a wide arc the next.

It had been a good number of years since Alec had actually fought anyone. Still, he had practiced daily to hone his skills with the blade. Donnel, overweight and out of shape, was no match for Alec's youth or experience.

Donnel lunged forward, his sword slicing through Alec's tunic. Alec used the moment to bring his sword down hard on the back of the man's skull. Stunned, growing tired, Donnel stumbled and fell to his knees.

Alec charged forward, just as Donnel was bringing his sword up to plunge it into the younger man's gut. Alec spun sideways, the sword barely missing it's intended mark. Before Donnel could make another attempt, Alec spun once again, and rammed the blade of his sword into the man's back.

A look of stunned horror exploded on Donnel's face. Alec withdrew his blade and watched as Donnel McLaren fell forward onto the cold stone floor.

He had just turned his attention toward Charles McFarland when the sound of Dougall's horn blared through the stillness of the morning.

Rutger withdrew his own sword at that sound. The blade scraped against the sheath menacingly. "What the bloody hell was that?" he bellowed, the sound of his voice booming off the walls, echoing down the hallways of the keep.

"That, brother, would be the call to arms," Alec said, keeping a wary eye on Charles.

"I gave no such order!" Rutger ground out. "Who is calling out me men?"

With his sword pointed at Charles, Alec chanced a glance at his brother.

"It be no' yer men he is callin'," Alec told him. "But a call fer the McLarens, Mackintoshes and Grahams to storm the keep."

Rutger's eyes grew wide, as wide as trenchers, as his mouth opened then closed again. "Ye traitorous bastard!" he spat out furiously. In his next breath, he called out for his guards. They swarmed into the room.

RIGHT BEFORE SOUNDING THE ALARM, Dougall disarmed the young man in charge of the drawbridge, knocking him unconscious. While the bridge was still lowering, he blew into the horn. 'Twas a booming yet plaintive wail that rang through the quiet hour.

As soon as Ian and his men heard the call, they kicked their horses into full runs and headed toward the keep. None of the inhabitants of the cottages came to investigate, thus allowing Ian and his men to run around the small village unimpeded.

They thundered across the drawbridge, shaking the timbers in their wake. Dougall met them at the first gate, swinging it open wide to allow their entry into the main keep. He then led them through the small courtyard, with Ian and Frederick in fast pursuit, and at least two hundred men following close behind.

Dismounting, they were immediately set upon by a hoard of Bowie warriors.

Metal crashed against metal, horses screeched and cried out in the melee that ensued. Ian felled two men, then a third, while he tried to make his way inside the keep.

Quickly scanning the wide-open space for his next victim, he caught site of someone running across the yard and toward the stables. Although he'd never met nor seen Rutger Bowie, he recognized the man's crimson silk tunic as well as the heavy gold chains that glinted in the torchlight. From Brogan's description, Ian knew at once the man must be Rutger Bowie.

Seeing that his brother and men had the matter of the courtyard well in hand, Ian raced away and headed toward the stables.

With his senses on high alert, his heart pounding in his chest, he stopped at the entrance to the long building. From within he could hear a man barking out orders.

"Saddle me horse at once!"

Carefully, Ian poked his head through the open doorway long enough to glance at the interior. Pulling back, he counted to ten rapidly, a trick he oft used to steady his nerves during battle.

Taking a deep breath, he stepped inside, his bloody sword at the ready. There, in the middle of the long row, was Rutger Bowie. The man was enraged, cursing at the boy who was working hard to saddle his mount.

"I take it ye be Rutger Bowie," Ian said as he approached the object of his consternation and fury.

Rutger spun at the sound of his voice, his face purple with rage. "

"I be Ian Mackintosh, chief and laird of Clan McLaren," he said as a means of introduction.

Rutger withdrew his sword clumsily. The lad scurried away, taking refuge inside the open stall.

"Out of me way, Mackintosh," Rutger said as he held out his sword with one hand while reaching for the bridle and reins that hung on the wall with the other.

Ian gave a slow shake of his head. "Ye'll be goin' nowhere this night, Bowie."

"Me brother said ye agreed to a peace accord," Rutger stammered as he tried to get the bridle on the uncooperative horse's head with one hand. "Are ye goin' back on yer word?"

Another slow shake and a few steps forward. "Nay, I be keepin' me word. Ye have to the count of three to make up yer mind, Bowie. Peace or death."

Fed up with the bridle, Bowie tossed it against the stable wall. The horse whinnied and stomped his foot. Rutger took a startled step backward, away from Ian. "I'll no' go down without a fight, McLaren."

With his sword pointed at Ian and a crazed look in his eyes, Rutger knew he was trapped. He tried retreating, but soon found himself trapped behind the horse.

Without a word, he growled and lunged at Ian, who was able to shove him away before the sword could do any harm. Thus, the battle between two enraged and obstinate men began.

Haphazardly, Rutger lashed out, his sword slicing through the air. On one downward motion, it landed hard on the dirt floor.

Ian met each of the blows by either blocking them or taking steps backward. To and fro, back and forth, most of Rutger's thrusts and jabs hit inoffensive air.

They ended up circling back, fighting betwixt the wall and the nervous steed. The black stallion pawed at the hard earth, screaming loudly at the combat taking place so close to him. He reared back, breaking one of the cross ties, just as Ian and Rutger made their way around him.

"I'll see ye burn in hell before ye leave this night," Ian declared, his voice determined, his jaw set.

"Then we'll both burn in hell, ye bloody bastard!" Rutger ground out as he lunged forward.

Ian pushed him back and away while thrusting his sword into the man's belly. Rutger landed against the horse, which screamed again and reared frantically. Before Ian knew what was happening, the horse kicked and pawed at Rutger, sending him to the earth beneath its hooves.

The chief's scream could not be heard over the violent sounds of the horse's cries, or as his hoofs trampled Rutger Bowie to death.

THIRTY TWO

Alec had managed to hold off several of his brother's guards, but not unfazed or uninjured. One of them managed to slice through his left forearm, tearing the skin to the bone. Hot, searing pain shot from his fingertips to his ears. Blood raced down his arm and off his fingertips.

Just as two men were coming toward him, Frederick Mackintosh and his men burst into the gathering room. The sound of wood splintering and men shouting drew their attention away from Alec.

He took the opportunity to slip out and make his way to the bowels of the keep. As he stumbled through the dark hallways, he ripped the bottom of his tunic with his teeth, tearing off a strip. Holding one end with his teeth, he tied the linen around his forearm as taut as possible to staunch the bleeding.

All the while, his heart pounded in his chest and he prayed that Rutger had not given the order to kill Leona.

Dizzy with dread and pain, he shook the images from his mind as he pulled open the heavy iron door that led to the dungeon. Removing one of the torches from the wall, he carefully made his way down the stone stairs. The large room was empty, save for tables and implements of torture left over from Eduard Bowie's rule.

The first three cells were empty, save for rotten rushes and the carcasses of rats. Holding the torch high, he almost missed her. She was lying on her side in the far corner of the cell, curled into a tight ball.

Searching feverishly for the key, he called to her. "Leona. Leona, I be here, lass."

She did not move so much as a muscle.

Cursing under his breath, overwrought with worry, he eventually found the key lying on a small table. Quickly, he returned to her cell, sheathed his sword and unlocked the iron door.

Shoving the torch into a wall sconce, he knelt beside her. "Leona." He called out to her in a harsh whisper as he lifted her head up, showing great care. Pressing his fingertips against her throat, he let out a relieved breath when he felt her pulse. 'Twas slow, but 'twas a pulse.

Pushing the hair away from her face, he gasped when he saw how badly she had been beaten. One eye was completely swollen shut, her lips cut in three places. Blood had dried and caked on her chin and her neck.

"Leona, lass," he said in a hushed, nearly reverent tone.

Her eyes fluttered, but she was only able to open one. 'Twas the dark green eye that stared back at him. "Alec," she whispered, her voice scratchy and low. "Ye came back fer me."

"Aye, lass, I promised ye I would."

IAN COULD NOT FIND IT IN his heart to feel any remorse for how Rutger Bowie had died. Although he would have preferred to disembowel the man, tie him to a stake and watch the ants devour him over the course of several days, at least he was dead. He could no longer harm anyone, least of all his Rose or their child.

Most of the fighting had ceased when Ian left the stables and went inside the castle. Inside, those cold, dark gray walls were many Bowie men, most but not all of them dead.

Ian scanned the space, looking for signs of Donnel McLaren and Charles McFarland. He found Donnel dead, hidden under the bodies of two other slain Bowie warriors. 'Twas another slow and painful death he'd not get to witness.

Seamus sought him out to let him know there were prisoners, and one of them was Charles McFarland. They were being held in the rear yard, between the castle and the kitchens. Ian wasted no time in seeking the traitor out. Mayhap, just mayhap, he'd get to punish at least one of the men responsible for his wife's kidnapping and the subsequent war.

Charles was sprawled on the ground. It took only a cursory glance of the young man to realize he was not long for this world. His skin was ashen, for he'd lost a good deal of blood from a large gash on his head and the gaping wound left by someone's sword that tore across his stomach and chest. Ian made a mental note to reward the man responsible for gutting Charles later.

"Ian," Charles called to him weakly.

Ian crouched low curiously.

"Ian, I be sorry. 'Twas no' supposed to happen like this."

Ian raised a brow. If the man thought he'd get absolution from Ian Mackintosh, he was sadly mistaken.

"They said they only wanted to steal a few head of cattle. I did no' ken about their plans to take Rose, I swear to ye, I did no' ken." He coughed, winced, and forced himself to continue. "By the time I knew, 'twas too late."

"And ye did no' think to come to me?" Ian asked. "To tell me who had her? Ye did nothin' to help aid in her escape."

"He would have killed me," Charles said, his voice raspy, the pain intensifying. "But I suppose it does no' matter now."

The man's skin was turning ashen. Ian knew he'd be dead soon. A long burning question loomed. "Who be the other traitor?" Ian asked.

Sweat formed on Charles's brow. "There be no other. 'Twas Rutger's way of playin' with yer mind, leavin' ye to trust no one."

Ian let out a quick breath though he shouldn't have been surprised. The Bowie chief was as much a liar as he was a thief.

With little time left, there were other matters to discuss. "Ye nearly killed Rodrick. He was yer friend."

He shook his head. "Aye, I did, and fer that, I will go to me death feelin' no remorse. Neither do I feel remorse fer takin' Eggar Wardwin's life. They had discovered the truth, ye see. I did it to protect meself and me sister."

'Twas as if he'd been kicked in the gut. Charles had killed Eggar? Fury burned in his gut, but there were still many unanswered questions. "Yer sister?" Ian asked. 'Twas the first time he'd ever mentioned a sister.

"Aye, her name be Muriel. Rutger and Donnel, they said they were holdin' her here, as prisoner." He coughed again, this time spitting up blood. "But I found out only days ago, she is no' here but on Skye, with Rose and Leona's aunt."

Rose and Leona's aunt? As far as Ian knew, his wife had no living relatives. "Rose has no aunt," Ian told him.

"Aye, she does. Rose's mum and Leona's were cousins, ye ken," he closed his eyes, his breathing becoming more labored as the moments passed by. "Leona's da? He be a cousin to Donnel. That is how I ken."

So his wife and Leona were cousins? That would explain the eerie similarities in their appearance. "But why does Rose's aunt have yer sister?"

"The aunt, her name be Kathryn MacCabe, she be Donnel's sister, the woman who has me Muriel. He lied and told her," he stopped talking, wracked by coughing he could not stop. "'Twas all fer lies," he said through deep gasps for air.

As he watched Charles McFarland take his last breath, Ian could derive no pleasure in it. If what the man said was true, he had lied to protect his sister. For that, the laird could not blame him. Still, he should have come to Ian and explained everything to him. He would have done whatever he could to help the young man. Instead, he chose another route and put his trust in the hands of madmen. 'Twas his own fault he was dead.

As for Rose and Leona? He could well imagine the beaming smiles they would have when they learned they were in fact cousins.

As for Ingerame? Why did he not mention he and Donnel were cousins when they first learned he was involved with all of this? Was it fear or was he also a traitor?

As fer Muriel McFarland? Until moments ago, he'd never heard of the woman. Or she could have been a young maid or a bairn for all he knew. He doubted he would ever know, for that information died with Charles. He could only hope, for Muriel's sake, that Donnel's sister was kinder than her brother had ever been.

He stood to his full height and looked about the yard. The two people he did not see were Alec Bowie and Leona.

Leaving the yard, he made his way back into the keep to search for them. Just as he passed into the gathering room, Alec appeared from one of the dark hallways. He had Leona in his arms.

HEALERS WERE CALLED FROM BOTH the Bowie clan as well as those Frederick and Rowan had brought with them.

Alec refused to leave Leona's side. "She be me responsibility," he yelled at Ian. "Tend to her first."

"If she dies, me wife will never fergive me," Ian told his brother as they both ignored Alec Bowie's protests.

Leona was laid out on the table in the gathering room. Someone had covered her with a blanket while someone else banked the fire. One of Rowan's men was tending to her injuries.

"Alec, if ye do no' sit down, I shall have ye tied to the chandelier!" 'Twas his own healer, a handsome woman Ian estimated to be in her early thirties.

Ian looked up and glowered at Alec. "Fer the sake of Christ, man, sit down! Ye'll do no one any good if ye die. Yer clan needs ye now more than ever."

"But it be me fault Leona was beaten," Alec argued.

"Och, it is, is it?" Ian asked. "Did ye beat her?"

"Of course I did no' beat her!"

"Then it be no' yer fault. Now sit down!" he barked.

Like a chastised child, Alec sat and allowed his healer to tend to the gaping wound in his forearm.

"If ye're lucky, ye'll live. If ye're smart and follow me orders, ye'll get to keep yer arm," she told him as she began washing the blood away.

Rowan's healer, Marcus Graham, finished his cursory examination of Leona. "Please tell me the man who beat her is dead?" he asked as he looked up at Ian and Frederick.

"Aye," Ian answered. "He is."

"Good," he said before returning to Leona's face. Dipping a cloth in the basin of water, he began washing the blood from her face and neck. She moaned something incoherent and batted his hand away.

"I believe she will live," he said. "But she will need plenty of rest. I do no' find any broken bones, thank the gods."

"Can she travel?" Ian asked.

"Aye, she can. But I'd let her rest here fer a day or two."

Rowan appeared by their sides to let Ian know all the surviving Bowies were accounted for and being held in the armory. "Do ye wish to take Leona to me keep?" he asked Ian.

Rowan's keep was a damned sight better than his own. At least there, Leona could get the rest she needed. And she could be reunited with Rose. "Aye, I think that would be best. But I do no' like the idea of leavin' her here alone."

Alec spoke up then. His face pale, his expression odd. "I'll take her to Rowan's," he said.

Ian, Frederick and Rowan cast curious glances among themselves.

"I do no' think ye're in any condition to travel," Frederick pointed out, with a nod toward the man's injured arm.

"This?" Alec scoffed. "'Tis but a scratch."

Ian doubted there was anything save death that would get Alec to change his mind. "Verra well," he said. "But I will be leavin' ten of me best men here to watch over her." What he didn't say was, *and to watch over ye.*

Alec looked relieved. His healer looked bemused as she muttered something that sounded like *daft men* under her breath.

LATE THAT AFTERNOON, IAN, FREDERICK, Rowan and their men crossed back over the drawbridge of the Bowie keep. In a few days, Ian would be back with his wife. He looked forward to telling her Rutger, Donnel and Charles were all dead. Never again would the bastards cast shadows on this earth. And never again would they bring harm to her.

He was also eager to tell her she had a cousin in Leona Macdowall, though he was still trying to work out that odd family tree in his mind.

He left the prisoners to Alec, to deal with as he saw fit. Chances were, no harm would come to any of them, for they were only doing as their former laird had ordered. They'd done what Ian and his men would have done: protected their families, their keep, against outside forces.

Though he was exhausted and mightily sore, he would not let his physical condition keep him from his wife. Kicking the flanks of his horse, he led the way to Rowan Graham's keep, riding off into the late afternoon sun.

For the first time in a very long while, he felt something more than despair or worry. Nay, his heart was filled near to bursting with the simple image of holding his lovely wife in his arms once again.

THIRTY-THREE

ose's escorts treated her with the gentlest of care. She knew they meant well, intended only to see her safely to Rowan Graham's keep. But that did not mean they had to proceed at a snail's pace.

At her insistence, they pushed on, rarely stopping. It was a long, lonely ride, with her heart filled with worry over her husband's safety.

By the time they reached the keep, she was covered in road muck and exhausted beyond measure. She would feel no genuine relief until Ian's return. Night had fallen and she could not remember now how many days she had been traveling. Everything was beginning to blur, one fuzzy image into another.

She had never been to the Graham keep before. Too tired to take any notice of the beautiful structure, her only thought was of a long hot bath before crawling into a warm bed.

Because she was barely able to stand or keep her eyes open, someone helped her down from the horse and led her inside. The gathering room was a grand yet warm and inviting space. Before she could clear her vision to take anything in, a familiar voice she had not heard in far too long, called out to her. It was soon followed by another.

"Rose!"

Aggie rushed forward and wrapped her arms around her friend. Rose's heart suddenly felt much lighter, her worries slipping away.

"Aggie!" As she held on to her dearest friend, she felt arms twine around her legs. 'Twas Ailrig, Aggie's son.

"Rose! Och, we have missed ye!" Ailrig declared as the three of them clung to one another.

Joyful tears fell as Rose sobbed uncontrollably. "I have missed ye so," she cried.

"Did ye miss *me?*" Ailrig asked hopefully.

Placing a hand against his head, she pulled him in more tightly. "Aye, lad, I did."

They stood for a long while, crying and embracing one another. 'Twas a reunion far too long in the making as far as Rose was concerned.

After her tears were shed, she pulled away to look at Aggie. "Ye're still as beautiful as I remember."

Aggie smiled warmly. "Ye're just as daft as I recall," she said with a giggle.

Just then, a very beautiful woman with long auburn hair stepped into Rose's line of vision. "Good eve," she said warmly. "Ye must be the Rose I have heard so much about."

"Och!" Aggie declared. "I have fergotten me manners. Rose, I would like ye to meet Lady Arline Graham. She be Rowan's wife."

After the introductions were made, Lady Arline said, "We have a hot bath and clean clothes ready fer you above stairs."

"Thank ye kindly, m'lady," Rose said with a curtsey.

"Ailrig, would ye be so kind as to ask the cook to have a tray sent up to Rose's room?" Lady Arline asked.

"Aye," he replied. He gave Rose another hug. "I be glad ye're home, Rose." He hugged her again before running off to the kitchens.

"Come," Aggie said as she took Rose's hand. "Ye look ready to fall over. Ye can bathe while we catch up."

ROSE DID NOT WANT TO FEEL, or to think, or to worry. She'd spent too much time these past few weeks feeling terrified, wondering what would happen to her and her babe, and worried over Ian. For now, she wanted to simply feel some measure of calm.

'Twas quite difficult to focus on what Aggie was telling her. The bath felt far too luxurious, far too relaxing. Bones that had ached with fire earlier, began to feel as strong as the water she sat in. Soon, she found it difficult to keep her eyes open.

The room grew quiet, the flames flickering softly in the hearth. Rose paid no attention as she began to sink farther into the tub.

"Rose," Aggie's soft voice broke through her restful peace.

Slowly, she opened her eyes. Aggie wore an expression of great concern. "Did they hurt ye?"

Rose knew without asking what kind of 'hurt' Aggie was asking about. "Nay, they did no'," she replied. "No' me person, anyway. But me heart?"

Tears pooled in her eyes again. "I do no' ken if I will ever truly get over bein' afraid."

Aggie dipped a pitcher into the warm water. Slowly, she poured it down Rose's back. "I lived most of me life in fear, Rose. I can tell ye, 'tis no' a place ye want to dwell in fer long. It can eat away at yer soul until there be nothin' left of ye but an empty shell."

Rose knew all too well the fear Aggie'd experienced, the life she had led. Prior to meeting Frederick and Ian, they'd both spent a good long while in that darkest of places. Thankfully, Aggie had Frederick to help her back into the light.

And Rose had Ian. At the thought of her husband, her babe decided 'twould be a good time to remind her he was still there. A firm kick, just below her ribs, then a twist. 'Twas not painful, just a sweet reminder of what love betwixt a man and woman could create.

With her lashes damp, she held back the urge to break down again. 'Twould do her, nor her babe, no good to allow the intense feeling of dread to drape over her like a heavy blanket.

"Ian will be well," Aggie assured her as she grabbed a drying cloth. "As will Frederick."

Aggie helped her from the tub. As Rose stood in front of the fire, her eyelids grew heavy. Aggie dried her off and slipped a warm nightdress over her head. "Remember *who* our husbands are, Rose," Aggie said as she combed her friend's hair. "They be Mackintosh men. No more stubborn men were ever born, aye?"

Rose had to agree. "Aye, they be stubborn."

"And if yer Ian be anythin' at all like me Frederick? No' even the devil himself could stop either of them from returnin' to us."

In her heart of hearts, Rose knew her friend was right.

EPILOGUE

With Rutger Bowie dead and Leona rescued, Ian Mackintosh, along with his brother, Rowan Graham and the army of men left the Bowie keep that cool, gray afternoon. Once they reached the border between McLaren and Graham lands, Ian's men, together with Alec, Dougall and Kyth, escorted Leona home.

Ian, Frederick and Rowan and the remaining army headed east. They had wives to return to. Ian in particular was eager to cross on to Graham lands, to get to his wife.

'Twas long after the midnight hour, days later, when they finally entered the Graham keep. With child again, this one due in early autumn, Lady Arline Graham met them in the gathering room. She was just as lovely as the last time Ian had seen her.

He refused her offer of refreshments. "She be in a room above stairs, the last door on the left," Arline said with an affectionate smile.

Ian took the stairs two at a time, all the while his heart pounding against his chest, his palms sweaty, his stomach in knots. All that he wanted was to climb into bed and hold his wife for the next decade or so.

Rose was fast asleep in a big, comfortable looking bed. A low fire burned in the hearth, the embers crackling and popping softly.

As quietly and as quickly as he could, he stripped off his clothing, washed up in the basin, and climbed into bed. Rose startled, gasped, and withdrew a *sgian dubh* from under her pillow. Pressing the point against his chest, she was fully prepared to plunge the blade with all her might.

"Wheest, wife, 'tis only me," he whispered raggedly.

Rose let loose a vexed breath.

"Ian!" she exclaimed breathlessly.

"I will have to disarm ye lass, before I can hold ye," he told her as he cast a glance at the small blade.

Tossing the blade away, it clanked on the floor, skittered and ended up where, she did not care. Her husband was alive and had returned to her.

For the next hour, they held on to one another. Between tender kisses, words of love and affection were spoken in low whispers. There was much she wanted to tell Ian about her time as Rutger Bowie's hostage. But for now, they would take the greatest joy in simply holding each other. In listening to one another's soft words of love.

As much as he had wanted to make love to his beautiful wife, he refused to do more than press sweet kisses against her lips. Until he spoke to the healer, he would do nothing to endanger either her life or their babe's.

They slept through the morning meal as well as the nooning. Exhaustion and relief taking equal toll on the two of them.

'Twas late in the afternoon before they awoke. The sun streamed in through the narrow window as dust danced in its beams. Ian woke first and for a long while he simply stared in awe at his beautiful wife and her large belly. The belly where *their* child hopefully grew well and strong.

Rose woke next, stretching languidly beside him. The sight of her, the way she moaned softly as she stretched was enough to make any man mad with lust, but he held back.

"Good morn," she said, her smile bright and filled with much joy.

"Good morn," he whispered, his voice catching ever so slightly.

The babe decided then to kick hard against her belly. "Och!" Rose said as her hand flew to her stomach.

Panic seized him. "What be the matter?" he asked as he sat up in the bed with a jolt.

"Yer son is kickin' like a donkey," she giggled.

He let loose the breath he'd been holding in a whoosh.

Seeing her husband's worry then relief made her giggle again. "Do no' fash yerself, Ian," she said as she took his hand and laid it across her stomach. His brow knitted for a long moment, until the babe kicked again.

'Twas by far one of the most wondrous sensations he'd ever experienced. Pride, joy, and adoration formed into one large lump in his throat.

"He does that when he is hungry," Rose explained. "Or when he simply wants to remind me that he is still there."

Ian quirked a hopeful brow. "Ye think it be a boy?" he asked.

Rose shrugged her shoulders and smiled. "We'll ken in May, aye?"

May. It seemed a lifetime away. Worry settled in around his heart again. What if she did not survive the birthing? What if something happened between now and then? What if another foolish clan chief decided to kidnap his wife again?

Rose let out a heavy sigh. "Ian, ye can no' spend all yer days worryin' about what *might* happen."

The crease in his brow knitted tighter. His wife had always had the uncanny ability to know exactly what he was thinking.

"If ye do, ye'll no' experience any of the joy this time in our life brings us," she said, caressing his cheek with much tenderness.

Her touch was balm to his often times tortured mind. It amazed him how she could both calm his nerves and unsettle him all with the same simple touch.

"Do ye ken how much I love ye, Rose?" he asked, taking her hand and pressing a cheek to her palm.

"I may have fergotten," she said cheekily. "Why do ye no' show me."

He knew *that* look. The *come hither and love me* look. "Not until the healer gives us permission." It took every speck of courage and strength he owned to utter those words.

Seductively, she batted her eyelashes at him. "I already spoke to Lady Arline's healer and midwife. Our babe is well and so am I."

"Ye tell me true?" he asked, his voice doubtful and hopeful all at once.

"Of course I tell ye true!" she exclaimed with a roll of her eyes. "I would do nothin' to bring any harm to our babe, Ian."

"I do no' want to hurt either of ye," he admitted.

A warm smile formed on her lips. "It has been months since last we joined. I think ye should worry *I* will hurt *ye*."

Thus the gauntlet was thrown, the challenge made. A challenge he was all too willing to accept.

THE BOWIE BRIDE

May, 1357, The McLaren Keep

Peace was tenuous at best.

Alec Bowie was loathe to admit it. Of course, he was loathe to admit many things of late.

Two months had passed since his brother had been killed. It had been a painful, horrible death. Had Ian Mackintosh's piercing blade not been enough for Rutger to succumb to, then the horse that trampled him into the earth finished the job. Even though his brother was mad with greed for gold and power, Alec still missed him. Besides the endless lines of cousins, Rutger was the last living kin he had. Now he was dead. Laid to rest in the family plot without much pomp or circumstance, near the loch. In death, as it had been in life, Rutger was placed between his parents. While their parents loved their sons without question, they often used them as weapons against the other. They were probably all three burning in hell. Alec couldn't be certain of course.

He had begged his brother on numerous occasions to take the opportunity to bring peace to their clan. To change the tide and bring the outside world in. But Rutger refused.

Too entrenched in the past, too afraid to take chances, too greedy and obstinate, it had been left up to Alec to give the clan what they needed most: a future.

A far different future.

A life without thieving, without terrorizing neighboring clans, a life without crime or prices on their heads.

And now he was their chief.

He'd never held any designs on being chief of any clan, let alone this rag-tag one filled with criminals, horse thieves, and ne'er-do-wells. How the bloody hell was he supposed to turn these people into farmers? Weavers? Whisky makers?

Mayhap 'twas folly. Mayhap 'twould all be for naught. But he had to — at the very least — *try*.

And that was what he was doing this day. *Trying*.

Trying to find a wife while trying not to wring his cousin Dougall's neck.

The man was mad. Daft. Delusional.

But he had a point. One more thing Alec was loathe to admit.

In order to bring ever-lasting peace to his clan, alliances must be made, friendships nurtured and cultivated, much like the seeds of barley he had planted a sennight after his brother's death.

So here he sat in Ian Mackintosh's tent, looking out at the McLaren and Mackintosh people. The tent, while quite large, was filled to bursting with curious people.

His fingers rested gingerly on a dirk he had hidden at his waist. Generations of murderous men and thieves ran through his blood. 'Twas hard to let one's guard down when one was used to an entirely different way of interacting with people.

Dougall and Kyth sat on his left, Ian to his right, and Brogan next to him. The long table faced out at the crowd and he had an odd sensation that left him feeling as though he were some mysterious creature on display.

Ian leaned in and whispered, "Are ye *certain* ye wish to do this?" for what seemed the hundredth time.

Alec gave a curt nod, which belied what he was truly thinking. *Bloody hell, no! I do no' wish to do this, but I must.*

With a sigh of resignation, Ian said, "Verra well, let us get started. But we must hurry, I do no' wish to leave Rose fer long."

Rose Mackintosh. Alec liked that woman verra much. Strong, blunt, and quite pretty. She was a week past when she should have delivered Ian's babe into the world.

Babes and wives. They would be the downfall of human civilization. Eventually.

While Ian fawned all over his lovely wife, worried and fretted over the life of their babe, Alec felt confident that he would never suffer such indignities. He was not here to find a love match. Nay, he simply needed to marry a McLaren lass in order to ensure peace betwixt their clans. That was why he was so bloody angry with Dougall. This had all been his idea — the bastard.

But again, he had to admit there was wisdom in the plan. No matter how ugly or deplorable the idea of marriage was to Alec Bowie, he had to find a wife. Hopefully, she'd be a quiet, biddable lass, who would understand the importance of peace.

She must also understand, unequivocally, that he had no wish, need, or desire for a *happy* home life. Nay, theirs was more a matter of business than a matter of the heart, and that was how he intended for it to remain for all the rest of his days.

That was if he could find someone brave enough amongst this crowd. With his luck — and he knew 'twas God-awful luck he possessed — he'd be married off to some mousey wench with missing teeth and moles scattered across her face. He shuddered at the thought. But again, he was not here to find a love match. Just a woman willing to marry him, bed him until she got with child, then leave him the bloody hell alone.

Outside, 'twas a clear, bright afternoon. A stark contrast to how Alec was feeling to his very core. Doomed. They might as well have been taking him to the gallows, such was his inevitable fate. For marriage was like that;

you lost your freedom and your mind. That was if you weren't careful and diligent.

Ian stood then, raising his hands to hush the murmurs of the crowd. When silence fell, he spoke. "I have called ye here today to discuss the matter of peace betwixt our clan and the Bowies."

Riotous laughter broke out amongst Ian's people. It set Alec's nerves on edge. This was not going to go well, not well at all. More images of a mole-covered wench flashed before his eyes. With his awful luck, she'd most likely be missing a limb as well.

A loud voice rang out above the laughter. "What do the Bowie's ken of peace?"

Another cried, "Ye can no' trust a Bowie as far as ye can pick one up!"

"Aye! All they ken is stealin' and reivin'."

Ian raised his hands once again and called for quiet. "I ken we be unused to the idea of a peaceful Clan Bowie," he began. "But they have a new laird. A laird who risked his own life to save Rose's."

That point hit home. Heads nodded as people murmured in agreement. 'Twas his only saving grace, that. Saving Rose Mackintosh's life. Rescuing her and bringing her back to her people. Of course, he couldn't have done that without help from the lass named Leona.

Upon thinking of her, he searched the crowd surreptitiously, but saw no sign of her. Earlier that morn he had asked Ian how the lass faired. But they'd been interrupted and Ian had not been able to answer.

No matter. The lass was far too intelligent to settle on the likes of him.

Ian speaking to his people pulled Alec back to the here and now. "I want peace with the Bowie's as much as they want it with us. I have spent time gettin' to know Alec Bowie and a few of his men." He cast a glance at Dougall and Kyth before turning back to the crowd. "I find them to be honest and genuine in their pursuits."

More murmurs from the crowd as they all stared at the three Bowies with curious and doubtful eyes.

"After a long mornin' of discussin' just how this peace can be everlastin' and ensured, we have come to the conclusion that a marriage is the best approach."

Stunned and uncertain silence filled the air. 'Twas as if the world froze in that instant.

Ian took a breath before going on. "This marriage would need to be betwixt Alec Bowie and a lass with McLaren blood." He let the words sink into the minds of his people for a moment. "The only true lass who qualifies is me niece, Ada Mackintosh. But since she be only a year old, that will no' work. So," he took another deep breath and rested his palms on the table, "we will be willin' to accept *any* lass from our clan, no matter her bloodline. Any lass of marriageable age."

The deafening silence stretched on and on.

Alec looked out at the crowd of slack-jawed, stunned individuals. Their expressions said it all: not only was the Bowie mad, but their laird was as well.

Before Ian could speak again, someone in the far back of the tent stood up.

"I will do it."

He could not see her face clearly, for she was in shadow. But he felt quite certain he recognized her soft voice.

"I will marry the Bowie."

Bloody hell, 'twas Leona Macdowall.

About the Author:

USA Today Bestselling Author, storyteller and cheeky wench, SUZAN TISDALE lives in the Midwest with her verra handsome carpenter husband. Her children have all left the nest. Her pets consist of dust bunnies and a dozen poodle-sized, backyard groundhogs – all of which run as free and unrestrained as the voices in her head.

Afterward

Ian's Rose marks my return to writing full-length novels, after more than two years of writing novellas. I do hope you enjoyed the story. *Ian's Rose* launches my new series, *The Mackintoshes and McLarens*.

In the next novel of this series, *The Bowie Bride*, Rose will have her baby -- with Leona Macdowall's help. Flip back a few pages and you will find the Prologue to that novel.

In the third novel of this series, titled *Brogan's Promise*, Ian's brother, Brogan, will gain a bride. And she will not be like any female character I've ever written.

I hope to have *The Bowie Bride* released by the end of this year.

The Mackintoshes and McLarens Series Titles:
Ian's Rose
The Bowie Bride
Brogan's Promise

You will find information on new releases at my website, www.suzantisdale.com. You may also follow me on Facebook at: facebook.com/suzantisdaleromance. Twitter@ suzantisdale.

ALSO BY SUZAN TISDALE

The Clan MacDougall Series
Laiden's Daughter
Findley's Lass
Wee William's Woman
McKenna's Honor

The Clan Graham Series

Rowan's Lady
Frederick's Queen

The Clan McDunnah Series

A Murmor of Providence
A Whisper of Fate
A Breath of Promise

The Mackintoshes and McLarens Series
Ian's Rose
The Bowie's Bride - 2016
Brogan's Promise - 2017

Moirra's Heart Series

Stealing Moirra's Heart

Saving Moirra's Heart

Isle of the Blessed

For HM Ward's The Arrangement Series

The King's Courtesan

The Brides of the Clan MacDougall

(A Sweet Series)

Aishlinn

Maggy (arriving 2017)

Nora (arriving 2017)

Coming Soon:

The Thief's Daughter

CPSIA information can be obtained
at www.ICGtesting.com
Printed in the USA
FFOW02n0217020916
27349FF